CAROLYN MITCHELL BOYKIN

THE
KNOWING

WWW.BLACKODYSSEY.NET

Published by
BLACK ODYSSEY MEDIA

www.blackodyssey.net
Email: info@blackodyssey.net

This book is a work of fiction. Any references to events, real people, or real places are used fictitiously. Other names, characters, places, and events are products of the author's imagination, and any resemblance to actual events or places or persons, living or dead, is entirely coincidental.

THE KNOWING. Copyright © 2024 by Carolyn Mitchell Boykin

Library of Congress Control Number: 2023919265

First Trade Paperback Printing: March 2024
ISBN: 978-1-957950-12-9
ISBN: 978-1-957950-13-6 (e-book)

Cover Design by Ashlee Nassar of Designs With Sass
To the extent that the image or images on the cover of this book depict a person or persons, such person or persons are merely models and are not intended to portray any character in the book.

All rights reserved. Black Odyssey Media, LLC | Dallas, TX.
This book or parts thereof may not be reproduced in any form, stored in a retrieval system, or transmitted in any form by any means—electronic, mechanical, photocopy, recording, or otherwise—without prior written permission of the publisher, excepting brief quotes or tags used in reviews, interviews, or complimentary promotion, and as permissible by United States of America copyright law.

10 9 8 7 6 5 4 3 2 1

Manufactured in the United States of America

Distributed by Kensington Publishing Corp.

Dear Reader,

I want to thank you immensely for supporting Black Odyssey Media authors, and our ongoing efforts to spotlight more minority storytellers. The scariest and most challenging task for many writers is getting the story, or characters, out of our heads and onto the page. Having admitted that, with every manuscript that Kreceda and I acquire, we believe that it took talent, discipline, and remarkable courage to construct that story, flesh out those characters, and prepare it for the world. Debut or seasoned, our authors are the real heroes and heroines in *OUR* story. And for them, we are eternally grateful.

Whether you are new to Carolyn Mitchell Boykin or Black Odyssey Media, we hope that you are here to stay. We also welcome your feedback and kindly ask that you leave a review. For upcoming releases, announcements, submission guidelines, etc., please be sure to visit our website at www.blackodyssey.net or scan the QR code below. We can also be found on social media using @iamblackodyssey. Until next time, take care and enjoy the journey!

Joyfully,

Shawanda Williams

Shawanda "N'Tyse" Williams
Founder/Publisher

PRAISE FOR THE KNOWING

Carolyn Boykin's debut novel is imaginative and arresting. This writer is unflinching in her development of characters who are searing and consume the pages with no boundaries. This makes for an unforgettable story that will stay with you—long after the book is closed. Get well acquainted with this work and the writer. Boykin comes onto the literary scene with a promising start for critical acclaim.

–Alexis Pride, Associate Professor of Columbia College Chicago and author of *Where the River Ends*

Boykin weaves a tale of supernatural suspense around a cast of characters who all deserve their own novel. She breathes a terrifying urgency into the age-old themes of co-dependence, hatred, and betrayal.

–Jeff Hoffmann, author of *Other People's Children*

In 1933, in a rural area outside of Rayville, Louisiana, the birth of a child was keenly anticipated. His coming has awakened spiritual forces seeking balance in the universe. Two entities in close contact are believed to have similar properties even after being separated, making it possible to manipulate one to reach the other. So it is with the child, Clyde, who will struggle between two powerful women. One believes in his inherent evil, while the other thinks she can nurture his salvation.

PART ONE
1933

CHAPTER ONE

A restless edge in her spirit pushed Cora's mind into a frenetic clash between will and want. Her knee bounced up and down beneath the table where she sat while her toe tapped against the wooden floorboards. Her hazel eyes gazed blankly around the room, unable to focus or fix on any one thing while the slight insistent tremor of what her grandmother called "the Knowing" gnawed within her.

Drawing in a deep breath, Cora reined in her thoughts, delved into her memories, and brought her eyes back to the journal opened on the table. Picking up her pencil, it raced across the page, recording her brooding.

June 6, 1933

Seem to me like sometimes, I spend just as much time writing as I do living what I writes about. But most times, I think if I couldn't talk on these here pages, I might go crazy. Lose my mind.

Joe sitting over there in his rocker watching me like he always do. It be a shame he never learn to read or write. I be glad, though, because I can say anything I wants to and don't have to worry none about him reading it. I tells him as much as I can, but there always be things of the spirit what ain't no way to explain.

Her pencil stopped, her sight fixed on the opposite wall, meditating on the events of the previous evening as they played across the screen of her mind. She thought about her boys, then paused, hesitant that if she complained, the Lord would consider her ungrateful for the blessing of their twins, David and Daniel, and then take them away.

She and Joe had long accepted her barren womb when they had miraculously swollen in her belly. Now, at two, the twins challenged her every day. Daniel had overturned the wash tub, and together, the boys had dragged the laundry through the mud, her screams and admonitions pushing their glee to greater heights. Not even the threat of Joe taking a switch to their behinds had deterred them from further mischief until she gave them milk mixed with molasses and valerian to force them into an afternoon nap.

Later, her body nearly collapsed with the strain of the day. Exhaustion dragged her down while her uncooperative brain refused to slow down. She wasn't asleep but caught in that twilight place between being asleep and awake, all the day's unfinished work playing across her nerves. She took a mental inventory of the herbs she was running low on, then let her thoughts chase themselves until they arrived at Fannie, making her shiver involuntarily before the pencil scratched across the rough paper again.

> *That's when the dreams come. I be standing in the field right back of the house, and I can feels something getting closer. It be real bad. I hear the Knowing louder each time, warning me about what I done. Telling me I got to make it right. This feeling of what coming is twisting up in my spirit. It ain't nothing about life. It all about death. And I know what coming is all my fault.*
>
> *I regrets it now, but not then. Wasn't nothing else I could do when they brings Fannie to me all tore up like she was. I still hears the*

Knowing pressing on me to let her die. I didn't listen. I couldn't. It wasn't no choice for me but to tends her. I is a healer, Lord.

The pencil slipped from her fingers, and Cora's hand rose to rub her chest, the cold foreboding an icy brick lodged over her heart. Joe rose from his chair, crossing the room to sit across the table from her, sipping his coffee. Ribbons of steam spiraled upward. The smoke from the scorching dark liquid obscured his curious stare as he watched her write, mystified by the swirling lines and circles that formed letters he could not decipher.

"What you putting down there, gal?" he asked before puckering his lips to blow on the coffee.

"Just writing. How your coffee?"

He made a loud, satisfied slurping sound before he answered, "It just like I likes my women, strong, black, and sweet." His voice held a hint of amusement, and a blush quickly stained the caramel tan of her skin. He chuckled out loud. It tickled him to see a woman as strong and competent as his Cora become so undone at a simple compliment.

Winking at her embarrassment, he waited for her response. Cora had a quick, sharp wit and always enjoyed their usual early-morning game of words and teasing. But none came. She didn't come back with a scathing comment meant to put him in his place as usual. She simply stared vacantly at the pages of the journal in front of her, and he stopped himself, sensing a more profound discomfort lurking below the surface of their early-morning banter.

Standing, he pushed his chair back from the table, thinking to ask her what was bothering her, then hesitated. She always told him things in her own time, trusting him to listen and believe. He waited another moment, hearing the pencil scratching across the paper, pride swelling in his chest as it always did when he saw her writing.

Moving across the room, he lowered himself back into the heavy rocking chair beneath the living room window. A warm, gentle breeze blew over him, the sun not having had a chance to heat the air to the temperatures that would later wring sweat from him until his face rained water. He slowly rocked back and forth, watching the curve of her bent back, her broad shoulders, and the profile of her face, her eyes narrowed in concentration. She was a handsome woman, her strong features carved into rich, caramel-brown skin, etching a face that confronted the world with fierce determination. Her strange hazel eyes seemed to stare into the depths of the heart, seeing beyond the limitations of human sight. The room was silenced, filled only with their synchronized breathing and the ticking of the mantel clock.

Cora jumped in her seat as a fisted hand slammed repeatedly on the frame of the kitchen's back door, making Joe lean forward in his chair. Through the grit and wire of the screen, he could barely make out the slender shoulders of a child. Slowly, he recognized him as Fannie's oldest boy, Don, hunched over on the step.

Rising from the table, Cora walked to the door and pushed it open so that Don could see her. He remained leaned over for another moment, his hands grasping his knees, air bellowing in and out of his open mouth. Finally, seeing her standing in the open doorway, he straightened up, nodding his head, first to Joe, still seated in the rocker in the living room behind her, and then to her. He rolled the broken brim of his straw hat around in his hand and jostled from one foot to another as he squinted at Cora. She waited for him to speak, seeing the wild panic and fear in his eyes.

"Muh, morning, Miss Cora. My mamma need help." He panted, his words stopping and starting, stuttering over one another as he struggled to get them out. "She-she in a real bad way. Th-that baby ain't coming right." Pausing for breath, he swallowed, slowed down, and began again, forcing the words to come out correctly. "They send me for you. Say you be the only one might can help."

Cora gazed at the distraught child, her eyes locking with his as she searched his spirit, his overwhelming fear cascading through him and reaching out to her.

"She been paining long, Don?" she asked. Her hands kneaded the fabric of her skirt, twisting the coarse cloth until it bunched around them, hiding the tremor that had begun when Don arrived.

"Since last night, Miss Cora. I ain't never heard my mama holler like that with none of my brothers."

Behind her, Joe shook his head "No" emphatically as he rose halfway to his feet. "Cora?" his voice rumbled a warning from deep in his chest.

"I got this, Joe." Cora moved to block Don's view of him, ignoring the part of her that wanted to agree and send the boy on his way. The Knowing prodded her. She sucked in a breath and spoke, her voice sounding firm and assured to her ears as she heard the thump of Joe's body falling back heavily into the rocker behind her.

"Don, go on and get you a dipper of water from the bucket outside. Then you go on back home. Let them know I'm on my way. I just got to get my bag, and I be right there."

She watched until he followed her directions, and she saw his feet kicking up dust moving in the direction of his house. Turning around, she stared at Joe, untangling her damp hands from the fabric of her skirt and rubbing them down her sides. Walking back and forth in front of the table, she began to pace restlessly.

Dread sent an icy chill spreading until it flowed down her arms, numbing her fingers, and settled just above her stomach. She could feel the weight of the Knowing dimming her vision and robbing the light from the room. Fear churned in her gut, forming an acid rush, burning as it rose in her throat. She swallowed the bitter gall, glancing from beneath lowered lids at Joe, her eyes silently beseeching him for understanding.

Joe cleared his throat, hawked, and spat into a large red handkerchief he pulled from his pocket before glaring in his wife's direction.

"You know them folks is all touched, Cora. Ain't not one of them right in the head. Not Fannie, Corinn, or any of them other girls. Only one seem like she got a lick of sense is Beaulah, and I ain't real sure about her."

"What you want me to do?" Her words rose, pitched high with her distress. "You wants me to let her die this time?"

Cora let the question settle in the air unanswered, then continued talking, her arms crossed over her chest, rubbing at the chill before giving voice to her feelings. "You know my granny, Mi, always said I got the gift. Say I was special, and it be a blessing." She stopped, holding Joe's eyes with her own, spinning the memory until he could see it clearly hanging between them. "Well, one day, when I was little, I got to smelling myself. Put my hands on my hips, reared back, and I told Mi I don't wants to be special, and I don't want no gift."

Cora paused, running her fingers down her cheek, the remembered sting from her grandmother's palm fresh and hot on her face. "She pretty near slap my face off." The corners of her mouth turned downward as she continued. "She say, '*I remembers when you was born, and I seen that veil covering you. Look like you ain't got no face. Damn near scare your momma to death.*'" Cora waited, assuring herself that he was listening, then continued. "And then she laugh, you know how Mi used to do, and she say, '*But the Knowing tell me how special you was gon' be. I ain't got it like you. It just be a little bit, but enough for me to see what in you. You got the healing; the sight and the Knowing be powerful strong in you. It a gift, and I be damned to hell before I let you turn your back on a gift God done bless you with.'"*

Cora sighed before turning away from Joe to stare back through the window. "She buried that veil right out there under that pecan tree," she finished, pointing at the towering branches of the large tree in their front yard. Her shoulders slumped, exhausted by the remembering.

Turning from the window, she allowed her feet to bring her to stand behind Joe's chair, her hand resting on his shoulder. "Choice ain't been give to me. I got to fight for it every time," she cried, her voice a hoarse whisper cutting the air.

Joe reached up, squeezing her fingers in his large hand, then bringing them forward to plant a gentle kiss on her knuckles, shame bending his head forward. As the mantle clock ticked off the minutes, Cora absorbed the range of emotions he tried to hide as his kiss tingled beneath her fingertips . . . anger, bitterness, and fear.

"Do what you has to do." He softened his words, forcing his emotions under control. He released her hand and watched silently as she walked into the bedroom they shared.

Kneeling to reach under the bed for her healing satchel, Cora felt the Knowing slam into her mind, clinching around her spirit. Rocking back on her heels, she brought her hand up to her throbbing head and gathered her breath.

Scooting backward, she clutched the satchel to her chest, then rose to stare through the bedroom's large window and opened herself to the Knowing. The divination of the birth descended into her, both a terrifying prediction and a deadly weight. *The child must die.* Cora cried out, her wail filling the room.

She waited, fully expecting to see Joe's big frame filling the doorway, coming to rescue her. Her soft sobs remained trapped in the room as the Knowing sealed the space around her, and she reconciled herself to the power that dwelled inside her.

She was afraid, a devastating fear manifesting itself in the rapid palpitations of her heart that threatened to crumble her where she stood. She feared the stain of darkness to come, feared what it might do to her. She wondered if it would warp her soul, take over her, and make her a part of its evil. Would she be any different than the corruption she sought to eliminate?

Cora wiped the tears from her face and stood, feeling in her pocket for her journal, and yielded to the Knowing. She was responsible for fixing the tear in the fabric of her world that she had unwittingly set into motion. Her mouth moved in soundless prayer, the vacuum around her dissolving. Striding across the room, she straightened her posture and returned to the living room.

Reaching Joe, she stopped, leaning down to kiss the irritation from his face, running her fingers along the stubble on his cheek. "You can let Daniel and David sleep some more," she said, sending a worried glance toward the other bedroom shared by their boys. "I only be gone as long as it take."

Joe leaned his head back, peering up into her eyes, unable to put his finger on a tangible reason for his fear. His eyes silently pleaded with her to stay; then, seeing her determination, shuttered in acceptance. Nothing would make her stay.

Straightening her back and squaring her shoulders, Cora walked away from him, placing the room's distance between them. Reaching the screen door, she pushed through it, letting it bang behind her. Joe felt another shiver of dread pass between them and crossed himself.

Before he'd met Cora, he'd never been a superstitious man. Now, it was a permanent fixture in his world.

Cora's feet turned from the dirt road leading from her house to the trampled path that would take her through the woods to Fannie's house. Anxiety cramped her stomach, making it ache. She stopped several times on the path, her reluctant feet digging into the grass, pushing up small tufts of earth, and considered turning back. She tried willing her body to return to the safety of her home, taking her back where she could feel Joe's arms wrapping around her, holding her close to his chest.

She sucked in a long, heavy breath, compelled by an invisible force to move forward. Another thread of the memory she had shared with Joe earlier floated on a thread through her mind until it became a picture of her younger self and Granny Mi.

She visualized Granny, her Cherokee features riding in her high cheekbones and flashing dark eyes. Her hair was parted in the middle and pulled into two long, tight black braids that hung almost at her waist. She let the sounds of Granny Mi's scolding voice resonate in her inner thoughts.

"*We is who we was made to be and does what us purposed to do*," she would say, then thump the edge of Cora's ear using her forefinger and thumb, followed by a reprimand that demanded she "*Shut up that noise and does what you told!*" The memory inserted its way into the fabric of her reality, banishing her useless desires.

Granny Mi was the one who told her she was born with a powerful strength in the Knowing as well as a connection to both the light and the dark. The Knowing was a force that absorbed and wove the light and dark energy of every being. It flowed through her, revealing and influencing the present and future of the lives around her.

The light unveiled patience, kindness, gentleness, love, and healing, possessed by all in varying degrees. In others, it disclosed a propensity for the darkness, leaning toward perversions, debauchery, anger, viciousness, and brutality. Life pulled on both forces as each person fought to keep them in balance. Viewed through her mind's eye that saw into the soul, the Knowing allowed her to discern them clearly.

Lifting her eyes toward the heavens, she began to pray out loud, her head thrown back, her voice climbing to the skies above and imploring the ancestors in the heavens for help. She brought her prayer focus to the enormity of the task presently before her. Today would demand both the dark and the light of her gift.

Standing there, Cora froze during her prayers as a wrenching scream pierced the stillness of the day, rising above her own cries and snapping her mouth shut. Her eyes stretched wide as the cry ripped through the air. It vibrated on the breeze, speaking of pain beyond human endurance, an agony that begged for a merciful end. Cora lifted her skirts and ran.

CHAPTER TWO

Cora came to a halt, panting, her shoulders heaving with each breath. One hand shading her eyes, she squinted into the distance until Fannie's house came into view. She took in the gray, weathered boards of the dilapidated two-room shack and how the sun beat down on its corrugated tin roof beneath the cloudless blue sky. The metal had rusted. In the sections where it had been replaced, it produced an overlay of new tin grafted on old in odd patches, making the house look as forlorn as she felt.

The Knowing reawakened in the recesses of her mind. It stretched and unfurled to burrow its way to the forefront of her thoughts, bringing with it again the awareness of what was to come. Her feet remained rooted in place as her spirit battled, clamoring between obedience to the Knowing, her will, and her want to perform her healer's calling. Another scream rang out from the house, and she succumbed, accepting both the curse and the blessing of the Knowing.

She straightened to her full height, drew in several deep breaths, and shook off the premonitions. Striding forward, she pushed through the sagging screen door and into the house itself, where she was immediately overwhelmed by the stench that saturated the air and assaulted her nostrils.

Beneath the shack's roof, the sun's heat formed the single room into an oven. It broiled the raw, pungent smell of Fannie's sweat, mingling together the stink of blood, mucous, urine, and feces that lay in a pool between her raised legs. Fannie lay thrashing on the bed.

"I ain't backing away from this," Cora whispered, crossing to the pump adjacent to the sink to wash her hands. Dropping her bag on the room's only table, she joined the family at the laboring woman's bedside.

Cora added the strength of her hands to those of Fannie's mother and sisters as they tried to restrain her on the bed. The woman screamed again as her back arched with the onset of another pain, bending her like a bow drawn tight. The other women looked across her body at Cora, shaking their heads, loss swimming in the unshed tears pooling in their eyes. Each waited for the death that lingered in the rank air around them, counting it a blessing.

Cora, who stood just under six feet in height, commanded the area around them. Sweat poured from her forehead, dripping from her chin. Sliding her hands up Fannie's arms, she took her by the shoulders and shook her before pushing her down onto the mattress.

"I be sorry, Fannie. I knows you hurting, gal, but you got to stop fighting me," Cora urged, speaking through clenched teeth. The muscles in her upper arm bulged and flexed as she grabbed Fannie across her back, rolling her to her side and pulling her to the edge of the bed. "Get that sheet out from under her," she panted.

The women grabbed the soiled sheet and yanked it swiftly from beneath Fannie's hips, then allowed Cora to roll her back onto the bare mattress. Once Fannie was on her back again, Cora used her strong hands to knead the round mass of her abdomen. It hardened with another contraction, and Fannie's heels dug into the mattress. She threw her head back, howling.

Cora traced her fingers over the taut skin of the woman's abdomen, staring at the outline of the baby's body seen clearly against the skin of her stomach, the head visible beneath her breast. She inhaled sharply. *Lord, help us. I know you got a plan.* She breathed out a prayer: *Give this child strength.*

She hesitated, the Knowing solidifying and manifesting itself in a warning within her to let both mother and child die that negated her plea. Cora continued stubbornly with her prayer. *You done seen this before we did. Show me the way, please, and thank you.* She sighed, seeking direction and solace, ignoring the strife between the Knowing and her Christian faith. Behind her, she heard a snort of derision coming from Fannie's mother.

Fannie's eyes rolled wildly, tracking from Cora to her mother and sisters, then finally fixing on her sister, Beulah. A pitiful whimper escalated in volume to become a shriek of despair as her head whipped back and forth.

"We gon' die." She wailed into the silent wall of the women's collective anguish, waiting for someone to refute her words. Her mother, Corinn, and her sister, Ruth Anne, lowered their heads and averted their eyes as she wept helplessly.

Beulah dipped a rag into the bowl of cool water on the nightstand beside the bed. After wringing it out, she wiped it across her sister's forehead and cooed soothingly. Her mouth worked in intercessory prayer, her heart twisting as she witnessed her sister's pain.

"Hush, Fannie, and be still. Ain't nobody gon' let you die." She murmured the words softly, her mouth close enough to whisper into her sister's ear. Her hands traced a path as she wiped her sister's brow, her head turned to avoid the judgment in the eyes of her mother and sister. Beulah squeezed Fannie's hand and continued pouring their hopes between them into the shell of her sister's ear. "He coming, Fannie. The one we done heard the Lord promise."

Fannie smiled weakly and squeezed her sister's hand in return before another pain arched her back, eliciting a long moan. Cora raised her chin and motioned the other women into place.

"Beulah, you, and Corinn hold her shoulders down. Don't let up," she ordered the women. "Ruth Anne holds her by the ankles. This gon' be hard."

With one hand pressed firmly against Fannie's stomach and the other thrusting upward through the hot, moist walls of her sex, she continued to push her hand upward, ignoring Fannie's cries and her own pain as another contraction squeezed Fannie's womb, feeling the tightening on her arm and wrist.

Panting, she waited until it passed and pushed upward until she felt the tiny feet of the infant. Opening her fingers, she grasped her hand tightly around them and yanked, putting all her strength behind it.

"PUSH!" she screamed at Fannie.

She felt the baby sliding forward as Fannie fought to rise on her elbows, her chin against her chest as she pushed down, the ripping pain tearing at her. Cora saw the genitals and grabbed the baby with both hands, turning him to ease his shoulders out, then pulled again until he lay in her waiting hands, facedown.

Fannie fell backward onto the bed and wished for death. The room had gone quiet, as though everyone had taken a breath they could not release. She waited to hear her child's cry fill the void.

Cora stood still, the silent infant lying facedown in her cold hands. Even from the back, she could see the effect of being forced and snatched from his mother's womb in the severely warped shape of his head.

His skin was pale gray, showing no hint of blood flow. She turned him quickly, then gasped at the sight of his nose squashed into his face, his bulging eyes, and his wide, silent mouth.

Her Knowing radiated outward, probing at the darkness emanating from the infant in waves as he struggled for his first breath, his body twisting with the effort. Cora felt the tendrils of the Knowing like snakes writhing beneath her skin, protesting the darkness as it judged the balance of the infant's spirit. Her eyes darkened, her body swaying unsteadily.

Corinn raised her arms in front of her, bent at the elbow, her index fingers crossed in front of her chest, forming the symbol of protection against evil as she recoiled at the sight of the horror in Cora's hands.

"Jesus, something wrong with him," Ruth Anne hissed, her arms and fingers crossed in imitation of her mother, taking a step backward. Beulah's eyes remained riveted on the child.

Cora trembled, feeling the slight weight of him resting in her palm. The Knowing thundered in her mind, loud and insistent, urging her to place her large hand over the infant's face, denying him the breath of life. Beulah, Ruth Anne, and Corinn stared, their mouths flapping without sound, horrified at the spectacle before them.

"What's wrong?! Give him to me." Fannie's words floated weakly to where Cora stood, breaking through the spell of the Knowing. Cora paused, then hesitated, her duty as a healer and the duty the Knowing thrust upon her grinding in conflict against each other. Fannie attempted to sit up, grimacing in pain, her arms reaching out for the fragile body of her son. Cora steeled herself as the Knowing asserted itself again, bending her to fulfill its demand.

The baby's eyelids slowly slid open, staring at her, unflinching and peering soul deep. The agitation of the Knowing grew, asserting itself beyond her spiritual gifts as darkness spread upward from the child through her arms, intensifying into a solid block around her heart. She felt the urgency of the Knowing ricocheting around her brain, demanding that she "*do it*" as she remained paralyzed in the newborn's gaze.

The smell of copper rose into the air as hot blood rushed from Fannie, soiling the mattress further and startling Cora—who blinked twice—freeing herself from her trance. She looked down at the baby, and the ramrod steel determination from the Knowing dissolved as the baby stared, unblinking. In his eyes, a separate and distinct darkness swirled in the depths of the obsidian orbs, obscuring the whites. His tiny chest began to rise slowly, his lungs laboring for air.

Cora stared, mesmerized, locked in the grip of his gaze. The words that would end him dissipated. Her body deflated. The Knowing went silent. The strength of her inner light melted and dimmed, withering under the child's darkness.

Hastily, she pushed the baby into Fannie's arms and turned, moving quickly to her bag, her large, heavy shoes making prints in the dust of the earthen floor. She rummaged, hands shaking as she searched for the herbs to pack Fannie's womb and stop the bleeding before she lost her, trying not to think of the baby's death as a blessing missed. On the bed, Fannie clutched the child to her chest. Glimpsing them from the corner of her eye, Cora could see him wriggling and knew he still lived.

Returning to the bed, Cora pressed against Fannie's abdomen until the placenta slid forward. Gathering it, she twisted it in a clean cloth, set it aside to be buried in the yard later, then packed a poultice of red raspberries into Fannie's womb. Finally, she tied a thick wad of white cloth rags between her legs. The herbs would control the bleeding.

As she worked, she felt regret niggling against her mind. Feeling opportunity sliding away, Cora cleared her throat, courage seeping back into her veins—the Knowing strengthening her for the moment—and began speaking aloud.

"Fannie, he ain't right, child. I got the Knowing, and I can feels it. He pure dark. Ain't no light in him." She stopped, waiting for the words to sink in, seeing the other women retreating farther. "You knows I got the sight, was born with a veil, and I sees how much dark in this one." The tension in the air threatened to suffocate her as her head reeled, struggling to inhale. The Knowing throbbed again, pulsing and insistent. Unlike before his birth, she saw her mistake. The darkness in the child was palatable, stronger than anything she had felt before, and now she had allowed it into the world.

"Give him to me and let me send him back before it be too late," Cora demanded, holding out her arms. Her head swiveled around, trying to catch the eyes of the women surrounding her, hoping they would raise their bowed heads and provide some support.

"You a witch!" Corinn screamed, pointing at Cora. At the sound of her mother's anguished cry, Ruth Anne's head jerked up as if snapped by an invisible string. "And you is a Jezebel spirit!" she yelled, her finger pointing at Fannie. "And he a whore son. Demon spawn before the Lord!"

Corinn's jaw unhinged, dropping open, her throat choking on silent words of outrage as her youngest daughter's disgrace solidified into a lump of humiliation. Her eyes shone with a venomous hatred as she stepped forward, her gaze scanning across Beulah, Fannie, Cora, and back to Ruth Anne, whose reddened face remained twisted and contorted in fury. In her head, she already heard the whispers of the townspeople wafting around her, reaching out to envelop her in shame.

"So, they was speaking truth about you and that man, and that there the proof in your arms," Corinn shouted, her voice escalating to a scream, bouncing off the walls and obliterating the baby's weak cries. She crossed herself hastily, her eyes searching the ceiling as if she could penetrate it and see the Lord in his heavens looking down on her with divine forgiveness.

Beulah whirled, screeching as she separated herself from her mother and sister, her teeth bared in a snarl as she faced them. "Don't you dare judge her or him." She advanced toward her sister, hands raised, stopping only when their mother inserted her body between them. "You ain't the Lord in heaven. He the one say who live and who don't and ain't none of you fit to judge, so you shut your mouth right now."

Corinn bumped them apart, using the girth of her chest and hips—leaving them to glare at each other—filling the small space with the sound of their angry breaths. She placed her arm around Ruth Anne's shoulder and sniffed indignantly in Beulah's direction, putting distance between them.

On the bed, Fannie clutched the baby's tiny body closer to her chest, scrunching down into the bloody mattress, shielding him with her own body, protecting him from the harshness of their words. She stared down into his distorted features—all too big, overpowering his face, his skin turning purple with the continued effort to breathe.

Clutching him tighter within the crook of her arm, she leaned her head down until her mouth covered his nose and mouth, then exhaled into him, watching his chest rise. She ran her fingers lovingly over the wrinkled crevices of his skull, down his cheek, and across his tiny body, and then repeated the process.

She allowed her hand to continue downward, stroking his shriveled legs and wondering if they would ever support his weight or if she would see him walk or run. Gazing into his eyes, she willed him to live, infusing him with her spirit, whispering and praying for the Lord to remember his promise that her baby was special and mightier than any of the darkness Cora prophesied or what anyone else thought they saw. She ignored the swirling she saw stirring in the depths of his eyes.

Looking down at her son and closing her eyes, she let her sister's hateful words slide away. Tears flowed down her cheeks, anointing his head and body. She vowed to make her son better and fix whatever was broken in him.

"He be all right. I make him be all right. The Lord done told me when he saved me." Her words, a ragged whisper, silenced the room, stunning her mother and sisters. "He the living proof of my redemption, and ain't nobody never gon' hurt him."

She curled her body protectively around her baby, a grunt of pain pushing through her lips. She glared at Cora, who still stood beside the bed, holding her arms out again expectantly. Her fingers and palm continuously rounded her baby's crown, smoothing the dented skull before stroking her fingers on either side of his nose, shaping it, and then moving to start again.

"Don't you come near him," she hissed at Cora, her breath blowing the soft, thick curls on his head.

"Least let me clean him off," Cora urged, the Knowing surging again, making her frantic and filling her with desperate plans. *When I go to clean him, he just gon' stop breathing. It be the Lord's will. All us could see how he was fighting for air.*

She reasoned it would be a blessing, the spirits sparing him from the crippled life his deformed legs promised him. The Knowing clouded her thoughts, assuring her *Fannie would understand and be glad he was dead.*

"You ain't touching him again," Fannie hissed, annihilating her plans. "Beulah gon' stay and clean him up. She the onliest one I can trust." Fannie gripped the infant tighter, shaking her head violently as though reading Cora's intent. "The rest of you get on out my house, and don't you never come back. You just gone and get. My husband make sure you get paid for coming, Miss Cora, but you can get out too."

The Knowing flooded Cora's mind with images of her yanking the child from Fannie's arms and dashing his head against the floor. Her mouth rounded in horror, the vision so real she could hear the thud of the baby's skull against the earth and feel his blood splashing against her skin. She recoiled, feeling her legs straining to move forward. She couldn't do it. She looked at the child, helpless in his mother's arms, and shook her head in defeat.

Cora turned away, her shoulders hunched, her face a closed mask hiding her frustration. The baby's breathing had eased, becoming regular and even. Fannie's mouth continued to move silently in prayer.

Corinn and Ruth Anne joined together, their faces drawn tightly in scandalized offense. Their malice toward Fannie and her child pulsed outward, forming a wall between them.

"We should have knowed when you brought that witch up in here what was gon' happen," Corinn spat in the dirt in front of her. "A demon cain't bring forth nothing but another demon," she intoned loudly.

"We gon' leave you to the Lord," she called back over her shoulder as she and Ruth Anne turned to leave. Beulah stood sentinel between them, shielding Fannie and the child.

Cora felt the Knowing retreat in the face of her refusal. Sighing in resignation, she watched as the women shuffled toward the door, glaring over their shoulders at her and Fannie. Gathering her things, she stuffed them back into her bag and left. No one seemed to notice.

Cora's long legs ate up the distance, striding through the wild grass surrounding her. Her leather bag bumped against her knees as she walked, the familiarity of the tall stalks tickling against her senses, giving her small comfort. She relished the connection between herself and the earth as her bare toes dug into the ground, the sandy dirt coming up in little puffs between her toes as she walked, her shoes draped over her bag. She looked down at her broad, wide feet, her lips pursed in disgust.

She had two pairs of shoes, one for Sunday and the everyday pair of men's work brogans that she wore when it was wet and muddy—or she had a distance to travel, like today. She let her thoughts wander to the tin tub Joe would fill with heated water and have waiting for her tired feet. A small smile curved the corners of her mouth at his thoughtfulness. He would add lemon juice and baking soda to the water and let it soak away the tough skin. Then he would massage her feet with castor oil, making them smooth before they went to bed.

Thinking about her big feet was easier than contemplating the sense of failure weighing her down as she walked, oblivious to her surroundings and trusting her body to find its way back home on its own. The snakes of raw power the Knowing sent had quieted, no longer contorting beneath her skin, and she felt a flicker of her healing light rekindle.

She chewed her lower lip as she replayed the birth in her mind, looking for any opportunity she might have missed, a time when she could have obeyed the Knowing without hesitation. When she held the baby in the palm of her hand, she thought she could have wrapped the umbilical cord around his neck and used her hand to choke off any air he could draw in. No one would have seen her. Or she could have let his slippery, writhing body drop to the floor. The different scenarios flashed back and forth through her mind, each one a boulder threatening to bury her. She had felt the darkness in him, and yet she had wavered.

Standing under the glaring heat of the sun, the Knowing flooded her vision with images of Fannie, taking her back to the child's creation, the same visions that plagued her dreams. She saw how the healing she had performed nine months ago had unwittingly shifted the balance of the light and the dark in the world.

She witnessed his parents in the backwoods in a small clearing, lying spent in each other's arms. His name was Nathaniel, and Cora could sense Fannie's feelings spreading outward. *Couldn't nobody love her like he did. When he touched her skin, the hard callouses of his hand tickling as he stroked made her feel like a real woman. With him, she was beautiful, not worn out from having babies one after another, cleaning, scrubbing, cooking, and taking in laundry. Before him, she'd felt as washed out as the endless work clothes she scrubbed.*

Cora heard Nate begging Fannie to leave James Henry and run away with him. She sensed both his misery and how desperately Fannie wanted to go, leave it all, and be free to live on the tenderness of his kisses and the warmth of his hands caressing her thighs.

She felt Fannie's immense regret when her desires slammed into the solid reality of leaving her boys behind. Her hands stroked Nate's shoulders, and she followed the trail of her fingertips with little kisses and nips of her teeth against his skin as she talked, using the soft tone of lovers.

I just needs to wait until they a little older. Then I can leaves. Her breath caught deep in her throat. *James Henry cain't take care of his own self. Ain't no way I can leaves them boys to him and my mama.*

Cora winced as each word pierced Nathaniel's soul, his anger rising, leaking darkness that peeled away his love. His body hardened against Fannie, swelling with fury as she spoke. Cora watched as Fannie turned her head at an angle to face him, seeing his eyes transform into a vortex of anger and hatred, growing with every word of her rejection. They became larger and darker, with a black mist swirling within their depths.

She saw Nathaniel raising himself, then scooting backward on his knees, staring down at Fannie, his fisted hand lifting, then coming down to smash her face. Cora flinched, feeling each blow in her own body, hearing the crack of bone as his fist came down repeatedly. Fannie grunted and screamed, throwing her arms across her face, attempting to protect herself from the blows raining down on her as she thrashed beneath him.

She heard Fannie praying aloud, her petitions for mercy tangling in the boughs of the trees overhead. Cora felt Fannie's legs being stretched wide as her hands batted at him, ineffective as flies against a window screen. Nate grasped her wrists together, holding them above her head, his knees holding her legs apart as he fumbled with his manhood, pushing it against her. She pleaded helplessly, her mouth a litany of begging, her eyes reflections of terror, her body bucking wildly.

Then the raw, searing pain came as tissue ripped and tore while Nathaniel pounded her body, claiming it for himself. His free hand wrapped around her throat, choking off her screams as he squeezed harder with each thrust until the last of his rage poured out of him, his seed flowing into her.

Cora squeezed her thighs together where she stood, her hands reflexively covering her womanhood. Nathaniel's darkness permeated her being, and she felt herself cringing away from it. It was the aura she'd felt in the infant today when she held him.

Mi had always taught her there wasn't a person born that didn't have both dark and light and a spark of the Knowing. The balance moved and shifted, depending on their choices and paths in life. Then there was that rare person Mi had warned her about, whose darkness smothered his light. There was no balance in people like Nathaniel. And now his seed had produced an heir, someone even darker than he had been.

The boy was the aberration the Knowing repeatedly showed her in her dreams. The baby planted in Fannie's womb that was not meant to be. Cora felt her body tremble, the shaking starting in her legs and flowing upward through her arms and into her hands. Her hands twitched uncontrollably, her eyes blinking open and shut rapidly. She felt like she was breaking apart, shattering into pieces that would fly into the wind and scatter into the universe.

The Knowing pierced sharply in her mind, a stabbing pain that forced her to reach up and grab her head, holding it as the deluge of memories continued.

The sour sweat of desperation wafted off them in waves when they arrived at Cora's door, Fannie's bloodied body drooping in James Henry's arms. Beulah wept. She and James Henry told her that Doc Adams had refused to treat her. Cora had snorted. Of course, he wouldn't. He had never been able to stand up beneath the threat of town gossip and the weight of the mothers' board of the church.

Town folks said Beulah, her sisters Fannie and Ruth Anne, their mother Corinn, and that whole Cooper clan were crazy as rabid coons. They walked the roads between town and their backwoods shacks, Bibles clutched to chests, heads covered, mouths working in prayer, convinced of their own holy righteousness.

Now, heathen, witch, and sinner that she was in their eyes, she was all they had. She saw again Fannie's battered and bruised body sprawled unconscious on her son's bed, the stink of Nathaniel's seed wafting up from her torn and mutilated body. She saw how the darkness had hovered over her skin, and deep purple bruises circled her neck. She felt the pause in her spirit again, feeling Fannie's life hanging by a precarious thread balanced on the edge of death. She had finally yielded, bending beneath Beulah's wailing pleas and the sadness that pulled down James Henry's features.

Cora's thoughts continued to chase themselves like wild squirrels, back and forth from branch to branch, until she was mentally exhausted. Shaking herself free from her reverie, she looked around, not knowing how long she had stood in the middle of the woodland grass, her arms hanging at her side, her features slack, the Knowing and the light embedded deep inside her body. Coming to herself, she squared her shoulders, straightened her back, and continued her walk toward home. She had the Knowing, but she also had free will. She had decided, and an abomination had anchored itself in flesh.

She would wait and watch. Only time would fully judge the weight of her actions. The Knowing had foretold that he should not be allowed to remain in the world, and she had rebelled against it, losing her opportunity to restore balance. She prayed that she would be given a chance to bring balance again. And if it meant taking his life force, she would yield. The Knowing would lead her in its own time, and she would trust that she would do what was right.

CHAPTER THREE

Clyde raised his hips to allow Fannie to tuck the blanket around his legs firmly, then patiently waited as she brushed the curls back from his forehead before planting a kiss there. At the age of six, even his diminutive size did not support his weight completely.

"Now, you waits here, Clyde. I'm going into the store, and I be right back."

He nodded and smiled up at her, reaching out to stroke her cheek, happy to be in town, away from the confines of their shack. He watched her back as she disappeared into the store and puckered his lips, attempting to whistle like he saw his older brothers do, his head turning to follow the comings and goings of the people treading on the rough boards that comprised the street.

Some of them stared as they passed, then turned away, whispering behind their hands. Clyde reached for the hat on the seat beside him and pressed it down on his head, protecting him from the sun's heat. He liked watching the people as they passed, wondering what it was like to have legs that went where you wanted them to go when you wanted them to. It seemed so easy for each of them, just like with his brothers.

He leaned forward, his arms resting on the edge of the truck, his chin perched on his folded arms. A short distance away, he heard laughter, followed by a small group of boys walking toward the vehicle. The footsteps abruptly halted as they reached where he sat.

Clyde smiled, a feeling of warmth and happiness filling him as he looked down into the three upturned faces, his thoughts filled with the hope of friendship. He remembered his mother telling him that you had to be a friend to make a friend.

"How you?" he asked, his voice uncharacteristically deep in the chest of a six-year-old.

The boys gawked, then laughed nervously, pointing at him. "Damn, you is ugly," one of them roared, slapping his friends on the back.

Clyde's smile slowly slid, turning his mouth down in the corners as he inhaled sadness. He pulled his arms back from the truck's rim, turning his head to look at the other side of the street where a woman stood watching him, two young boys running in circles around her. He held her gaze, willing her to help him, disappointed when she turned away. Behind him, the young boys continued, boisterously ridiculing him while his ears burned with shame. He regretted coming along on this trip. It was no different than the ones before.

"You still ugly, even from behind!" another boy guffawed. "Ain't you that monkey boy we done heard about?"

He heard six feet pounding the dust of the road to come up on the other side of the truck where they could stare at his face. He wished he could stand and face them, leap from the truck, and dare them to call him another name. But his legs remained twisted under the blanket. Today was a bad day for him, and the pain rendered them nearly useless.

He fought against the urge to hurt them, hoping by ignoring their taunts, they would grow weary and leave. Maybe they would feel ashamed enough to stop so he could try again to be friendly.

Instead, the words became more hurtful, stinging slurs hurled against him.

Clyde felt the darkness rising within him. It edged into his mind and swirled there, wanting to reach outward. The darkness knew just what to do. It knew how to stop them.

From across the street, Cora felt the Knowing stir and turned to see Clyde sitting in his father's truck. She felt the tendrils of joy she'd first felt dissipating from him as the darkness grew. Reaching out, her hands snatched Daniel and David to her, holding them against her long skirts. Her heart twisted in anguish as she felt Clyde's hurt, the boys taunting him from beside the truck, his anger growing with the darkness rolling through him.

Suddenly, she saw Fannie running toward the truck, her face twisted in anger. "YOU BEST GET YOUR LITTLE BAD ASSES AWAY FROM HERE!" she shouted, waving her handbag toward the boys as they ran away from the truck, scattering in different directions. She lifted her skirts, climbing into the back before duckwalking over to her son. "It all right, baby boy. They ain't gon' hurt you."

Clyde allowed himself to be pulled into his mother's embrace, inhaling the comfort of her scent, rose sachet, and mother's milk. His muscles relaxed, and the darkness released its hold on him. He watched trails of it following the boys as they ran away from the truck. Then he turned his head and saw the woman watching.

Cora exhaled, grateful tragedy had been averted. She'd felt the raw power of the darkness in him, watching it dancing and gathering around the boys outside the truck. She pinned Clyde with her gaze, then drew away before Fannie could see her, pulling her boys with her. She turned one last time to watch Fannie wipe the tears from Clyde's face, feeling the darkness recede from him.

"I thought we was going to the general store," David whined, unable to release his wrist from Cora's firm grasp.

"We'll come back tomorrow," she said, tugging harder, "and if I hear another word, you won't be with us."

Cora had visited this dreamscape so often that it no longer startled her. Instead, it felt safe and familiar. She stared around her. The soft sobs that had drawn her to this location carried through the twilight air toward her, and she began walking in that direction until she caught sight of Clyde hunched over in the tall grass, his head cradled against his knees.

She observed him from a distance, the Knowing drifting to enfold him. His aura pulsed green, tinged on its edges with purple, imbued by his overpowering need and his sense of confusion. He looked so small sitting there. His sorrow and loneliness were tangible to her, and she despaired, recalling his tear-streaked face the day before as he sat in the truck, trapped by his crippled limbs, unable to flee the insults of the boys around him.

In the years since his birth, she had followed him through town gossip, the occasional sighting, and through his dreams. She witnessed the dark Knowing manifesting within him in minuscule increments, often when he was frustrated, angry, or afraid.

As always, he remained blind to her, unable to see or sense her, disconnected from the divine in himself and others. Nothing reached him except the darkness.

Looking at him, she renewed her vow to remain vigilant. She trusted that she would know what to do if the time came. The Knowing prodded her, pushing her to see what he would become. She pushed it away.

Fannie shuffled from the stove to the small table in the center of the room, humming a little hymn of gratitude for the blessing of another day as she glanced over at Clyde sitting on his stool in the corner. A warm glow spread across her chest as she smiled at him. The Creator was as good as he had promised he would be. She had her special boy.

She harrumphed deep in her throat, recalling the viciousness of the words thrown at them over the years since his birth. They called him "bastard" and "demon," making the sign of the cross anytime they passed him in town. Before yesterday, she hadn't taken him to town with her since he was four, and others had taken to throwing rocks at them.

She stared at him, his head perfectly round beneath the mop of thick, black curls. His feet swung restlessly in the air, thumping against the legs of the stool, and his hands gripped the seat. He was humming tunelessly, trying to imitate the sounds that she made. His eyes followed her movements as she kneaded the bread dough on the table, dusting it with flour and then pummeling it.

"What you thinking about over there, baby boy?" she asked, waiting for his head to lift and acknowledge her words. His feet stopped in midair. "The Lord done made you able to walk when they said you never would."

She wiped her hands on her apron and picked up the bottle of healing oil from the windowsill. Leaning over Clyde, she rubbed his head, her hands following the familiar shape of his skull she had spent rounding since his birth. Kneeling, she rubbed both his legs with the oil, kneading it into his dark skin and praying as she did. She got it from a healer in the next town and had been using it when she stretched and pulled the muscles in Clyde's stunted legs. She rose to stand before him, dropping the precious oil into her apron pocket and placing her hands on her hips.

"You been sitting there most of the morning. Why you don't go on outside and play with the boys? Go give them legs some use. I knows they feeling better today, ain't they?" she asked before cupping her raised hands around her mouth and calling out, her voice escalating until it could clearly be heard outside. "SIMON! SIMON?"

Simon appeared in the doorway, his hands grasping the frame, breathing hard, his eyes rolling in panic. "You call me, Mama?"

She wiped traces of the remaining oil from her hands, leaving smears on the front of her dress before placing them back on her hips. "Take Clyde on outside with you so he can get some air. He don't need to always be in here up under me."

"Mama, you know he cain't do nothing. Why I got to take him?" Simon whined, annoyance momentarily displacing his fear of his mother.

Fannie crossed the short space to the door and cuffed him sharply on the side of the head before he could move, then grasped his left ear, twisting it between her fingers. "Boy, you back talking me?"

Simon squirmed, then stilled as the pain in his ear increased, huffing out air. "No, ma'm, no, ma'm, Mama," he squealed, his heart pumping madly in his narrow chest.

"Then takes your brother out like I said. If you cain't take him, then you stays in and play with him."

Simon lowered his head as his mother gave his ear a final twist, being sure to hide his glare from her as he considered his options. Finally, rubbing his tender ear, he held his hand out toward his brother.

"Come on, Clyde."

Clyde eased his body forward, looking first at his mother and then at his older brother. Simon was only eight, but he towered over him. Clyde began his slow, shifting gait, his knees knocking together with each step, his torso shifting from side to side. He stopped as he approached his mother, leaning into her, inhaling her smell as he wrapped his arms around her knees. She nudged him until he was an arm's length away, prying his reluctant arms from her knees and bending down to stare into his eyes.

"You go on, Clyde. It be all right," she said, her voice hushed, her breath whispering against his cheek before pushing him toward the door and Simon.

Fannie stood, her eyes hardened, losing all the softness they had held when looking at Clyde. "You watches out for baby boy and remembers what I done told you. And he better not get lost neither." She fixed Simon with a glare that froze the marrow in his bones, his body going rigid. "The Lord be watching over you both," she said, her gaze gentle again as Clyde took his brother's hand and left Fannie to return to her baking.

Once through the door and outside, Clyde strained, struggling to keep up with his brother's longer strides. Walking made his legs hurt worse, using up his little store of energy. "Wait for me, Simon," he called, the distance between them increasing. Simon scowled and hesitated, hearing his friends ahead of him, deeper in the woods.

He glared back at his brother, resentment rising as it often did when his mother thrust his brother on him. He hated the way Clyde made their lives.

Clyde had always been a problem for him, starting when they came home after he was born and saw him mewling and pathetic in his mother's arms. He and his two older brothers, Don and James Junior, had looked at the mashed-up face snuggling against their mother's breast, not liking him even before they learned any reasons to hate him.

Clyde sucked every minute of their mother's attention. His squalling screams startled the whole house awake each night, shredding the air and hammering against their ears throughout the day, demanding comfort. He was at her breast, on her lap, or held against her hip in a sling while she prayed for him.

She would forget about Simon, his brothers, and their father for days at a time, leaving them to find their own way in the shack, forage for food, and beg from their auntie Beulah, the only family still talking to them. There was no peace. Since Clyde was born, all he had known was hunger, humiliation, and the sound of his family falling apart.

His parents' fighting peppered the air of their shack, weaving the threads of discord around them from daybreak to can't see. Their arguments escalated into loud, brutal battles that ended with broken furniture, bruised bodies, and his father stomping out of the house and not returning for days or weeks.

At first, the other aunties and cousins had come around, trying to talk to his mother even when she screamed curses at them. Sometimes, they brought the preacher with them, standing outside and sprinkling holy water around the house, chanting prayers of salvation to disperse Clyde's demons.

Once, he'd seen his mother throw boiling lye water out at them, aiming for the preacher and screaming the name of the Lord. The preacher ran, holding his Bible over his head for protection, hollering and calling Fannie a blasphemer. That stopped the visits, leaving them to see family only at the rare gatherings.

Then came the final time when Clyde was about two. Auntie Beulah had just about got down on her knees and begged his mama to come for Christmas, crying and quoting the Bible about forgiveness. Then they had all gone to Granny Corinn's house.

When they arrived, the house smelled of roasted turkey, ham, and sweet potatoes, and the collected body odor of too many people pressed too closely together in a too-small space.

Fannie had scanned the room suspiciously, cutting her eyes around the place, her back up, waiting for the first openly hostile word. Eventually, she found a corner for Clyde. Whipping out the small quilt she carried with her, she placed him gently upon it, caressed his face, and left him staring at the crowd around him. The feet on his crippled legs pointed inward, not allowing him to crawl from the spot where his mother placed him while the family skirted around him, keeping their distance.

The cousins snickered and pointed at Clyde when Fannie wasn't looking, whispering behind their hands about his brother. Simon flinched and shushed them harshly, not wanting anything to set off Fannie's anger and force them all to leave. His mouth watered as his eyes roamed over the feast his grandmother had laid out on the table. His empty stomach growled in anticipation.

That was why he didn't see the mouse creeping toward Clyde, its fat brown body slung low to the floor, head raised, and whiskers quivering in the air as it made its way to the hole in the wall adjacent to the quilt Clyde sat on. Clyde bent forward, reaching out to snatch the wriggling creature faster than the mouse could react, bringing it up in front of his face. The movement caught the attention of the other children, causing them to look again toward Clyde.

Clyde stared at the mouse, his eyes glazing over, growing darker and rounder. As the frightened animal struggled to get free, it bit down on the tender skin between his thumb and forefinger, and he grunted loudly. His hands began to squeeze, seemingly unaware of the high screeching sound of the mouse, the small bones crunching, or the blood oozing through his fingers.

One of his cousins screamed, and the room erupted into chaos. His uncle Charles ran toward Clyde, attempting to swat the dead mouse from his hands. Fannie leaped on her brother's back, her hands reaching around to scratch his face, bellowing, "Don't you touch my baby. You better not touch him, Charles."

Uncle Charles had twirled in circles, trying unsuccessfully to buck her from his shoulders until his daddy had muscled his way through the crowd to grab Fannie around the waist. He carried her—twisting and thrashing—to lower her in front of Clyde.

Fannie crouched, her teeth bared in a feral snarl as she shielded her boy. Clyde continued to sit, the blood running over his closed fist, a smile turning up the corners of his mouth.

Fannie turned and grasped his wrists, shaking them until he loosened his grip on the dead rodent, wiping his hand on the front of her skirt. Lifting him from the floor, she wrapped the quilt around him and strode for the door.

The family, who had formed a dense circle around them, moved aside and cleared a path for her. Simon walked slowly behind her, his head lowered, avoiding the horrified looks of his aunts, uncles, and cousins, their whispers crawling against his back. That was when Granny Corinn stepped forward and blocked the front door.

"I done told you that boy an abomination, Fannie, and you knows it." She wagged an accusing finger in Fannie's face. "The whole town know how you was whoring round with that boy, Nathaniel, gapping open your legs." She stopped, her eyes shadowed with a moment of repentance before hardening again when looking at her daughter as she continued. "I be sorry, James Henry, and I don't means to offend you none, but you knows it too, and that boy ain't right. She should have let that witch Cora lay him to the side to die."

Fannie's hand shot out, striking her mother across the face, leaving a four-finger print, the echo of the blow resonating through the room. Corinn's head rocked back on her shoulders before she stumbled forward, falling onto Ruth Anne. Fannie's chest heaved with each breath—her body rigid, Clyde huddled against her chest—eyes blazing as Ruth Anne tried to rush forward, pushing against her mother's restraining arm.

Corinn's eyes bored into Fannie's as she pulled herself up to her full height, looking down at her daughter's petite form. Her words chopped through the air, whittling at Fannie. "You best be going, Fannie, and you don't never come back here no more. You ain't no child of mine. I ain't claiming you or that demon sin boy no more. I done prayed for you, and that's all I can do."

Fannie's head went back and sprang forward on her neck as she spit in her mother's face.

"That for you and your prayers," she shouted, then shouldered her way past, avoiding the hands that reached for her, leaving her mother with the glob of spittle sliding down her face.

Simon took a chance to look backward as he stumbled after her through the snow, seeing his aunts gathered around his grandmother, his auntie Ruth Anne being held down while she screamed, "Let me go! I'm gon' kill that no-good bitch, spitting on my mama." Tears streamed down Aunt Beulah's cheeks as she shook her head in dismay.

Reaching home, his daddy had shooed him and his brothers to their pallets, pulling the curtain that divided their sleeping space on the floor from their parents' bed. He could hear Clyde breathing on the other side of the curtain where he lay near their mother's side of the bed. He listened to her pacing, mumbling incomprehensible words to herself before he heard his father clear his throat and speak.

"You was wrong, Fannie, and you knows it." His words were followed by the sound of something flying through the air and crashing against the wall.

"You gon' takes her part against your own?!" Her voice was shrill, making him want to clap his hands over his ears.

"I'm guessing us all know that thing ain't mine." His voice was heavy with a finality Simon had never heard before, followed by a screeching scream that knifed his mind. His body became tense with fear.

The heavy tread of his father's boots moved toward the curtain before he pushed it aside, staring down and meeting Simon's terror-filled eyes for a moment before he strode to the door, Fannie's unholy shrieking following his bent back. Daddy left them for the last time.

After that, he would sometimes return and give his mother money or take the older boys to town with him. Later, the big boys went to town and stayed with him permanently. He claimed they were old enough to work in the shop with him, but he always left Simon behind. Said he needed to stay and help his mama. James Henry still sent money home when he could, leaving Simon stuck there with Clyde.

Simon felt the heat of anger and frustration burning his cheeks as he pushed the branches back from the clearing, seeing his friends gathered there. That was four years ago, and they hadn't seen his mother's family since then. Four years of having his gut twist with fear living in Clyde's shadow. He took a deep breath, swallowing his emotions and pushing his way into the clearing to stand before his friend, Robert.

"Oh, man, why you got to bring him?" Robert twisted his mouth in disgust, groaning as he stood up and brushed the dirt from the seat of his tattered overalls. The other two boys' faces were twisted in distaste as they looked over Simon's head at Clyde.

"Damn, that boy funny looking. He about the homeliest thing I done ever seen," Robert said, laughing loudly as he walked around Clyde, looking at him from head to toe. The boys behind him joined his laughter, nodding and pointing toward Clyde.

Simon shrugged his shoulders, his face coloring in embarrassment, the familiar taunts sticking to his skin like hot tar and mingling with his recent memories. "My mama say I got to bring him," he mumbled.

Being the oldest of the group, Robert took leadership and stopped, looking down at Clyde and shaking his head. "How come his arms so long and his legs so short? He look like some kind of monkey. If he had some hair somewhere beside on his head, he be a monkey all right."

The boys bent over double, holding their stomachs, their laughter raining down around him and Clyde. Simon wanted to shove his brother away and join his own laughter with that of his friends, to let the words hurt only Clyde and not him. Instead, he held his ground silently and waited, hoping they would lose interest and stop if he didn't defend himself.

Clyde swiveled his head, looking up into the boys' faces, feeling their disgust, recognizing them as the same ones who had surrounded the truck on that last awful trip into town. He looked at his brother, Simon, waiting for him to say something back, ignoring his sorrow when he didn't. He knew Simon didn't like him, hadn't wanted him to come, but Mama did, and Simon feared his mother. Clyde suspected maybe he feared him too.

Mama always said he needed to get more air, like there wasn't enough air in the house. All he really wanted to do was stay with her, stay close to the house where nobody laughed at him, and the bad feelings didn't come rising like they were now.

"Leave him be, Robert. He ain't gon' bother nobody. Just let him sit over by the pond," Simon spoke at last, grasping Clyde's hand, surprised as he always was by how large it was. Clyde's short legs gave him the height of a four-year-old, while his torso was bigger than all the older boys around him, including Robert, who was nine. His large head seemed way too big to be supported, even on his thick neck. Nothing on him seemed to match.

Leading him to the edge of the pond, Simon pushed down on his shoulders until he was sitting down. Removing his shoes, he arranged Clyde's legs so that his feet could dangle in the water. "You sit here. We gon' be playing over there." He pointed at the area behind him. "I come back and get you when it be time to go home."

Clyde nodded, forcing the bad feelings down until he couldn't feel them anymore. He listened until the laughter and talk from the boys subsided, flinching when he heard Simon's laughter joining in. The trees closed in behind the boys as they walked away, giving him his last view of them jostling and wrestling one another as they walked. It was always like that, always had been for as long as he could remember. People pointing and laughing at him, groups that he was never a part of.

Clyde lay back in the grass surrounding the pond, spreading his arms out and feeling the sun hot on his upturned face, his feet cooled by the water. One hand covered his face as he traced his features: the close-set bulging eyes, broad nose, and full mouth. He knew his brothers said he was ugly, and the other boys called him that too. He saw how people turned away from him on the rare times his mother had taken him into town and how they moved away from the truck where he sat.

He came to understand that "ugly" was a bad word that hurt him to his core. He also knew what it made him feel when people said it, bringing with it the desire to make them feel the same pain that he did. The desire he fought every day.

Then there were the days when he lost the battle, and he had to pour the darkness and the hatred into living things that could not fight back. Tears of remorse leaked from the corners of his eyes, running down into his ears to water the dry grass beneath him.

His large hands fisted, pulling up tufts of the brittle stalks, feeling them crumble as he gazed at the puffs of white clouds drifting across the blue sky above. He found himself wishing he could float away with them; wishing he was back home in the kitchen with Mama, smelling the fresh bread baking in the oven; waiting to feel her warm hand caress his cheek and feeling the darkness pushed away.

Pulling himself back into a sitting position, he looked down into the surface water of the pond, squinting to see his reflection. Mama didn't have any mirrors in the house, said they didn't need any. If he wanted to know how he looked, she said, all he had to do was ask her, and she would tell him.

He tried to compare what he saw in the murky waters with his brothers' faces, running two fingers along the outline of his nose. *Nothing alike*, his mind screamed. His palms rubbed against the dark skin of his cheeks, so unlike the smooth tan and creamy caramel of the rest of his family. He grasped his head with both hands and moved it back and forth, watching the reflection do the same. *Ugly must look like me*, he thought, sticking out his tongue. Running his fingers through the water, he watched as his reflection began to ripple and distort his features further.

"Boy, that face ain't gon' change staring at it." Robert cackled loudly as his open palm slammed into the back of Clyde's head. He was momentarily stunned when the blow didn't move the boy's body at all.

Clyde turned slowly, shaking his head and feeling the darkness rise unchecked, molasses thick in his veins. His hand lashed out, wrapping itself around Robert's ankle and yanking him forward.

Robert danced off balance on his remaining foot for an instant, his long, angular limbs flailing before he felt himself leave the ground and sail into the stagnant water of the pond. His body submerged, then came up, spewing water from his mouth and nostrils, staring with bulging eyes at Clyde, whose chest rose and fell rapidly, his dark eyes rimmed in red, still seated in the grass.

"GET YOUR BROTHER, SIMON," he yelled, his arms flying up and down, splashing the water around him.

"I done told you leave him be," Simon muttered, sitting down to place Clyde's shoes back on his feet before gently placing his hands upon Clyde's shoulders. He turned his brother's face toward him, speaking softly the way his mother had taught them to—to the darkness that lay deep within him—and hoping he could reach him like she did.

Clyde's breathing slowed, the red of his eyes abating until the whites looked normal again. Simon continued, relieved, still stroking with one hand and lifting his brother to his feet with the other. He guided him toward the worn path that would lead them back home.

"Damn, that boy strong," Robert mumbled as he struggled back to dry ground, his face burning hot under the laughter of the other boys. Scowling, he shouted after Simon and Clyde's retreating figures.

"You know something wrong with him!" He inflated his chest, pounding against it in a show of bravado meant to suppress his humiliation.

"I think you best leave that boy alone, Robert." Jason smothered a chuckle as he pulled wet leaves off his brother's clothes. Robert smacked his hands away, whirling back, his fist balled for a fight. The other boys were bent over laughing, pounding each other on the back, only stopping when they happened to look up and catch Robert glaring at them. He eyed each of the boys, daring them to continue laughing as he seethed, plans of vengeance seeding his thoughts.

Fannie turned, hearing Clyde's sobs and the door opening. Her hand flew to her mouth as she dropped the chicken to the table she had been seasoning. Clyde stopped just inside the shack's front room, his shoulders drooping and his eyes cast down at the floor. Darting across the room, she took him in her arms and felt him trembling against her, his body shaking with soft whimpers as she stroked his back.

"Mama, why God make me like this?" He wept, the words hitching in his throat. Fannie held him an arm's length away from her, her eyes blazing with anger, her head swiveling from him to Simon, who stood statue-still in the doorway.

"Simon, what them boys say to him?! Did *you* say something?" she demanded, the questions ground between clenched teeth.

Simon almost leaped into the air, startled by the venom in her words. "No, ma'm, Mama. It weren't me. It was Miss Emma's boy, Robert. He the one did it. Say he the homeliest-looking boy he done seen." Simon's eyes rounded in fear, then squeezed shut. He held his breath, his body tensing in anticipation of the explosion to come and the blow that would accompany it. His heart beat out the time.

Nothing happened, and Simon exhaled, cautiously taking a step backward and edging closer to the door. Fannie's attention was riveted on Clyde. She dropped to the floor, her dress pooling around her legs, and pulled Clyde onto her lap. She held him close, his head resting on her chest, her chin rubbing against the thick, coal-black curls of his hair.

"Don't you pay that little fool no mind, Clyde," she whispered, her breath ruffling the silken strands on his head like bird feathers in the breeze. "His momma one that be homely. Got a face like a mule just like that old bucktooth boy of hers. Everybody know that, and she gon' get hers one day. The Lord gon' see to it." She stopped and patted his chest, then started again. "But God don't look at thangs people look at. He looks and sees the heart. And your heart be beautiful, Clyde, just like you. When he look at you, that's all he see, and all we see."

Simon lowered his head. His face squelched up involuntarily, and he quickly looked at the floor to keep his mother from reading his expression. To him, Clyde had an ugliness in his spirit that was not so much a physical attribute as it was a profound corruption of his soul. Something that seemed to come over him and render him dangerous. Sometimes, Simon would look up and see him staring at him with those red-rimmed eyes, and fear would ice his bones. He didn't know how she couldn't see it.

Like yesterday, he'd come across Clyde sitting in the woods just behind the house, holding a squirrel up by the tail and watching the small animal squirm and struggle to get free. Simon had frozen, his mind flashing back to the mouse on Christmas Day. He forced his feet to move, easing behind a tree where Clyde couldn't see him. He waited and watched to see what Clyde would do, an uneasiness settling in his heart.

Clyde smiled and slammed the animal against a rock protruding from the ground. Blood and gore splattered, splashing up into his face, making the smile he wore look that much more gruesome.

As he repeatedly slammed the squirrel into the ground, its gray brain matter added to the slime covering his hands while his smile grew wider. Wisps of darkness drifted up from the ground where Clyde stood. When he turned in the direction of the tree Simon hid behind, Simon saw those smoldering, dark eyes rimmed in red and that same horrifying smile he wore on that Christmas night at Granny Corinn's.

Never before had he thought when he saw the mangled, torn bodies of animals in the woods that the predator stalking them had been his brother. He'd assumed a wolf had gotten to them. Now, the reality that it was Clyde all along weighed his mind, a brick of certainty. He had been the one slaughtering them all along.

Simon gagged and swallowed, fighting the urge to vomit into the bushes, fearing Clyde would turn his darkness on him if he were heard. He sucked in a shallow breath and waited, his heart pounding wildly, to see if Clyde would look directly at his hiding place. The wrongness of his brother that he'd heard people whispering and talking about in school or town echoed in his thoughts, weaving together with what he was seeing.

He shivered, fear caressing his spine, frantically wondering who he could tell. Who could help him? Maybe he could tell his daddy the next time he came. He knew something was wrong with Clyde. Maybe his brothers had seen something too. His daddy might finally be able to get through to his mother. He shook his head at the improbability of Fannie believing anything bad about Clyde, and the hope evaporated as quickly as it had come.

Clyde stared down at the remnants of the squirrel, nudging it with his toe. He lifted his head abruptly as though listening to a sound only he could hear, then took off in his shambling run, moving toward their house. Simon had exhaled in relief and collapsed at the base of the tree, eyes glued to the dead squirrel.

"Ain't that right, Simon?"

Simon jumped again, startled out of his reverie, his head bobbing up and down rapidly as he swallowed hard and tried to refocus on his mother's words. "Yes, ma'm, Robert be right ugly."

Clyde lifted his head from his mother's chest, turning his brooding gaze upon his brother, pinning him with his stare. Simon felt the same chill in his blood he'd felt when he was hidden behind the tree, and his body trembled with fear. He felt searching fingers crawling and probing his mind, making him shiver harder, and instinctively knew that it was Clyde. Somehow, he thought, his brother was reading his mind, knew what he had been thinking, knew what he had seen him do. Simon pressed his back against the wall of the shack and cringed, his breath hitching in his throat.

Clyde slid his gaze away from Simon's terrified eyes, breaking the connection. He lowered his head to rub against his mother's chest, hiding his lips curved into a smile. He listened to the rhythm of her heartbeat, letting it lull him, pushing down the pain and the darkness and his knowing about Simon. The new power asserted itself, filling him with a sense of satisfaction.

He envisioned himself smashing a rock into Simon's head, seeing the bones shatter and his brains squish. Better than a squirrel, he thought as the image danced across his mind, then ebbed slowly as the darkness drained away under the gentle strokes of his mother's hands. The darkness was growing.

He did not see Simon as he backed up slowly, easing his body silently along the wall, then through the crack he had pushed between the door and the frame. He lifted his head slightly at the sound of Simon's feet pounding on the dry earth as he ran away from the house.

Outside, Simon threw his head back—arms and legs pumping as he ran—not looking back, pulling the threads between him and Clyde taut until they snapped free. He was back in the clearing when he stopped, panting, thoughts racing through his head. He leaned forward, heaving the meager contents of his stomach until nothing came up but bile.

Fear and hopelessness threatened to overwhelm him. He saw the look in Clyde's eyes again and knew he couldn't go back in there. That home was lost to him forever. Raising his head, he sighed and wiped at the tears raining unchecked and dripping off his chin. He looked toward the opposite path that led to the road to town and started walking. He would make it to his father and brothers, and he could be safe.

Clyde lay his head back on his mother's breast, feeling her nipples harden beneath the thin fabric of her dress. He inhaled the scent of her milk and let all thoughts of Simon drift away.

CHAPTER FOUR

Cora sat on a lightning-blasted tree stump, her chin cupped in her palms, elbows resting on her knees, staring into the stark blue sky. She stilled her thoughts and opened herself to both the world on this plane and the one that lay beyond it.

The Knowing could not be forced. It moved at its own volition, unbound by time, unbothered by her demands or will. It came in fits and starts, often silent as the seasons bled into one another, sometimes becoming years.

Then it returned like now, to snatch her relentlessly from her sleep with dark visions of blood and death, bathed in sweat and tangled in her bed sheets. Over the previous nights, visions of Clyde had been awakened, plaguing her. Something had changed.

By early morning, when the first rays of sunlight had touched her eyelids, she shot straight up in bed, aroused by the awareness that Clyde was growing worse. It sank into her, gripping her heart with a paralyzing jolt that left her panting, glad that Joe had already risen from the bed and she would not have to explain it. She dressed quickly and started breakfast for the family, eager for them to leave so that she could be about her business.

Cora stood up. The Knowing had beckoned her to these woods, lurking, following, seeking a trail of darkness that teased and enticed her to follow it. Moving, she stood behind the trunk of a giant oak, as thick around as three men standing side by side, alone in the deep grass. The trees surrounding it were burnt stumps struck by lightning like the one she had been resting on. Bush grass grew waist-high around this peculiar sentinel left standing amid the chaotic destruction of previous summer storms, effectively concealing her behind its girth. Her heart drummed rapidly, and she tried to take deep breaths to calm its racing while feelings of shame rolled through her. She had been derelict, rebelling against the Knowing, managing to convince herself that Clyde wasn't part of the foreboding premonition given to her. Her empathy had hidden the clarity of her purpose from her path.

Early on, she had followed him off and on once he was big enough to walk through the woods unaccompanied. Fannie had let him wander, knowing that his paraparesis wouldn't let him go too far. From a distance, she would probe him, sensing the edge of darkness that followed him . . . waiting . . . watching.

Over the years, she had observed no outward signs of the level of darkness she'd witnessed at his birth manifesting itself in him. Instead, there was only the persistent goldenrod aura of guilt and self-destruction permeating striations of darkness that always seemed to circulate around him. That, and a God-awful smell that seemed to cling to him. A smell that she had come to know as uniquely his own. She wondered how Fannie and the rest of them could bear to be around him in the closeness of that small shack.

She continued to delude herself that maybe her failure had not been a failure after all. Maybe the Knowing had been wrong. Maybe Clyde was just a mangled mess of a child born with lame legs and a peculiar face.

She studied his features intently. Taken individually, they showed a unique perfection: delicately shaped ears, thick yet finely arched eyebrows, skin like smooth dark chocolate, and a mop of curly hair. Yet, his wide mouth and full lips seldom smiled to display his small, even white teeth, and his large, protruding eyes disturbed it all. Taken together, the discordance of his appearance formed an unattractive whole.

Every now and then, she had heard whispered stories from town, like the one about Clyde and the mouse killing at his grandmother's house a couple of years back. By the time the town was finished with the tale, it was a rat the size of a small house cat that he had killed and drank its blood. She put that story and the others down to the town gossip of people happy to see the misery of anyone other than themselves. As time passed, everything surrounding him and his birth had taken on the texture of a nightmare dream, which she pushed to the farthest parts of her memory.

Until today, when the Knowing's urging became so intense that she'd felt it in her bones, she lifted a prayer that she was following her path, and now, that long-ago prophetic purpose would be revealed as truth.

She knew Clyde immediately when she saw him, that big man's chest stuck to those little boy legs—and that smell, like skunk and sulfur. Looking at him, she shivered, a new and irrational fear that he was stronger than she was flowing through her blood, making her body shake until she feared she would lose control of her bladder. Cora took a deep breath, her muscles tightening as she stood to her full height.

She shook herself free of her fear and straightened her posture. No matter his look, she told herself, he was still a six-year-old boy. She was a woman grown and filled with the power of the Knowing.

Peering around the tree trunk where she hid, she could see that he was looking at something near his feet, the shadows cast by the leaves overhead momentarily hiding the expression on his face. He stood, straightening his body as much as his crooked limbs would allow, and stared toward the tree.

Cora drew back, making her body as small as she could, holding her breath, waiting. An awareness of the escalation of the darkness in him resonated in her soul, making her wonder if it would allow him to see her through the tree trunk or hear her heartbeat thundering in her ears.

He stared at the tree where she hid for a long moment, then turned his attention to whatever was on the ground. Cora adjusted her position, daring to peek around the tree again until she could see him clearly, the dappled spots of sunlight illuminating his face. His mouth was spread in a disarmingly wide smile.

She cringed, shrinking farther behind the tree. His smile did not touch those bulging eyes, yellow instead of white around the brown irises, rimmed with red and sitting beneath that wide nose spread across his face, conveying a look of pure gratification.

She stared at him. Her thoughts meandered, remembering his birth and how Fannie kept stroking the soft curls of his head, rubbing his misshapen skull. Even then, she had noticed the thick, black coils. She contemplated whether that thick mop of curls obscured a head still dented and sunken in. What a waste of good hair.

This close, the Knowing informed the darkness of him upon her spirit, a simmering miasma of fear, hopelessness, and rage that absorbed portions of her light. It clouded her mind, radiating from him and suspending her in a trance.

Cora blinked rapidly, attempting to clear her thinking as Clyde moved farther away from her, his hands shoved in his pockets, his knees knocking together, whistling off-key.

She concentrated, reaching for her gift, desperate to correct the dark impurities circulating in her spirit. Searching, she found her light was pearl gray on the edges, pitted with spots of charcoal blackness. Sinking cross-legged on the ground, she rested her hands on her knees and began breathing deeply, in and then out, focusing on the dark spots. She centered her breathing and worked to purge the darkness she'd absorbed from him until it was gone.

Sighing loudly, she stood, stretching her limbs to ease the tension from her legs and shoulders, and moved farther from her hiding place, the long grass scratching against her calves.

She stepped forward, needing to know what he was looking at, what had caused that hideous grin to spread across his face. She began to chant under her breath, a deep certainty that she already knew what she would see taking firm possession in her mind as she walked.

She had reached the place where he had been, and though the smell had begun to dissipate, it lingered along with a light purple mist rising from the spot and marking it as Clyde's territory. It wrapped itself around her ankles and traveled upward, freezing her face and severing her connection to nature as she stared down at the remains of a wild rabbit.

The small animal's head was twisted, almost off its neck, its body crushed, bones sticking through the fur. Cora recoiled. He had done this. He had savagely killed the animal not for food but for sport. She had watched him smile over his kill, then leave it there to rot.

Leaning down, she touched the rabbit's fur, the kill so recent that it hadn't stiffened yet. Grabbing it by the ears, she dropped it into the bag hanging at her side and continued to trail behind Clyde as he made his way home.

She thought about how many deaths like this she had seen over the years, rejecting the truth the Knowing placed before her. It wasn't Clyde. He was too young. She had assured herself that animals died all the time, victims of predators bigger and stronger than themselves. As she thought about it now, a flush of shame rushed up to color her cheeks for covering the travesty of his kill pattern with a thin veneer of denial. The slaughters were always close to Fannie's, and there were far too many for it to be natural. No signs of teeth or claw had marred a single carcass.

As she walked, she collected several more remains. He seemed to be leaving her a trail to follow, mocking her, daring her to do something about it. She continued to stalk him with no clear plan, simply a determination to know the truth for herself.

Arriving at Fannie's door, she stared at the gray boards that formed the frame around it, beaten down by sun and weather until it appeared soft. She had not been there since his birthing, fleeing from her impotence at his birth and allowing Fannie's unspoken curse to reduce her to prey.

The place looked more dilapidated than she remembered, the structure and the land suffering the neglect of men. James Henry and the older boys had abandoned it long ago, moving to Rayville. The scuttlebutt shuttling through town was that Clyde was a danger to be around. James Henry, fearing the ass whopping the boy deserved or that one of his other boys would get hurt, kept them with him in town.

Fannie endured, struggling to make a living, taking in washing and baking bread that she sold in town. It allowed her to keep Clyde close to her. Cora thought about the youngest one, Simon, and if he might still be there. She shivered, imagining the horrors he could have been living with if he were.

Standing outside the door, breathing deeply, Cora gathered the light into herself, feeling it spread and push back the darkness. She brought her fist down sharply, banging against the door frame, feeling it shake and hoping it was the wood and not her trembling hand.

Fannie opened the door, brushing flour from her hands onto her apron as she pushed the screen door wide enough to fit her body, blocking Cora from coming inside and making it clear that she was not welcome. Cora glanced over Fannie's head at Clyde sitting on a stool in the corner. He bowed his head, his hands twisting in his lap.

Fannie stared up at Cora, whose big body filled the small porch, blocking the sun behind her and dwarfing the woman in front of her. Cora's nose wrinkled at the smell that had grown strong again, noting that Fannie didn't seem affected by it.

"How you, Miss Cora? What bring you out this way?" She clapped her hands against her apron, flour floating in the air between them. "I don't mean no rudeness to you, but you know you ain't welcome here."

Fannie didn't move, forcing Cora to step back, craning her neck to look over Fannie's head into the room. Snakes of darkness and deep purple writhed across the floor, drawn to Clyde.

"What you looking at my boy for?" Fannie hissed, raising up on her toes to further block Cora's vision.

"I expect you knows what he is, Fannie. Ain't no use in trying to hide from it. He just gon' keep getting worse. The older he get, the worse it be. Somebody gon' have to do something with him."

"And who that somebody gon' be, Miss Cora? You?" she demanded. "Is you come to kill him like you was gon' do when he was born?" Fannie's eyes bored into Cora, her words making the other woman flinch, the hard truth lashing into her. Had she not, in fact, come to do just that?

The Knowing pressed the truth into Cora, a swirl of blue coloring her thoughts. There was no other solution. She could no longer deceive herself that the Knowing misspoke. Clyde wasn't just sin ugly with some strange ways. He was his father's darkness incarnate. He needed to die.

Wrenching open the bag hanging beside her, she looked down at the visible truth it contained, one Fannie could not deny. Using one hand to hold it open, she allowed Fannie to see the grizzly carcasses within, the blood staining the sides of the bag.

Fannie's eyes rounded in horror, staring back and forth from the contents of the bag and back up at Cora. She reached out and snatched the bag, catching Cora off guard with the sudden movement, wrestling it from her shoulder. Cora stumbled backward as Fannie stepped back behind the screen, into the house, and slammed the door in her face, leaving her blinking outside.

Regaining herself, Cora moved to the side of the house and stood beneath the only window of the shack, a few feet from the door. Stretching her neck upward, she peered inside, grateful for her height. Fannie's back was to her. Clyde was still crouched down on his stool, his eyes searching the floor. Their voices carried clearly to her as Fannie shook the bag in front of him.

"Did you do this, Clyde?" Fannie asked, shaking the bag. "Look at me! Did you do this?"

Clyde pulled himself in tighter, his knees pulled up to his chest, his bowed head resting on them. The darkness swirled around him, twisting vapors slithering across the packed dirt. Lifting his head, Cora felt his stare drilling into her just before dark mists shot across the room toward the window where she stood.

Falling backward, arms flailing, she landed on her butt, the darkness piercing the walls. Clyde, she realized, had grown stronger than she had perceived, apparently able to manipulate and utilize the darkness.

The dark Knowing swirled over her until it covered her completely. She felt it pushing down her throat, making her gag, tasting it like the rot of desecrated flesh. She pulled her light, sucking it from deep inside and blasting it outward into the darkness, straining against its power.

In the distant woods behind her, a light flared, flashing toward her, causing the darkness to retreat. Coughing and spitting, Cora staggered to her feet and began running toward it, her long legs churning and eating up the distance.

As the woods closed in around her, Cora slowed her pace until she was walking, her whole body slumping in defeat. Reaching the light hovering in the trees, she watched as the brilliant orb transfigured into a human form before her, startled as she recognized the face.

"Mi?" Cora whispered, her lower lip trembling while tears pooled in her eyes, causing the image to waver in front of her.

"How many times you gon' run?" Mi's voice demanded, steeled with the rod of discipline so familiar to Cora that she ducked, anticipating a flick to the lobe of her ear.

The image flickered, becoming distorted, and then became her grandmother again. She felt the acidic burn of her shame pulsing through her blood with each heartbeat. The truth was affirmed, yet she had run, not fighting the darkness but fleeing it.

"I done taught you better." The voice she remembered as Mi resounded around her, clipped and strident.

Cora's head lowered, avoiding looking directly into Mi's deep black eyes. Mi drifted forward, her feet not bending a blade of grass. Her wrinkled fingers settled beneath Cora's chin and lifted it, forcing her to look at her.

"Why you leave me?" Cora sputtered. "It been so long."

"Child, you know I ain't of this world no more."

Cora stared as Mi's features bled in and out, flickering in the air, the Knowing embodied in her familiar form. Questions raced through her mind as she tried to sort out what she wanted to say. Ideally, she wanted direction, a plan, a surety of action that left no room for doubt, and the strength to execute it as opposed to the uncertainty that made her waver.

"I know the truth now, but I still don't know if I can do it."

Mi's features hardened. "Stop all that crying and whining before I take a switch to you."

Cora felt a chuckle of disparagement climbing upward in her throat, then—remembering her grandmother's quick backhand—smothered it before it could escape.

The darkness had bent her light, fractured it, and she had run like a whipped dog. Her thoughts rolled over one another as she remembered the darkness swirling across the room to reach for her and the other thing she had seen when Clyde locked his gaze with hers. In his eyes, she had seen her death coming.

"You done always had a head hard as a rock, but you gon' do what you was told." Mi's words reverberated inside her brain before the apparition stretched upward, the light elongating her form until she towered over Cora. "He your mirror, and he wasn't never meant to be in this world with you. He the opposite of everything you is," she chided. "He ain't supposed to be."

Regardless of what physical form the Knowing took, she felt inadequate for the task. The dark Knowing was growing within him. Reaching down, Mi lay one hand on Cora's forehead, allowing her radiance to flow around the edges of her granddaughter's brain.

"Balance!" reverberated in Cora's mind.

"You knows the truth now. The Knowing strong in you." The brilliance of the light expanded, filling the air around her, then seeping into her pores. "Now you ain't fighting it no more. It be all right." The last words echoed, floating disembodied as Mi's form dissipated into the air. "You ain't gon' fail."

Cora struggled to hold onto the images of her grandmother, of the words, of the Knowing, of her purpose. As it faded, her last thoughts melted with it. She found herself alone, staring at Fannie's house, visible in the distance, still double-minded.

CHAPTER FIVE

Cora closed her journal and put it back into her skirt pocket. She had written enough for the night. Emptying herself of words had not helped. She wanted to seek her bed and join Joe, but there was no rest in her sleep. The darkness from Clyde would be there to fight her. It tugged at a corner of her mind, then fell away, leaving her anxious and agitated.

Walking across the room, she pulled the large tin tub from its nail on the wall and set it in front of her chair before going back to the pump at the sink. She pumped water into her biggest pot and heated it on the stove.

"Want some company?" Joseph asked, standing in the doorway of their bedroom.

"No." She shrugged, her shoulders moving up and down. "Ain't no point in both of us not sleeping."

Joe walked over to where she sat, scooping a stool beneath him and pulling her feet into his lap. He began to rub them, his hands strong, massaging deeply. Cora leaned back and closed her eyes, a soft moan escaping her mouth.

"Just let old Joe take care of you. Talk if you wants to. Don't if you don't."

She felt her shoulders relax while her body sagged into the comfort of the old wing chair, unaware of Joe going to the stove to retrieve the hot water and pour it into the basin. The scent of tea tree oil floated in the air as he eased her feet into the tin tub.

"Let the water work its magic," Joe instructed, his hands rubbing her calves, alternating from leg to leg, his eyes lifting to hers occasionally. She allowed herself to connect to his spirit.

"I ain't never knowed nothing like him before, Joe. He got a dark power in him. Evil. No other word for it."

"You ain't God, Cora. This ain't your battle." His thumb rubbed a deep massage against the ball of her foot, making her moan in relief. "You needs to stay away from them folks."

"I been trying, Joe." Air blew softly from between her lips. "But the dreams I had done started getting worse here of late. I waked up this morning with the feeling that the day coming." She leaned her head against the back of the chair, stretching her neck.

"How come you ain't say nothing about it this morning?" he asked, switching expertly to her other foot.

"Because I figured what you was gon' say."

Joe pulled one foot into his lap, drying it with the towel he had brought with him. He picked up a bottle of castor oil from the floor, pouring a little into the palm of his hand, and began rubbing it into the skin of her heels.

"Well, you done did all you can for now. Ain't that what you was saying?" He waited for an answer that didn't come. Then blowing air noisily through his lips, he abruptly changed the subject. "Did I tell you I was talking to James Henry when I was in town the other day?" His hands continued to massage, and Cora thought about how her feet didn't feel big in his hands. Small groans of comfort filled the air around them, an undercurrent to their conversation.

"He say the last time they went out to the house, Clyde went after the middle boy, James Junior. He start beating him, then choked him. Took James Henry and them other two boys to pull him off. He say if Fannie hadn't come and started rubbing him the way she do, he believe he would have killed Junior."

Joe stopped, his gaze locking with hers, watching her eyes change from gray to green until she was forced to look down. She studied the oil floating on the surface of the water. Shaking his head, Joe kneaded the heel of her foot, his story not finished.

"He say Clyde strong, stronger than his big brothers, and he ain't made seven yet. Said he hated he left Simon out there so long. You know what? Crazy as it sound, I think he still love that woman. I keeps telling you it something real wrong with them folks, and especially something special wrong with that boy and his mama. He ain't natural."

"We knows that," Cora said, sighing as she lifted her other foot and pressed it against his chest. She felt his heart beating through the sole of her foot and waited as the rhythm synchronized with her own. A small smile lifted the corners of her mouth, and she sighed. "I don't know what I'm gon' do, Joe, but I ain't gon' give up. I'm gon' keep on praying that the Knowing give me the strength to do what I got to do. I didn't ask to be chose and two times, I done failed already. I cain't live with that."

She pulled her foot from his chest and forced the other one from his hand, splashing them both down into the water. Joe sat back, blowing air through his lips again in exasperation at her stubbornness. He scooted on his stool, leaning back as she removed her feet from the water and stood, walking around him to pace her agitation out on the wooden floorboards.

"How I be so stupid, huh? What I think was gon' happen? I'm gon' walk up in there and strikes him down? Fannie gon' say, '*Oh you right, Miss Cora. Gon' ahead and kill my boy.*'" She studied the strong lines of his face, his high cheekbones peppered with a smattering of freckles, courtesy of the reddish-brown coppery hair on his head. "I would have had to kill Fannie first."

"All I ask," Joe said, standing and catching her in midstride, holding her by her shoulders, "is for you to wait until you get a sign that it be the right time to go after him again." He continued to stare into her eyes until she nodded her agreement.

Cora flexed her fingers as she stretched her hands out in front of her. Internally, she reached for the light, at first feeling nothing, the space where it usually resided, hollow and empty. Something skirted around her brain, sparking and shorting out, then flaring back to life. The Knowing settled, and she accepted the choice the truth had left her.

Clyde still sat in the corner of the shack's large front room, unaware of how many hours had passed. His abnormally broad shoulders touched each side of the wall in the tight space. Looking up to the room's only window, he shook his head, confused by the day's events. He wasn't the same.

He remembered the face of the healer. How the darkness rose within him and fed on the fear that shimmered in her eyes, how he had sent it to claim her, and how good it had felt.

The darkness had freed him to despise her, his hatred forming a knot that twisted in his stomach and strangled his mind. The feelings rose from a place unreachable within his conscious mind, a place from before this time and this body. Primal memories spoke to him of danger, warning him that she was his destruction.

The dark whispered across his mind, causing him to squirm on his stool. She wanted to destroy him. She would make his mother hate him too, taking away the only light he possessed.

He pulled his body tighter, trying to disappear into the darkness where his mother would not find him, where he couldn't see her look at him with such hurt and disappointment. He tried to hold on to the hope that she would forgive him today and just love him like she did when she told him he was her special boy, her good boy. Then she would hug him, and he could feel her light brushing against the darkness. It would wrap around the bad feelings, muffling them.

He sat there on his stool, watching her. She retreated to the only table and chair in the room. She sat, opening the worn family Bible, resting in its place of honor on the white lace cloth covering the tabletop, leafing through the pages. The light from the sky had dimmed, turning to full dark as she sat, her mouth moving in silent prayer, her eyes occasionally lifting to the ceiling and then casting back down to her Bible.

More time passed, and Clyde could hear her breathing as she rose to cross the room to him. He counted the spaces between her breaths. If they were long with a little sigh at the end, she was unhappy—not angry—and he was safe. There would be no pain. If they were short and rapid, she was bringing the Lord's wrath to him. She stood, arching her back to relieve the ache of having sat for so long, then bent to pick up the bag, walking to stand in front of him. She shook it at him, the smell of decay and blood exploding into the air with each shake, and his eyelids fluttered involuntarily with pleasure.

"Did you do this? Clyde? Did you do this?" She began questioning him as if no time had passed since she first asked him the question.

He remained mute as always when she confronted him with his sins. She tossed the bag to the floor, some of its contents spilling out. Stepping over the grizzly remains, she reached out for his hand.

He wanted to resist, to bypass this part and get to the other side where she would hold him on her lap, his legs dangling above the floor and his head resting on her chest. He could smell her musky milk scent mixed with the rose sachet that she wore.

He awaited the gentle stroke of her hand on his head, moving down to the length of his nose and finally caressing his cheek. He would hear her voice, low and warm, as he listened to it with his ear against her heart. He lifted his head and raised his arm, his hand reaching out to her.

Fannie took his hand, leading him to the center of the room. He remained there, rooted in obedience, with his head hanging down. He waited as she crossed to the wall, reaching for the heavy leather strap she kept hanging from a nail by the door, its surface marked with dark streaks of dried blood.

She knew that he would not move or attempt to run from her. He never did. Tears streamed down her cheeks as she wrapped the strap tightly around her fist and walked back toward him, her head shaking from side to side. "Why you make me do this, boy?" she asked, the belt smacking against the palm of her hand. He tried not to cringe at the sound, but his muscles quivered with remembered pain. She stared at him for a long moment and then began again, the belt whistling through the air as she spoke.

"He that don't use the rod hate his child; but he who love him, beats him until the devil gone out of him." The words flowed over him as the leather came down against his skin, the smack of it aligning itself with her last words. He grunted, waiting for the next blow. It would be harder than the first but not as hard as the next.

"Get behind me, Devil. You demons gets away from my boy and leave him be!" Her voice escalated with each blow, sweat pouring from her brow, stinging her eyes and blurring her vision as it swam with her tears. She sobbed as the belt slammed against his flesh again and again.

He tried to take it, to let the darkness strengthen him and absorb the pain, not allowing it to turn against her. She was his mother, his light, and the only love he had ever known. His lips began to tremble, and he felt the first scalding tear burn a trail as it slid down his face—felt his mouth twisted as pain raged through his body, and the welts rose on his skin. Rushing under her next swing, he threw both arms around her waist, burying his face against her and sobbing loudly.

"I sorry, Mama, I sorry. I don't means to be bad. I don't wants to be no sinner. Make me right, Mama, and I won't do it no more. I ain't gon' do it again. I won't sin no more. I promises." He gasped, the sound rough and muffled. He was on his knees, dropping his arms to clasp his hands in prayer in front of her. "Please, God, make me right for Mama, please." He wept.

Fannie dropped the belt in midswing, collapsing to the floor and pulling him onto her lap, ignoring the fact that his upper body was as big as hers. One hand began rubbing around his head before lowering to stroke his nose and finally resting on his cheek, where she cupped it and waited for his shuddering to stop. She rocked him back and forth.

"Shhhhhhh, baby boy, shush now. It be all right. I knows you gon' do better."

After a moment, her hand began fumbling with the buttons on her dress, exposing and lifting out her breast, pushing the nipple toward his eager lips. As he began to nurse, she nestled her nose in the thick, black curls that covered his head, inhaling his fresh scent and whispering her praises to God for his deliverance.

CHAPTER SIX

"**C**lyde, when you done fetching that water, you go on and finish reading them Proverbs I give you the other day, then get ready for school."

"Yes, ma'm, I be almost finished." Clyde felt the pull of the full buckets straining the muscles of his arms as he made his way to the wash tub, his lopsided walk causing the water to slosh over the edges.

He didn't complain; he was the man of the house now, not some weak little boy. He set one bucket on the ground and then used both hands to raise the other bucket and tilt it into the tub. Lifting the other bucket, he repeated the process, thankful that the steam from the hot water hid the scowl that covered his face.

"Does I have to go, Ma?"

They had the same argument since she sent him to school two years ago. Fannie moved to stand beside him, trying to wrap her arm around his shoulder, then letting it fall. At ten, he was a little taller than her, his shoulders too broad for her to comfortably embrace.

"Now, we done been through this, Clyde, and I ain't saying it no more. I done teached you all I can. You need a real teacher, one with book learning." The corners of her mouth turned up momentarily before she stopped, suppressing the sin of pride as it welled upward. "You ain't gone be dumb like your daddy and your brothers who don't know how to do nothing but wallow in grease all day or work this no-good land. You is ten now, and before you knows it, you be a full-grown man. God done made you special. He got plans for you."

Clyde shrugged and turned to go back into the house, dragging the empty buckets behind him. Gathering up his schoolbooks, he turned toward the door, ignoring the open Bible on the table, and left for school, his feet dragging through the dirt.

Sitting in the back of the class, Clyde tried to shrink his body into the small seat, his shoulders folded in and his head down as he looked around at his classmates from beneath lowered lids. His gaze flitted from child to child, searching for a friendly face and finding none. His hopes drained from him as they did each day, shattered against the wall of callousness they presented and replaced them with simmering resentment.

He detested them all, each and every one. Hated their perfectly shaped limbs, their legs proportionate to their bodies, their arms that hung just so, and the perfect alignment of their features on the smooth, brown skin of their faces. Even Robert— held back in the fourth grade twice because he really was stupid, with his buckteeth separated by a giant gap—thought he was handsome compared to Clyde.

Sometimes, when he grew bored and distracted, he let bad thoughts come. He would think about the animals that came to him, unaware they would be dead in mere minutes. He would hear their dying screams in his mind and smile until his mother entered his mind, making him stop, guilt gnawing at him.

If he could just get through the day and get back home, everything would be made right. Mama would sit and listen to him recite, excited to hear what he had learned that day, or listen to him read. Her face lit up with the pride she attempted to hide. He was her special good boy. He turned his attention to the teacher at the front of the class, determined to ignore the others and push the darkness back.

Four rows up, Robert turned to look at him, dropping his arms to his sides, sticking out his lower lip, and making silent monkey sounds every time the teacher turned to write on the blackboard. Hearing the other children snickering, Clyde's ears burned in humiliation. He watched them grow quiet when Miss Lilian spun around, her eyes scanning the room for the source of the disturbance. Her gaze rested on him first, hesitated, and then moved on as he sank lower into his seat.

When she turned again to continue writing the multiplication problems for the day, he saw Robert tear a page from one of his books and begin writing across the bottom before passing it over his shoulder to be grabbed by the student behind him. Each child would look at the page, laugh, and pass it on. Clyde ignored them, concentrating on the math problems and working the sums in his head, not allowing them to chip away at his resolve until the page landed on his desk faceup.

Clyde stared down at the picture of the gorilla: the large, black, hairy body and the long arms dangling down; the big hands and knuckles nearly scraping the ground; the short legs; the wide nose; and the mouth that stretched all the way across the animal's face. He saw his name, an arrow, and "Clyde's daddy" scrawled in large letters. He could feel everyone's eyes on him, hear their smothered laughter, and his determination withered.

His blood grew thick and hot, feeling heavy as it pumped through his body. It took its own sweet time, in no hurry to reach his heart with the madness he was feeling. He let the darkness come as his head pivoted from left to right, letting his murderous gaze stop on each of his classmates until they lowered their heads. The laughter on their lips died, replaced with a trembling fear that rapidly tainted the air of the room with the smell of terror. Clyde breathed in a deep lungful, the pleasure roiling through him as the darkness fed. His eyes rolled upward until only the whites showed. The darkness pulled at their fear, and he absorbed it, tasting their anxiety on his tongue. He licked his lips, savoring it.

Robert twisted around in his seat, laughing . . . until Clyde caught his eye and held his gaze, pinning him in place. He watched the boy's face grow ashy as the color leaked from his skin. Robert sagged in his chair before abruptly spinning around to face forward, his eyes riveted on the teacher.

Clyde leaped from his seat, the sound of his books slamming to the floor like a gunshot in the room's silence. He noted with satisfaction that Robert cringed in his seat. Miss Lilian turned from the board, her eyes sweeping the room before coming to stand in front of her desk, staring at him where he stood.

"Clyde Henry, you pick those books up right this minute," she demanded, trying to hide the tremor in her voice. He could smell her fear mixed with the sweet scent of a rose sachet, like the one his mother sometimes wore. She cleared her throat and repeated her demand again, conscious of the eyes of all the children watching them.

His hands gripped the desk by its edges, raising it high over his head, the gorilla picture fluttering to the ground before he slammed it back down to the floor. He bent, reaching down to scoop up the picture, then ripped it until it was a handful of tiny shreds he tossed at his feet, grinding them under his heel before storming past Miss Lilian and out the door.

He could hear Miss Lilian's voice shrieking his name from the spot where she remained rooted in alarm. He didn't turn around. He didn't care. He gave that cursed place his back, knowing he would never see it again.

Clyde stumbled out of the building and stood there panting, his vision temporarily clouded by the dark rage that boiled around him. He pushed his bent knees into a shambling run that took him toward the woods and home.

Hours later, he sat in the woods adjacent to the pond. Thoughts crawled and spread across his brain, an uncomfortable, irritating rash that rubbed it raw without relief. He raised his hands to the sides of his head and kneaded hard with his knuckles, then squeezed before leaning sideways and pounding his left ear, trying to shake the thoughts free. But they were stuck, rattling around and chasing each other like squirrels loose in the trees.

None of them knew him. None of them cared to know him. All anyone ever saw was his face and his legs. They took one look at him—his mouth hanging open, his red-rimmed eyes staring into the distance, air rattling in and out of his wide nostrils, his thick tongue that had trouble forming words—and thought that he was dumb. They looked at his stunted legs and thought—crippled.

Clyde sighed, tears flowing unchecked down his cheeks. He was weary of fighting against the darkness. Tired of the inevitable failure of trying to fit in where he was never wanted. He relinquished and let the darkness that had pursued him all his life claim him.

The power thrummed in Clyde's veins, the darkness rimming the edges of his vision and blocking everything in his periphery. Peering through the tunnel of his memories, he saw the morning in the schoolhouse playing on the screen of his eyes, bringing a hot flush of mortification to his cheeks. He heard Robert's ridicule.

Clyde blinked, focusing on the dragonflies drifting in the air—hanging in midflight, their iridescent wings beating the shimmering heat—as he pushed himself farther back into the bushes. He made sure he was totally concealed but close enough to the pond to hear Robert and his friends when they approached his hiding place and began to plan. He wasn't dumb at all.

He leaned back, his arms extended behind him, his face pointed toward the sun. The sun didn't care how he looked; it shone on him just like it did on everyone else. It never hid itself from him, running behind clouds to get away. And sometimes, when the hot rays of light touched his skin, the dark would recede momentarily. He wondered if this was what other people felt like: the darkness not chasing into every corner of their mind, showing them bad things, helping them kill, or using their mother's soft voice, encouraging them to be the wrath of God. In those moments, he was not trapped in a purpose not his own.

But then, they weren't him, chosen by God—specially touched. He imagined the feel of his mother's hand, stroking and smoothing, her warm breath, and the sweet smell of her milk as she spoke the messages she received from her God. *"Let those who love the Lord hate evil."* He let her words form a balm, covering his spirit, soothing and affirming his plan.

Robert was evil and full of sin. And today, Clyde would be the hand of God. Payment was due. He would wait, hidden from their sight, knowing the near summer heat demanded they stop by the pond for a swim before going home. Soon. It would happen soon.

Clyde's ears perked up, alert to the sounds of multiple pairs of feet first shuffling through the grass and then along the sunbaked ground moving toward him. He sat up quickly and quietly, securely concealed behind the thick growth. He watched Robert, Jason, and Sonny walk along the dusty road, their schoolbooks banging against their legs as they ambled along, occasionally bumping shoulders as they walked, their three heads bent conspiratorially together. He strained his ears to hear their words as they stopped a few feet from where he was hidden.

"Did you see monkey boy's face? Man, I thought that Negro was gon' lose his mind." Robert laughed, hopping on one foot as he began taking off his shoes, followed by his pants that he threw toward the bush where Clyde crouched unseen.

"I don't know, Robert. I think you better leave that boy alone. He pretty big, and he was mad as hell." The voice was followed by more pants snagging on the branches.

Robert snorted and punched his younger brother, Jason, in the shoulder. Jason unexpectedly grabbed his arm and pushed back, surprising him and forcing him to hop on one foot before regaining his balance. "Mama done told you to leave him be. I don't know why you don't listen," he said, his face twisting in frustration as he looked up into his older brother's face.

"Forget it," Sonny said, moving quickly to wedge himself between the two. He, like Jason, stood a head shorter than Robert, both two years his junior and closer to Clyde's age. "What you fighting about? He long gone, and he probably won't be back to school." He pushed back, using his butt to force a further separation before continuing. "I seen Miss Lilian talking to the principal. He done went too far. He gon' be expelled."

Sonny crossed his arms, stood, and waited, the peacemaker of the group. Robert tended to bully his younger brother and Sonny too when he had the chance. After a few tense moments, he felt them relax.

"That's right. We ain't gon' have to look at that monkey mug of his after today." They both guffawed loudly.

Sonny exhaled his relief, joining their laughter as he spoke, "Come on, fools, we ain't got all day. I got to get home and do my chores."

"Ain't but one fool here today. That be monkey boy, and he ain't here." Robert snickered, then cackled loudly, slapping the smaller boys on the back.

Their words struck Clyde like bristling spears, their stinging venom further poisoning his mind. The darkness clouded his vision again, nearly obscuring the sight of the three naked boys easing themselves into the pond. They tread water until they reached the center, where they dove underneath, chasing one another as the muddy creek provided a brief respite from the heat.

Shaking his head to clear it, Clyde crawled silently on his hands and knees, creeping through the grass until he grasped Robert's pants. He licked his lips, closed his eyes, and searched for the vision playing across the insides of his eyelids for hours. Opening them, he reached for the two dead frogs lying in the grass beside him.

If his plan went right, he wouldn't be returning to that school, but neither would Robert. Chuckling to himself, he carefully placed a small dead frog into each pocket of Robert's pants, then pushed them back before retreating to his hiding place.

An occasional roar of laughter rent the air as the boys splashed, sending sprays of water into their faces. Resentment rolled up and down Clyde's spine, chilling him as he observed their unfettered joy. Such play had never been a part of his world.

Clyde's eyes narrowed, his breathing slowed, and time crawled with each breath. The boys swam to the edge, clamored up the embankment, then ran, jostling one another, elbows shoving as they made their way to the clothes dangling from the tree branches and piled in the grass. A faint breeze chilled their wet bodies, forcing them to dress quickly. Jason's voice drifted through the trees.

"Hey, Robert, you got some money?" Sonny shoved his bare feet into his shoes and rubbed his stomach as it growled its emptiness. He skip-stepped to catch up with Jason, walking ahead of Robert. "We gon' stop by Miss Mason's candy house before we go home."

"Broke-ass Negroes always begging." Robert sniggered, stopping on the dirt road and simultaneously ramming his hands into the pockets of his jeans. His fingers searched for the few loose

THE KNOWING 71

coins he had filched from his mother's purse that morning. As
his hands plunged deeper, sliding against the coarse fabric, his
fingertips stopped, brushing across something foreign.

The cold, bumpy skin of the frog imprinted itself on the
sensitive pads of his fingers, first touching it, then clutching as they
closed and spasmed around the fragile bones. His eyes widened,
bulging, and his mouth opened in a soundless scream. His body
stiffened, muscles tightening.

"F ... F ... Fr ..." The fractured sounds stuttered into the air
as spittle foamed white around the edges of his mouth, running
down his chin, his eyes wild marbles rolling around in his head.

Within his chest, his heart hammered an erratic arrhythmia,
his throat working to make a sound. Pain gripped his chest as his
heartbeat changed and thundered. His breath rasped in and out of
his lungs, and darkness danced before his eyes. His fingers remained
locked around the frog, squeezing as he choked on the words.

"Boy, what's wrong with you?" Jason shouted over his shoulder
from his place a few feet ahead of Robert. Receiving no answer, he
turned to walk back to him, huffing out his exasperation. "I swear,
your stingy ass ain't got to do all that if you don't want to share."

Sonny pivoted on his heel and turned as well, both boys
kicking up dirt, mumbling and griping while he prepared to
intervene if the brothers went at it again. Jason raised his head,
almost bumping into Sonny's back in his haste to get to Robert,
stunned by the sight before him. Robert's mouth flapped like a
grounded fish, issuing undecipherable grunts, his skin an ashy gray.

In front of him, Jason hesitated, then threw himself forward,
running to close the short distance to his brother. Reaching out, he
grasped empty air as Robert's body went rigid, then fell back, dead
weight slamming to the ground and dust billowing up in a cloud
around him. Sonny and Jason dropped to their knees beside him,
pushing against his stiff shoulder, shaking him—screaming in his face.

"Get on up, Robert!" Jason coaxed, his voice tapering off as breath rattled in Robert's throat . . . until it ceased abruptly . . . and finally. "Stop playing, boy!" he shouted into his brother's still face.

The boys stared across his body. Their eyes roved back and forth from Robert to each other and then back to Robert's sightless eyes fixed on the sky above them, his mouth still open.

"Shit, man, what done happened?" Sonny cried, his eyes filling with tears. Leaping to his feet, he grabbed Jason and pulled him along with him as he began to run for home, Jason's shrieking cries for his mother startling the birds from the trees.

Clyde stepped from the thick covering of the bushes and trees, stopping in front of Robert and nudging him with his toe. The body did not move. Leaning down, he tried to pull Robert's hand from his pocket, unable to bend the hand at the wrist, finding it frozen in its position, clutched around the frog. He reached inside his pants pocket, tried to pry the fingers loose, and failed. He sniffed the air, smelling the boy's loosened bowels and smiling, satisfaction spiraling through his body.

"W . . . W . . . Who th . . . the dummy now, Robert?" The words stumbled over one another, and his face colored in frustration. He stared down into the boy's open mouth, examining the bulge of his eyes. "You . . . You n . . . n . . . needs to c . . . close your mouth, boy."

He stopped and sucked in a breath, struggling to control his words. Laughter rose from the depths of the darkness as he pushed Robert's chin upward and watched it fall back open. He waited for some acknowledgment to come, the feeling of success, but felt only the pit of darkness still churning inside. His work was not done. The darkness continued to cry out for more.

Clyde's hands spasmed, opening and closing, a new urge for violence overwhelming him. Even in death, he could still see that bucktoothed smirk and the desire to wash it from his face crashed in waves over him. Seizing a large rock from the ground, Clyde raised it over his head, then paused as the darkness whispered to him, providing him with a new plan. He grinned and heaved the body over on its stomach.

He loomed over Robert, the energy of darkness swelling and rising within him as he lifted the rock over his head and brought it down on the back of the boy's head. The loud and gratifying *thunk* of bone being crushed and the warmth of blood splattering across his face pulled a sigh from his lips.

He placed the rock back on the ground and rolled the body onto its back until the head rested neatly against it, fitting like a puzzle piece. He laughed.

Clyde scrambled, disappearing through the bush, tree branches slapping into his face until he stumbled onto the trail leading him home. Stopping, he cocked his head to the side and listened intently. In the distance, a wild cry climbed into the air, escalating in despair and interspersed with the heavy thud of feet pounding the ground.

The screams cut off, knifed into silence, then exploded in a shriek wrenched from the womb. They were the wailing sobs of Miss Emma, Robert's mother, and he smiled, the darkness appeased.

CHAPTER SEVEN

With hands that trembled, Cora removed her hat as she listened to Joseph outside talking with their sons on the porch. The three of them sat in a semicircle of chairs she had arranged before leaving for the service. Their voices were quiet and subdued, affected by the emotions wrung out of them over the last two days since the discovery of Robert's dead body in the woods.

Images of her and Joseph with the family at Emma's house following the burial lingered. The offering of words to lift the spirits, knowing that none could, swam in her mind. An air of solemnity had hung in the room, pressing people into the depressions of the sofa cushions, the hot, dim corners of the room, and the cane bottoms of the chairs outside on the sagging porch. Whole hams, cakes, pies, and steaming pots of vegetables weighed down every available space in the kitchen and the dining room table as friends and relatives tried unsuccessfully to push food into their bodies to fill the hole that death had drilled into each of them.

Back home and alone for the moment, Cora picked up her journal, sat at the table, and began to write.

It feel like I'm losing my mind. I cain't imagine what Emma feel like. My breath cut off just thinking about Daniel or David being dead. It ain't natural burying your child. It happen, but it just don't feel natural. Alls I can hear is the sound of Emma crying out for her dead baby like the sound of her voice could bring him back. And Jason just sitting there, staring at that casket, not moving, not a bit. It be like somebody just stuck him there and say, "Don't you move."

I was sitting in the back, trying hard to close off the noise of all them feelings around me, the air heavy as syrup, sweat dripping off my forehead, praying for Pastor Raleigh to hurry up. I closed my eyes for a minute, and when I open them back up, there be Robert, standing in the corner behind the pulpit.

Robert was looking right at me, dressed in his overalls he be wearing all the time, not the new suit his mama done bought him to be buried in. He lift one arm, and I can see the fingers on his hand is curled like he be holding something and he shaking his head no. I turns and follow to where his hand be pointing and look right at Clyde Henry, sitting next to his mama, swinging his feet, and, sweet God, it look like he smiling.

I keep waiting for Robert to fade away, but he don't. He still standing there when they close that casket, and Miss Emma throw herself on top of it. She set that whole church up to hollering and screaming, and Fannie took Clyde out, her hands covering up his ears, and she pressing him to her side.

He look back to the front of the church at that casket and at Robert in the corner, and that smile get bigger. He look dead at me when they go past me. I smell that smell strong on him and lift my finger to rest it under my nose. He see the Knowing in my eyes. I look back to the corner, and Robert still there, watching us both.

Cora sighed and closed her journal, staring into the corner—just beyond the window curtains that stirred in the light breeze from the porch—where Robert stood.

Glancing surreptitiously through the window, she saw that everyone still sat with their bodies leaned forward. Joe reached out and squeezed Daniel's shoulder as the boy wiped a tear from his cheek.

"Robert, was it Clyde?" Cora asked, whispering the words, speaking to the apparition, sure that no one was listening. "It be him what did it?"

Robert nodded, and she watched his body slowly lose shape and fade. Falling heavily into the rocking chair, she waited for this day to end and a new day to begin. The Knowing pressed upon her.

Clyde moved his head from side to side, rubbing his nose against the rough fabric of the overalls covering his raised knees. His constant presence in this spot in the dreamscape had formed a depression in the earth, the tall grass dead beneath him. He raised his eyes to stare at the sky overhead, tinted goldenrod and trimmed with green.

The ground and sky heaved as turbulent as his thoughts, guilt attempting to burrow inside. He sighed, his feelings in turmoil. The solitude of self was lost to him, even here in his dreams, and he felt tears welling in his eyes.

The righteous certainty he'd felt when he was executing his plan leaked from his pores, draining into the ground around him.

He listened for the sound of his mama's words from the book of Job, "ruin for the wicked; disaster for those who do wrong." He shook his head, confused. He needed to talk to Mama, be reassured that it was Robert who was wrong. The boy was evil, and he had brought his own damnation on himself.

The darkness rumbled in his chest, filling Clyde's drifting thoughts, expanding in the spaces where doubt lingered. He closed his eyes, turning his ear inward, letting the dark soothe him, growing stronger. It whispered that Clyde was the judgment.

Clyde wavered, panic shooting through him, loss setting an alarm in his soul. He had felt it before when he picked up the rock to bludgeon Robert, a rage that would not be satisfied until it had been obeyed. He sensed it changing him, pushing him to a place he could not return from.

The air around him thickened, the skies growing dimmer and an invisible wind picked up, flattening the tall grass. A prickling of fear flowed along his spine, forcing Clyde to sit upright, his head swiveling from left to right, surveying the dreamscape. In the distance, a body approached.

Cora felt herself moving toward Clyde, unable to stop, discerning that she was completely visible and vulnerable to him. She watched as his eyes locked on hers, drawn into the swirling darkness of his gaze.

"You," he cried out, pushing himself into a standing position. He felt her emotions flying around her, a swirl of fear and anger. She knew. Knew what he had done to Robert. Knew about the darkness in him. Knew that he had to die. And he knew that he would have to kill her first.

In her bed, Cora shuddered, her thundering heartbeat slowing as the fingers of the dream released her from their tenuous grip. She gulped down a deep breath and shoved herself against the security of Joe's body curled around her in the bed. Her mind settled itself into her surroundings, set free from the dreamscape. She allowed her breathing to synchronize with Joe's. She stared through the bedroom window and waited for dawn.

Cora shuffled from the stove to the kitchen table, rubbing sleep from her eyes, watching Robert where he stood in the corner. His face remained somber, fear etched across his expression. She stirred the eggs, scooped them onto a plate, and then turned and poured Joe his coffee.

"What's wrong, Cora? You done had that same hang-dog look since the funeral yesterday. I know it hit you hard, but talk to me," his voice pleaded as his hand covered hers and squeezed.

"It ain't nothing, Joe. I'm just feeling for Emma. You know I brought that boy into the world, then had to stand over him while they buried him," she replied, gently extracting her hand and kissing his forehead, feeling his resistance. His eyes searched hers for answers that she could not provide. Finally, he lowered his head and began sipping his coffee.

"You didn't sleep hardly none last night, huh?" he continued, his slow, syrupy voice tingling through her and tickling her insides in the way it always had.

"How you know? You was calling hogs every time I look your way," she answered with a low chuckle.

"Because you was up reading the Bible when I got up. I just figured you didn't sleep none. Is them dreams back?"

"It gon' take me a bit to get over it. Just give me some time. That's all I need. You don't worry yourself none, Joe. I be all right," she said, attempting to steer the conversation away from her dreams, the disturbance in her spirit playing across the background of her thoughts. "You needs to take David and Daniel and gets to working them fields, or we won't have no crops this year."

An enigmatic smile teased her lips but did not rise to her eyes. She reached for the Knowing, cloaked in Mi's image. She allowed it to renew the strength of the light, letting it banish the flashing visions of death that had continued to chase her through the night.

Joe stood, slapping his battered hat against the leg of his jeans before placing it on his head. His eyes lingered on his wife a few minutes longer before shaking his head and leaving to meet Daniel and David in the fields. Cora followed him out to the yard, where she'd left the family laundry to soak, stopping at the large tin tub she had set up earlier that morning. She watched him until his figure was a small speck in the distance, then began the soothing and repetitive motion of washing the clothes.

Cora's hands pushed the bunched fabric against the metal rungs of the washboard, up and down, then back again, the sun hot on her bent back as she leaned over the tin tub resting on a large tree stump in her yard. Plunging Joe's shirt into the soapy water, she continued the process until she was satisfied that it was clean.

The details of the dream forced their way to take precedence as her hands continued to work automatically. Last night, everything had changed. The darkness had increased in Clyde, a magnitude of power that allowed him to see her and invade her mind.

Pulling the shirt from the tub, she twisted it in her powerful hands, wringing it until it was free of even the slightest residue of moisture. While she vacillated, divided against herself, and serving two masters, Clyde had succumbed to the darkness born in him.

Tossing it into the basket at her feet, she leaned back, fisting her hands into the small of her back, kneading and stretching the kinks that had knotted her muscles as she washed. She cursed the duplicity of her life. Raised in the church and nurtured in the spirit of the Knowing, she had walked a fine line, thinking she could keep them separate and equal in her heart. Catching movement in the trees from the corner of her eye, she lifted her hand to shade her vision, fully expecting to see Robert emerge from the trees.

"Joe, is that you?" she called, irritation coloring her voice. It would be just like him to have doubled back and try to sneak up and check on her. She had too much on her mind to play along with him today.

Nothing else stirred while her eyes scanned the sky, a clear blue, the color of truth. An unnatural silence descended around her, making her voice sound oddly loud. Something was wrong. No sounds of birds singing, no fluttering of wings, no buzz or whir of insects, no skittering of small animals over the brittle, sun-dried grass of the woodland floor marred the absolute stillness.

Lowering her hand and leaning over the tub again, Cora shook off the foreboding. She lifted another shirt, slamming it against the corrugated surface of her board, if for no other reason than to hear a sound beyond her own ragged breathing. Her eyes roamed around her surroundings, alighting briefly on each object. The faded wooden walls that formed the back of her house remained blank, with no shadows riding across the surfaces. Yellow curtains blew in and out of the open window of her kitchen as a slight breeze passed through the yard, cooling the sweat that dripped from her forehead.

Her hands lifted a polka-dotted shirt from the water, and she grimaced. She had always hated it. Some whimsical purchase of femininity with lace trimming the collar and cuffs meant for the woman her husband saw when he looked at her. It always made her feel that people were laughing behind her back at how silly she looked in it, the bright pink and white stretched across her broad shoulders. She'd worn it to church last Sunday, enduring the stares as Joseph beamed with delight, her arm held tightly in the bend of his elbow. Closing her eyes and squeezing the water from the fabric, she allowed her inner eye to search, amplifying her other senses.

A repugnant scent wafted toward her, causing Cora to sniff the air, her nose wrinkling in disgust. The odor drifted on a current of air, faint at first but growing stronger. It was the rot of death long in the ground, of moldy, desecrated flesh moving closer. She searched within herself frantically, pushing through the fog of her conflicting thoughts. Today, she would choose.

The Knowing flared, her light growing stronger and saturating her being. Mi's face flickered in front of her, and Cora's lips moved in gratitude. The light blazed, the fullness of her power aligned with the Knowing. Her God knew what she was. Had he not created her?

The Knowing intensified in her spirit, and the fear and conflict that had constantly gnawed at her diminished, evaporating into nothingness. She took a deep breath, stood tall, and leveled her shoulders.

Cora squinted into the trees that bordered their property, observing a figure drawing closer. She saw an aura pulsating around a form, light purple, deep purple, green, then black, rippling against the natural light of the sun until she could discern that it was Clyde. Emerging from the woods with his steady, shambling gait, he stopped some five yards away, the blistering sun glistening on the dark skin of his bare torso beneath his overalls.

The legs of his pants had been altered to accommodate the shortness of his lower limbs, while the larger size of the overalls barely contained the barrel chest and heavily muscled arms of his upper body. He was a cruel joke of creation, a broken man and child pulled apart and put back together. His massive head balanced on a short, squat neck.

Clyde's dark eyes fixed on her, and his lips curled upward with that horrible smile, the same one she had seen at the funeral. It was the one that followed her into sleep and formed the substance of her nightmares; the one she had seen just before she had awakened in the quiet hours of the dark night.

Thick ebony ribbons of darkness flowed forward, a tsunami crashing over her, drawing on the residues of the darkness in her own soul. It beat against her light as she threw her hands up, bending under the attack and forcing her to the ground.

Cora collapsed and lay in a crumpled heap, her voluminous skirt pushed up to expose her thighs and her bare legs. Her arms and hands were still wet and soapy from the washtub of clothes that sat close to where she had fallen. She watched through lowered lids as Clyde moved closer, now no more than the length of her own body away from her. He stood with his hands shoved in the back pockets of his jeans, whistling off-key as he stared down at her.

He took a step closer, the malevolence of his gaze sending a chill through her as she struggled to sit up, seeking her voice. Forcing her mind to calmness, Cora oriented herself to where she was—still behind her house, on the hard-packed earth that was her yard. Her mind worked rapidly, forming and discarding plans. She crept closer to the tub, scooting, preparing to grab its edge, fling the water at him, and then using the empty tub to batter him.

"What you doing here, Clyde? Do your mama know you here?" She waited for him to draw closer, buying time. Her hands pushed down her skirt as she struggled to her feet, groping for the tub's edge. She pushed herself forward until she was standing, using her height and size to intimidate him. Her blazing eyes never left his, the color shifting from gray to green.

"Naw," he growled, his words slow with the effort to speak. She could see the frustration as his throat bulged, the words seeming to force their way out. "We both know why I be here."

"You ain't got no business here." Cora inched forward with each word, giving up the idea of throwing the water. Her weight shifted to find balance. "You ain't right, and you knows it. Your mama knows it too."

"You remembers when you made her beat me. She b . . . beat me real bad." The words were broken, starting and stopping. "She ain't know nothing about them critters before you come waving them around."

"I ain't made her do nothing. That between you, her, and the Lord," Cora said, baiting him with her words. Rolling her shoulders and moving her neck from side to side, she planted herself firmly in front of him. "You got a chance to go on back home, Clyde. It ain't too late for you." She blew air noisily between her lips, her hands rubbing up and down the fabric of her skirt to dry them.

Clyde continued moving forward with a speed that belied his size and stunted legs. He lunged forward into her, surprising her and knocking her off balance.

"Sweet Lord!" Cora screamed, her arms pinwheeling as she stumbled backward, attempting to keep herself from falling to the ground again.

"DON'T YOU SAY HIS NAME!" Clyde shouted so close spittle sprayed her face, his eyes rolling crazily in their sockets. He ground his teeth, his tongue catching on the words. "You. . . You the one wh-wh-what wants to kill me." His lids blinked rapidly over his bulging eyes in confusion. Cora continued to back up and put space between them again, bringing herself closer to the back door of the house. Her mind raced as she regained her balance. She quickly glanced behind her, gauging the distance between her and the back door, turning to dash toward it.

"And I know you seen him," Clyde sneered, his words freezing her in place. Her head swiveled to stare into his eyes. Death floated there in the dark, swirling mists.

Cora stopped moving away from him. Her feelings ranged across her features, betraying her thoughts and causing him to smile that hideous grimace again. Her head swam with the dizzying déjà vu of her recent dream where she had seen this death coming.

"What you talking about, Clyde?" she asked, straightening again to her full height and pushing her emotions away. He was close now, standing in her shadow. The odor emanated from him overwhelming her, thick in her lungs. She slowed her breathing to prevent gagging. It was the stink of death, like the smell of those lifeless carcasses she had discovered all those years ago left rotting in the woods and marked by his presence. The final dredges of the fear he imprinted drained from her.

He raised an eyebrow. "You didn't finds no more, did you?" A sly look passed over his features, and Cora hesitated, letting his deception sink in.

"And I seen you in my dream," he stammered. "I know you seen Robert when we was getting ready for the burying. He told you about me."

"So what?" Cora said, her voice hardening, not flinching in the face of his declaration, denials, or failures, shrugging her shoulders. She could feel how his power had grown, the dark throbbing and pulsating as she slid her feet sideways over the hardpacked earth.

"We all got what us purposed to do. I done missed mine before. But you think a boy like you gon' keep me from it this time?" Laughter barked from deep within her chest, deriding him, goading him into making a foolish decision, and giving her an advantage.

"You scared, ain't you?" Clyde asked, inhaling deeply, his chest expanding. "You tryng to hide it deep down, but I c . . . can smells it on you." He cut his eyes in the direction of the fields. "Ain't nobody c-c-coming to save you, neither."

"I ain't needs no saving." Her mind churned, then found its peace as she allowed the Knowing and the light to flow throughout her being, strengthening muscle, bone, and sinew with its power.

The darkness writhed around Clyde, pooling around his feet, swirling around his hands, and flowing from his mouth. Cora felt it nudge against her mind and shook her head to free herself before it could invade her and attach itself.

Cora's arms lifted—elbows bent, the palms of her hands facing outward—as light exploded from her hands, blinding in its intensity. It shot forward at Clyde, slamming into his darkness and absorbing it.

She felt the Knowing and the light pressing, pushing, and bending the darkness, a smile spreading over her face. Her mind reveled at the prospect of victory. There would be no failure today.

She would not relinquish. Her death was a worthy price to bring back the balance his destruction demanded.

And then, she felt her power being siphoned from her as the light flowed outward. Clyde bellowed, seeming to grow stronger as they fought, darkness against light.

"SINNER!" he thundered. His stuttering was gone, and his words flowed unobstructed, rolling off his tongue as though the impediment had never existed. Cora's mouth twisted, and her eyes widened in disbelief as he inched forward, his darkness fragmenting her light. "WITCH!"

Images swam between them, and Cora saw him nestled in her hands, an infant straining to suck in air, his tiny fists waving ineffectively in the air. She saw one hand coming down toward his tiny face, hesitating for a fraction of a thought.

"HOW YOU DO THAT? HOW YOU GON' KILL A LITTLE BABY?!" he screamed, his eyes rolling back in their sockets.

Her light melded into the darkness, sucking in the image with the light. He seemed to swell as he took her powers into himself.

"NO!" The words tore from Cora's throat as Clyde threw himself forward, his large hands reaching through the darkness surrounding them. The weight of his body carried them both to the ground, where she landed flat on her back, the air whooshing from her lungs.

His big hands locked around her throat and silenced her screams while she fought to free her last words and thoughts. His body pressed down on hers, his hands continuing to squeeze. Her heels drummed on the ground as she twisted and bucked, trying to free herself, the pulsing light from her hands slowly ebbing.

"You is gon' die." She rasped her last words as he crushed the cartilage in her throat.

The image of Clyde swam in front of her eyes as Cora's internal light began to dim with her vision. Her fists beat weakly at his arms, then tried feebly to pull his hands from her throat, flagging against his strength. Words no longer came from her. She felt failure and regret. She stared into his face, mottled purple beneath his dark skin, just like it was the day he was born. She saw the darkness writhing in his eyes, felt the snakes of power twitching beneath her own skin cease . . . and then she felt no more.

Feeling her body go limp beneath him, Clyde pushed himself into a standing position. Looking down at Cora, his heart thundering in his chest, his hands hanging loose at his sides, he let the rage funnel around him. He raised his foot and kicked her hard, listening for the crunch of bone.

Instead, his toe jammed against something unyielding within the tangles of her skirt. He leaned down, digging through the voluminous folds of fabric to find the pocket concealed there. He stared momentarily at the leather cover, worn soft over the years, then opened it.

His eyes darted rapidly across the tight, neat script as he flipped through the pages. His name appeared on almost every page, a chronicle of condemnation, damning his existence. He read until the words blurred before his eyes, swimming with tears. Slamming the book shut, he raised it over his head, prepared to hurl it to the ground, then stopped.

He pushed it into the large pocket in the front of his overalls. He would keep it. He would use it to learn what she knew, using it to take her power. He lifted his foot high, the dark energy flowing down his limb, and kicked Cora again. His foot connected solidly with her temple, ensuring she would not rise again. Finally, he felt the darkness receding, the rage satisfied, his vision clearing. They were safe from her.

Fannie sat on the small front porch of the shack she shared with Clyde, waving absently at the flies that buzzed around her head. It seemed to her that it was mighty hot for May, the sun blazing against her skin. She had made a fan from the pages of an old mail-order catalog, waving it back and forth in front of her face. It did little more than stir a slight breeze, giving her little relief. Still, it was better than the heat from baking bread in the oven. The thought of the five additional loaves needed for Clyde to make his deliveries to the general store in town melted her further into the chair.

She watched listlessly as a figure materialized from the woods, moving along the rough track she and Clyde had trampled with their going and coming over the years. She squinted into the distance, anxiety worming into her thoughts until she recognized Clyde's walk, his knees knocking together, giving him a side-to-side gait. She watched, observing how his head and shoulders drooped and his steps dragged.

Before he had completely crossed the dry brown earth that was their front yard and reached the bottom step, she shot out of the chair, her arms encircling him as much as the width of his body would allow.

"Clyde, what's wrong, baby?" She took a step back, her voice escalating. "Did somebody bother you? I say, what's wrong?"

Clyde stood a head taller than Fannie, his broad shoulders and chest dwarfing her in size, balancing on his truncated legs. As he looked down at her, she studied the features on the broad plane of his face. His mouth was wide, the lips full and pink, and stretched across the width of his features. His thick nostrils flared beneath the flat bridge of his nose that divided his bulging eyes. She saw a glimmer of joy and pleasure mixed with fear and remorse in those eyes.

"I'm gon' ask you again. Why was you walking like that? You scaring me."

Clyde hesitated, uncertainty flickering across his face for just an instant, filled with the self-loathing Cora's words had implanted.

"Is I'm bad, Mama? I just did what I supposed to do. I makes a sinner pay."

Fannie's heart lurched, then fell with the pain of his words. Her eyes narrowed, her mouth pulling into a pout. She reached up, her palm cupped his cheek, and he leaned into her hand.

Clyde allowed her to lead him to the edge of the porch, where he perched on the rim, Fannie sitting back in her chair. His head rested in her lap, her hands tracing a pattern on his scalp.

"Tells me what done happened, Clyde. What make you think you bad?"

"The dream said she gon' kill me. She a sinner."

Fannie's hand stopped, and she leaned back until she was rigidly aligned against the back of the chair. "I needs you to tell me what sinner, baby boy?"

Clyde grabbed her hand, pulling at her fingers, hungry for the soothing they offered as Fannie continued questioning him. "I thought we was gon' talk about it if God was speaking to you again. You remembers?"

He nodded and began, "It was what the dream said, Mama. She come to my dream place, and I seen her. I seen in her head what she was gon' do to me. Then . . ." He stopped, swallowing the words that threatened to choke him before he continued speaking. "He done put her right there in front of me, Mama, in a dream. Wasn't nothing to do but his work. Why he tell me about her if it ain't time?"

"But who, baby? Who was it?" Panic and worry began to build again as Fannie tried to sort out the truth from him, her eyes casting rapidly—wildly—as she searched his face. She took several deep breaths, not wanting to rush him but needing the truth.

"Was that witch, Miss Cora," he spat, the poison of his hatred putrefying the air between them. "You know her, Mama?" Clyde's eyes probed hers, eager for approval, judging the impact of each word as he spoke it. "It come to me in my dream last night. I knowed she was gon' kill me."

Fannie sighed, breath released from her like a slow-leaking balloon. She felt tension easing from each portion of her body along with the fear that had resided in her since his birth. Cora. Of course, it was Cora. All these years, she had lived in trepidation that somehow she would take Clyde away from her. She rolled her head around, then relaxed her shoulders, aware of taking the first long, deep breath since the day Clyde was born—when Cora told her he had to die.

Apprehension slid off her in waves. Grabbing Clyde more firmly, she clasped him to her chest, patting him on the back, great wrenching sobs shaking her body.

"Why you crying, Mama? Did I do bad . . .? Huh? Did I?" Clyde wailed, climbing to his knees and turning his face into her skirts. He felt the darkness beginning to churn, and he fought against it, hugging his mother tighter.

Fannie lifted his face, smiling through her tears, raining kisses on his forehead and cheeks. "Oh no, baby boy. You did just right." Her fingers began the familiar salving dance, rounding his skull, sliding down both sides of his nose, her hands caressing his cheeks, and then starting again.

"Now you tell Mama what happened. Don't leave out nothing."

Clyde rested in Fannie's embrace, the darkness receding for now while his mother made it right. It curled inward and waited.

CHAPTER EIGHT

Joseph found himself humming as his feet pounded along the dirt road, his metal lunch pail swinging against his thigh, empty of its contents. He imagined Cora—bent over a pot on the stove, stirring whatever she had cooked up for their supper—leaping as he snuck up behind her and embraced her around the waist. Thoughts of her stirred his loins, and his steps quickened.

"Pawpaw, wait up for us." David and Daniel yelled simultaneously, panting as they ran up behind him. Joseph smiled, warmed with the pride of fatherhood they always brought. He looked into their similar faces, one reflecting Cora and the other reflecting him, a double blessing sent when they had given up on having their own child.

"You need to get them long legs to moving. You know your mama don't like to keep supper waiting. She ain't gon' be fussing me out!" He laughed, grinning into his sons' faces before striding ahead of them again.

Approaching the turnoff to the road leading to the back of their property, he became aware of an odd stillness descending, abruptly cutting off their laughter. Joseph's eyes roamed across the barren ground between him and the house, coming to rest on the overturned wash tub, the deep puddle, and the damp circle around it.

He crossed the short space, his stride reducing the distance in seconds. He gazed down into the puddle of water, seeing the film of soap scum floating on top. Cora would never leave the tub like that or the wash sitting on the muddy ground. Fear iced his bones.

"CORA! CORA!" His voice rose, grating against his ears in the stillness. David and Daniel stood a few feet behind him, his unease telegraphing to them as they began shouting for their mother.

"You boys go look on the side of the house and see if the truck is gone."

They leaped into action, spreading out, each taking a different direction. They shouted, hands cupped to their mouths, and walking quickly.

Joe lifted his gaze from the tub, staring forward at a barely discernable lump in the tall grass near the back wall of the house. He wanted to turn away—not discover what it really was, not allow it to become a part of his reality. His feet trudged forward, weighted by an unreasonable fear. Cora's name continued to pour from his mouth, a low mewling litany of sound that would not stop as the bundle resolved itself into limbs, a torso, and a head twisted at an impossible angle.

Joseph dropped to his knees, pulling Cora's body to his chest, lowering his face to her hair to muffle the scream that escaped with his sobs. Behind him, the sound of the twins' footsteps thudded toward him, slamming to a stop as they reached their father's bent figure and the horror that confronted them.

"Momma!" the boys cried out simultaneously, their voices blending with their father's sobs.

"Is she breathing, Pawpaw? Huh? Is she?" Daniel asked, his words breathless.

David punched his brother in the shoulder hard enough to rock him on his heels. "Don't say nothing like that. She be breathing, Pawpaw, ain't she?"

Joseph ignored them, scooping Cora into his arms. He stood carefully, arranging her so that her head lolled against his chest, and stepped lightly to keep it from rolling around on her broken neck.

He did not answer his sons as he walked, keeping his eyes fixed on the house in front of him, focusing only on reaching his living room where he could lay her down. Entering the back door, he passed through the kitchen and into the front room, laying her gently on the couch. Staring down, he counted with each of his own breaths, waiting for the sight of her chest rising with her own corresponding breaths. They had been breathing as one body for so long that his mind snagged, revolting at the thought that this synchronization no longer existed.

Straightening her head to appear more natural, he laid his hand on her still chest, and the pain roared out of him. His body collapsed across hers, oblivious to the keening wail of the boys behind him.

It became impossible to draw in air, a clean breath that would fill his oxygen-starved lungs and remove the spots dancing in the darkness before his eyes. Joseph felt himself sliding, swooning into a puddle on the floor beside the couch where Cora lay unmoving and devoid of breath. Sobs strangled in his throat, and he choked as his body struggled with the contradiction of trying to breathe and cry out.

He wanted to pull himself together for his sons and be strong in the face of his loss. Instead, his body violently trembled as he sat up, pulling his knees to his chest, lowering his head, and covering it with his arms—unmanned.

"Daniel, you best call the sheriff and Mason." David rubbed at his eyes, his palms pressing into the sockets before calling to his brother. Daniel stood paralyzed across the room, unable to come nearer. David lowered one hand to his father's shoulder. He felt his shuddering reverberating through his arm, echoing his sorrow as he stared at his mother's remains.

Dark bruises stood out on her throat, and her eyes were frozen open, permanently staring into the unknown, a grimace of terror locked on her face. He reached out with his other hand, gingerly trying to lower the lids. Cora's eyes remained stubbornly open, fixed on her last vision.

Daniel remained incapable of movement, his feet rooted on the spot where he stood, until David's voice forced its way into his mind. It urged him forward, his voice taking on a hard edge and asserting his natural dominance.

"Go on now. Get down to Miss Rachel's store and use they phone," David barked.

Daniel moved forward—his long limbs tangling as he got his feet stumbling toward the door—glancing back into the face that mirrored his own. Both reflected the deepness of their shared sorrow. He saw the glimmer of wetness in his brother's eyes before he turned away, taking a final look over his shoulder before scrambling out the door.

The fabric of David's world was irrevocably torn. Didn't matter that he was twelve. Today, he was a man. Born fifteen minutes earlier than Daniel, he was in charge as the eldest.

His mother was dead, and his father, his rock, was a quivering heap on the floor. David sucked in his breath, strengthening his core, and listened to hear his mother's voice echoing inside his head, guiding him. It did not come.

Looking down at his father, he felt his body deflate, helplessness pulling the form from his bones until he felt himself collapsing beside his father. David encircled him with his arms as he rocked him back and forth.

Time crept, measured in the ticking of the mantle clock over the fireplace. The sun had moved away from the window, and a cooler breeze blew in to raise the curtains as footfalls sounded on the porch, accompanied by heavy voices. The screen door banged open, and Sheriff Jesse entered the room. He was a big man, standing six foot four, his frame molded with muscle, and his bulk seemed to fill every available inch of space in the door frame.

He cleared his throat, uncomfortable as he took in the sight of David and Joseph on the floor and the body of Cora lying beside them on the couch. Men sobbing unnerved him. It wasn't natural. Behind him, Elder Mason, the town's undertaker and quasi coroner, tried to peer around him.

Joseph looked up, his eyes red-rimmed and puffy. A momentary flicker of embarrassment and shame passed over his features as he saw the pity in the sheriff's eyes. Gathering his strength, he pushed away from David and attempted to climb to his feet, turning his head to avoid looking at Cora. Jesse stuck out his hand, and he accepted it, allowing the man to help him up.

"Joe, I'm sorry to hear about Miss Cora. My condolences to you and your family," he spoke as he walked closer to the body, taking up the space that Joseph had vacated.

David was now on his feet, crossing the room to embrace Daniel, whose body broke anew.

"How long ago this happen?"

"Don't know." Joseph shrugged his shoulders. "We found her in the back of the house when we come home for supper and brung her in here. What time it be now?"

"Almost seven. So, you saying it been at least two hours?"

Joseph's shoulders moved upward again, his head hanging and his limbs drooping toward the floor. He felt the need to sit but couldn't find anywhere that didn't scream of Cora's presence. He tried to focus and hear what Jesse was saying to him, answer his questions, while his mind raced toward an answer.

Jesse lifted Cora's hand, examining the nails and the blood embedded beneath them. That Cora had fought her assailant was apparent. She'd fought hard, raking and gouging from the look of the ragged and broken nails on her fingers. His eye roved upward from the bruises on her neck to her face, frozen in a contortion of fear, anger, and defiance. She had fought to her last breath, he thought, not giving in even as life fled her body.

"You knows anybody could have done this, Joseph?"

Joseph hesitated, and the image of Clyde filled his mind, his hands stuffed in his overall pockets and his mouth twisted in a grin. He shook the image free from his mind before he answered. "Nah, I don't. Cora help everybody she could. Who would have done this?"

He hugged his thoughts of Clyde to himself. This was not for the sheriff to deal with. This was something he had to settle for Cora. Resolve renewed him, and he straightened, mentally seeing his shotgun in the corner of their closet.

Elder Mason elbowed his way through the bodies of the men that towered over him, making his way to the deceased. He tried to shove down the feelings of titillation that bubbled to the surface as he prepared to examine the body. Murder was something he didn't often see in these parts. Some deaths might have seemed suspicious, but this was the first blatant murder he had come across.

He leaned down, sniffing the corpse as he prodded and examined it. Like old meat sprinkled with cheap perfume, the smell of rot with an underlying sweetness rose immediately. He pulled out the stethoscope he carried with him to verify the lack of heartbeat and used a penlight to check if the pupils reacted. As was expected, he found nothing and observed that the muscles had begun to stiffen in early rigor mortis. Rocking back on his heels, he prepared to turn and inform the sheriff that he could move the body to the morgue, where he could provide him with more information. However, a flicker of movement from the corner of his eye caught his attention.

He could have sworn Cora's mouth had twitched, the dry lips rubbing together. He looked again, wondering what muscular contraction could have caused it. Then her eyes squeezed shut . . . and opened, rapidly blinking as she bolted upright on the couch. Her arms extended outward, fingers on her hands splayed defensively, bulging eyes searching her surroundings.

"Sweet Jesus, have mercy!" Elder shrieked, his voice an octave lower than high soprano, and stumbled backward, crashing into Jesse and Joseph in his haste to remove himself from the reanimated corpse.

Daniel and David hurled themselves toward the couch and their mother, reaching for her as Joseph leaped forward. He tried to wrap his arms around her, simultaneously shaking and pulling her close. Cora's eyes looked out wildly at him, her mouth working to form words before she collapsed against him.

"What in the name of hell and damnation is happening here?" Jesse yelled, the macabre scene pushing reason from his mind.

Joseph felt her chest rising and falling against his own, her heart beating against his, the rhythm finding his, and tears rolling down his cheeks. He held her that way for a long moment, afraid that if he moved her, he would find this was a dream, his desperate brain trying to bring her back to him.

"It ain't possible. It just ain't possible," Elder babbled, his words rapid and tumbling over one another in their haste to get out. "What kind of juju is this, Joe? She was dead!" He kept repeating it. "I know dead, and Cora was dead." Elder shook his head in dismay, keeping his distance across the room. "Her neck was broke. She wasn't breathing, and you could smell the death on her. Ain't no way she could have just raised back up and be sucking air. It just ain't."

Joseph eased her body back down to the couch, watching the rise and fall of her chest. He rubbed her arm, feeling the heat return to her skin. David leaned in and rubbed her other arm.

Elder recovered enough to force his way through Joseph and his sons to examine Cora again. He repeated his previous procedure, listening to the steady beat of her heart and feeling her pulse. Lifting her eyelid, he checked the pupils and saw them retract at the intrusion of the light. Unlike before, he had to raise the eyelid, as she was no longer staring sightlessly at the ceiling.

Behind them, Jesse towered over them and looked down at Cora. "I'll just be damned. Ain't nobody going to believe this. Cora done come back from the dead."

I ain't never seen no dark like this here. I cain't see nothing. Cain't feel me neither. I just knows that I am. I don't know how long I been here. There ain't no day or night, no up or down. The only thing I have is my feelings. I be mad and sad at the same time. Mad because I know I been taken from someplace, someplace I cain't remembers too good; sad because I done lost something. I keeps hearing my name, least I still got that. I know I called Cora because I be at a crossroads like Corinth in the Bible. I can remembers that too. Somehow I knows who be calling me, and I want to answer them.

"Miss Cora, that you?"

"Robert?"

He sound lost, scared. Ain't nothing to reach for, no hand to hold, no shoulder to squeeze. It just be what I hear. So, I calls out to him, and he call back. I start asking him even when the Knowing already there. I wants to hear it.

"Where we at?"

"We dead, Miss Cora. We both us dead."

I feels weighed down. I is sinking in the blackness. If I keeps going, I knows there won't be no more me ever. Robert be fading, and it hard to hear him, but he calling me back. He keep on telling me: don't be scared. I keeps listening, makes myself wants to hear him.

"Don't you do that, Miss Cora. You gon' fade and not come back. Way we is now, least sometimes I can gets people to see me. Well, I could before, but now you dead, and won't nobody see me but him."

I knows right off who "him" is. I say, "Him what put me here? Him what I was told about? Him I was supposed to stop? Clyde?"

Robert's voice change. He sound like me now. Mad and sad, but most mad.

"It him. He put them frogs in my pantses, then smash my head with that rock. Monkey boy did it. You the onliest one I could tell."

His last words begin to fade again, and I reach with my mind, trying to hold onto him. Then I starts hearing other voices, and I sees a little teeny piece of light, a pinpoint in the black darkness around me. I moves toward it. It pulling me so fast, too fast.

Pure white light around me, and I can see again. My heart slam in my chest, and I feel my body buck with the force. My mouth twitch with the need to holler out. I feels my eyes blink and stretch wide with all the remembering coming back. Then it black again.

Joseph stopped, staring at the weather-beaten boards of Fannie's shack. The sun blazed against the one small window that looked out into the yard. His shotgun hung at his side, the barrel pointed toward the earth, the muscles of his right arm tense in preparation for firing it. Fannie or Clyde would tell him the truth today, one way or another.

He should have come sooner, left as soon as he knew that Cora was breathing again, back on the other side of the veil where he could feel her and hold her. But he had been too afraid; afraid to let her out of his sight; afraid that if he got too far away, she would lose the rhythm of his heartbeat and be gone again, this time not coming back.

Raising his left forearm, he swiped it across his forehead, feeling the coating of sweat on his skin. His eyes squinted, searching for movement or any signs of life. No smoke rose from the chimney. The window was shut tight, the door closed, and he felt his body heating up at the thought of the sweltering furnace that had to be building up inside.

Striding forward, he used the butt of the gun to beat against the door, then stepped back as the last blow splintered it from the force. The rusted-out lock hung useless as the door flew open, banging against the inside wall.

He had to be sure. He had to silence the persistent voice that told him Clyde had been the one who attacked Cora. He had waited, hoping she could tell him herself, but she remained silent as death lying on their bed.

"Fannie? Fannie, you here?" he shouted, poking his head inside and scanning the room.

Inside, an odor formed a solid wall, roiling outward to engulf him, seeming to seep into his pores, choke down his throat, and cause his eyes to water. He turned—trying to spit out the smell that coated his tongue, dragging in the air from outside—before crossing the threshold, the rifle's muzzle leading the way.

The room was almost barren, except for a table canted to the right, one of its legs shorter than the other; a three-legged stool stood in the corner, an iron stove and a sink taking up the wall beneath the back window. He took shallow breaths of the tainted air and moved forward.

Lowering the gun, he allowed it to drag behind him as he crossed the cramped space, pushing aside the curtain that separated the front room from the bedroom. As he stared at the single bed and the bare mattress, he remembered his last conversation with James Henry, his tongue loosened by liberal shots of whiskey and a six-pack of beer while they sat in the back of his garage.

I unlocks the door. And there they was, laying together curled up on the floor, him with her tit in his mouth, sucking at it in his sleep. He must have heard me, because his eyes slide open, and he stare at me.

Recalling his words, the wrongness of the room and the people who inhabited it rang in Joseph's soul. He shook his head to free it of the images cast clearly in his mind's eye, continuing to scan his surroundings.

The pegs on the wall were empty on this side of the curtain. Against it, a dilapidated dresser leaned precariously, its open drawers like broken teeth hanging from its frame. Lifting the shotgun to his shoulder and sighting down the barrel, Joseph fired, watching it explode into pieces, his cry of frustration ringing in the still air. They were gone, just as he had feared.

He sniffed the foul air like a bloodhound, desperate for any trace of Clyde or Fannie. He stopped, standing still in the center of the room, his head lifting, then turning to the right and the left. The rank smell he had been wading through since he arrived seemed familiar to him. He shuffled through his memories, certain he had smelled it recently.

The shotgun clattered to the floor, falling from his nerveless fingers as the sensory memory of the rancid smell clicked into place in his brain . . . why something so repulsive was so familiar. It had clung to Cora when he found her, been in her hair when he breathed her in, in her clothes as he lay her down on the couch. He'd thought it was the stench of death before.

The smell affirmed it. Now he knew. It was Clyde's smell. The stench hung in the air of the house, pressed into the cracks of the walls and the dirt on the floor. He would not forget it again. When he found it, he would finish Cora's work for her. He would kill Clyde.

CHAPTER NINE

Fannie glared into the eyes of the man standing before her. He chewed on the end of the cheap cigar clamped tightly between his teeth, the end wet with saliva. Rolling it around, he blew a ring of smoke that drifted lazily toward her face. Instead of backing up, she leaned in, a smile curling the corners of her mouth, her index finger stabbing the air between them and emphasizing her words.

"I done told you, Jacob, we'll take this place. My boy, Clyde— he do all the fixing up here and your other places for you for taking down the rent."

"How old that boy of yours be?" he asked, pushing his hat back and scratching at the bald patch on his head, seeming to consider her offer.

"He ain't but ten, but he real big for his age. Strong too." She flicked her head sideways toward the door, and his eyes pulled in that direction as she continued. "His daddy done teached him how to fix most anything round the house."

Jacob looked through the door at the hulking figure standing at the rail. He would never have guessed him to be ten years of age. The boy looked up, his red-rimmed eyes connecting with his. It made him look away quickly, not wanting the perplexing fear that tingled in his gut to show.

"You asking too much as it is, but I ain't paying no more than twelve a month. Plus, you ain't paying no wages to Clyde," Fannie continued, stepping back so she would not have to bend her neck to look up at him. "This here ain't nothing but a shack, nohow."

"I cain't go no lower than fifteen, Fannie. Take it or leave it," he said, clearing his throat, aware of Clyde still standing silently on the porch with his hands shoved in his pockets.

"I guess I be leaving it then," Fannie said, turning to give the man her back.

"Shit, woman, wait. You got the money now?" His voice dropped until it was a whispered shout. He felt sweat beading under the rim of his hat, glancing uneasily from the door and back to Fannie. He had never seen the boy before today, but he knew of him, had heard some whispers about the strange boy out at the Henry place outside of Rayville, the next town over—stories told by the Henry boys when they'd had a few drinks at the Doll House. The way the boy glared at him from under his brows, his body tightly coiled and ready to spring, forced him to shuffle his weight from foot to foot nervously.

Fannie turned back, her head lowered to conceal the smirk of satisfaction on her face and dug down into her dress pocket to pull out a faded and twisted handkerchief. Pulling the knot free, she extracted twelve crumpled one-dollar bills and placed them into Jacob's waiting palm. He counted them twice, cleared his throat, and handed her a set of keys.

Fannie took them, looked at the lock, and snorted to herself. She doubted if the dilapidated lock served any purpose besides decoration, declaring rust was the only thing keeping it together.

"You getting a deal as it is. I'm giving you all the furniture with the place."

Fannie laughed out loud this time, air snorting through her nose as she surveyed the furnishings. A full-sized bed resided in one corner, its mattress sinking in the center to form a dangerous concave that would only allow an individual to rest at its most extreme edges. Stains of various sizes and shades covered what may have once been blue and white stripes while an explosion of metal coils and stuffing erupted from its surface. Beside the bed, five large wooden pegs had been hammered into the wall to hold clothing, a battered trunk sitting beneath them.

A round, wooden table sat in the center of the room, the least battered item in the place. Surprisingly, two beautifully hand-carved chairs adorned either side.

Jacob sucked his teeth, then grinned at her, showing brown tobacco stains, genuine pride sparkling in his eyes. "My daddy carved that there table and chairs hisself. That been here since him and my mama was here. I got one, but it way bigger with six chairs."

Fannie listened to the man brag as she ran her hand over the smooth, sanded surface of the wood, marveling at the texture and the craftsmanship.

"And I thanks you. Now that we done come to an agreement, I take good care of it."

"You best do that," Jacob said, turning surly again, avarice sidling up beside his pride. "I'm gon' have to charge you if anything get broke."

"I done said we take care of it." Fannie bristled, casting an eye toward Clyde, who had begun moving forward, his face registering the distress he heard in his mother's voice. "What you thinking?"

Jacob shifted uncomfortably as Clyde shuffled into the room, anger blazing in his dark eyes. Jacob's eyes roamed from the apparent strength of the boy's upper body to his face, tightened in anger, and then fell into the depths of darkness in Clyde's eyes. He could not stop himself from recoiling as he stared, the fear transforming from a tingle to a surge threatening to liquefy his legs. Jacob swiveled abruptly, skirting around Clyde to reach the door in two quick strides.

"I didn't mean no harm, Ms. Fannie. I knows everything be took good care of." Sweat poured profusely, rivulets sliding into his beard. His words came swiftly as he tried to read the expression on her face, gauging her anger level.

"I leaves you all to get settled," he called over his shoulder, not caring that he was running now, feeling the boy's eyes boring into his back. Fannie chuckled, the laughter rumbling and threatening to overflow, but stopped when she saw Clyde, his shoulders slumping now that the threat to her was gone. His sadness tugged at her heart.

Clyde broke off his staring after the fleeing man, the darkness swirling inside wanting to reach out and bring the man back—show him that he couldn't talk to his mama that way.

"Th . . . This where we gon' be staying?" he asked as Fannie stepped close to him, running her hand along his cheek, letting her corral the darkness.

"Yeah, baby boy. We gon' have to work real hard, but we can makes it. I got the same folks buying bread from me and might get a few more now that we in town. I can takes in laundry too. You be able to hire out in the fields and around town. Plus, your daddy and brothers got the shop. I know they help out too. We be all right here."

"It don't feel right." Clyde sank into one of the chairs, his shoulders heaving, and Fannie feared he might cry. She walked closer, reaching down to lay her open palm once again on his cheek, stroking softly.

"We gon' fix it up, and pretty soon it feel just like home. Don't you worry none. Mama gon' fix it. That witch gone, and we safe. You safe. Don't nothing else matter."

Clyde gazed into her eyes, which glistened with tears, and he shrank back, afraid he had hurt her feelings. She was trying hard to make it right for them. He grasped her small hand between both of his and then stood, towering over her petite form.

"And don't you forgets, you my special boy, give to me by the Lord. He ain't took his hand from around you."

"O . . . OK, Mama." He choked the words out.

Fannie turned her hand inside his until she could lead him gently across the room, sinking down to the edge of the bed and guiding him until he was next to her, then lay his head in her lap. Clyde listened to the soft whisper of material sliding over the front buttons of her dress and inhaled deeply. The musky smell of her skin and her milk blended, and his head swam in ecstasy, his eyes shut tightly. He felt his lips puckering in anticipation as she lifted his head and pushed his eager mouth to her breast, both sighing aloud.

Fannie rocked him gently, one hand still stroking his head and rubbing it in a circular pattern, trying to ignore the throbbing between her legs that pulsated through her sex with each tug on her nipples. Easing backward, carefully avoiding the dip in the mattress, she curled herself around her son, where they remained until darkness filled the windows and sleep claimed them both.

Clyde stopped in the shadows of the alley, the last building at the very edge of the town's main street. He stretched his feelings, allowing the fingers of darkness to extend outward, searching the area around him. The dark powers within him had grown. He could sense it in others, sometimes lying dormant, waiting for a spark to ignite it. In some, he could reach out to it, draw it to him, or feed on it. He had discovered that everyone carried darkness in them. Sometimes, he felt that he was learning to control it. Other times, it strained to overwhelm him.

He had promised his mama. There would be no more slipups. He was good. He wouldn't succumb to the desires the darkness kindled. If God spoke to him in a dream or through the darkness, he would tell her first. He would not be bad again.

He bent his neck backward, craning to see the top of the two-story structure, and squeezed his eyes shut in silent prayer. This building had to offer up some work. If not, he would head out to the farms that bordered the town.

A smile crept over his face as he anticipated seeing the woods again, getting away from the closeness of the buildings, the crush of people staring at him, the constant mud, and the smell. Hearing the coins jingling in his pocket from making grocery deliveries, he forgot his dislike of the town and began whistling, thinking how happy Fannie would be.

Hearing the slide of a window sash being raised overhead, he stepped back just in time to avoid the contents of the slop jar being hurled from the window. A head full of brown paper bag curlers poked out after it, the eyes in the round face beneath them squinting at him first, then the face's open mouth howling in laughter.

"Boy, what the hell you doing standing out there in the dark? Black as you is, I damn near cain't see you, and you was about to be covered in shit and piss."

Clyde blinked rapidly, his mouth hanging open. "I, uh . . . I mean, why come you talks like that? I ain't never heard no lady say them kind of things."

The woman threw her head back and laughed even louder as two more heads joined her at the window. She held onto the arm of one of the women to support herself, pointing downward, talking loudly between guffaws of laughter.

"That little fool down there say don't no lady talks like that."

"Boy, don't you know where you is?" the other woman managed to snort out the words.

Clyde shook his head. "I was just walking around town looking for work, and I stop back here. Does you got anything for me?"

The three heads withdrew and conferred before the brown curlers reappeared. "Come on over to the side door. I'll come down and get you."

Clyde moved slowly to the door cut into the side of the building and waited, bouncing awkwardly on the balls of his feet. The door opened, and a pale brown hand and arm grabbed him by the shoulder and pulled him inside. He followed the woman attached to the arm into the dim light of the lamp she held, trying not to watch the sway of her buttocks visible beneath the sheer fabric of her robe and night dress as they made their way up a set of creaking stairs leading to the second-floor level.

The smell of tobacco, whiskey, and perfume mingled thickly in the air, and Clyde wrinkled his nose in disgust. At the top of the stairs, they followed a floral carpet to the end of the hall, passing several closed doors. Wisps of darkness swirled beneath each one. Reaching the end, the woman opened the last door, and bright light spilled into the hallway, silhouetting her body's ample curves.

"Come on in, honey. Don't get shy now. Ain't nobody here gon' hurt you."

Clyde eased into the small, cramped room, his head down and his hands finding their way into his pockets, afraid to look up at the three women. The one who had led him up the stairs turned and sank into a chair in front of a vanity table with a large mirror. The other two women lounged on their beds, their legs spread apart beneath the layers of lace on their gowns. Clyde could see the shadow of their womanhood beneath the reds and blues of their garments. He felt his face coloring in embarrassment.

"My name Baby Doll. What they call you, boy?" the woman with the paper curlers haloing her face asked, leaning over to place her finger under his chin, lifting his face. "Jesus, boy, look at you." She laughed, dropping his chin back down.

"Girl, stop. He cain't help the way he look. And it ain't all that bad. Just way too much of it!" The woman she had been talking to at the window clicked her tongue between her teeth, shaking her head from left to right. "It a damn shame, though, to have all that pretty hair and nothing fine to go with it," she said as she rose and walked toward him, first running her fingers through the thick black curls, then placing her hands on both sides of his face as she lifted it, studying it closely. "My name be Sugar." She clicked her tongue again, and Baby Doll shook with silent laughter, the paper curlers softly rattling as Sugar continued studying his face, finally concluding, "You right, though, Baby Doll. God ain't do him no favors when he give him this face. What your name?"

"Clyde." His voice was barely more than a whisper.

"Speak up, honey. Don't be ashamed. You done met Baby Doll and me. Her over there be Sweetness."

Clyde cleared his throat, glancing at the woman sprawled on the bed, then averted his eyes as he spoke again. "I'm obliged to meet you ladies."

All three women burst into gales of laughter again, Sugar collapsing onto a plush burgundy velvet armchair near the window. Clyde stared at them, confused.

"You just keep on calling us ladies, and you sure can work for us," Baby Doll gasped, sucking in deep breaths and trying to control the mirth that kept rising.

"B . . . But, you is ladies; you all ain't mens," he replied, his words stuttering over themselves.

This caused another bout of hilarity, the women holding their stomachs and sides, reaching up to wipe tears from their eyes. Clyde narrowed his eyes and unleashed the darkness, feeling it stretch out, siphoning from the women. He detected the darkness building as the laughter fell around him, his head sinking lower, his chin resting on his chest.

"Clyde, how old is you?" Sugar asked, taking a deep breath.

Clyde lifted his head and pulled himself up straight before he answered, "Ten."

"Shit, but you big for ten. You almost the size of a grown man, excepting them legs. What wrong with your legs?" Sweetness asked, her eyes roaming from head to foot, looking at him from her place on the bed across the room, her hand waving the red feather boa that draped over her negligee.

Clyde refused to answer, his face coloring with shame, the dark swirls of anger swimming in his head. His hands clenched to fists inside of his pockets.

"Don't mind her, boy," Sugar said, rolling her eyes in her friend's direction before looking back at Clyde. "Well, you old enough to know what this is, child. This a whorehouse."

Clyde's features remained blank as he looked from one woman to another.

"Damn, he stupid too!" Sweetness harrumphed loudly, crabbing backward toward the headboard and ignoring Sugar as she slapped at the air in front of her.

"You really don't know, do you?" Sugar asked, her voice soft as she began to explain. "This where men comes to be with women. You know?"

Across the room, Sweetness let her body lean against the brass railings that formed the headboard, supporting her torso while allowing her legs to sprawl open farther. Holding Clyde's gaze with her own, she lifted her hand to her mouth, sucking her index finger until it glistened, then dipped it between the dark cleft between her thighs. Bringing it back, she waved the finger in front of her face before curling it to beckon to him. "All mens wants something sweet every now and then," she purred, her words throaty and sensuous.

Clyde violently shook his head, looking down at the floor, his eyes searching wildly for an escape. The darkness brought the full stain of the women to him, rolling over him in waves, revulsion crawling over him as Sweetness continued to rub herself, touching her private place.

He could smell it, the scent like the one he had sniffed on his mother one night, lingering beneath the usual smell of her skin and her milk. The one that caused a stirring, like the one he felt now. He remembered that time with his mother, when his man parts had stiffened, and she had pushed him away, screaming at him that he was bad, demanding to know if he had been touching himself.

Mama had beat his hands until they were red and swollen, then cried, her tears falling on his hot flesh while she beseeched the Lord not to let him lose his soul and prayed for his return to purity. She had made him kneel on hard white rice all night, praying for forgiveness and redemption.

His body jerked forward as he felt a hand on his shoulder, rubbing softly, a cloud of perfume swirling through the air with it. But beneath it was that other smell.

"Stop being so nasty, Sweetness," Baby Doll scolded. "You see the boy don't know no better." She had moved from her seat at the vanity and now stood behind him, pulling him closer to her. She took up where Sugar had left off. "It where men pays women to sex them, Clyde. They comes here when they wants to drink and has a good time. We gives it to them."

Stepping in front of him, she was close enough for Clyde to feel the heat from her body, smell the rank odor beneath the overpowering scent of the perfume she wore. Her breasts pushed against the fabric of her gown as she inhaled and exhaled.

Snatches of conversations he'd overheard from his older brothers filtered into his awareness, of them smoking behind the garage, drinking whiskey, and talking about some place called the Doll House and who had been there last. They would howl and grab their privates, challenging each other, calling their privates "dicks," and asking who had the biggest dick and who could do the most with it. The words and images slammed together with the memory of his own hands touching himself, Fannie's beating, the biting pain in his knees as he prayed, and the women in front of him.

Clyde's head snapped up, and his eyes rounded in horror. He knocked the hand from his shoulder and began backing toward the door, his arm raised and his finger pointing in accusation. "Harlots! You all is Jezebel womens. My mama done told me about you. You all is sinners!"

The laughter ceased abruptly, sliced in two by his words. The women's features hardened, becoming one collective, carved into masks of anger, each an effigy of rage and resentment. Baby Doll, who had been leaning forward to talk to him, uncurled to her full height, standing a head taller than him and trembling with rage. Striding toward the door, she threw it open, then held it in place.

"Boy, get your little righteous ass out of here," she screamed, her mouth contorted in a snarl. The softness had left Sugar's face, and she glared at Clyde as he turned and passed by her. He avoided looking at Sweetness on the bed altogether.

Intent on escape, he did not see Baby Doll as she lifted her foot, slamming into him with such force that he could feel the pointed toe of her slipper digging deep into the crevice of his buttocks, pain shooting up his tailbone. He fell face-first on the musty hall carpet, inhaling the smell of stale vomit as she shrieked, "Who the fuck you think you is?"

Clyde heard her words, a string of curses, behind him as the door slammed shut. Crawling slowly, he remained a few feet outside the door for a few minutes and let the rage gather in his chest, feeling it pitching through him. The palms of his hands burned in remembrance of the punishment for sin—the knowledge that these women did "things" with men and would have done them with him if he'd let them. He pushed to his feet using his hands, ignoring the pain radiating up his back and embracing it as he stood.

The darkness emerged, engulfing him with rage. His eyes burned, and he knew that if he could see them, they would be ringed in red, the pupils pitch black. He let it consume him, incinerating his promises and controlling him.

The darkness of the hall around him gathered to join his own, and he sucked it in as it swirled toward him from the various rooms he passed. Clyde let it comfort him and drew it to him, the mist gathering around his feet and mingling with it.

CHAPTER TEN

Fannie moved the flat iron from the stove and pressed it against the damp sheet on the ironing board, her face lost in a cloud of steam. She pressed the iron hard against the fabric, smoothing out any wrinkles, and watched Clyde through the vaporous cloud.

Since he'd come home, he'd been sitting in the corner on the stool she had found for him, his broad shoulders wedging him in the space and his feet dangling just above the floor. It was taller than his old one, but he seemed comfortable with it and had not complained. His head lowered, and she studied the perfect roundness of it, covered with the thick, jet-black curls that swirled over his scalp, fighting the urge to cross the room and run her fingers through them.

"What you thinking about over there, baby boy?"

His head lifted, and she raised the iron, holding it in midair, arrested by the anger in his eyes. She moved the iron to the end of the board and walked over to the table. Pulling out one of the two chairs, she dragged it across the room to sit, facing him. Her hands went instantly to his head, enjoying the silken feel of his curls, and rubbed in a circular motion before dropping to stroke his nose and cheeks. She could feel him relaxing against the pressure of her fingers and saw the darkness in his eyes receding.

"What wrong?"

He flinched, and she hesitated. "I say, what wrong, Clyde?"

"I don't want no whupping, Ma; I don't." Clyde twisted his hands that were pressed together inside of the bib of his overall, wondering if he had gotten all the blood out from beneath his fingernails. He had stopped at his father's shop before he got home, using the harsh lava soap to scrub them.

Fannie stood and waited for his confession. Her head was down, her hands clutched tight beneath her apron, rubbing her knuckles, an unconscious mimicking of her son. Clyde stared at the part down the center of her hair, which was pulled tight and twisted in a rolled braid on each side. Her thick brows knitted together over large brown eyes that darted restlessly over his face. She waited for him to tell her how he had strayed, her bosom heaving with each breath. Her body began to rock back and forth, the hem of her dress sweeping over her black leather shoes. He noticed, not for the first time, how small her feet were.

"Us ain't got no secrets, baby boy. Just tell me." She stopped again, and he made himself look away from her breasts, seeing Baby Doll leaning toward him again. He focused on her voice.

"I knowed not to bring you here. I should of never brought you here. This town a wicked place. Wicked." She tried to calm herself, to remind herself that her God was not a God of fear. That was the devil's work.

Clyde stared into her eyes, struggling against the darkness and the guilt of breaking his promises to her. His mother's touch soothed him. Her light stilled some of the anger inside and pushed away the feel of the woman's foot hard against his backside and her words.

"It was them womens, Mama." His confession finally came, his eyes cast on the floor. "They was nasty, Ma. Real nasty talking and showing they privates."

Fannie shot to her feet, the chair falling back to slam against the floor. Her smooth brown skin flushed red, her mouth a round "O" of disgust.

"What you talking about, Clyde?"

He told the story, his embarrassment causing him to stop and stutter repeatedly as Fannie visualized the woman throwing shit on her child and imagined the words they used, the ones she tried to keep away from Clyde—the ones she sometimes said in her head but never aloud.

"They was Jezebels, Mama. Just like you done told me."

"You did right, baby boy. Flee from evil, that's what the word say." She was pacing back and forth before him, and then stopped. "They didn't touch you, did they? They didn't foul you, did they?"

Clyde shrank into himself, pulling his head down into his shoulders and folding in upon himself. "One of them she was touching her privates and stuff." His whole body shuddered as he spoke. "But I didn't look no more, Ma, and then that other one, the one brought me in who say her name was Baby Doll, she put her hand on my shoulder, but I jerk it away. Then she kick me in my hind parts."

Fannie drew in short, sharp breaths that seemed to inflate her where she stood, towering with rage. Her eyes burned, staring at the juncture of Clyde's thighs.

"Did they touch your man parts, Clyde? Tell me true."

Clyde covered his crotch with both hands, horror swimming in his eyes. "No, ma'm, Mama. Ain't nobody touch me there. You done told me."

Fannie deflated, lifting the chair from the floor before sagging into it. Her son was still pure, still special, and free of sin. She patted his knee absently, humming softly.

"Don't worry, baby boy. God gon' take care of it. But don't you go back there. Not never, because they can tempts you."

Clyde nodded in agreement, then lowered his head to his knees, swallowing the truth before his mother could see it shimmering in his eyes. He recalled the part he didn't tell.

How he had sat there in the alley, burning with anger and embarrassment, staring up at the lit window, and letting the darkness whisper to him, telling him what he could do to the three women. How the window had lifted, and Baby Doll had begun calling into the night, her voice shrill and worried. "Princess, Princess, come on in."

Voices blended in the background, urging her to pull her head in. Her head swiveled around on her shoulders as she snapped, and he heard, "Shut up, bitch, this ain't about you," before she turned back and began to shout, making sucking, kissing sounds with her puckered lips. After a few long and silent moments, she had withdrawn her head and slammed the window shut, cutting off the women's loud conversation.

He wondered if any of them would come down if he threw a rock, especially that one who called herself Baby Doll. The darkness demanded her, making his body vibrate with the need to break her, to show her what the cost of her sin really looked like.

He started, his body jerking forward at the sound of boxes toppling to the ground a few feet to his left. He looked at the closed window, waiting for it to open, but it remained shut against the night. Peering hard into the darkness, Clyde saw a pair of green eyes staring at him from the shadows. A moment later, a round gray cat uncurled itself from the darkness and stepped toward him.

Her plump body spoke of meals that didn't rely on the alley or the kindness of strangers. Around her neck, a collar sparkled, diamond bright. The cat sat down a few feet away and began to lick its paws, swiping at its face, unconcerned with his presence in her alley.

He knew it had to be Princess. That was who Baby Doll had been calling. A stupid cat. He stared at the animal, waiting as his dark thoughts congealed into a plan—studying its sleek fur, the collar on its neck, and how fat it was. Anger and resentment grew disproportionately inside of him. The damned cat probably ate better than he did, he thought. Clyde chastised himself for swearing, then reconsidered. "Damn" was one of the three cuss words you could find in the written word, along with "hell" and "ass." He reasoned that he could use them in his head as long as he didn't slip and let his mother hear them.

Puckering his lips, Clyde made a sound imitative of the one he had heard Baby Doll make when calling the cat.

"Here, Princess, come here, girl. Clyde got something for you, something for the pretty kitty." He cooed, cupping his hand as if it might conceal food and watching as the cat approached, sniffing at his closed fist.

Clyde whipped his hands out, grabbing the cat and snapping its neck before it could emit a growl, and he was stunned by his own speed. Lifting the cat by its back legs, he slammed it into the dirt, listening to the dull thud of the head meeting the unyielding soil until the brains and blood oozed out to water the earth. He had continued slamming its head to the ground until it was a mass of fur, brains, blood, and bones, and his anger was depleted. He swooned in ecstasy at the familiar smell of the blood.

Breathing hard, Clyde stared at the mangled remains at his feet and thought what to do next. Looking around, he spotted a flattened cardboard box among the litter. He used it to scoop up the carcass, ensuring that none of the gore remained and that he got it all. Shuffling carefully, he approached the side door and lay the grisly mess directly in front of it, arranging the collar so that there would be no mistake about what it was.

Backing away, he searched the ground for a couple of fair-sized rocks. Stepping back into the deep shadows of the alley, he took careful aim and hurled the stone at Baby Doll's window. It hit with a resounding thud, cracking the glass pane, and Clyde took off running, his short legs pumping. Behind him, he heard someone screaming. "Who that? Who down there?"

A few minutes later, a scream rent the air and caused a smile to curve his mouth as he continued to run.

No, Clyde couldn't tell her that part, not at all. Swallowing again, he leaned over and rubbed his face against his mother's apron, waiting for the touch of her hands rubbing his head. She leaned down and kissed the back of his head, then quickly pushed him away. "Go on, wash up. I'm gon' finish these sheets, then I wants you to run them over to Miss Shirley's. When you come back, I has your dinner on the table."

"Yes, ma'm." He strolled toward the wash basin and began to scrub his hands and face. Baby Doll had just started to pay.

Clyde stood outside of the Doll House, the morning sun showing the flaking paint of the sign outside the red-painted door. He stepped aside, letting people pass by him before creeping around to the side of the building to the back alley, staring up at the cracked windowpane that was Baby Doll's. He stood in the shadows as the window was raised and a pair of skinny arms pushed out into the air, holding a porcelain chamber pot and hurling its contents into the yard. The urine steamed on the brown grass, and Clyde's face wrinkled in disgust as the window closed, and he saw the person walk away.

Clyde waited patiently, softly whistling until the side door opened, and Baby Doll strutted into the sunlight, her girl running behind her to keep up. By the leanness of her frame, he guessed this to be the body that belonged to the skinny arms he had seen earlier. He followed silently in their wake, weaving himself between the shoppers on the other side of the street, just out of their sight. He listened absently as two women walking from the

Mercantile stopped, their mouths twisted in a sneer as they glared across the wide dirt road at the Doll House.

"Lord's shame we have to suffer a place like that, right here on Main Street," one woman said to the other, lifting her chin to peer from beneath her hat. The other woman nodded, her hand fanning her breast.

"At least you don't have to worry about running into any of them"—she put her hand to her mouth—"because them heifers, forgive my language, Lord, they don't get up most days to near about sundown."

"Wonder what she doing up then?" The woman glanced across at Baby Doll, then quickly back to her friend.

"What's done in the dark always come out in the light, though. But me, for one, be glad they keeps it in the dark. I wish I would catch my boy up around here."

She watched as Baby Doll stopped to stare at her reflection in the store window. Her face stared back, a perfect oval canvasing large dark, almond-shaped eyes, a petite nose, and a plump mouth slashed with vivid red lipstick. Her rouged, pink cheeks blazed on skin as pale as milk, framed by long, black ringlets of curls. She grinned impishly as men ogled when she walked past, her hips swaying hypnotically.

"It best not be my man nowhere near here," the other woman chuckled, unaware of the change in her friend's attitude. A whiff of anger and hatred lifted from her as they approached Clyde. He was startled, her dark emotions permeating his mind, floating back to him on a black ribbon.

Both women clicked their tongues loudly, shaking their heads and walking on, giving Clyde a sideways glance as they took in his short legs. Clyde ducked back between two stores, staring after them, noting the trails of darkness that followed them. It was in them too. Everyone carried it, he reminded himself before turning his attention to the plan formulating in his mind. He would find a way to get Baby Doll without disobeying his mother. The darkness would have its due from her. Sin had a price, and he would make sure she paid.

So, every day, he watched, obsessed, as Baby Doll exited from the red door, the small, thin, brown-skinned girl walking rapidly at her side and taking two steps for every one of Baby Doll's long strides. He recorded the woman's movements, etching them into his mind along with the memory of her foot planted deep between his buttocks.

CHAPTER ELEVEN

Clyde awakened slowly, the hint of a smile curving his wide mouth. His brain burned as the darkness fed his need for retribution, which would release Baby Doll from her wretched existence and deliver the freedom of absolution only he could provide. The darkness called to him, growing insistently daily as he prayed and waited, enduring the continuous assault on his psyche that demanded action.

He rose from his bed and saw that Fannie was awake, standing at the stove. The smell of freshly baked bread filled the shack, and his stomach grumbled in anticipation of the morning meal.

"Gets washed up and eats your breakfast, baby boy," she insisted, speaking over her shoulder. "I needs you to deliver that bread and picks up the wash from Miss Shirley," she continued as she bustled back and forth from the stove to the table.

His smile broadened as opportunity blossomed before him. He nodded and crossed to the waiting basin, splashing the water over his face and then cupping his hands to pour it over his head. Grabbing a flour sack towel, he scrubbed himself dry, gathered his clothes, and sat back on the edge of his cot, whistling.

Fannie leaned over as he put on his boots, running her finger through his hair and kissing the air above his bent head. "Somebody woke up real happy today."

He rose, crossed the room, and picked up a tin plate from the table. Then he dipped the thick chunk of bread into the syrup, covering its bottom, and mashed butter into the mixture. Stuffing it into his mouth, he savored the sweet taste, garnering a smile from his mother as she watched him.

"I'm gon' get my wagon and load it up, Mama, then I be gone." Clyde stuffed the last of the bread into his mouth, following it with a glass of cold milk that waited beside it.

"And make sure you goes around the long way, so you don't be near that bad house. You hears me?" Fannie warned as if she could read his thoughts.

"Yes, ma'm." He nodded vigorously, keeping the deceit from his eyes. Mama didn't understand. The darkness did.

Now, he stood where he would not be noticed in the shadowy spaces the Mercantile offered. He licked his lips, the glee buoyant at the nearness of success. Today was the day. He had seen Baby Doll strutting inside, and the darkness throbbed in his veins. It writhed and swirled at his feet, agitated by an unexpected movement outside the store window.

Peering from the gloom, he saw a woman standing there, her back leaning against the boards of the Mercantile store. She stared blankly in the direction of the wide window in front of her, ignorant of the dark mists that gathered around her ankles.

She turned, staring past him, looking into the sun hanging high in the cobalt sky, then turned back to the window. Clyde scratched his scalp and squinted, trying to place her face, his eyes stretched wide as he remembered. She was one of the two women who had stood across from the Doll House, the one who swam in the darkness that he could feel. He took a wary step back deeper into the shadows.

The woman took several deep breaths and rubbed her hands that shook visibly on her apron. Sweat glistened on her face, collecting under the band of the white rag that wrapped her hair. She wiped her palms on the apron she wore over her dress, and Clyde watched, mystified, as she withdrew the handle of an ice pick from the pocket, then shoved it hurriedly back inside, her eyes never leaving the window where Baby Doll could be seen completing her purchases.

From his hiding place, Clyde's eyes wandered over Baby Doll's brilliant red dress, the color screaming against his eyes even with the window and distance separating him from her. The bodice held a deep décolletage that squeezed the woman's ample breasts, pushing them up until it seemed she could rest her lowered chin on them. He watched the clerk fumble with her items, unable to raise his eyes, which caused him to drop everything and start the bagging process over repeatedly. Baby Doll leaned on an umbrella. Its fabric matched her dress, as did the hat perched precariously at an angle on her head, topping the riot of black curls.

Clyde heard her laughter as she walked toward the door, speaking over her shoulder. "Don't worry about it, Zeb. My gal ain't with me today. Little pickaninny say she sick, but she just lazy, I expect. But you know I ain't about to carry no bags. Just send it over to the house. You know where we be."

She winked, and the clerk's face brightened with color as he ducked his head, causing Baby Doll to laugh harder and add an extra wiggle to her behind, knowing he was watching.

As she turned back toward the door, she cocked her head to the side as if listening to something the man inside was saying, then sashayed forward onto the wooden boardwalk, the umbrella striking the boards with each step and adding to the rhythm of her walk.

Clyde's heart thundered in his chest, and his plan unfurled in his mind. When she reached the corner of the wall, he would grab her—his hand over her mouth to prevent her from shouting out—then drag her to the alley, where his hands would wrap around her throat and squeeze the sin from her. He licked his lips, quivering in anticipation.

Baby Doll's footsteps stopped abruptly as the woman stepped directly into her path, causing her to draw back, startled.

"You Baby Doll?" she demanded, forcing the name through lips twisted in disgust.

"Who want to know?" Baby Doll asked, taking two steps back to look down at the woman, who stood half a head shorter than she did. She assessed the odd little woman standing before her, whose hair was pulled into a tight bun beneath a white wrap, making her narrow face appear more severe. Her clothes screamed homespun. She gripped her umbrella's handle harder, prepared to use it as a weapon.

The woman was breathing hard, unintimidated by the contempt on Baby Doll's face, haughty tone, or height.

"I don't gives my name to no harlots," she sneered and spit on the ground, just missing the toe of Baby Doll's red shoe. "But you the one been with my man!"

Baby Doll stepped back, raising the umbrella to her shoulder, preparing to swing, studying the woman's face. She searched her memory, wondering which crazy-ass wife this was coming to settle a score about her man.

"You needs to be talking to your man. Ain't nobody making him come," she sneered, allowing her gaze to rake the woman from head to foot before barking out a laugh. "But by the looks of you, I can sure see why he come."

"Harlot! Jezebel!" the woman screamed, spittle flying from her mouth with the force of her words. Her eyes seemed to glaze over before she spoke again. "You is a corruption to men and boys, dragging them into sin!"

Baby Doll frowned. She didn't recognize the woman, but then again, she had little use for the frumpy townswomen like her, smug in their righteousness. Still, there was a familiarity there, something in the way she spoke and the words she used.

A bolt of remembrance shot through her brain of a boy in the alley, inviting him upstairs, and her features scrunched tight, red-hot anger mottling her skin until it blended with the rouge on her cheeks. She saw Clyde again, screaming, his finger pointing. She leaned down into the woman's face, yelling. "You must be some kin to that uppity-ass little holy roller. If you ain't, then you should be." She pulled herself back to her full height, rolling her eyes at the woman. "You all cut from the same 'my shit don't stink' cloth—"

The sentence went unfinished as searing pain flared from the corner of her eye and down her cheek. One hand flew to the side of her face. Her mouth gaped open in shock, and she felt hot blood seeping through her fingers. The woman followed the slashing blade, throwing herself forward, toppling both her and Baby Doll to the ground. Air whooshed from Baby Doll's lungs with the force of their fall, her head slamming hard against the boards.

Trying to gather her senses, Baby Doll pushed and shoved against the woman on top of her, amazed at her strength, her hand trying to reach the razor she carried strapped to her thigh beneath her dress. Unable to get it under the flurry of blows raining over her, she pitched her body violently, feeling the trail of stinging agony as the ice pick tore flesh.

"Get your crazy ass off me. Get off me!" Baby Doll had gathered her breath and was screaming the words, causing a crowd to stream forward, drawn to the chaos. The woman rose abruptly—her chest heaving—and backed up to hug the wall as she moved away from the sound of pounding feet moving toward them. Her eyes were wild and bewildered. The bloody ice pick remained clutched in her fist, and her head swiveled from side to side as people began to approach.

"You best get gone from this place. You leave my husband be. Does you hear me?" she hissed, feeling the edge of the wall as she reached its end. "I kills you if you don't!" she screeched, tears leaking down her face.

"Sweet Jesus! Somebody calls the sheriff," someone hollered from the growing crowd, drowning out the sounds of agitated whispers.

Baby Doll moaned and tried to get to her feet, rolling to her side, then slipping back down on one elbow as pain coursed through her shoulder and blood leaked from a half dozen stab wounds. She collapsed in a growing pool of blood.

The store clerk had made his way to the doorway, his frightened gaze going from the woman standing far back against the wall to Baby Doll lying on the boardwalk. Her blood-splattered dress was pushed up to expose her legs, and the rolled stockings were held in place with garters. He moved quickly to kneel beside her. Lifting her head and shoulders, he held her against his chest.

"Let go of me, fool," she slurred, moaning again loudly but too weak to protest.

"You all best be calling Doc Adams too," he yelled into the still-growing crowd of bodies wedged tightly against one another.

Feet hammered the boardwalk, lured by Baby Doll's screams of alarm, and the woman tried to push herself further backward. She wiped the sweat from her brow.

The clerk whipped his head, looking back and forth from Baby Doll on the ground and the woman shrinking into the gathering crowd, barely visible. She pressed against the wall, blood splattered across her face and staining the front of her white apron.

"Catch her before she get away!" he cried as the woman reached the adjacent alley, turning to run. Hands reached out, grasping at her, succeeding in wrestling her to the ground where they held her, thrashing against their restraining grip. Spots of darkness danced across her closed eyelids. The black rage bled through the slats in the wood, draining from her mind and leaving her dazed and confused. She waited for the sheriff to come, her eyes jittering from person to person.

Clyde pressed himself deeper into the crevice that hid him, still in the cover of the shadows, the others oblivious to his presence. His wide eyes locked on the swirling darkness oozing beneath the woman held on the ground. Her head turned toward him, her struggles ceasing as she saw him. Her eyes widened, then went blank as her body deflated and went still.

She was yanked, unresisting, to her feet, and she stumbled forward awkwardly, trying to keep her balance. Her fingers remained clutched around the ice pick in her apron pocket. She pulled it free, staring at the mixture of blood and rust that coated the slender, wickedly pointed metal. The crowd gasped and stepped back, leaving a circle around her and the sheriff who had arrived in their midst.

"Just hands that to me, ma'm," Jesse commanded, standing before her. He held his hand out toward her, suspicious of the blank expression in the woman's eyes. "This the sheriff."

She looked back at him, blinking rapidly, and saw his other hand braced on the butt of his gun. "You just hands it to me, miss. Ain't nobody gon' hurt you."

She sighed, her head dropping forward, and let the ice pick clatter to the ground.

"You got a husband or somebody you wants us to call?" he asked, stooping to lift the ice pick between two fingers—avoiding touching the handle—and passing it to a deputy who had stepped up beside him. The woman threw her head back and howled like a wounded animal, followed by a bark of hysterical laughter. Jesse locked the handcuffs in place, and the crowd parted, allowing him to lead her away, shoulders sloped downward in defeat, screaming and sobbing inconsolably.

The crush of townspeople began dispersing quickly once Sheriff Jesse and Doc departed, one with a prisoner, the other to accompany the wounded. Each person scurried away, eager to chew the details over supper tables or wash them down with a swig of beer.

Clyde waited patiently, then moved from one pool of darkness to the next until he was well away from the scene. Soon, he was full-on running as fast as his legs would allow, losing himself in the trees, the sound of the few remaining people diminishing behind him. The branches thrashed against his face, scratching his cheeks as he ran, afraid to slow down, adrenaline pushing his legs faster, his heart pumping furiously, and the darkness leading him.

Clyde finally collapsed, his back braced against the nearest tree, feeling his frame swell in frustration. It should have been his hand. But instead, he'd remained concealed from sight, licking his lips and savoring the sound of Baby Doll's screams. Even now, he could still smell the blood, see the woman's arm rise and fall, the ice pick finding its mark repeatedly. His hatred and the blood lust overtook him then, his eyes rolling back in his head in bliss.

But she still lived. He'd seen her chest rising and falling with shallow breaths as they carried her away. Her sin cried out for redemption. The darkness pulsed, dissatisfied, repeating that his hand should have been the one to deliver Baby Doll.

CHAPTER TWELVE

Joseph lifted Cora until her shoulders fit securely between the wide back of the wing chair in the living room. His eyes strayed to the window, taking in the sight of the tall green stalks of sweet corn waving in the distance. It was hard to believe that they had just begun planting when Cora was attacked, and now the harvest was almost upon them. He'd pulled down an ear just yesterday, peeling back the silky brown head and sheath to pierce a kernel with his nail. The creamy white that bled onto his fingertip told him the corn was ready.

During these three months, she had made some progress. She no longer lay rigid on the bed, staring at the ceiling. Bit by bit, some suppleness had returned to her limbs, and she allowed herself to be maneuvered until she could sit up. Now, she had reached the point where she could remain seated upright without pillows cushioning her to keep her from listing sideways. He looked away from the window and back to the gaunt face and skeletal remains of the woman he had married. Swallowing his sorrow, he scrubbed it from his face and voice.

"I'm gon' leave the curtains open so you can feel the sun on you. Put your feets up here," he said, pulling the hassock close and raising her feet to rest upon it. He arranged her hands in her lap, then stepped back to look at her.

Her skin sagged on her body, yellow and lifeless, the glowing pecan hue a distant memory as the weight had melted from her frame until there seemed to be no layer of fat between skin and bones. The small amounts of broth and thin stews they could spoon into her were sufficient to sustain life but not weight. He tried hard not to count each disappointing day as it passed, but he couldn't help it. He marked ninety-three days and nights since he had found her, nights he had prayed for a miracle, days of sinking into sadness. He told himself to consider it a blessing that she was still alive, still with him.

Turning his head back to face her, he saw that her eyes stared straight ahead, occasionally moving from left to right as though she followed the movement in the room of something no one could see but her. He waited for her to blink and acknowledge that she saw him, gripping the arms of the chair as he stared into her face before he began speaking to her.

"This sister Betty's day to stay with you. She ain't gon' be able to get you on the pot, so if you got to go before I gets back, just go on," he said, speaking into her blank face, his Adam's apple sliding up and down as he swallowed his pain. "It be some real thick rags under you. I gets you changed when I get back. Don't be ashamed and make yourself sick and not go."

He knew he was rambling and should be able to stop himself, but he could not. The words tumbled forth, brimming with the hope that the right combination would trigger something in Cora's stalled brain, and she would begin to talk back. "Me and the twins working that cornfield on the south end today. It gon' be a real good crop this year." He stopped, his gaze drawn back to the window again, then sighed. "We in the path of some good for us." He waited a heartbeat for a flicker in her eye. Seeing none, he finished his thoughts. "Don't you worry none. Miss Betty gon' make us supper too. I told her you can sit some by yourself. Maybe when the crop come in and sold,

I'm gon' gets that radio I seen in town. Then you can have something to keep you company when ain't nobody around."

Her silence beat against him, interrupted only by the sound of someone pounding against the screen door's frame. Betty pushed against it, poking her head inside, smiling brightly, and waving at him and Cora. He turned and waved his hand, sighing with the relief of straining not to stare at the dregs of his wife.

Crossing the room in three long strides, he pushed the door open to admit Betty's large, round body.

"She all ready for you, Miss Betty. We be back at the regular time."

"Ain't no rush, Joe. I got some sewing here in my basket that need to be done, and then get supper for you and them boys." She held up a large basket affixed to her arm. "Look like a lick a cleaning might not be bad neither."

Joe's head lowered, chin to chest, and his face colored with embarrassment. "Me and the boys—we ain't much on house chores, Miss Betty. We tries, though."

Betty slapped him softly on the shoulder and laughed out loud. "Don't you worry none. You is menfolk. I don't expect nothing different."

Joe allowed her to step fully into the house and strode forward to occupy the space she had been in. He stopped suddenly and turned back, returning to lean over Cora. He kissed her gently on the cheek, then walked back out the door. Cora stared after him, her eyes locked on how his broad shoulders fell as he passed from her field of vision, leaving her thoughts to press in upon her.

Joe a good man. A real good man, but I be so glad to see him go every day. If I had some tears left to cry, they be dripping like rain. It hurt me that bad to see the look in his eyes and the weight of me on his shoulders. When he lift me up, I knows I don't weigh nothing no more. But it ain't my physical body. It the caring for me that be breaking him down. Nothing I can do about how much I weighs. Food don't go down. Feel like I'm choking every time. And Joe, he sit there just as patient as a saint, trying to spoon it into me. I feels it dribbling down my chin, and he just wipe it and keep feeding me.

The boys, they stay gone. Don't hardly come near me, and when they do, they scared of me. They helps Joe, but they cain't abide being by me. I ain't mad about it. They just boys. On them times they here, I sees they eyes be so full of sad; I be glad when they look away. I wish I could look away, but I got to wait until somebody move me. I cain't turn my head. If I could talk, I tell them that I ain't in no pain, and I can hear them real good. I cain't answer is all.

I can feels the sun on my skin, the breeze from the window, and I can hear every thang inside and out. Blessed Father, at least it ain't all black no more. It just a pale kind of gray that cover the room. It be way better than the black, though. I don't never want to go back there.

I ain't felt the Knowing so much since I been this way. I still prays to see it come back as Mi, then I knows the light done forgive me some. Least that's what I figure when it brung me back from the dead and from the dark. I believe it giving me another chance. Excepting I cain't talks to a living soul. I be stuck here in this body that don't want to do nothing for itself.

I hears a sound off in the distance, coming closer until it be right there in the room with me. It ain't Miss Betty. She stomp cross the floor like a team of mules. I waits for whatever it be to move where I can see it.

"Miss Ma'm, can you tell me where I is?"

I cain't make my body move, but sometimes when a spirit come, I be moving just like these folks who as stuck as me. It always feel like I be floating. Only thing is they dead and going to stay that way, but they souls don't know how to let go. Me, I be the living dead.

"I be Cora, and who you be?" I ask real slow like so she don't get spooked.

"Baby Doll. Where we at?"

"*Child, you is dead. What happen to you?*"

While I waits for her to answer, I studies her real good. Folks always shows up the way they remembers being when they was living. That the reddest dress I done ever seen she got on. I knows I ain't never seen that one in the church pews.

She sure is pretty, though; look like a doll baby. All that pretty hair and them big old eyes. Shame she be dead. She stare at me a long time, drifting around the living room. She pass right through Miss Betty, and that old woman shiver like she cold and pull her shawl close around her shoulders. Miss Betty wear that shawl every day, cold or hot. Well, mostly cold in here because all the dead come through here to see me.

I sees her lift all the way to the ceiling where I cain't see her, then stand back right in front of me, hands on her hips with a mouth what could chew up nails.

"*That stuck-up little bitch done killed me over some raggedy-ass man she cain't hold on to.*" *The words hiss from her, her lips twisted in a snarl. They all comes to me sooner or later. They all has to tell they tale in they own time, they own way. I wait for the telling. Waits to hear if Clyde gots a part in all this.*

She flit around the room, sit on the couch right in front of me, then float back up to the ceiling. I cain't bends my neck, so I just stares at where she was and see if she come back. Sometimes, they be gone for a long time. Sometimes, they been dead for a long time, sometimes not. Hours, minutes, days, weeks—that time don't mean nothing in this place. I count the passing by Joe bringing me from the bed, then bringing me back to sit some more.

They so mad sometimes when they come. But some of them be different from the rest of them. They most just be sad and lost, still trying to hold onto life, hoping I can talk to they folks for them. They full of words they needed to say before they left the world and ain't get no chance to. Each one have they own little bit of light. I guess that why they here. Me, I been waiting for Clyde's next kill.

"Cora, you feel a chill in here?" Miss Betty asks, her dentures flashing as she smiles, her voice perpetually cheerful as she grins at Cora. "Seem like it get downright cold in here sometimes, hot as it is outside. You wants I should get you a blanket?"

Miss Betty blinked rapidly several times, twisting her hands and grasping her shawl, then seemed to remember that Cora could not answer. She bustled into the closet in the corner of the room and pulled out a crocheted Afghan, which she draped over Cora's lap, resting her hands on top of it. Nodding her head in satisfaction at having solved the problem, she began talking again as she walked toward the kitchen.

"I'm gon' get on these dishes and start supper. A good stew be something that stick to your ribs, and Lord know you needs to fatten back up." She disappeared into the kitchen, leaving Cora staring into the air.

The mantle clock tick off the minutes like it always do. I feels hot liquid seeping between my legs onto the rags Joe done piled beneath me. Shame done left me a long time ago. It funny, how we take things for granted, going to pee, moving your bowels. I be glad my menstrual ain't coming. I don't want Joe having to do that for me. I breathes in that strong ammonia smell and listens to the clock some more.

"It ain't right, you know?"

"What ain't right?" I ask, pulling myself back into her story.

"Dying that way. Nobody giving a damn but that little gal a mine. Everybody else just glad to see me go, take that last breath."

She back where I can sees her again, fading in and out. Sometimes, she look solid; other times, I see right through her. She stop flicking back and forth, and it look like she going to stay this time.

"I can listen to you if you wants to talk." I stare straight at her. My mouth don't move when I talk. She hear me, though, like our minds is talking. She ain't forgot about when she was still alive, so she still move her lips when she talk. Robert do that too.

I don't stops them when they telling they stories. I listens real close. While she talking, Robert come in and stands behind her. His eyes and face got that sorrowful knowing. Sometimes when he get like that, he bawl like some little old baby. I hopes he don't start that. I give him the hard eye I used to give my boys, and he straighten up some. Baby Doll she still talking, not paying him no mind.

She close her eyes and keeps on talking. I know she reliving the whole thing. I done it often enough myself. Seeing Clyde choking me, fighting him. I let her wait, let the words fill her up until they needs to come out. A shadow come down and cover her face, her pretty fading under it, her face shrinking down, and her eyes sunk in like two dark holes. Her hair done turned thin and brittle looking, the skin hanging on her bones where a fever done burned her from the inside and took all her with it. A plump gray cat jump up in her lap and curl up. Her hand stroke it gentle-like, and she grin; a demon dead, nothing human in that smile. The way that cat head laying ain't natural neither, sitting under her shrunk-up bosoms, but she don't pay it no mind; just keep talking.

"Her and that little bastard. I wish I had never laid eyes on him. Left his ass out in that alley, maybe somebody would've cut his throat. But no, me and my big-ass heart, always trying to help somebody. Had to bring him inside. And look where it got me." *Her eyes glaze over, and she pause while she stares over my shoulder, then begin her story again.*

"First, after I got stabbed, it seem like I be all right. Doc say I needs to rest, and I heal fine, being a big, strong girl. He say, 'Baby Doll, you too damn pretty to die. Them stabs ain't as deep as I thought they was. You be all right. Stay in that bed.'

"Old quack don't know his ass from his elbow. They should've took me to the hospital up in Monroe where they could see what was wrong. After a few weeks, the fever start. They brought Doc Adams back again, and he shake his head and say he don't understand what went wrong. Then he scratch his head and start hemming and hawing, say, 'Might've been something on that there ice pick she done stuck you with. Maybe it was dirty or rusty.' Dumb son of a bitch." She hawk and spit.

"Them dick suckers what own the Doll House. Put me out my room in this broke-down shed that got a bed in it. My gal come out there and take care of me. She there day in and day out, putting cool rags on my head, even when I start talking crazy. Sugar and Sweetness stop checking on me, say the whole place stink of death. Them miserable heifers was probably too busy stealing my things.

"By then, my heart want to fly out my chest, it beating so fast, and I cain't catch my breath most the time. The fever don't never leave. I cain't get up, barely can move. Then my body start shutting down. I can feels it. Feels myself dying, but I cain't stops it.

"The last day, I was lying on that broke-down-ass bed, feeling the life leave me. It wasn't but one window to the place, and when I look up, I sees him. That boy, grinning down at me like he been doing every day.

"He ain't right, the way his eyes be looking at me. It feel like I be staring straight into hell. Then when I looks again, he gone. I hears the door opening. The light coming in hurt my eyes, and I squeeze them shut. When I opens them up, he standing over me, looking down and grinning. He yank the pillow out from under my head, twisting it in his hands.

"'Who stupid now? Who don't know the price of they sins?' he say. He talking real slow. Got that stutter when he talk, but he ain't doing it. I see him bring that pillow down, and I wants to scream, but ain't no sound coming out. I be too weak to move, cain't even turn my head away. Just feel that pillow cover my face, then my lungs burning for air. 'Jezebels got to die and be ate by dogs,' he say. Last thing I hear is dogs outside howling like the dead. He the last thing I see before I be in that dark place. Then I be here with you."

The only breathing in the room be mine as she fade until ain't nothing left. She gone, the cat gone, and Robert—he drift off too. I be left in my chair to sit in my own mess and wonder what Clyde do next. Them two dead and me, trapped with the dead.

CHAPTER THIRTEEN

Clyde stood—waiting—behind the whorehouse just outside the shed, hidden by the edge of the building between the wall and the wooded area stretching out behind it. He mollified himself with the knowledge that he was not at the whorehouse and was not disobeying his mother, not wanting to add disobedience to his broken promises. The sun had shifted in the sky, and he guessed less than an hour had passed since Baby Doll died. He smiled, still tasting her death on his tongue, wishing he could have prolonged it more.

He recollected silently pushing the door open and listening to the sound of Baby Doll's laborious breathing, which he had become accustomed to on his frequent visits to check on her. He would listen through the gaps left by the uneven placement of the panes, allowing sound to travel clearly to the crates where he stood outside the window.

Inhaling the sweet scent of her death as she died, he'd watched the darkness overtake her bit by bit, a layer hovering above her. It swirled around her now, covering her entire body—sliding up her nostrils, into her ears, her open mouth, and even working its way into her eye sockets. It would have been better if she had struggled and fought him. Instead, she was too weak, her death quick.

That little skinny girl who worked for Baby Doll had run screaming from the shack, letting him know that Baby Doll was,

in fact, dead. His ears rang with the sound of her screaming for
Jesus, praying loudly, "Please, Lord, helps my Miss Baby Doll;
don't let her be dead." As if God would hear prayers from her
mouth for that nasty whore.

Clyde shook his head, freeing himself from the pull of his
memories, knowing that his time was short, assuming the little
ninny had gone for help. She would be back, bringing the sheriff,
the undertaker, and anybody else who would listen. He still had
work to do. Her judgment was not yet complete.

Opening the door wide, he whistled loudly, a sharp sound
that brought a pack of dogs running swiftly from the woods, their
bodies held low to the ground. They were starved, ribs sharp over
their caved-in stomachs, their jaws open and slobbering, desperate
for food. He'd kept them out in the deep woods with him, feeding
them nothing but the darkness in preparation for this day.

They shot past him, howling and snarling, biting at each
other in their rush to get to the corpse while Clyde stood in the
doorway and embraced the sight. Closing the door behind him, he
whispered, "And dogs will devour Jezebel's flesh."

His mouth stretched in a wide grin, and he worked hard to
keep himself from whistling as he waited, hidden. Inside the shack,
low growls and occasional thrashing split the still air. The urge
to peek inside the window and witness the sight surged through
him, so intense that he was forced to push his hands down into
his pockets to hold himself in place. The sound of several people
moving toward the shack, followed by a young girl's frightened
voice, arrested his desire. He pressed his face and body against
the back wall of the shack, once more invisible, his mother's Bible
teachings and the darkness swirling in his head.

"No, sir, I ain't going back in there no more. I come to get you,
but I cain't see her like that again."

From where Clyde stood, he could see the girl trembling, her body trying to shake itself apart. She wrapped her arms to her elbows and hugged herself, her head whipping vigorously from left to right as she looked at the sheriff.

"I done told you. I went to get some more ice for the fever, and when I come back, she be dead already. Eyes open wide, staring up. I cain't look at her like that again."

Sheriff Jesse drew in a long breath, looking over his shoulder at Elder Mason, pulling up his holster, and placing his hand on his gun before striding to the door of the shack. Mason was close on his heels. Deep guttural growling rose and fell on the other side of the door, followed by pained whimpering.

"You all got dogs in there?"

Gal shook her head violently again. "Nah, sir, wasn't nobody here but Miss Baby Doll, and she ain't never like no dogs. She had that cat, Princess, but somebody done killed it a few weeks back." The girl clutched her dress tighter around herself, using it to hold her vibrating body together. "I swear I ain't do nothing wrong. Did I?" Her fear rose, choking off any additional words until only frightened squeaks came from her compressed lips.

Tightening his hand on the gun butt, Jesse crossed the patch of dirt between the back of the Doll House and the shack. Reaching the door, he applied his shoulder to it, the force sending sharp pain radiating down his arm and through his back. The door slammed inward, ricocheting off the wall and allowing a small stream of sunlight to enter. It took his eyes a moment to adjust to the dimness within and illuminate the sights on and around the bed. Jesse's eyes rounded in horror as the writhing shadows congealed into shapes.

The four dogs raised their heads in unison, blood and gore dripping from their muzzles, the sound of cracking bone coming from their jaws. Their bodies tensed, lowering themselves close to the ground, preparing to defend their prey.

The first dog sprang toward Jesse, causing his arms to fly up defensively before the dog's powerful jaws clamped down on his left forearm. Using his right arm, he yanked his gun from his holster, firing directly into the dog's eye, the vibration from the gunshot traveling up his arm. The dog fell to the ground, its back legs scrambling in the dirt as its body convulsed. Jesse stumbled back and dropped to one knee. Gulping in great gasps of air, he used his forearm to take direct aim at the remaining three animals, striking heads and hearts. The dogs growled, twitched, whimpered, and then lay still in pools of blood.

Jesse stood shakily, his legs threatening to collapse as he walked backward until he had backed up to the open door, his back pressed against the door frame. He dropped his hand to his side, noticing the trembling as he attempted to holster his revolver. Once it was secured, he mopped the sweat from his forehead with his arm, feeling the blood dripping from his wound. His breath whistled loudly. Mason and Gal stood in the doorway just to his left, blocking the sun's light, their breaths trapped within their bodies, holding back their screams.

Behind the shack, Clyde stepped deeper into the shadows as he listened through the thin pine boards that separated them, peeking out intermittently. The silence that had followed the gunshots was now broken by a guttural scream of terror issuing from within, followed by the sound of retching as Elder Mason staggered away from the open door to lean against the wall, heaving violently until nothing but the sound of dry gagging remained.

Elder took a large white handkerchief from his jacket pocket and wiped his forehead and then his mouth. He finally saw Jesse stomp out. The sheriff pushed his hat backward until it sat near the back of his head, dangerously close to falling. His hand pinched the bridge of his nose, holding it for a long minute before he spoke.

"Them dogs is all dead. I got them all. You coming in?" His eyebrow arched skeptically, taking in the pallor of Elder's skin and the sheen of sweat on his face.

"You gon' need to give me a minute, Jesse. I ain't never seen nothing like that in all my days." Elder shuddered, and his Adam's apple moved convulsively up and down as he struggled to keep the bile down.

"Me neither, Mason." Jesse exhaled, shaking his head. "And four of them. Just going at her. I don't know if you gon' have much to work with." He looked at his ragged shirt and the puncture marks left from the dog's teeth. He would probably need a shot, and he hoped the dog hadn't been rabid. "It's a good thing they was weak."

Elder Mason shrugged his shoulders. "From what little I seen, it wasn't much of her to begin with. I heard tell she been real sick, but I ain't have no idea it was bad as this."

"But how them dogs get in there? Gal, did you leave the door open?"

The girl jumped. "No, sir. She cain't stand no air on her. I keeps the door closed no matter how hot it be in there or how it stink."

Seeing the girl shrink back into herself, Jesse adjusted his voice. "What is your name anyway?"

"Miss Baby Doll ain't never called me nothing but Gal, and my mammy didn't give me no name. I been in the whorehouse since I was born."

Both men stared at her emaciated form, noting the rags that draped her body, the ashy skin stretched over bones that hadn't matured yet, all elbows and knees. Tears pooled in her eyes. "I guess I ain't got nowhere to go now that Miss Baby Doll dead."

They shifted uncomfortably in the face of her misery. Elder Mason moved forward and rested one hand on the girl's shoulder, patting it awkwardly. "You wait here, Gal. When we finished in there, me and Sheriff Jesse find something for you to do. Somewhere you can go."

The sheriff nodded and walked past them back into the shack where the dogs still lay in a heap where they had fallen. Huge chunks of flesh had been torn from Baby Doll's thighs and her side, leaving gaping raw wounds that spilled more carnage onto the floor. Her wide eyes stared up toward the room's window, and he wondered what she had seen as she died. Had she seen death coming? Were the dogs already in the room, stalking toward her as she lay defenseless on her bed? And who had closed the door, locking them in?

He waited just inside the doorway, taking shallow breaths of the foul air as he waited for Elder to join him and pronounce the obvious, that Baby Doll was, in fact, dead.

Outside, Clyde slowly ambled away, waiting until he was far enough to allow his whistling to begin and go unheard. The darkness swirled around his feet as he walked. He sped up, heading for home.

Mama said he had packing to do. They would be leaving this miserable town behind, taking the Greyhound to Jackson, Mississippi, for a while and then returning to Delhi. Nobody knew them in Delhi. Mama's uncle Simeon on her father's side said they could stay with him.

A flicker of guilt flitted across his heart. He had surrendered to the darkness, letting it have its way. Part of him reached toward it while a sliver clung to Mama. He felt the need to be her special boy, anointed to do a great work, but the dark was powerful in him. It slithered around his spirit, satisfied with the corpse that lay inert inside. He felt himself stretched between her and the darkness.

Could killing be God's work? Was *this* his anointing? He pushed the contrary thoughts away. He would confess to Mama, and she would purify him. Then they would begin again, away from this miserable town. She would help him to control the darkness. It would be better when Mama fixed it.

PART TWO
INTERLUDE

CHAPTER ONE

Mae let her feet drag, clutching her books to her chest, mentally scolding herself for her frequent absences from class. She was sixteen years old and already the oldest student in her classroom. But she was determined that she would graduate. Gaps of weeks and months would not deter her, she thought furiously while she waited to answer the summons from Miss Norma, the principal.

Standing just outside of the open door, she shifted from one foot to another, her hands shaking, waiting for Miss Norma to look up from the papers stacked in front of her on her desk. Finally, she lifted her head and motioned for Mae to come in, pointing to the chair in front of the broad cherrywood desk.

Mae sat, placed her books on the floor beside her chair, and loosened the buttons on her coat, fighting the urge to sit on her hands to keep them still. Her protests and excuses gathered in her mouth, ready to pour out at the first opportunity.

Miss Norma fidgeted with the glasses that dangled from the gold chain around her neck, lifting them to peer at Mae and then allowing them to fall back to the lace of the blue-flowered dress covering her sagging breasts. The lines in her lemon-yellow skin spoke of an age that aligned itself with the rumor that she had been teaching at the school since it opened its doors, some forty-nine years ago, in 1904. Clearing her throat, she pulled her thin lips into a line that caused them to disappear and spoke, her eyes riveted on Mae.

"How are you doing today, young Miss Mae?" she'd asked in that crisp, efficient voice that often echoed in Mae's mind late into the evening, bent over the wash basin at home. She would repeat the lessons, striving to master each repetition in preparation for the next time she was permitted to go to school.

"I'm fine, Miss Norma. No reason for me to be complaining about nothing." She was careful to pronounce the "*g*"s on the ends of her words like Miss Norma taught them.

"About anything," Miss Norma corrected, lifting her glasses to look over at Mae, her mouth rigid with the disapproval she reserved for poor grammar. Mae slumped lower, folding into her chair, embarrassment coloring her cheeks.

"Yes, ma'm." Mae felt beads of sweat trickling from her armpits and down her side to pool in the band of her wool skirt. She waited, the unease building steadily as Miss Norma seemed to assess her, pause to think, and then evaluate her further before she spoke again. Her mouth relaxed to show the fullness of her lower lip and turned up in the corners in an uncharacteristic smile that left Mae bewildered. Her heart tripped rapidly.

"I'm sorry about missing so many days in school," she blurted, leaning forward farther. "It ain't, I mean, isn't my fault. I be in school every day if Verna didn't stop me."

Miss Norma's eyes widened in disbelief, and she sat up straighter in her chair. "Children don't call their parents by their first name, even if they are our stepparents," she declared, her eyes piercing Mae and watching her squirm where she remained pinned until she sensed contrition on her part.

Mae's stomach twisted into knots as she prepared for her expulsion. She'd shown herself to be rude, illiterate, and disrespectful. Her body tensed for Miss Norma's following words as if awaiting a physical blow.

"Well, it seems," Miss Norma continued, seemingly oblivious to Mae's distress, "that although you have missed many days of instruction, you have somehow managed to obtain the highest test scores of any of the students in your class. You apparently have a propensity for learning that is unequaled."

Mae's mouth dropped open, and her eyes rapidly blinked as she struggled to understand, leaning more on tone than the words themselves, the meaning of some of them escaping her.

Mae sat up straight in her chair, her mouth falling open with comprehension. She stared at Miss Norma, half-stood, then dropped back into the chair.

"You mean I'm not getting expelled?" she asked, her words rushing out with a sigh of relief.

"Of course not. Whatever made you think that?" Miss Norma blinked owlishly at Mae, picking up the disparate threads of the conversation and piecing them back together for clarity. "As I said, it seems that you have managed to impress most of the faculty with your acumen and have been chosen as a candidate to take the teaching exam. We usually take the younger girls, but we've decided that, despite your age, you will be groomed for a teaching position at the Rayville Colored School."

Mae struggled to understand everything she said, feeling like she needed a dictionary to decipher the big words Miss Norma spewed, finally seizing on the fact that she had been chosen to become a teacher. Her heart lurched in her chest, throbbing with hope. The whisper of a dream that she could escape this place coalesced, the one she thought had been buried in the grave with the remains of her dead mother.

She clenched her hands on her lap, the knuckles yellow beneath her tan skin, her body angled forward, eager to capture every additional word as a warm glow filled her, and Miss Norma continued.

"We do understand that there are some limitations in your home situation." Miss Norma stood and walked around the desk to lean down and pat her clenched hands, clearly uncomfortable with this part of the conversation. Mae inhaled her scent of pressed powder and topaz sachet, her body relaxing back into the chair, feeling comforted.

She looked into the round, protruding eyes behind the lenses of Miss Norma's glasses, reflecting pools of sympathy before she blinked, erasing it. Straightening, Miss Norma walked back, putting the desk between them, a barrier between position and emotions. Pulling out a handkerchief from her bodice, she coughed into it.

"I have devised a possible solution if you and your family are amenable to it." She waited, and Mae moved to the edge of her seat. "You know Pastor and his wife Lena never had any children of their own?" she asked, pausing again to wait for a response.

Mae nodded, "Yes, ma'm. It's a shame her being barren as a rock and sweet as she is."

"Yes." Her features arranged themselves to include that disapproving stare that rolled over Mae again, and she flinched. Miss Norma coughed into her handkerchief and sniffed before continuing, studying the rising blush coloring Mae's cheeks. Satisfied that her silent chastisement had been received, she went on. "Well, they do have an extra room, and they said they would be willing to open their home up to you during the new school year. We'll just need your folks to say yes and agree to the arrangements. Then we will be able to put everything into place. Is that something you think that you might want to do?"

A bright light ignited, illuminating within Mae's head, bringing with it a swimming sensation that almost toppled her from the chair. She wanted to shout and run around the room. Instead, she choked out three words.

"Yes, Miss Norma." She paused, overcome, additional words sticking in her throat.

Mae stood rapidly, arms stretched wide, to wrap around Miss Norma, then halted, stopped by the horrified expression on the woman's face as she leaned away from the embrace. She settled for extending her right hand, which Miss Norma shook firmly, her mouth working itself back into the tight smile she had displayed earlier.

"Be here first thing on Monday morning and bring your father." She returned to her paperwork, signaling Mae's dismissal, an air of accomplishment settling around her. "And congratulations, Miss Kennedy."

Picking up her books, Mae managed to walk sedately from the office, her steps measured and soft until she reached the front door, where she broke into a run. Kicking up dead leaves as she skipped through them, she threw back her head, her mouth open in a wordless scream of joy. God had finally answered her prayers.

Now, forty-five minutes later, she stood in her front yard. Her arguments and courage had evaporated with each step that brought her closer to home. She hugged the thin material of her ragged coat tighter around her slender form. The wind slipping through the threadbare fabric chilled her skin, causing her to shiver as she picked up her steps and moved more quickly toward the house. The light that had sustained her began to fade, rolling away in waves, leaving her bereft of her previous joy.

She took deep breaths and pulled her lower lip between her teeth, chewing it lightly in agitation. She lifted a silent prayer as she twisted the large white knob, letting the door swing inward to bounce off the wall.

"Close that door, fool. I swear you ain't got the sense you was born with, or was you born with any?"

Mae's eyes narrowed as she glared at her father's second wife Verna, sitting on the small, faded green sofa pushed back against the wall of the cramped living room. It stood a few feet from the black potbellied stove that took up the center of the same wall. Verna's hand rested on the small mound of her fourth pregnancy swelling beneath her house dress. Around her, two-year-old Sarah and three-year-old Josiah crawled and scooted quickly across the pitted linoleum covering the wooden floor, scrambling toward their sister.

"A fool know enough not to let all the heat out. And is you cutting your eyes at me?" Verna demanded, leaning forward as if to stand. Mae schooled her face into a look of exaggerated remorse, taking the venom out of her own gaze and replacing it with one of subjugation. Satisfied, Verna sat down again, her mouth puckered as if she had just bitten sour lemons.

Mae quickly closed the door, stepping over the tangle of her younger siblings as they reached toward her legs and the hem of her skirt.

"Why you late this time? You been out there with that boy, Moses?" Verna sneered, her eyes rolling in Mae's direction as she sucked her teeth, searching her face for evidence of guilt.

"No, ma'm, Sweet Mom." Mae muttered, the endearment bitter on her tongue as it left her mouth. "It was Miss Norma at the school what kept me late."

Verna's eyes moved upward to lock on Mae's, lingering on the almond shape of the girl's dark eyes, the upturned nose, and the deep lines of the dimples that showed even when her plump mouth was at rest. A scowl swiped across her own sharp features as she drew herself up straighter on the couch, her hand rounding her stomach. At the same time, she smiled at the honorific she demanded of Mae, though she usually preferred to think that they could pass for sisters rather than mother and daughter, considering herself far to young to have a child as old as Mae.

"It ain't nothing but a waste you spending all that time up at that school noway." She stopped, her eyes moving around the room until they landed on the door leading to the back porch. "You needs to be working. The washing piling up, and them folks be needing they stuff back." Her eyes returned to settle on Mae, lingering as the animus built between them. "I cain't lose no customers because you late."

Mae's anger ignited and flared, the words releasing from her tongue and flying into the air before caution could stop them from spewing into Verna's face. "Miss Norma say I might can be a teacher at the Colored School. And she can get me a room with the preacher and his wife until I finish."

She watched Verna wince as if the words had weight, the color first draining from her face, then her skin turning scarlet with rage.

"I know you ain't putting no store in what Miss Norma say. She been at that school since Mary met Joseph." She spit out the words, simultaneously reaching down to the floor to snatch her daughter, Sarah, and put her onto her lap. She had unknowingly crawled into the crossfire of bitterness between them. "Probably ain't nothing right in her head, especially if she think your dumb ass can be a teacher." Her hand rose and came down to slap the child's round thigh as she tried to wriggle free.

Frustration sprouted in Mae's spirit, bringing with it a deep-seated desire to nullify Verna's poisonous criticism. She let her eyes soften while her mouth relaxed, then channeled scathing words wrapped in sarcasm. "Why you say that?" she asked, her expression fixed into a masque of innocence. "Did she tell you the same thing when *you* was in school?"

Verna recoiled, her eyes narrowed, her breath coming in quick, short inhalations. A moment later, a howl split the air as Sarah received several more sharp, heavy-handed slaps.

"Shut up that noise," Verna screamed, squeezing Sarah's back against her chest, one hand over her mouth to muffle the sound, ignoring how the girl bucked against her restraining hand. Sarah's head struck Verna's breastbone repeatedly until she was finally wrestled into silence. She and Mae glared at each other in the thick silence of the room.

Mae glowered at Verna, wanting to pull Sarah free from her lap as Verna continued to pinch the child's legs. She could see bruises on the child's tender flesh as Verna peered from beneath her thick, lowered lashes at Mae.

She knew she was being baited, Verna daring her to move, punishing her with the child's pain. Her hands balled into fists at her side. Pushing her shoulders back and steeling herself, Mae ignored Sarah's cries, locking her mouth closed and refusing to exchange any more words. She needed to put some distance between Sarah's tear-streaked face and herself before she lost the barely maintained slender threads of control left within her.

Turning on her heel, Mae threw open the door, stepped outside, and heard the resounding clap as it slammed shut behind her. With the door between them, her shoulders slumped, and she allowed the tears to fall, dripping down her face, the remnants of any joy she had felt earlier beginning to leak out with them.

"Damn it all," she swore to herself as she stomped across the porch, pounding out her frustration on the rotting boards. Nothing had gone the way she'd planned while walking home. It had all fallen apart as soon as she had seen Verna, swollen and squatting on the couch like a toad. Her plan of coming in on her best behavior, starting her chores, and smoothing the way for the conversation dissolved into madness. She should have figured that Verna could mess up hell itself.

Standing still, she counted to ten in her head, breathing in and out the way Miss Norma had taught them at school. Bending from the waist, she picked up the uneven pieces of wood from the stack, oblivious to the slivers leaving splinters in her hands. Inside, three-year-old Josiah had joined his bawling to that of his sister, and she stopped to peek in the side window, then stepped back, horrified. Verna was kicking at the boy to silence him. Josiah flinched, hiccupped, and stilled at her feet, mouth trembling and choking on his cries.

Mae's eyes rounded in fury, her patience snapping as the wood slid from her arms and clattered to the porch. She raced forward, her open palms slammed against the door, this time heedless of how it swung inward and ricocheted off the wall. Entering, she crossed the space in three quick strides to stand over Josiah, nestling the boy between her spread feet, then yanking Sarah free of Verna's lap and into her arms. Her chest heaved, the heat of her anger blazing in her eyes.

"Don't you hit neither one of them no more," she hissed from between clenched teeth, holding Sarah balanced on one hip with one hand, her other hand balled into a fist raised over her head. "What's wrong with you? These is babies! How you gon' hit and kick them like that?" Mae yelled into Verna's upturned face as she fell back onto the cushions of the couch, her hands raised defensively to cover her face and stomach.

"What the hell going on in here?" Her father Ben's thundering voice filled the room, halting Mae and Verna, freezing them into a tableau of acrimony.

They turned to stare at him as he filled the open doorway, his eyes swinging from one to the other. Ben was a big bear of a man, broad shoulders straining against the wool of his coat, his large hands hanging inches below the sleeves of his jacket. His once-handsome face was lined, etched with the pressure of years of providing sustenance for his family, the loss of one wife, too many babies who never drew breath, the demands of the young girl he had taken as his second wife, and the balm of the whiskey that soothed the raging disappointments that ate his soul.

"Cain't a man get no peace when he come in his own selfs house?" he shouted, his head rotating on his thick neck, glaring at both women.

Verna's eyes instantly filled with tears, her mouth quivering as she shrank further into the cushions, a look of wild-eyed hysteria distorting her features.

"Oh, Jesus, Ben, you gots here just in time. She was gon' hit me," she shrieked, tears pouring liberally down her face as she sobbed. "I done told you before I be scared to be with her. Ain't no telling what she gon' do," she cried, wrapping her arms around her upper body and rocking back and forth as she spoke through quaking lips.

Mae's father's eyes locked with hers, wildly searching hers for understanding. "Mae, Mae, what going on?"

"I was just trying to stop her. She was hitting Sarah, and SHE KICKED JOSIAH!" Her voice steadily rose until she screamed, first holding Sarah out toward him, then pulling her back against her chest, rubbing at the reddened flesh on the child's thighs. Stepping back, she eased Sarah to the floor to place her next to Josiah and smoothed her skirt from where it had bunched up on the side. She lowered her head, eyes cast to the floor, unable to meet her father's accusing glare.

"She telling a tale!" Verna wailed, leaping to her feet to press herself against Ben's tall frame, weeping convulsively into his chest as his arms encircled her. He leaned down, kissing the crown of her head, murmuring soothingly, his hands running up and down her back.

Sweeping his arms beneath her, Ben turned, lifted Verna, and walked back to the couch, lowering himself to the cushions and cradling her against his chest. Mae remained standing, a forlorn figure isolated in the center of the room, the toddlers crawling between her legs, oblivious to the drama unfolding over their heads. Her shoulders sagged.

"Now, Verna, sugar, tell me what happened," he demanded before turning his gaze back to Mae, pinning her with a withering look. Her feet anchored her to the shame and disapproval pulsing between them, helpless as Verna hitched and stuttered out her tale.

"She come in here late again." She paused, watching the contours of his face tighten, letting the information dig at him. With each damning sentence, she would glance at Mae, then shudder before continuing. "I ain't been feeling good today, what with the baby and all." She pulled Ben's hand to rest over her stomach as she talked, using her thumb to stroke the rough skin on his palm. "I was sitting here waiting, and she wasn't here, and she know I needs her help. I cain't do this by myself, and you already working hard as you can. We need that little bit of money I make. She done left me with all them clothes on the porch still needing to be washed."

She moved her hands upward, allowing them to wind themselves in the rough spun cotton of his shirt as she talked, looking up to give him the full benefit of her direct gaze. "I bet you anything she been mooning over that boy, Moses, again, even after you done told her to stay away from him."

Mae saw her father's back go rigid, his shoulders pulled back, and she felt her dreams burn to ash. Nothing she could say now would persuade him differently once Moses' name had been mentioned. Verna's words tumbled around her, burying her deeper in a tomb she could not extricate herself from. She wanted to bawl at the injustice, knock Verna from his lap, take her place, and beg him to understand. Why couldn't he see Verna for the conniving, miserable heifer she was? The words swam around in her mouth, eager to be spit free.

"And I told her so about what you done said about that boy." Verna continued, unable to conceal the undercurrents of deception and her manic glee from Mae while her father remained deaf to it. "Then I ask her to change Sarah's diaper, and she tell me to change my own stinking baby. That ain't her job. Next thing I know, she slapping Sarah's legs, and then she gon' start hollering about how she ain't washing nothing, she ain't watching no babies, and she gon' be a teacher." Her words rushed out in her haste to paint a vivid picture of her victimization, her body attuned to the hardness of Ben's muscular frame against her, feeling his anger fueled by her words.

She chose her next words carefully, playing his emotions against him, inhaling the whiskey fumes coating his breath. "Miss Norma done fill her head with some craziness about her being a teacher herself. Now, she too good to be with us." Verna drove in the final stakes to his pride with her last sentence. "She say she ain't gon' end up with some poor-ass hick farmer getting swolled up with babies like me."

Mae's eyes bulged, her mouth dropping open in amazement as she listened to Verna, her ears unbelieving.

"Nah, Papa, that ain't true. It ain't happen like she say." Stuttering, she began to refute her stepmother. She should have stopped her sooner. "I mean, that part about Miss Norma saying she think I can be a teacher, that part be true, and I was gon' tell you soon as you come in," she cried, scrubbing her hand down her face, an unconscious reflection of her father's own gestures of frustration. Mae stopped, searching his face, hoping to see a glimmer of understanding relax his features.

Nothing came, and she pushed on. "What she say about me maybe staying with Pastor Brown and his wife through the semester, that be true too, but it ain't what we was fussing about. She fibbing, Papa, I swears before God. She was the one hitting Sarah. Look at her legs if you don't believes me."

Mae lifted Sarah, holding her thigh toward her father so he could see the faint traces of red welts against her golden skin and igniting a new round of wails from Sarah, her brother joining in. "See them marks what she left?"

"YOU CALLING ME A LIE?" Vera screamed, her wails escalating over Mae's voice and the children's cries, creating a cacophony of sounds that threatened to drown reason from Mae's mind.

"You saying you ain't call me no baby-breeding heifer, not fit to do nothing but pop out babies?" Verna wept. "Look at her now, standing there all high and mighty. Grown enough to call me a lie. After I done did my best to be a mama to her."

"YOU AIN'T MY MAMA!" Mae shouted, her hands tightening back into fists at her side, her eyes narrowed to slits, focused on Verna. She did not see her father moving, sliding Verna from his lap and pushing her gently to the side as he leaped to his feet, moving impossibly fast for a man his size. He stood and faced his daughter, towering over her diminutive form, his hand rising and coming down in a blow that rocked her backward on her heels. She stumbled, clutching at the air, her arms pinwheeling to catch her balance and not fall on the children underfoot. Mae felt her cheek exploding in pain, the side of her face swelling instantly. Both hands went to hold her cheek, scalding tears spilling over her hand, hoarse sobs wrenched from her throat.

Ben breathed in deeply, rubbing his hands across his face, then again down the front of his pants legs while his breath bellowed in and out. "Little gal, you done lost your mind. Where the hell you think you is when you can talk to your mama like that. This *my* house! Mine. And Verna is your mama now. Your little grown ass better be knowing it."

"But she fibbing, Papa," Mae muttered, feeling the skin around her eye tightening and throbbing, seeing the blur of his hand raised again as she squinted through her good eye. She flinched, ducking away from the anticipated blow but still unable to stop her treacherous mouth from speaking. "You know I won't never do nothing to Sarah or Josiah," she pleaded, her uninjured eye swimming with tears. "And I ain't been seeing no Moses neither." She finished petulantly, her lower lip sticking out, trembling with the effort to staunch her weeping.

"So, what was you fixing to do when you was standing there when I come in with your fist raised?"

Her eyes lowered to the floor. She had no defense to his question. "I'm sorry, Papa," she said softly.

Ben hesitated, his eyes softening momentarily in the face of her remorse. He took a step toward his daughter, his arm outstretched. "Mae?"

"You taking up for her?" Verna wallowed from side to side, struggling to stand, brushing past Ben. "So, now you calling me a lie too? I guess I knows what I needs to do."

Startled, Ben reached out for Verna's arm as she passed, stopping her progress. He spun her around and pushed her back down to the couch, his face hardening again. "Just sit the hell down, Verna. I'm sick to death of being stuck between the two of you. Cain't get a minute of peace!" Anger, frustration, and pain churned across his face as Verna angrily swiped at her tears.

He stood back so that he could look at both of them. "Mae, I done seen how grown you thinks you is right here. Heard it for my own-self. Old enough to start hollering at grown folks in my house and calling them a lie." He leaned forward to glare directly into her face. "You sure as shit done start smelling yourself, and you likes the smell. But you ain't grown yet."

He patted his pocket and felt the hard, familiar shape of the whiskey bottle within. Pulling it free, he twisted off the cap, put the bottle to his lips, and threw his head back to take a long swallow. He felt the comforting burn down his throat and sighed as it settled into a pleasant warmth radiating through his stomach.

"So, a poor-ass hick farmer like me ain't man enough to takes care of you no more? That's why you needs Pastor Brown taking care of you? I ain't man enough to take care of my own, right?"

"It ain't like that, Papa. It's just Miss Norma say maybe I could be a teacher." Mae watched his Adam's apple moving up and down, hearing the gurgle of the amber liquid as he drank. She saw that more than half the contents were gone when he lowered the bottle to retwist the cap and return it to his pocket.

Her words trailed off as she looked into her father's eyes, looking for the love that sometimes sparkled there, that had been her everyday due before Verna entered their lives. Reason faltered in the face of his liquor-fueled accusations. Each word from her only served to twist the maze of Verna's half-truths and innuendos. The sly and calculating look of drunkenness stared back at her, and she wondered how many bottles had preceded this one.

Ben paused, sucking in a deep breath as he searched the ceiling for words that would bring his world back, a world where his daughter looked up to him, where he could be proud of what he did as a man, the living he scratched out of the unyielding earth. He weaved slightly before focusing his gaze on Mae. His words slurred slightly, his voice escalating until it thundered in the room. "Ain't nobody gots to take care of me or mine, Mae!" He pounded his chest to emphasize his statement. "You knows that. Ain't no way I'm gon' let no man, preacher or not, come in like I cain't take care of my own. Especially not no uppity-ass bitch Miss Norma." He paused, then shook his head as if clearing away the thoughts. "She ain't never like me. Say none of us Kennedy boys was worth cat piss."

Mae felt her heart folding in on itself, shriveling under her father's rant. She willed new tears not to fall, refusing to relinquish that final victory to Verna.

"And far as you talking to Verna like that, she still your mama whether you thinks it or not, and you gon' respects her." He stopped, breathing deeply, then continued. "That boy probably have been sniffing around you, got you acting a plumb fool."

Ben sighed, the whiskey spinning his thoughts, then stopping. His eyebrows arched upward, his features alight as his next thought sprang forward, taking precedence, painted by the shame Verna's words had planted in his mind.

"And you know what?" He did not wait for her to reply. "You through with that school. You too damned old to be going no way." He gritted the words out, slamming his fist into the palm of his hand, his aggravation finally finding an outlet in his decision. "We needs you here at the house. Verna got the baby coming, and we needs the extra money you can bring in. You grown enough to do that."

Mae's mouth dropped open, stunned. She stared at her father, dumbfounded, as the last flicker of hope was snuffed out in her eyes. Behind him, she saw the corners of Verna's mouth raised briefly in a triumphant smile before she lowered her face into her hands and continued sniffling loudly.

"You done had enough book learning. It be time for you to be done with that foolishness and come down off that high-ass horse you been riding today. You ain't no better than nobody here. Now, you get yourself right. Then maybe we sees about somebody coming to court you."

"But, Papa," she began. "Please, I can get the work done and still go to school. Please don't make me stop. I just wants to finish."

"Ain't no buts," Ben interjected, breathing the whiskey fumes into her face and ignoring the hurt in Mae's eyes before she turned and moved stiffly forward.

"Get on outside and pick up that wood on the porch." His voice rose again, climbing back to the rafters as he seemed to consider all that had transpired in the room.

"AND CLOSE THAT DAMN DOOR. Letting all the heat out with it standing open." He called to the slumped curve of her retreating back. "And don't you never let me see you raise a hand to Verna again, or I'll whip the skin off your ass myself."

Mae felt her father's anger and disappointment burning a hole in her back as she walked away and wondered how she had allowed everything to dissolve into such disaster and misery. The possibility and promise from the early afternoon shrank and shriveled her heart into nothingness.

Her shoulders fell, pulled by the gravity of her defeat, her hands dropping to her sides as she felt the tears she'd been holding back begin to fall. Stepping carefully over Sarah and Josiah, she made her way through the open door, closing it carefully behind her, making sure that it did not slam.

She gathered the discarded pieces of wood into her arms, her tears splashing down to land on the cold pile. She stood, too weary to brush them away, staring toward the woods that bordered the land their house sat on. Her sight lingered on the small crosses nestled against the tree where her mother was buried. She couldn't read them from where she stood but mentally traced the letters carved into the smallest one, "Samuel Kennedy," Verna and her father's firstborn son. The boy he had always wanted. The boy she had never been and could never be.

Her memory conjured the roundness of his limbs and the sound of his laughter as she bounced him on her lap, bringing him through the mists of the past. She remembered him screaming incessantly. His little face was perpetually beet red, his arms flailing, and his back stiffening when Verna tried to hold him, only quieting when she thrust him into Mae's arms.

She'd only been twelve herself, Verna, a mere nineteen. The baby seemed to baffle and confuse Verna, the constant demands of his care wearing against her, whittling away at her happiness. She became mean, shunting more and more of her demands onto Mae. Mae didn't mind. She loved Samuel. Loved him until the day she came home and found Verna sprawled across the bed, sleeping peacefully, Samuel lying beside her, still and blue.

People said it was an accident, that Verna must have rolled over on him in her sleep and smothered him. Others said it just happened sometimes. Babies stopped breathing. They took a breath in and never let it back out. Mae didn't believe it.

She had seen how Verna looked at him with anger and frustration when she would order Mae to take him, mumbling under her breath that he stank and needed to be changed. Mae had seen how Verna glared at her when she watched her cooing at Sammy as she cuddled him in her arms or he grasped her finger tightly in his chubby fist.

Only she had witnessed Verna shaking him, yelling in his face before dropping him onto the bed she shared with Mae's father, things she never did when he was around. The empty space held in her heart for Samuel pulsated, longing for him, and Mae sighed aloud. Verna had taken him away from her. Verna had taken Mama's place. Now, it looked like she had taken Papa and her future too.

CHAPTER TWO

Clyde stood, dusting the dirt from his hands. He lifted the shovel from the ground, carefully tamped down the earth, and looked around for loose brush to cover the fresh grave. He felt the darkness receding, and his breathing slowed. He worried for a moment. Had he buried her deep enough? The last thing he needed was some animal digging her up.

It had been six months since the last woman died. He'd wrestled with the darkness, fasting, and praying for six months, conflicted by the revivals his mother insisted on dragging him to. Preachers flew across the hastily raised platforms, saliva flying over the congregants as they shouted accusations of punishment for their sins.

Mama pushed him up front each night, forcing him to stand with the crippled, lame, and sin-filled heathens to seek repentance. Standing beneath the hands of the fiery preachers, he prayed to do what was right in God's sight. The darkness writhed inside him, drowning out the sounds of their words as they anointed his head with oil, and he felt the sign of the cross scalding his forehead, burning him.

Afterward, he'd stumbled home, crawling into bed where the darkness followed him into his sleep, entering his dreams, coercing him to hunt. Climbing out of bed on silent feet, it led him to the woman, smelling her scent before he reached her. He sought her in the juke joint where she sat, voice thick with cigarette smoke and whiskey, perched on the edge of a bar stool, her legs spread in invitation, the darkness swirling around her ankles. He felt the darkness inside of her drawing him closer.

From the corner where he sat, he turned his attention to the room around him, cradling the beer grown warm in its mug. He'd ordered one when he arrived, nursing it, pretending to take small swallows. His eyes searched until they rested on her, the one the darkness marked, listing sideways as she attempted to get off her bar stool, pushing her would-be companion away. The man whispered something inaudible into her ear, making her bristle.

"I knows my own way home, and I don't need you sniffing your way to my door," she slurred, unsuccessfully tugging at the hem of her skirt that had risen on one side.

He waited until the man turned in his seat, his mouth fixed in a smile for the woman sitting on his right. The woman staggered to the door and left. Clyde waited a few minutes, then followed, tracking her on silent feet as she stumbled from the juke. Walking through the darkness, she swayed drunkenly, her heels catching in the dirt and grass. Singing loudly and off-key, she held a rambling conversation with the man she had left behind, having forgotten she was alone. She never heard Clyde until it was too late.

"Who you?!" she slurred as she lurched into Clyde, who stood, legs spread, in the middle of the road. She blinked stupidly, her wet mouth open in surprise. She leaned to the side, the juke's cheap alcohol blurring her fear. She seemed to look around, searching for her friend. Clyde stepped behind her and wrapped his hand around her mouth, cutting off the scream that belatedly made its way to her throat.

Throwing her to the ground, he straddled her, watching her eyes clear as she lay sprawled beneath him. All traces of drunkenness evaporated, replaced by terror. His nostrils flared as he breathed in the stink of sin that permeated her body, rising into the air around him. His hands tightened on her neck, squeezing, feeling her writhing beneath him, her nails clawing at his forearms. Life leaked slowly from her until her dead eyes lost their last light. He remained on his knees, savoring the darkness he had drawn from her, then stood and dragged her body to the spot he had picked out earlier.

Glancing at the finished grave one last time, he prayed to God to forgive her of her wickedness, then collapsed with his back against the gnarled surface of a large tree of heaven, the one they called a stink tree.

He stared at his large hands, the feel of her slender neck imprinted on his palms. He saw the flow of darkness crawling across the earth. It wasn't enough. It would not sustain him. He groaned, dropping his head into his hands. He was tired. The darkness and the death left him weary. Time drifted around him. He slept.

Panic overwhelmed Clyde, and his heart beat erratically as he startled awake. He was sure Mama would be looking for him by now, and she would be mad. He had been disobedient again, succumbing to the darkness, showing his weakness. He lumbered slowly to his feet, his muscles aching in protest at the time spent on the unyielding earth. His feet found their way through the familiar woods, away from the grave.

As he walked, he listened to the sounds around him, leery of the small creatures scurrying from his path, sensing the alpha predator among them. He stopped, cocked his head, arrested by an unfamiliar sound. He waited, sorting it, then followed it, the dark pulling him along.

Hiding in the shadow of a large water hickory tree, he studied the source. A girl sat slumped over her raised knees, ragged sobs tearing from her throat. He stared at her, waiting for the darkness to grow, inhaling deeply . . . then hesitated. Her scent was different. He stepped forward, drawn by the sounds of humiliation and pain that painted the early-morning air between them.

Her head snapped up, her eyes bright and alert as a branch cracked beneath his foot, alerting her to his presence. He cursed his heavy foot and stepped hastily into her sight, one hand raised, his head shaking from side to side. Gasping, she scrambled backward, putting distance between them as he shuffled toward her.

He imagined her heart palpitating in her chest, the feel of her pulse throbbing in her neck as her eyes widened. The darkness awakened in him.

"Wait." The word leaped from his lips unbidden. "Don't be scared."

Clyde continued to move forward, one hand reaching toward her the way he did when he lured in timid animals, the ones who should have sense enough to run but didn't.

He stretched one finger of his other hand forward, touching her wet cheek. A tear slid onto the tip. Clyde raised the finger and studied it, turning his finger from left to right, then looked back at her, his head turned quizzically to the side.

"What wrong?" he asked, his voice gruff but surprisingly low. The darkness churned in his chest as he grappled against it, pushing it down. He didn't want her fear.

Now, it was her turn to study him as her emotions overrode her natural impulses. Instinctively, she knew she should run but did not. Oddly, his words were the first kindness she had heard in days. She took in his broad, sloping forehead, the thick brows bridging the protruding eyes glowering at her, his tight jaws, and his long arms dropped at his side, his hands like shovels. Her breath hitched in her throat, tears spilling down her cheeks as he watched her, and her body vacillated between flight and remaining in place.

Clyde hesitated, the dark thrashing inside wanting to break free and be sated. It searched the small girl, finding only dots of darkness, no full threads to pull on. Confused, he looked around, searching the trees, sure his mother would come rushing through, screaming the Lord's wrath. The girl settled back into her position, sitting in the glen, her face open and inviting, a small smile tugging up her lips, her face still wet.

Her shoulders rose and fell as she shrugged, sat up straight, and reached out her hand toward Clyde, tugging him gently. He saw her swallow her fear, then allowed her to pull him, falling down hard next to her. They sat together and silently apart, the sounds of their breath synchronizing. Tension and fear drained into the soil around them.

Clyde had never been this close to a living female other than his mother. He sought them only when sent, driven by need and purpose. Then the darkness demanded their sin be eradicated quickly and without mercy. He never knew them. But not this one.

This girl he found on his own. The dark had no control of it, no control of her. He could feel the warmth of her skin radiating and tingling against his own. The darkness tried to push its way between them, then abruptly halted, fizzling in his brain as if extinguished. He shook his head, puzzled.

"Why you crying?" he asked again.

Mae drew in a long, unsteady breath and stared at the stranger beside her. "He say I cain't go back to school no more," she confessed, her voice a shattered whisper. The finality of her father's decision solidified into reality as she spoke it into existence.

"Who?"

"My daddy." Mae sucked in the tears that pushed against her eyes.

School had been her hope, the promise of a future, a way out of her miserable existence. She was now stuck with Verna's squalling babies and the backbreaking toil of scrubbing urine-stained sheets and shit smears from other people's underwear. Her despair deepened, and she poured it out to Clyde until she felt empty. She found herself rattling off her pain to him, her apprehension diminishing while he listened. She searched his face while she talked, the way that his head dipped, his eyes avoiding hers. Silence sat comfortably between them until he spoke again.

"I don't goes to school no more. Don't need it," Clyde informed her, his eyes focused ahead of him into the woods. "How much schooling you got?"

"I was gon' be a teacher when I finished next year," she said, pride lacing her words.

"You smart." He turned his head to look at her, pulling his head down into the neck of his shirt. "Ain't you scared sitting out here with me?" he asked suddenly, his eyes casting back into the woods again. "Most everybody scared of me."

Mae stopped and considered what he said, shamed by her own initial fear. "Of you?" she asked, her lips forming a coy grin. "Should I be?"

The question hung in the air between them as he contemplated it. He'd felt her stop the darkness in him. Even now, it sat dormant in the corner of his mind, occasionally pressing against him, otherwise trapped.

Mae's small hand covered his, and he startled, springing away from her. "It don't seem like it nothing to be scared of," she said softly, speaking to herself as much as to him.

Clyde settled back beside her, allowing her hand to remain on top of his, looking at it and then at her.

"My name Mae. You ain't never even tell me who you is, and I been bawling all over you like some big old baby. What your name?" she asked, lowering her head in embarrassment.

"Clyde."

She smiled again, a luminous glow forming beneath the creamy caramel of her skin, touching her eyes. "You a good listener, Clyde."

Confusion clouded his thoughts, flooding him with a longing to be near her mixed with self-loathing as the darkness attempted to assert itself and faltered again. He stared at her small hand covering his, then watched a deep dimple appear on both cheeks to accompany her smile.

Mae was tenderhearted, a light child. That's what her mother's family had called it when she was growing up. She felt a swell of compassion ebbing and flowing from her toward Clyde, and she leaned toward him, her head resting on his shoulder.

"It show enough is good having somebody be nice," she declared, looking at their clasped hands.

"I figured you was just deep down hurt is all." He turned his hand over to cup hers and shook his head. "I knows about hurt," he finished, his expression shuttering as he closed his emotions against her.

The dark inside him shuddered and was silent. Clyde scrambled away from Mae, his heels digging into the earth in his effort to gain his feet. Panic filled him as he frantically searched for it, feeling lost.

Clyde turned away, walking as rapidly as his legs would allow, leaving Mae sitting alone.

"I sorry. I didn't meant no harm." Mae called after him, watching him walk away, her spirit wounded.

Clyde crept around the main room of the shack he and Fannie shared, hoping not to draw her attention to him. He walked to the basin resting on the sink, picked up the thick bar of homemade soap, and began lathering his hands and arms to the elbow. His fear that Fannie would detect Mae's scent lingering on him forced him to scrub harder, leaving his skin raw.

"Where you been, baby boy?"

Clyde kept his body still, his breathing even, his head down, studying the film coating the water in the basin.

"In the woods."

Fannie stared at him for a long moment, stewing in a storm of emotions. He was different. He was hiding something from her. She couldn't put her finger on it, but a wrongness resonated from him, a discordant chord between them. She snorted loudly, filling the air with her doubts.

Clyde let the words sit. They weren't a lie. He had been in the woods but not alone. He kept the knowledge that he was with a woman named Mae deep in his mind lest she ferret it out.

Fannie continued to stare at him, suspicion itching her soul. She walked to the room's only table and chair, pulling the big family Bible into her lap. After a moment, Clyde crossed the room to sit at her feet, his head bowed. He felt his mother's fingers combing through his hair and heard her say, "Do us need to pray, baby boy?"

"Yes, ma'm." He swallowed hard. "I sorry, Mama. I couldn't stops myself."

Fannie stilled her hand. She'd sensed it like she always did. "Tell me what kind of woman she be? Was she one like the Lord be showing you. One like might try to spoil you?"

He nodded at the look of smug satisfaction on Fannie's face as he spun his tale for her, concealing his new truth. He felt the warm tingle of Mae's presence gliding through him, holding the darkness at bay. He kept his head down where his mother would not see the slight smile curving his lips.

Clyde stomped toward the glen where he and Mae had met, cursing himself for a fool. He had returned to the woods every day, only to find it empty of everything except the remnants of her presence, flitting through the breeze like fireflies. He'd gone every day, filled with an uncommon hope, followed by the devastating descent into disappointment when she wasn't there. On those days, the darkness mocked him for believing she had any interest in him. It thirsted to be released, manifesting itself in a hunger that left scores of dead animals scattered in the woods and a restless desire to visit the juke. The darkness told him she was a Jezebel like the rest.

Until today. Today, he'd found her sitting, a look of melancholy on her face replaced by a look of pleasant surprise as he stepped into her line of vision.

"Why, Clyde Henry, what you doing back here?" she asked, flashing her dimples.

"Walking." He glanced down at his knuckles, searching for traces of blood. Finding none, he shifted uncertainly from foot to foot while she stared up at him. She patted the ground next to her and smiled, her face radiant in the smattering of sunlight coming through the leaves overhead.

"I ain't been able to get back here for these past few days, but I was hoping you might come back. I was thinking I might have said something wrong the last time."

He dropped down next to her, aware of the heavy sound of his body hitting the ground, watching her from the corner of his eye. She looked tired, her eyes drooping despite her smile, her skin sagging on her frame.

"Why you look so tired?" he barked.

Mae rubbed at her face, suddenly self-conscious, folding her legs beneath her dress. "Verna, them babies, and washing all them clothes done wore me out, I guess," she exhaled noisily. "I swear it seem like she done got lazier since Papa make me quit school."

Clyde felt the darkness surge, the palms of his hands itching for Verna's throat. He looked away as Mae laughed lightly, a sound that imitated humor where there wasn't any.

"She ought not be doing you like that," he demanded, his hands curling in his lap. Mae's slender fingertips stroked the tops of his hands, soothing him. "It all right," she whispered.

"It ain't neither," he protested, feeling the darkness retreat at her touch, just as it had done before. Inside his mind, the dark slithered around in turmoil, fighting to loose itself from the tether that suddenly bound it. He pushed it back easily, controlling it.

His thick brows drew together with his thoughts. "How you do that?"

"Do what?" Mae asked, still stroking his hand, perplexed by his expression.

Clyde lifted her hand to his face, holding it there, trembling with pleasure. Mae stroked his cheek, moved by his response to her distress.

"I thanks you for caring, Clyde. But it do be all right. Don't none of us gets what we want. We just gets what is," she said, gently extricating her hand from his.

Reaching around her other side, she pulled a small basket onto her lap. Lifting the cloth that covered it, she rambled through the contents. "If I had knowed you was gon' be here, I would have brought more to eat. You looks like you can put away food real good."

Clyde stared at her outstretched hand and the ham sandwich it held. His mouth salivated as the smell of the thick bread and meat wafted on the wind. He took it, tore it in half, and handed the other portion back to her, happy when she smiled, dimpling both cheeks again.

"Don't mind if I do," Mae said, opening her mouth wide and taking a huge bite, chewing with obvious pleasure. He watched, biting into his own half.

"You eat good too," he observed.

Mae fell back, laughing loudly, her hand waving through the air in front of her, her heels drumming the ground. "Yeah, I do. My muhdeah say she don't know where I puts it all."

They sat in companionable silence, finishing every morsel of food in the basket. Mae leaned against him, rubbing her stomach contentedly, then sighed.

"I guess I best be getting on back home. My work be piling up while I'm sitting out here." She got to her knees, first gathering her basket, then standing. "Maybe us can meet here again tomorrow, and this time, I brings enough for both us."

He wanted desperately to hold her to him, keep her from leaving. The darkness rallied; it could keep her.

Mae smiled at him, light radiating around her, an aura framing her against the sun. She touched his cheek one last time, then turned. He shook his head violently, dispelling the darkness. Standing, he walked home, his dark thoughts trailing him.

Reaching home, Clyde pumped the sink handle vigorously, metal grinding against metal, the water pulled up from the well beneath it, filling the basin. He scrubbed his hands and rinsed away the remaining soap before wiping them on the clean rag hanging from the peg on the wall, wary as before that Mae's smell clung to his hands. Fannie would sniff it on him like a hound. He could feel her suspicions crawling up his back and doubted his ability to deceive her again.

"Your supper be just about cold," she scolded, slamming his plate on the tabletop.

"I ain't hungry noway," Clyde mumbled, trying to move past her.

"What you mean you ain't hungry? You ain't ate since this morning." Fannie's questions pulled him into a trap, stripping the joy from the afternoon.

"I done ate a bunch of apples I finds," he responded quickly, latching onto the first plausible memory he could pull from their past. He fixed his features, willing them to reflect discomfort, rubbed his stomach, and bent forward, prepared to risk Fannie's wrath if his deception failed.

"Boy, what I done told you?" she cried. Her skepticism vanished, replaced instantly by worry. "Now you done gone and made yourself sick." Rushing closer, she placed the back of her hand against his forehead, fretting out loud. "Gets me the castor oil."

Clyde groaned, already feeling the oil coating his tongue and mouth, knowing he would be belching the foul taste for the remainder of the day. He moved to the small shelf holding a few brown bottles and chose the one she requested. Returning to where Fannie sat holding a large tablespoon, he leaned down and let her dose him.

"You go on and lie down. Let that oil works you. You be better by tomorrow."

Clyde nodded and went over to lie in their double bed. After a while, he felt the other side of the bed sink and Fannie's back pressed against his.

He remembered how it felt when Mae had leaned against him and pulled his body away from his mother, suddenly uncomfortable, clinging to the edge of the mattress. Listening to the sound of her snoring, he followed the threads of his thoughts as they led him away from her. The dark snarled and fought in his head, waiting to invade his dreams.

The glen was familiar. If he breathed in deeply, he smelled Mae again . . . lavender, vanilla, and a light musky scent unique to her. He lifted his head from his knees, eyes searching, hungering for her presence. He was sure he could push back the encroaching darkness if she were there.

Fear invaded him, robbing him of his newfound strength. The dark wanted to hurt her, pull the light from her, and ravage her body. He heard himself whimper out loud. He had to keep her safe. She made him stronger. Better. He felt the darkness tremble as he thought of her and smiled.

He felt a nimbus of light around him, growing as he recalled her gentle touch and how she listened to him. There was no fear in his remembrance, no loathing. He lowered his head back to his knees. The darkness could not reach him here. He and Mae were safe.

CHAPTER THREE

Fannie seethed, concealed deep within a cocoon of bush plants, the images of Clyde and that girl seared into her brain, paralyzing her where she stood. Her mind replayed how the girl's hands touched and stroked his face, arms, and hands, and fluttered over his chest, drawing sighs and moans from him.

Her mind struggled to reconcile what she saw and heard. Her Clyde, her precious baby boy. Her chest heaved, and dark spots danced before her eyes. When had her vigilance dropped? Why hadn't she come sooner, followed him, demanded more from him when she saw his sudden moodiness or the way he'd begun to snarl his answers to the few questions she asked?

Clyde stood, helping the girl to her feet, brushing grass and leaves from her skirt before leaning in to kiss her cheek, then turning to walk away. She waited until the sound of him moving away on the path faded, then turned to walk in the opposite direction. Silently, she followed the girl.

Mae stopped outside a small house with a sagging porch and steps that bowed in under the weight of the woman sitting on them. Beneath her dress, her legs spread wide, forming a concave tent over her legs. After a moment, Mae's face broke into a grin, and she ran forward, nearly bowling the woman over as she hugged her.

"Muhdeah, what you doing here?" Mae asked, dancing back and allowing her grandmother to stand and hold her at arm's length.

"I done come to see about my gal's only child and this boy who been courting you."

Before Mae could say a word, a piercing howl split the air, startling them into silence as a woman came hurtling toward them, her teeth bared, her hands hooked like talons.

"HARLOT!" she screamed as Mae's grandmother pulled her behind her back, standing to her full height and slamming a stiff arm into the rampaging woman's chest to stop her. Fannie halted, rocking back on her heels, and glared at Mae's grandmother.

Mae peered around her grandmother Lula's broad back, staring at the small nut-brown woman reaching for her, clawing the air, trying to come around her. The snow-white rag wound tightly around her head now hung loose over her braids.

Lula pushed Fannie backward farther, using her height and body to keep her away from Mae, and then shoved her to the ground. She knelt and placed a knee on the thrashing wild woman. She raised one large, meaty arm to wipe the sweat from her brow and looked down at the woman's face, twisted in anger.

"Woman, who the hell you?"

"She done spoilt him!" Fannie screamed. "She done spoilt my boy. How he gon' do God's work now?" Tears rolled down Fannie's cheeks as she bucked against the weight of the woman holding her in place.

"You must be Clyde's mama." Mae rolled her eyes heavenward, complete understanding illuminating her heart.

"You needs to calm yourself some," Lula ordered, her tone ringing with authority. "Well, is that who you is?"

"She Miss Fannie Henry, Muhdeah," Mae interjected. "Her boy Clyde the one what been courting me. She his mama."

"You done ruined my boy," Fannie hissed, her voice ragged as she labored to breathe.

Lula laughed out loud, her head thrown back, her jowls shaking with humor. "Gal, that ain't no boy. He a full-grown man."

"He still a boy!" Fannie snapped. "And he pure. This little whore trying to ruins him. I smell the stink of sin on her."

Lula's face hardened, any humor evaporating as she leaned forward, close enough that Fannie could smell fresh spearmint on her breath. Her eyes narrowed.

"I think you best watch your mouth when you talking about my granddaughter. Now, her daddy ain't worth shit, and that dumbass gal he done took for a wife worth less, but Mae, she sure enough special to me."

"I know what you is, Lula, and know she using juju on my boy."

Lula eased up, incredibly agile for a woman of her size, pulling the smaller Fannie up to her feet as she did so. "You ain't had no trouble with what I is when you was getting salve for that boy's legs."

She stared hard at Fannie, who cast her eyes to the ground, mumbling incoherently. Lula twisted her lips in disgust. Fannie was like all of them, wanting you to help and save them, asking for salves and potions, approaching your back door in the dark of night while disparaging you during the day. She hadn't known her name then, she was just another phantom customer in the shadows.

Lula continued. "I done seen Clyde in town since he got growed. He ain't much to look at, but he work hard, and far as I can tell, he loves Mae."

"He don't knows nothing about no love. She been sexing him for sure." Fannie spat in the dirt in front of them.

Lula raised one hamlike fist, bringing it back for the blow, itching to knock sense into Fannie. She only stopped when Mae touched her arm.

"You ain't gots to hit her, Muhdeah. Me and Clyde ain't done nothing wrong except maybe some little petting in the woods. We ain't been together like that."

"I think you best be getting off this place, Miss Fannie. Your son a grown man and old enough to see who he please." She stopped and let the heat of her anger traverse the space between them. "And if I hears you done bothered my granddaughter again, you won't have to come looking for her *or* me. I'm gon' *find* you."

Fannie nodded absently, feeling her muscles relax as she sagged, ignoring Lula's threat. She wasn't too late. She hadn't failed. She could still save her boy. She turned away from the two women, her step lighter as she returned to the woods and the path leading her home.

Mae shook her head and hooked her arm through her grandmother's as they watched Fannie walk away.

"I hopes you know what you getting into. That woman sure enough trouble," Lula said, squeezing her granddaughter to her side. "You ain't gon' let that tender heart of yours lead you into trouble, is you?"

Mae gave her a lopsided grin, hugged her tightly, then answered, "I won't, Muhdeah."

Lula kissed the top of her head, then stared at the figure retreating into the woods. She shivered as a shadow passed over Mae's face.

Fannie strode through the woods, unaware of anything around her. The need to get to Clyde pushed her faster and faster through the trees until she finally saw their shack in the distance. She stopped, attempting to pull the threads of her thoughts together as fear shredded them. She turned her face to the sky, praying aloud, "*Lord, we done kept baby boy safe these long years. Be a fence around him, Lord. Don't let him fall to the temptation of this Jezebel spirit.*" She continued to pray the words as her steps resumed, taking flight through the grass, the spirit of salvation aflame in her breast.

Opening the door, she found Clyde perched in the corner on his stool. Over the years, his legs had grown long enough to reach the ground when he sat, and he tapped his foot nervously against the hard-packed earthen floor, waiting for Fannie to run out of words and tears.

"Baby boy, you ain't thinking right. She done puts you under a spell," she pleaded, her hands unconsciously kneading her breasts, producing blotches of milk to stain the front. "I hear tell her grandmother deal in juju," Fannie said, moving closer to him and forcing him to look at her. Reaching out, she grasped his chin. Clyde looked away, turning his eyes to the floor.

"Mae a good girl," was all he would say.

Fannie eyed the strap hanging on its hook, looking from it to Clyde. His eyes grew dark, the lids lowering as he followed the direction of her stare. The darkness rose within him, and he growled deep in his chest.

Fannie recoiled, her hand dropping to her side, her voice wheedling. "If you just don't sees her no more, everything be fine. We be like we was before."

Clyde said nothing, tamping down the darkness, squeezing it into a place where it could do no harm. Slowly, he stood up, making his way to bed, thinking of meeting Mae in their special place tomorrow. Behind him, he heard his mother dropping to the earth. When he chanced to look back, she lay prostrate on the floor, praying to her God that he deliver Clyde's soul from damnation.

Mae sat between Clyde's spread legs, feeling his body hard against her back, the throbbing of his manhood pulsing against her buttocks, the cloth of her dress the only barrier between them, his breath hot on the top of her head. The last two months had flown by, marked by clandestine meetings in the woods, wrapped in his comfort, love, and protection. She'd felt the temptation growing steadily between them.

"You still wants to be married with me, Clyde?" she asked, her voice whispery with heat, the juncture between her thighs wet and moist. She wiggled against him, listening to him groan. She smiled, safe in his embrace, feeling both desired and loved, wondering how a man as immense and powerful as he was could be so gentle and kind. The scowl he wore looking out on the world fell away whenever he looked at her. A pale blue dress and matching shoes lay on the blanket beside them, his latest gift to her. She released her hold on one arm to run her hand over the soft fabric of the dress.

"You knows I do." His voice was heavy with the lust flowing through him, obliterating the darkness, leaving only Mae. He pulled her arm back, resting her hand on his forearm, rubbing his face in her hair. He shifted, squirming away from the feel of her round, firm behind against him. He prayed she would sit still, unsure he could resist having her right here, right now.

The darkness whispered, urging him toward the wicked disobedience that would soil her, mimicking the sound of his mother's voice. He pushed the dark away and stood hastily, grabbing at the small suitcase sitting beside her on the grass.

"I got my daddy's truck so we can gets to the justice of the peace," he called back over his shoulder. "You gets changed, and I wait for you."

Mae stepped behind a thick grove of bushes, trusting Clyde not to peek at her as she pulled the worn calico she had arrived in over her head. Sliding the smooth silk of her new dress over her slim form, she relished its coolness. She stepped into the shoes, then picked up her old things, tucking them under her arm.

Mae made her way to the road where the truck was hidden in the trees. She looked around, searching for her father or, worse yet, Fannie, to leap out of the woods, determined to stop them. Clyde sat behind the wheel of the truck, leaning over to open the passenger door and helping her inside.

"Is you scared?" she asked, not for the first time.

Clyde shook his head. He didn't know fear when he was with Mae. Not the darkness, not his mother. He was sure of her. Since they'd been together, he hadn't been to a juke, hadn't wanted to be there, or felt the desire to release the darkness. Even now, he could hold it in place when the dark clawed relentlessly at him.

He wouldn't let the darkness blind him. Every day, his mother chipped at him, grinding against him, wearing him down. But each time, Mae renewed him, and his resentment against Fannie grew incrementally as she tried to divide him from Mae. She pretended she didn't know women like Mae existed, berating her and filling his ears with judgment. "*Mae a bad woman, full of sin. She the same as the ones God done sent you to purge from this world; she full of darkness.*"

Today, it would all be fixed, he thought. "We gon' gets married," he said aloud over the sound of the engine roaring to life and the persistent voice of his mother burrowed deep in his subconscious. "We ain't gon' sin."

Three hours later, Mae stood in the living room of her family's house for the last time, running her hand over the skirt of her dress, gripping a small bouquet close to her chest. It had been a moving little ceremony, standing before the preacher, speaking the words that bound her to Clyde. Verna's eyes surveyed her outfit, then moved on to Clyde, sniffing contemptuously.

Mae smiled inwardly. She didn't care. She was free. Clyde stood beside her, clasping her free hand, his brooding gaze fixed on her father and a red-faced Verna. Her father cleared his throat and looked at the paper she had handed him when they entered, the one declaring that she and Clyde were legally wed.

"I guess it ain't nothing can be done about it now," Ben declared, his eyes roaming over the print on the page, recognizing it as a marriage license. He shoved it abruptly back at Mae, who folded it and pushed it back into her purse.

"Ain't that your mama's handbag?"

"Yes, sir, it is." She clutched the handbag more tightly under her arm. "She left it for me, and no, sir, ain't nothing to be done," Mae said quietly, the regret in his eyes touching her heart. "And I be sorry, but I be legal age to marry. Clyde done ask me, and I say yes."

Ben surveyed his new son-in-law, taking in the bow of his legs, the barrel chest, and the heavily muscled arms. Clyde glowered at him, his anger flaring. Ben swallowed, refusing to be cowed, and spoke, "I done raised her once. If you don't like the job I done did, you sends her on back home. Don't put your hands on her."

"Like you did?" Clyde asked, pulling Mae closer before turning her toward the door. "She be my wife now, and I takes care of her."

Rebuttal hitched in Ben's throat, stunned by what Clyde said. His face colored, and he glared at Mae, swallowing his humiliation, wishing for a drink. Without looking, he could feel Verna bristling next to him.

"Don't you lets him talk to you like that in your own house!" Verna screeched. "She probably pregnant anyway," she seethed, poking her own enormous belly forward. "I bet you done let that thing knock you up. Ain't no other reason anybody marry you, even him!" Mae flinched, the insult falling on her and Clyde.

Beside her, Clyde roared, and Mae felt him go rigid, his eyes clouding with darkness as he turned toward Verna. Ben leaped between them, shielding Verna.

Mae yanked hard on Clyde's arm, suddenly fearing the violence etched on his face. Reaching up, she turned his face toward her, stroked his cheek, and whispered his name, tears pooling in her eyes. "Clyde, she ain't worth it, honey, she ain't worth it," she whispered, desperate to get his attention, straining with the effort to hold him. Clyde saw the wisps of darkness floating around Ben and Verna, some thick strands and some barely visible.

He heard Mae's voice penetrating the darkness from a distance, calling to him. His breathing slowed, the murderous rage beginning to recede. Feeling him relax, Mae moved them toward the door, letting it close behind her, refusing to give Verna the satisfaction of looking back at her.

She took a deep breath as they stepped off the porch and walked to the dusty road dividing the dilapidated shotgun shacks into two parallel lines. At the intersection of the next alley, they turned right, making their way out of town to Fannie's house. They passed an empty rental on their right, and she looked at it longingly. "Soon," she kept repeating the mantra to herself. But first, they would have to face Fannie.

Mae squeezed her hands over her ears, trying to block the venom filling the room as Fannie flew back and forth, raging first at her and then at Clyde, who stood, his head bent to his chest under the onslaught.

"That little bitch gon' be the end of you, Clyde." Fannie's voice was a high-pitched scream. Her nostrils flared wide, and sweat glistened on her forehead, her voice blistering in Mae's ears and making her heart thump erratically.

Her eyes shot daggers at Mae, then pinned Clyde. "You cain't see what she doing with her smell all up in your nose. Ever since that little whore done spread her legs, you ain't been able to think straight."

Clyde let her words hang between them before slicing into his heart, staggering him under their weight. He looked down into Fannie's furious eyes, his own pleading.

"Mae's uncle done found us a place here in Delhi and put in a word for me to get a good job when we gets to Chicago. Mae say—"

"Mae say, Mae say?" She cut into his words, her arms windmilling and waving as she spit curses. "Don't tell me nothing else that bitch say. She just trying to take you away from me." She howled the last words.

Clyde's head snapped up. His eyes clouded over again, narrowing as he leaned into his words.

"Don't you say nothing else bad about Mae, Mama," he hissed, teeth clenched as resentment rose, rendering him full to bursting with his mother's poison. He growled low in his throat, his hand raised, poised above her. "You shut your mouth right now."

Fannie's eyes rounded as she saw his fist begin to descend. Inhaling, she shrieked her alarm, staring into the perfect replication of his father's eyes, darkness writhing in their depths. She saw the hatred there, felt the fear breeching the chasm of time to paralyze her heart.

Clyde felt his rage growing, the darkness leaking black tears down his cheeks, his mother wavering in his vision. He lowered his fists and ground them against his thighs, his muscles bulging with the strain of his desire to pummel her and smash her words back down her throat. He saw himself, his hands tight around her throat.

"What you gon' do?" she shouted, backpedaling away from him, her hands flying up to her throat. "You gon' hit me? You gon' hit your own mama?"

Her words had become ragged. Her throat constricted as though invisible hands wrapped around it, choking the life from her. "Look what she done did! Look what you doing to me." Fannie rasped the words from her constricted airway, struggling to get them free. "Me what birthed you and done protected you all your days." The words trailed into a choked silence.

Mae cringed, lost in the battle between them. She crept closer to the door and then fled through it to stand on the porch, feeling like a coward. The blistering hatred flowing between them smothered her. She would wait here for Clyde.

Inside, Clyde recoiled, a flash of Fannie's memories telegraphing to him from her fading thoughts. He saw her sprawled and torn on the ground, a behemoth of a man crouched between her thighs—his buttocks clenching—and pounding into her body. The man had Clyde's face, stretched over smooth skin, and Clyde's body, with long, muscular legs attached to a powerful frame. He twisted his head until he could look over his shoulder and fixed his eyes on Clyde's, staring at him.

The phantom hands released Fannie's throat, allowing her to crumple to the ground. He shook his head violently to rid himself of the vision as Fannie pushed up to her knees, dragging in the air and crawling after Clyde's retreating figure.

"You gots to listen to me," she screeched at his back.

Clyde swayed toward the door, his head down, seething with the darkness surging around him that still demanded he silence her vitriol. He had to get to Mae.

"Don't goes with her. You knows I be the only one what care about you, Clyde. Just me," Fannie wept, her chest heaving and her hands reaching out almost close enough to grab at him.

"God give you to me and that damned Jezebel done spelled you." She was howling now, holding the back of his pants leg, her arms already aching with the emptiness of his leaving.

"Please, Clyde," she cried, sinking back to her knees, her hands grabbing her breasts and wringing the flesh. Her mouth twisted as she desperately tried to form the words to save him. "Sweet Jesus, you just like him. You be him." Her voice floated to him, a dejected whisper of defeat.

Clyde stopped, turned, and stared down into her upturned face, shuddering as those alien images floated through the darkness across their mental connection. He felt himself merging into the dark, swirling depth of the man's eyes, twisting and tangling until his spirit joined the violence against his mother, and it became his own memory, pounding flesh until bone broke.

Clyde's hands tore at his hair, pulling until it threatened to free itself from his scalp, and his voice climbed to the ceiling on the edge of hysteria. He dropped his hands to his face, his fingers clawed at his eyes, trying to snatch out the offending scene. "I sees him, Mama. Who he be?" He wept.

"Him?" Fannie sucked in her breath, narrowing her eyes at the shared memory, then spit the words at him. "He your real daddy. He the murdering sonofabitch what made you." Snot dripped from her nose and gathered on her top lip, mingling with her tears while the memories played themselves uninterrupted. "Bastard damn near killed me. He the one what made you, but I be the one what saved you—me!" Fannie's eyes rolled wildly. "First, God saved me from him, using that old witch what tried to kill you. I saved you from her too."

Fannie spit on the floor. "I put away my ownself's peoples for you, and all those nasty-ass peoples in Rayville. God done give you special to me!" Fannie's hand slammed against her chest, the sharp sound of flesh against flesh reinforcing her words.

She collapsed back to the floor, folding her body into her voluminous skirts and shaking with the force of her cries. "She don't love you no more than he loved me." Her words spiraled down to a whisper. "She done spoilt you, and now, you just like him." She sobbed.

Clyde's heart lurched, thudded, and shrank within his chest, watching the wreckage of his mother puddled on the floor. Fannie trembled, both hands reaching for her stomach, clutching at it and rocking over the hollow emptiness that filled her. Her head snapped backward, yanked on an invisible cord, pain jolting through her brain as she felt the connection between them snap, the wire severed and dangling in a black hole.

"Get on out and take that skanky-ass whore who done cursed you," she howled. "Go your ass to Chicago. You deserves what waiting for you!" Fannie's head dropped, her chin resting on her chest, her breathing becoming shallow.

Outside on the porch, Clyde stumbled toward Mae, his arms outstretched, screaming. Mae rushed to him, pulling his head down toward her as his hands clutched his head, pain ravaging his skull, the darkness filling him. Dropping to his knees, he felt the warmth of her hands, stroking. He saw the glow beneath her skin, growing brighter, and felt the darkness leaking from every orifice. Bending his spine backward until his head almost touched the floor, he strained until he felt the cord of darkness snap.

Finally, he slumped against Mae, his weight pulling them both to the porch floor. She held him against her chest, rocking him, whispering his name, stroking his cheeks, worried that he'd had a fit. Could she have married him and lost him on the same day? Was life that wicked to take happiness from her at every turn? From inside the house, she could still hear Fannie's broken sobs.

Clyde slammed the darkness behind the door of his mind, shutting it away, drawing strength from Mae. He stared through the screen door at Fannie and searched his feelings for her, reaching for his power and finding nothing. The space she and the darkness had always held in his mind was empty, a void. He was alone with Mae.

"It be all right," he said, climbing to his feet and pulling Mae up. Her eyes searched his, her mouth trembling. He placed one hand on the small of her back and guided her toward the steps.

Fannie's cries were a hard rain pounding against his back, dwindling to periodic silence as he and Mae walked away from her. His gaze fixed forward as they returned to the road to the rental where their new life would begin. Everything he had believed about being special remained behind him in the wreckage, with his mother groveling on the floor. One final wail pierced the air, and then . . . stillness.

PART THREE
1955

CHAPTER ONE

Cora raised her hand to shield her eyes, squinting into the waning light of the evening sun. The blue sky had faded to shades of orange and yellow tinged with pink, heralding the coming of night. In the distance, Gal's slender frame was silhouetted against the changing light, growing larger as she strode toward the house, limbs gangly and awkward as they had been since the first day she had come to care for Cora twelve years ago. She waved wildly in Cora's direction and sped up.

"Hey, Miss Cora, how you this evening? Your legs feeling some better?"

Cora tried to smile, the right side of her mouth drooping downward as only the left side moved, making her words come out slow and mangled.

"Some," she managed, then looked up at Gal standing in the dirt yard beneath the porch and shrugged her good shoulder. Gal stepped back, not pushing for further conversation.

Aggravation ground against her spirit as Cora's thoughts fired rapidly, stalling between her broken brain and mouth. She watched Gal take the two steps in one, even move and come up behind her wheelchair. She straightened the heavy shawl around Cora's shoulders to fight the chill that permeated her body, checked to ensure both of Cora's feet were secure on the footrests, removed the brake, and spun her around to take her into the house.

Cora leaned forward, her eyes darting quickly around the room, checking for the wisps of floating spirits. Exhaling softly, she realized that only the living inhabited the space for the moment. Realizing that Gal had been talking almost nonstop for a few minutes, she cocked her head to the side and began to listen. She raised her eyebrow to indicate that Gal needed to start again.

"You ain't never gon' guess who I done seen back up in Rayville, Miss Cora." She waited for a breath, then answered herself. "Miss Fannie, you know the one what had that little boy everybody used to talk about some years back?"

Cora's left eye bulged, and her bent forelimb, resting on the arm of the wheelchair, jerked. Her hand flew up to cover her heart, and her mouth formed a startled half circle. Gal continued talking, oblivious to her distress.

"Yes, ma'm, there her was, strutting down Main like she ain't never left here. I wonder where she been at. You know, I always was thinking that boy of hers had something to do with them dogs being let loose on Miss Baby Doll even if cain't nobody proves it." She stopped and stared into the air in front of her. "And I bet all I got he had something to do with that woman what stabbed Miss Baby Doll."

Cora flinched. It had never occurred to her that Gal had any insight into her mistress's death. But then, she had never asked her. She alone knew the truth that Gal seemed to have intuited for herself. Cora searched the ceiling, waiting for Baby Doll to appear, then shuddering in relief when she did not.

"Anyway, Miss Hattie in the general store say she back up in that same old shack she used to live in. I wonder what make her come back here. God know if I ever gets out of here, I ain't never coming back." She laughed and pushed Cora's chair to its usual spot near the window, facing into the room.

Gal turned on the radio, moving the knob back and forth until she found a strong signal broadcasting her favorite soap opera. She smiled at Cora and clapped her hands in delight.

"Ma Perkins coming on. I loves her. Don't you, Miss Cora?" Gal giggled, dropping down on the sofa across from Cora, her conversation about Fannie forgotten, evaporating as she lost herself in the daytime drama. "She always know just what to do."

Cora grunted, her dismissal of Ma Perkins's homespun wisdom lost in the garbled tangle of her tongue. She felt shivers running through her body, jangling her nerves and making her good leg and hand tremble simultaneously with enough force to shake the Afghan free of her shoulders. She stared down at it, wondering if Gal would notice.

A flicker of light in the corner nearest the door caught her attention, and she began to moan, drool dripping from her open mouth. She wished desperately she could rise from this wretched chair and confront what was coming on her own two feet, standing tall and strong.

The light resolved itself into shapes and sounds. More than thirty women now flitted in and out of the room, wailing, moaning, and screaming out their rage and despair. They were the steady stream of tragedy that had stained her days and nights until they had abruptly ceased a year ago. Now, they arrayed themselves around her again, eyes staring accusingly and boring into her.

Cora felt her heart race, slamming against her ribs, and she groaned again. So much time had passed since some new lost soul drifted in—time when she had continued to do her penance for her failure, her mind trapped in the remnants of this shattered body. Time that she allowed herself to believe that something had stopped Clyde, praying desperately that death had claimed his darkened soul.

Then last night, she had seen him in her dreams again. Her disembodied form floated, reminding her of the out-of-body experiences that had plagued her for as long as she could recall. In the beginning, they had frightened her, feeling like death, until Mi had explained them. She said they allowed her spirit to travel. Anchored in this body, she welcomed them as she felt her limbs become firm and powerful, functioning as they had before she was caught in this hellishness between existences.

She felt herself drifting down in a familiar clearing, her eyes adjusting to the murky twilight around her. A tingle ran down her spine as she felt the toes of her bare feet dig into the soil, her body solidifying further. She extended her hands upward over her head and stretched, a smile blossoming on her face. Inhaling, she breathed in the scent of the woods around her and listened to the sounds of birds and insects swirling in the air.

Breathing in deeply, she stopped, a new scent assaulting her nostrils. She followed it, and it became stronger, leading her forward. It was him ... Clyde, slowly moving as he stalked through the woods. His arms filled with the burden of the body he carried, the head and arms hanging toward the ground, the lifeless eyes staring upward. She noticed that his legs had grown stronger and straighter, if not longer.

She watched him. His body stiffened, and he glanced backward over his shoulder, cringing at the aura of light that hid her from him. After a moment, he proceeded forward again, whistling. Studying his aura and how he moved, Cora realized she was not seeing the present but a shadow of Clyde's past playing in a dark loop.

As her spirit rose, separating her from her form, a thrill ran through her. This time, she saw Clyde huddled in the long grass again, his body hugging itself the way it had when he was young. But now, a bright aura surrounded him, encapsulating him and the darkness. He sat, unaware of her presence. She felt the light returning to her. They were small increments, and for the time being, she remained helpless, unable to do anything but observe him.

Cora fell back against her chair and pounded her closed fist on the arm of the wheelchair. No, he wasn't dead, and whatever had caused him to cease killing and give them a respite was over. For the first time in a year, she felt Clyde stirring. The darkness was gathering in him again. She would meet it. She would not let it win.

CHAPTER TWO

The first rays of the sun slid over Ruby's body, cocooned beneath the crisp white cotton sheet of her bed. One parchment-colored hand pushed the sheet down to reveal the mint-green peignoir she wore. Her fingers smoothed the material over her full breasts, her nipples tightening as memories flitted through her mind of her husband, Amos, and how he used to stroke them each morning. Sighing, her hand dropped to the empty pillow beside her, sorrow washing through her body.

She should have been accustomed to it by now. Hell, Amos had spent more nights out of their bed than he had in it during the last years of their marriage. Still, this aching emptiness was different from what she'd experienced then, the ones tinged with a dark anger as she imagined him out tomcatting in the street. Discernment was not her friend. She would swallow her emotions and say nothing, letting the darkness be her companion. Now, the memories of him swam around her, darkening her hours and days and tinting the world gray.

She remembered lying in their double bed, afraid any movement might conceal the sound of his return, wishing and waiting to hear his footsteps sliding quietly across the room, trying not to wake her. When he finally arrived, smelling of bourbon, the scent of another woman's perfumed body lingered on his skin. Still, it was preferable to this never-ending loneliness that pervaded her days and nights. He had left her nothing but this darkness.

Rolling onto her back, she scooted to the edge of the bed, dropping her legs over the side and staring down at them as she eased her feet into her waiting slippers. His spirit was all around her today, filling her thoughts and the room with his absence. She let *Good Amos's* voice tickle the back of her mind, teasing, *Gal, them there ain't legs. They's baseball bats. See, they big at the top and skinny at the bottom.*

She pressed her middle two fingers to her lips, then moved them away, placing them on her husband's face in the photograph on the bedside table. For a moment, the image disappeared, turning completely black, forcing her to blink and bring it back into focus. When she looked again, the picture had righted itself. She saw his hat tilted at a rakish angle, his smile broad, and his eyes glinting with the mischief that always seemed to linger there.

In the picture, he was frozen in time, where he would always be her *good man*. When she resurrected him, her mind selectively eradicated the imperfections of the man she had buried a year ago. Pushing away the pervasive darkness that made day and night seem the same, she wrapped her thoughts with the solid cloth of denial she had built around her memories. She found herself rocking on the edge of the bed, her hands cradled in her lap, determined to push back any truth that would not align with her new reality.

The pain and the darkness felt strong today. Sometimes, she swore it lurked in the corners of the room, remnants of his passing that refused to relinquish his hold in this world, too stubborn to let her go, even in death. It tore and devastated her like it had the morning she awakened to find him cold and stiff beside her. The breath of life had fled his body during the night. That same day, he had become perfect.

Shaking herself free of her reverie—choosing to ignore the premonitions channeling their way into her mind—Ruby stood, found her balance, and shuffled toward the dressing table, her walk far older than her actual age. It was silly, she knew, to still dress herself as though her *good Amos* was waiting for her to join him in their bed or assessing her appearance each day. Averting her eyes from the mirror, she conveniently forgot his constant derision, his hands pummeling her when she failed again to meet his expectations, beating her for who she was not. She cast a critical eye at her reflection, noting that the peignoir showed signs of repeated wear and washings; how the translucent material revealed the sag of her breasts and stomach, which were no longer tight and supple. She twisted her mouth in disapproval, hating what she saw.

She poured water from the blue-flowered porcelain pitcher into the matching basin and began to wash her face and body. The tepid water shocked her into full wakefulness. Then she went to the closet to search for clothing for the day, her eyes searching for something that conveyed the authority of her position as the building manager. Her spirit lifted momentarily, and she preened at the title.

It had been Amos's job before he died, leaving her with no way to support herself. But her mama didn't raise no fools, and she knew she was the one who had been taking care of things all along, Amos being either drunk or hungover most days. She had harangued and nagged Mr. Elliott, the building owner, until he had reluctantly allowed her to maintain the title.

Once she'd proven herself by working hard—showed her capabilities of taking care of anything that came up in the building and accepted a lower wage for doing so—he had bragged as though the choice had been his all along.

Those years of dragging along behind her father from sunup to sundown, fixing up sharecropper's shacks in Louisiana, had proven an unexpected benefit. What she couldn't repair herself, she used a network of her husband's old friends to do, letting her body ply them with hints of favors that would never come to pass, dangled just close enough to keep them coming back.

Sitting at her dressing table, Ruby pulled the cinnamon-red stockings up her leg, rolling the tops down and knotting them at the knee to keep them from falling. She stood and smoothed her dress down over her narrow hips, making sure the hem covered her stocking tops, then slipped on her pumps.

Seating herself again before the mirror, she began working her straight black hair into a tight bun, ignoring the silver-gray strands that wove themselves across her scalp. Her mother's face stared back at her, and she wondered when she had become this old when her youth had fled, and how she had ended up here, alone. Her hand brushed across her lap, and the soft paunch of her stomach held the memory of the child that should have swollen within. Barren as a desert, she thought. Amos had made sure of that: empty womb, empty heart, empty life. Regret added itself to the sorrow in her eyes.

She grabbed the small can of snuff from the table, pinching a little and placing it in the pouch between her lower gum and her bottom lip. Another small sigh escaped her, this one of satisfaction, as she crossed the room to make her rounds through the building.

Air rose inside Ruby, pushing from her lips, the melancholy from the early morning clinging to her as she stared through the dusty grit of the screen door leading to the outside porch of the rooming house. Weak sunlight, now obscured by clouds, could not penetrate it, leaving a dark, murky view of the trees outside. Random thoughts of Amos framed in darkness continued to skitter in and around her mind as she considered getting a pail of water to clean the screen. The dirt was a personal affront to the cleanliness and order she usually maintained. She turned, picked up her snuff can, and moved toward the storage closet, her thoughts and gaze drifting to the spotless rose-patterned carpet in the hallway, reaffirming why Mr. Elliott believed in her. She wouldn't let him down.

The sound of mingled voices floated up from the stairs outside, and she turned back to the screen, rubbing her open palm against the thin film of grit to get a better view. Mr. Elliott, the building owner, used one thick arm to pull his ponderous weight up the steps, the rail providing the extra leverage he required. His pale cheeks bellowed in and out, turning scarlet as he strained to reach the landing. Behind him, a diminutive, slender woman followed, sandwiched between Elliott and the hulking form of the man behind her. Her oval face, dark, almond-shaped eyes, and plump mouth seemed to glide toward Ruby, her body blocked by the two men.

Ruby shook her head to free it of the image of the woman's flawless features and spit a stream of snuff into the small coffee can she held in her right hand before lowering it to the floor and gently kicking it into the corner with the toe of her shoe. She arranged her expression into what she hoped was a pleasant smile and swung the screen door open, stepping back to allow Elliott and the couple to squeeze past her.

"Mr. Elliott, I wasn't expecting to see you today."

"Got some new tenants here, Ruby, so I brought them myself. This here is Clyde and Mae Henry from Louisiana by way of Mississippi." He nodded toward the couple and then back at her. "This is Ruby. She manages things for me. If you have any questions or need anything, you just go down and knock on her door," he said, looking over his glasses to peer first at Ruby and then down the hall as if searching for something amiss.

Ruby took that time to study the couple in front of her. The woman vibrated, seeming to glow with energy, a look of sheer happiness radiating from her as she bounced on her toes, reaching for her husband's massive hand. As she found it, Ruby noted the contrast between the slender pale appendage locked under the thick paw of the man beside her.

Mae looked down at their intertwined hands, her hair falling forward. Good hair, Ruby thought. Not out of a jar, but natural like her own. It was cut into a bob that framed her sharp features. She smiled at Ruby, deep dimples appearing on both cheeks, and Ruby found herself smiling back. Mae's free hand was extended out toward her.

"How's you, Ms. Ruby? I'm Mae, and this here is Clyde Henry, my husband. We so glad to meet you." Her honeyed voice poured over Ruby, warm and inviting, the direct opposite of the look of the man towering over her, who glared under brooding brows.

Ruby looked fully at Clyde while he was distracted by his wife, allowing herself to stare at him, withholding a shudder. Beneath an incongruous unruly mop of thick, black curls, a broad, sloped forehead shadowed a face that looked like it had been smashed by an immense pan, squashing his nose flat so that it spread across his face, his nostrils mere slits. His mouth stretched just as wide beneath his nose, his lips thick and wet with saliva.

His head rested on a short neck connected to broad, powerful shoulders, long, heavily muscled arms, and a barrel chest. Clyde's protruding eyes found hers, the whites yellow, the rims red, and the irises a piercing brown that penetrated bone and marrow.

He stared back, and Ruby felt her face collapse, her smile sliding downward, and her chin lowering, gravity pulling on her cheeks. Her lips quivered, endangering the snuff pocketed in her lower lip. Behind her back, she held out her right palm and folded her pinkie and ring finger in a symbol to ward off evil.

Hatefulness radiated from him, marking him with what her mother had called "ugly ways." Ruby felt that familiar feeling of darkness gathering, pulling from the very air around her. Wisps of it drifted, then rested above Clyde, morphing his features until he resembled Amos, finally disappearing and leaving traces of her dead husband to remain in his posture.

As she continued to stare, she saw a swirling darkness in the depths of Clyde's eyes as his hand grasped his wife's smaller one, pulling her protectively to his side. She thought it could have been love, but Ruby only saw his possession and ownership. She saw the *real* Amos in him.

Clyde grunted, and Ruby took a step backward. Suppressed memories fought to surface from the locked depths of her mind, memories of Amos when he was *not* a good man. Dead Amos continued to grin at her beneath Clyde's face.

Pulling away from Mae, his large hands dangled from the sleeves of the battered, faded cotton shirt he wore beneath his overalls. In them, she sensed the same subdued violence that had emanated from Amos, a darkness rushing below the surface. It would explode on those nights he came home late, lipstick smudges bright red on his shirt collar, breathing sour whiskey fumes over her just before his big, calloused hands slapped her for forcing him to leave that other woman's bed.

Mae moved closer to Clyde and pressed her hand tight against his cheek, stroking gently and smiling. Her eyes sparkled with affection, and Clyde's mouth lifted at the corners in a returning smile, transforming him for a moment, displaying straight white teeth. His muscles seemed to relax, and his left arm reached to encircle the tiny waist of his wife.

Looking over Mae's head, his smile dropped, his nostrils flaring as he inhaled deeply, his nose and mouth twisting when he scented an offensive odor emanating from Ruby. His eyes locked with hers.

Ruby felt herself trembling, her knees liquifying and threatening to collapse her to the floor. She turned back toward Mr. Elliott to break the contact, apprehension congealing in her stomach. An inexplicable dread rolled through her again for herself and for the girl.

Mr. Elliott cleared his throat and moved his omnipresent cigar to talk around it, bringing her back from her thoughts. "Rent's due on Monday of every week unless you're paying by the month. Then it's due on the first. I don't take no excuses. Your rent isn't paid, you're out. That's it."

"Won't be no problem. I works, and I takes care of my responsibilities," Clyde growled, looking up into the man's face, his own fixed in a rigid scowl. Mr. Elliott flinched, his eyes blinking rapidly behind his glasses.

Mae watched color rise in his cheeks as she dropped her hand from Clyde's face and pulled at his hand, still beaming at Mr. Elliott. "Don't mind Clyde Henry. He ain't nearly as mean as he seem. He just tired, that's all."

Clyde huffed and stared down at his wife. He hated it when she talked for him, making him feel like an imbecile. The urge to snatch his hand away and stalk back the way he'd come pushed to the front of his mind. She reached up again, the soft skin of her palms rubbing against his cheek, and he felt the anger deflate and recede as she stroked and stared into his eyes, soothing away the bad feelings.

"That's just Clyde's way," she said as she turned her full smile back to Mr. Elliott, hoping to ease the tension from the situation.

They might be in the North, but she knew Clyde had seriously overstepped his place.

"You don't need to worry none about us paying our rent. Clyde—he work on cars, and he work for the railroad. He a mechanic and can fix anything that got a motor. He make good money." She continued to stroke the side of Clyde's face as she spoke. "We understand the rules here, and we be sure to abide by all of them."

Clyde reached into the back of his overalls to pull a stained leather wallet from his pocket, and Ruby realized what had seemed so off-putting about his size. It was his legs. They seemed disproportionately short for his upper body, which was huge. Moving her eyes back to Mae, Ruby hoped they had not seen her staring. Clyde counted several bills carefully into Mr. Elliott's hand.

"That for the first month. We have your money every month on the first."

Mr. Elliott nodded, his aggravation forgotten as avarice danced in his eyes. He counted the cash twice before dropping the keys into Mae's open palm. Ruby tsked internally. The bastard was double charging them, twice as much rent as anybody else paid. She tucked that information away for a time it would become useful.

"Ruby, they have the room right next to yours. Why don't you show them the way?" he said, turning away from them, walking quickly toward the back door, and exiting the porch. He mumbled a hasty goodbye.

Ruby started moving down the hall and looked back over her shoulder to see Clyde shuffling in the same direction as Mr. Elliott, shadows swimming around his feet. Mae followed directly behind her.

"Our stuff downstairs on my uncle's truck," Clyde called back over his shoulder. "I'm gon' go down and get it while you opens up the room, Mae." He turned away without another backward glance, his hands shoved deeply into his pockets.

Clyde moved slowly, his feet barely lifting from the worn carpet covering the wooden treads of the hallway, his hands opening and closing into tight fists, and his breath filling his broad chest. The vision of Ruby's sour face swam before him, stoking his anger. Casting his gaze downward, he watched his feet. Toes turned in to point at one another as they did when his legs grew tired from overwork. From the corner of his eye, he caught movement and hesitated. He watched as an achingly familiar darkness slid from beneath Ruby's door, slithering his way and flowing into the shadows.

The darkness was here, and it wanted him. Clyde shuddered, quickening his steps. He'd felt the city's wickedness as they were driving in, the darkness visible to him everywhere. It blew in on a breeze through the open window as they drove in, coating his skin. Only the nearness of Mae, her hand resting on his thigh, chattering brightly, kept it at bay.

Forcing his legs to move faster—limping and loping, his shoulders touching the wall as he swayed with each step—he held his dread trapped behind his teeth. Banging through the back door, he hurried down the steps to his uncle's truck, leaning his head against the hot metal, breathing hard, and reliving that last nightmare scene with his mother. Her parting words rushed into his mind, bleeding into his present. "*Go your ass to Chicago. You deserves what waiting for you!*"

He huffed out his fear as long-dismissed temptation probed him. He turned his head from side to side, watching the darkness surreptitiously, his heart palpitating in anticipation as a faint longing for something lost planted itself within him. Deep in his spirit, he felt its siren call, pulling at the loose tether dangling from his soul.

Looking up at the red brick building and the gray weathered wood of its back porch, he shivered against the fear inundating his spirit. Maybe Fannie was right. Doubt chipped away the façade of his dreams with Mae. The silent tendrils of darkness murmured behind the locked door of his mind, begging for access. The darkness felt him weakening, filled with anxiety that this city was not and would never be his home.

Looking around the street in front of him—weeds fighting through the cracks in the concrete slabs—Clyde's brain was a cacophony of twisting memories and terrifying prophecy informed by the darkness. As people passed him on the sidewalk, he heard their jeers and laughter carried on the wind as they hurried by, glancing over their shoulders. He sensed their derision, that they were talking about him, heard their ridicule as he turtled his head into his shoulders. Dark thoughts ran rampant. Same as always. Never any different, his mind screamed. Not in Rayville, not in Delhi, not in Jackson, and not here in Chicago.

He'd been stupid, his runaway thoughts told him, daring to let himself believe, his hopes born along on Mae's promises of how good it would be for them when they got to the big city. For once, she assured him they would be away from all the stares and snickering laughter, away from the fear.

He pictured Mae's mouth pressed against his ear, her soft breath against his lobe, the length of her body soft against him, making it all seem possible. The darkness that had begun to infiltrate his dreams again and threatened to return would shrink away from her, shriveling against her light, and the hungering need would scatter. He could fight it, he told himself. Mae made him believe that.

Then the vision of Ruby filled his brain. He saw her looking at him again, disgust dripping across her features. The darkness surged, pressuring the widening crack and swirling on the ground at his feet, issuing a hum of satisfaction.

The smell of Ruby remained in his nose, assaulted his olfactory memory, her stench invasive. He narrowed his eyes, searching for the window that looked into his new apartment. She was upstairs now with Mae, her stink enfolding them both and infecting his wife. He could feel her corrupting Mae, eroding her love for him with her words.

The darkness throbbed, misting up from the concrete street and ensnaring his ankles, caressing him lovingly. He breathed deeply, opening himself, and felt it leaping and leeching into him. The darkness seeped through his pores, traveling upward, and embraced him. He wasn't afraid anymore.

Clyde pulled Mae's trunk toward him, feeling his biceps bulge as he lowered it to the ground. He loaded two more boxes on top of it, then squatted to lift them, pushing aside the flash of betrayal that tried to assert itself.

CHAPTER THREE

Ruby halted in front of the dark mahogany door, the fourth one down on the left, then stood patiently aside as Mae stepped in front of her to insert her key into the lock and push open the door. She stopped, a little chuckle bubbling in her chest as Mae's mouth fell open, and a little gasp of wonder escaped as her eyes took in the room and its furnishings. The cherrywood of the tables and the chest of drawers sparkled under the bars of afternoon light streaming through the window.

"Lord Almighty, I ain't never seen nothing like this before. This room is so nice. I ain't never expects we would find nothing like it," Mae said, running her finger across the wood of the side table near the window, then looking over at Ruby.

"Oh yeah. It a good place, all right. Mr. Elliott, he pretty fair." Ruby preened as she spoke, her eyes roaming covetously around the room. "But I run this place and make sure it stay a good place."

"You the manager for real? It must be like they say. A body cain't help but do good in the North." Mae hesitated, waiting for a response, then began again without it, "Where you from, Ms. Ruby? We just come from Mississippi, me and Clyde. That ain't where I met him, though. That was in Louisiana. Him and his brothers worked on cars in his daddy's garage. Like I said, them Henry boys can fix anything with a engine in it. I know he seem like he kind of old for me, but he ain't old as he looks. He ain't but twenty-two, and he a good man." She kept talking, not seeing Ruby cringe when she said the words "good man."

"Shoot, he got me away from my stepmama, Verna, and all them kids of hers."

Mae seemed to realize she was rambling and stopped, taking her first full breath since she had begun talking, that quick blush Ruby had seen before staining her cheeks again. "I knows I talks too much, but I cain't help it. My muhdeah used to say it took me a long time to say my first words, until I was most two years old, and I ain't stopped since." She laughed, the sound tinkling in her throat before it became a full belly laugh, bending her in half.

"I'm from Louisiana too," Ruby answered, pronouncing it so that it sounded like *Loosiana,* just as Mae did. "Monroe."

"Delhi, just before Rayville and right outside Monroe. You drive too fast, you go right by it," Mae laughed.

"Gal, you know you right. I might have some peoples in Rayville you could know. You know any of the Williams?"

"You ain't talking about them whats got the still right outside of town? They do more drinking than selling!" she laughed.

Ruby found herself laughing with her, a rusty, ragged noise foreign to her own ears. She could not remember a time that she had laughed like this since Amos died. She eased herself into the overstuffed chair in the corner of the room, still chuckling softly, her eyes following Mae as she moved around the room.

"So how you meet up with somebody like Clyde?" Ruby asked, hoping her voice sounded curious and not offensive.

"Huh?" Mae, who was staring out of the window through the lace curtains, spun around to give Ruby her full attention. "Oh, I guess you wondering because of the way he look."

Ruby lowered her head and shifted uncomfortably in her chair, cleared her throat, and lifted the snuff can resting at the foot of her chair to spit.

Mae smiled. "No need to be embarrassed, Miss Ruby. I know how he look. He ain't handsome or nothing. Back home, folks laugh at me for being with him. Say things like, 'Be careful, Mae, you gon' end up with babies look like they supposed to be in the zoo messing with monkey boy.' That's what they called him. He say they been doing it since he was little. It a damn shame folks be like that. Won't let a body grow and be. But you know, he ain't rough with me at all. He real tender-like."

Ruby grunted and spat into the can again, eyeing Mae over the rim, age and experience giving the lie to what she heard. She pushed down her disbelief and started again. "Oh. So, how long you been knowing him?"

"We been married for a year, but I ain't from the same place as him. Us moved there a few years back when my daddy lost his share-cropping place we had. Got us another shack back outside Delhi, and that where we meet." Leaving the window where she had been watching Clyde leaning against the truck, she pushed aside the anxiety telegraphing from him to her, knowing that this move frightened him.

It would be all right once they got settled, she told herself. Mae pulled up a chair in front of a box on the floor and began extracting linens from it, carefully creasing and folding each piece. Her eyes misted over as she stared into her past, searching for the words to convey her feelings.

"Back when Clyde was courting me, every time he come, he bring me a little something. One time, it was a necklace, then some sweet-smelling perfume, and on the day we was married, he brung me a dress. Say somebody pretty as me should look pretty all the time. After a while, I couldn't see nothing but the heart of him.

The heart what love me." Her voice trailed off, her eyes clouding for a moment. "He say I be the only one excepting his mama ever really see him. He love me, Miss Ruby, and I loves him."

Mae eyed the older woman, uncertainty shadowing her features and her hands nervously plucking at the material in her lap. Ruby felt an uncharacteristic maternal rush flooding to the surface and branching out to Mae, causing a desire to reach out and touch her. She wanted to stroke her hair, feel the softness of her skin, and make her laugh again, displaying those deep dimples.

A loud thud resounded through the room, and they both inhaled sharply, looking toward the door. Clyde filled the frame, a large trunk at his feet. His head swiveled between them, his eyes questioning. Mae stood abruptly, the towel she had been folding falling to the floor, and quickly closed the space between them. Ruby watched as her hands instantly touched his face, stroking his cheeks.

"Thanks, honey. Me and Miss Ruby was just talking. You know, she say she might have some peoples we know from Rayville. She from Monroe." She paused, focusing on stroking his face, two fingers following the length of his nose, before she began again. "It a good thing this a strong trunk. You gon' have to be more careful with them other boxes what got the dishes."

"Something stink in here," he grunted, turning to walk back out the door. He glared at Ruby, sending another shiver through her.

Ruby and Mae both remained silent. She thought she caught a fleeting glimpse of something in Mae's eyes, but when she looked again, it was gone, replaced by her radiant smile that she beamed at Clyde's back.

"Clyde got some funny ways, but he all right," she continued. "I'm telling you, Ms. Ruby, he a good man." Mae's hands fluttered uncertainly, looking for a place to land as she glanced from under-lowered lids, suddenly nervous.

Ruby shrugged, keeping her feelings to herself. "I'm gon' get on out your way," she said, standing and stretching. "I needs to check the rooms and get some work done round here today. If it be all right, I stop and see you tomorrow. Maybe we can talk some more."

Mae continued staring long after the door had closed behind Ruby, wrapped in the scent of the perfume that lingered in the air. As she breathed it in deeply, her mind contrasted how different she seemed from her stepmother, Verna. Ruby was more like the memories she had of her own mother.

Simultaneously, she banished the glimpse of darkness she'd seen in Clyde's eyes, something she hadn't seen in a year. She stopped herself from borrowing trouble—choosing to count her blessings instead, letting her mind drift only to the goodness in him—and a small smile lifted the corners of her mouth. Clyde be all right, she chided herself, shoving away her worries. She allowed her expectations of this new place to reestablish itself, kindled by the spark of hope flickering on the breeze of that sweet sachet smell Ruby left behind.

Downstairs again, Clyde turned his back on his apartment and returned to the truck. The tether of light between him and Mae stretched thin as he moved away from her. He could feel the darkness nipping and tucking at his heels, having found entry and growing stronger.

He breathed in, his chest expanding until the material of his shirt was stretched taut across his chest. The urge to violence crept silently down his arms. Exhaling, he slammed his fist into his palm, repeating the action until the pain overcame his desire to punch something or someone.

His mother's voice eased into his head, startling him, not a memory, but a faint cry across miles. With it came the image of his mother lying on the floor of their cabin, her face pressed into the dirt and imprinted on the darkness. It called from the spiraling dark depths and pushed with his desires, both chiseling and cutting at any remaining resistance.

Movement along the sidewalk caught his attention as a young woman passed just beyond his uncle's truck. Her stiletto heels clicked against the concrete, her hips swaying with each step and undulating against the tight material of her pencil skirt. He sniffed the air, recognizing the mixed scent of sweat from her lady parts combined with a cloyingly sweet, cheap perfume riding the air. He knew that if he got nearer, he could smell the aroma of multiple men on her skin.

Just like Ruby. The unique stench marked her as the Jezebel she was. Sniffing hard, he felt his loins harden instantly, straining against his trousers. Clyde groaned out loud, appalled at these new thoughts. Mae was the only woman he ever thought of in that way. He didn't know what was happening.

She glanced quickly in his direction, an almost imperceptible move of her slender neck toward him. If she'd been closer, she might have seen the red rimming his eyes as Clyde glared at her. Still, an unease transmitted itself across the distance, forcing her to look fully into his face.

Her head quickly snapped forward as she visibly recoiled, his visage scalding upon her sight. Shuddering, she picked up her speed, first walking rapidly, then full-out running as fast as her heels would allow.

Clyde felt the dark rage pump through his body with each beat of his heart, demanding he follow her and show her what *real* fear was.

"Sinner!" he muttered; his teeth clenched hard enough to make his jaws ache.

His hands itched to be around her throat, pressing until the cartilage was crushed to nothing, and he could hear the gurgling of her blood while she struggled to breathe. He would choke the sin from her, saving himself and any other man she might tempt while giving her redemptive life through death.

He shook his head violently, willing the thoughts away, a stabbing pain splitting his skull and blurring his vision. He whimpered, needing to get back to Mae to feel her touch against his face, to smell her lavender and vanilla scent.

Looking up to the first-floor window, he thought he saw Mae standing there, staring at him. He imagined her hand on his cheek, the familiar ritual, stroking and soothing him. He told himself that the darkness was not in control anymore, not since Mae had changed him. She was all that he needed. She was enough. Her light would still keep the darkness away. He was the master of the darkness, he told himself.

He turned back to the truck, pushing the images and the whore's smells from his mind, feeling his manhood shrivel. Pulling two more boxes toward him, he lifted them and made his way back up the stairs to Mae, to her warmth and safety, hoping that dried-up old wench wasn't still up there with her.

In their apartment, Mae flinched as Clyde dropped the last box, startling her from where she had collapsed in a tired heap to sit in the middle of the floor. She raised her hands over her head, stretching the kinks out of her muscles from an afternoon spent unpacking and making the room look and feel more like their own while he hauled up the boxes.

She noticed that Clyde was unusually quiet even for him, his brooding gaze falling on her for long, uncomfortable moments before she looked away. She stood, unfolding her body from her position on the floor and crossing to him. Her hands rose to cradle his face, fingers moving gently across his features and entwining themselves in the thick curls of his hair in a soothing ritual. She leaned onto him, feeling the tension draining from his body as he relaxed beneath her ministrations. Standing on tiptoe, she pressed her mouth against his.

"This our place, Clyde," she whispered. "I be so happy, ain't you? It be just you and me. Nobody but us."

Clyde felt the swirling eddy of darkness within him subdued. The turbulent vortex calmed at her touch. It slithered across the floorboards and into the walls.

He felt the heat rising in his loins again, his blood coursing and hardening his manhood again as she rubbed against him. Looking over the top of her head, he stared at the large bed pressed into the corner of the room. Lifting her into his arms, he was across the room in three strides, placing her gently on the white chenille bedspread, never allowing her hands to break their contact with him, allowing him to pull on the glimmer of her light.

His own hands fumbled with the buttons running down the front of her dress, pushing up her bra until her breasts were free. He leaned down, his mouth encircled a nipple, and he sighed heavily, hearing her moan and feeling her wriggling beneath him. He sucked hard, imagining the sweet taste of the milk she would one day have when he put a baby in her.

Like the first time he had ever touched her and known her as a woman, he felt his insides explode with want, searing away his mother's curse, the need for the whore, and the need to be a savior again serving the darkness. She had changed him, showing him what it meant to be loved, and he clung desperately to it. Mae's light flickered dimly amid his burgeoning darkness, and he sighed.

Mae rolled away from the warmth of Clyde's body, listening to the rhythmic sound of his snoring as she lay on her back and stared at the ceiling. Her conversation with Ruby echoed in her mind. She brushed it away, ignoring a shiver of trepidation.

Clyde and this place were her new dream; this time, nothing and no one would take it away. In the gloom of the room, her eyes lingered greedily on the shadows of the rich wood furnishings and the lace of the curtains hanging at the window, illuminated by the moonlight. He shifted, pulling her until her back was flush against him, her buttocks fitting into his body's curve. Sighing, she closed her eyes and let sleep claim her at last.

CHAPTER FOUR

"I tell you, Mae, that boy a country Negro, and you ain't never gon' be able to take the country out of him." Ruby huffed around the clothespin held in her mouth as she and Mae hung the sheets to take advantage of the late-spring sun's warmth. She smiled, relishing the intimacy of their friendship. "Y'all been here most three months now, and I swear he going out the world backward."

"Shame on you, Miss Ruby. He ain't that bad. And you shouldn't be talking about a body when they ain't here to defend theyself."

Ruby harrumphed again, more loudly this time, before continuing her diatribe against Clyde. "Horse shit! You listen here, gal, and stop making excuses. Truth be truth, and you knows it." She clipped the sheet to the clothesline and bent to pick up another, giving Mae a penetrating glare as she straightened up. "Look at you. You done started talking more proper-like and you can get around on the buses and trains anywhere you wants to go. You all been here the same bit of time, but you different as night and day. He ain't even trying to fit with the rest of the good folks around here, not like you do." Silence filled the space between them, and she hesitated, wondering if she had gone too far.

"It ain't the same, me and him. I mean, he ain't had the same schooling I had. I was gon' to be a teacher before I married Clyde." Mae sighed as she bent to pull another sheet from the basket that rested between them, her face veiled with a sadness that shadowed her eyes for the briefest moment before she continued.

"So, you telling me you stopped going to school to marry him?" Ruby asked, her eyebrows climbing upward, skepticism sweeping her features.

Mae shook her head, the memories once again firing and popping through her mind as she sucked in a deep breath, then forced a smile that deepened her dimples. "Naw, ma'm, it wasn't him."

She stopped, her eyes hardening and sweeping past her memories of Clyde and resting elsewhere. She bit and chewed her words before spitting them out. "That was my own self's peoples what did that. If Clyde hadn't come when he did and took me away from all that mess, well, it would have been a sorry life for me, and well . . ." She paused, looking up at the cloudless blue sky, and inhaled deeply, a smile breaking across her face—"Then I wouldn't never have made it to Chicago. I wouldn't be living here, and you and me wouldn't be friends, Miss Ruby."

Ruby stopped, a damp sheet clutched against her chest, then grinned. "Girl, you is a natural mess. What I'm gon' do with you?"

The utter darkness Amos had left, staining her soul, receded a step further as a bright aura blazed around Mae. Ruby shook her head and searched for her snuff can. "I ain't never gon' understand you and him together. But if you likes it, I loves it."

"You just cain't see him like I do," Mae said, seeing the doubtful look on Ruby's face. "I know, I know. He ain't no good-looking man, and his legs ain't right, but they stronger than they was. He do pretty good, long as he don't push hisself too hard, and they start paining him, make him limp bad." She hesitated, stared into the distance, and then chuckled. "But it be something about him what strike my heart kind of pitiful about the way they treated him back home. He ain't deserve that. Nobody do."

Mae pulled the clothesline down so she could stare at Ruby over it, her words moving up and down the scale with her emotions. Everybody got a story, Ruby thought, and she could feel Mae's story straining and wanting to be told.

Both women dropped the sheets they held into the basket, and Mae approached the other side of the clothesline. Together, they backed up and fell heavily into the two cane-bottomed chairs on the porch, pulled by the weight of their stories. Mae fanned her hand absently in front of her face, stirring a slight breeze as she gathered her thoughts, then spoke.

"That first day I seen him in the woods, he had this look, you know, how a dog look what's been beat all the time. That be him. Shoot, I'm ashamed to admits it, but him coming up on me like he did, not making no sound, did scare me. I near pissed my britches seeing him standing over me. He got them big old hands, them long arms, and Lord Jesus, it be something about his eyes and the way they looks at you." Her face paled with remembering, her eyes growing large as they stared into the past.

"Anybody with some sense would have start screaming and running. But he look more scared than me. Seem like he was the one ready to run off." Her mouth twisted at the incongruity as she conjured the scene into reality. Ruby leaned forward, scooting to the end of her chair as Mae continued.

Mae had that faraway look Ruby often saw when she was reminiscing about Clyde. "Like I said, I think I scared him more than he scared me. And there he was, come to save me. I just didn't know it yet."

"I bet you didn't." Ruby controlled an involuntary shudder as she tried to picture Clyde as either afraid or a savior.

"I had done heard about him a few times since we moved to Delhi," Mae continued, ignoring Ruby's response, "but I hadn't never actual laid eyes on him until that day. And, Lord . . . Well, I gots to tell the truth and shame the devil, Miss Ruby. I understands why folks said some of what they did. He look like somebody you don't wants to get on the bad side of. I mean, he ain't never been like that with me, but it . . ." She paused, sorting through her words to find the ones to convey her meaning. "Sometimes, it's like something come up in him. A dark feeling come over him, and I can sees it."

Mae lifted her hand, whipping back and forth through the air as if to wipe the harshness of her words away. She continued her recollection of their meeting, the wonder in his eyes as he looked at the wet tip of his finger and then back at her, how gentle his touch was, contradicting the look and size of him. She picked up the threads of the story. "He wipes at my tears, and I wasn't scared like I should have been. Well, I might have shrunk up a little. But he was so tender, like I was a flower he was touching what he don't wants to crush. Made me stop crying, and we just sit there, looking at each other, breathing each other's air."

Mae's eyes blinked rapidly, and Ruby watched her expression change. Her mouth became a straight, hard line, and her eyes sparkled with anger. "Next thing I know, his head jerk around, and he up on his feet." Mae sucked her tongue in disgust and continued. "Then this other time, when we was up in the woods, Fannie come. I swear that man could hear his momma calling from the grave. I didn't hear her at first, but Lord have mercy, when she got close enough, I could hear her hollering his name like she was coming to fight Satan hisself. Clyde took off running. I should have knowed then she was trouble."

Mae paused in her retelling, reaching through the tangles of her memories and separating Fannie from Clyde in her mind. Her face hardened as anger threaded itself into her narrative.

"Fannie Henry ain't never had no use for me. But me, I thinks me and Clyde done saved each other. He save me from my daddy and Verna. I save him from his mama."

Ruby stared at Mae, her thoughts stewing as a flood of tumultuous emotion blossomed beneath the surface. She'd convinced herself years ago, when her own child bled out into the toilet in big clumps of blood that looked like raw liver, that any maternal feelings died with her child. Amos had beaten it out of her, along with any yearning she had for happiness.

Mae could easily have been that child. Hope fluttered within her empty womb as she bent her body forward, rocking back and forth protectively. Her features softened as she listened, and Mae continued, each word filling the space.

She sighed, consumed with a desire to comfort her. What would it feel like to let her fingers stroke her skin and feel the silkiness of her hair? Would they be as soft as they looked? Shaking herself, Ruby coughed.

"So, how you say you and his mama get along?" she asked, pushing back to the subject of Clyde's mother. Mae's eyes narrowed, and Ruby moved forward, almost falling off the edge of her seat in her eagerness to have the story continue.

Mae's tone changed abruptly, the lightness and humor gone from her voice. "His mama, Miss Fannie, hate my guts," Mae spewed, venom hissing between each word. "She think I done used some bad juju on Clyde to take him away."

Ruby sat up straight, eyes large and round as she stared up at Mae, first dumbfounded, then angry. It was anathema to hate Mae. In the months since she had met her, she'd not known Mae to fail to offer help or have an unkind word to say about anyone until now.

Indignation rang in Ruby's voice when she spoke again. "What you mean?" she asked, swallowing her angry thoughts, afraid that any stray words would cause Mae to stop talking.

Now that she had started, nothing would silence the runaway train of her words as Mae poured out the vitriol that lay like rot in the roots of her relationship with her husband. "I mean, she hate me. She ain't never want me with Clyde. Seem like she ain't want him with nobody but her."

Mae paused, folding her arms beneath her breasts, her mouth fixed in a hard, straight line, the expression out of place on her usually placid face. Mae's hands squeezed her upper arms repeatedly.

"I should have followed my first mind about her when he start telling me about her. Yep. God knows, I should have. But nah, dumb old me, I kept going back to the woods to see Clyde again."

Acidic bitterness churned in Mae's stomach, then splashed up to burn her throat. "And that there be the problem between us. Miss Fannie cain't stand him loving me. She cain't take not being the woman in his life. But he ain't her boy no more. He my man." She released her hold on her arms, the print of her fingers leaving a red stain behind.

"Miss Ruby, I ain't never met nobody like his mama, Miss Fannie, or them sisters of hers. They swears the Lord done picked them out special, and his wisdom and salvation is only for them. When she found out Clyde done been with me, she say I done been the ruination of his life. She say I'm gon' end up just like all Jezebels, shit on the ground."

Ruby wished in that instant that the woman, Fannie, was there with them now. She'd claw the ugliness from her throat, ensuring the woman could never say another hurtful thing to Mae again.

Ruby released the breath she was holding and rolled her eyes heavenward. "I ain't never been able to abide by no holy rollers. The Lord don't got no special picks." Ruby lifted her snuff can from beside her chair and spat the taste of Fannie into it with the brown stream of tobacco juice. "Come on with it. I know you got some more to tell. What else she be like?"

Both women leaned in conspiratorially. "Well, you ain't gon' believe this, but when I met Clyde, he was still sleeping in the same bed with his mama." She stopped to let the words fall on Ruby, whose mouth hung open in disbelief.

"Sure enough? Girl, no!" Her mouth continued to open and close, waiting for more words to convey her doubt and disbelief. "Ain't you say he more than twenty years old?"

"Yes, ma'm! He was living with his mama between Rayville and Delhi, just him and her in a house back up in the woods. It wasn't too bad, three rooms and a little kitchen with a pump inside and a stove." Her hand flew to her mouth, and her head twisted from side to side, searching for hidden eavesdroppers before she continued. "Didn't have but one big bed, and I heard from some gossiping folks Clyde was still sleeping with her. Now you know that ain't natural. What kind of woman be sleeping with her grown son?"

Ruby made a choking sound of incredulity as Mae continued, the words spilling forth, a river damned up for too long.

"Uh-huh. When I ask Clyde about it, he act like it wasn't nothing wrong with it. He say they always done slept in the same bed ever since his daddy and the rest of his brothers left. Afore that, far as he can recollect, even when his daddy was with them, he been sleeping with her since he was borned."

She stopped, pausing to gather her words. "Clyde say, 'Mae, ain't nothing wrong with it.' And that be the first time him and me ever got into it. The first time he got mad with me. Say I was listening to them heathens in town, the ones what hated him. Say I'm just like them. That the first time I seen that mad look on him. We didn't talk for a spell, and Fannie was strutting around happy as Christmas."

Mae had made her way to lean on the porch railing, the story seeming to drain the energy from her body. "But Clyde come back to me and ask me to marry with him. I puts my foot down. Say if you want to be with me, then you got to get your own self's bed until us gets married."

"He went and bought hisself a cot that day and start sleeping on it." A satisfied smile spread across her face, deepening the dimples in each cheek. "Then we start seeing each other regular again. Miss Fannie just about bust a gut. I swear the woman going to lose her mind when he tells her he was going to marry me." Her head shook in denial of the remembered reality.

"That old cow come to my daddy's house, cussing me and mine. But my muhdeah was there. And, Miss Ruby, she done already warned Miss Fannie before not to come around me no more. Don't nobody mess with my muhdeah." Laughter bubbled up in her throat at the recollection of Fannie yelling outside the house, face gone purple in an apoplectic fit, and Muhdeah cussing the air blue. "She got her straight real quick and run her straight back into them woods, waving the wood ax the whole time. Muhdeah don't take kindly to nobody hollering at her children or grandchildren but her." She watched as Ruby bent forward, guffawing loudly and stomping her foot.

"Don't laugh, Miss Ruby," she demanded, then chuckled and gave Ruby a moment to collect herself. Eventually, the older woman subdued herself, the sight of Mae's face flushed red, embarrassment coloring her cheeks, sobering her.

Ruby scooted back into her chair until her back rested against the wicker, the wet laundry bunched on her lap and forgotten, both fascinated and appalled by the tale. Looking into Ruby's face, Mae stopped talking abruptly, her face going a deeper red with the realization of what she had revealed.

"There I go, running off at the mouth again, telling all my business," she said, her open palm attempting to rub the embarrassment from her face while moving to snatch another sheet from the basket. Glancing upward, she noticed how the sun had moved across the sky during their conversation. "Anyway, she the main reason why we here. We had to get far as we could from his mama. You know the Bible say, 'leave and cleave,' but I guess, holy as she is, she don't read that part." Her face closed, her chin jutting forward, and her eyes glittering. "I be his family now."

Taking a deep breath, Mae cut off her words, stuffing them back where she stored them. Pulling up a smile that remained only on her lips, she lifted the basket onto her hip.

"It getting late, Miss Ruby. I best be getting Clyde's dinner on." Her right hand picked nervously at the few sheets on the bottom of the basket that she would need to rewash. "I'm gon' see you tomorrow. And you can tells me all about your husband. You said he was a good man too, right?"

Ruby cleared her throat and gazed at Mae for a long, awkward moment. Her truth pressed at the base of her throat, scratching to get out. She swallowed it back down. Turning her eyes to the floor beneath her, she felt the bitter taste of deceit on her tongue.

"I need to be getting on inside before these here flies eat me for they dinner." She avoided Mae's eyes as she stood, stretching her arms upward, startled by how knotted her muscles had become sitting in the chair. "Oh, you be baking any more of that banana bread? Girl, you put your foot in it!" She laughed as she followed Mae inside. "Or you done sold it all?"

"I sees what I can do." Mae laughed, speaking over her shoulder before escaping inside.

CHAPTER FIVE

Time dragged forward for Clyde. The spring breeze that warmed the air when they arrived in Chicago had yielded to the dog hot days of summer. He ignored the heads turning toward him, watching him shuffling through the train yard, eyes lowering to search the floor in front of them, avoiding his. The weight of disappointment bore him closer to the ground as he remembered those days when his life brimmed with hope and promise.

Some days, he successfully widened his stance and kept his posture erect. But as the day wore on, the stress and burden on his muscles weakened his legs, pulling his knees together and forcing him into the familiar lopsided gait that was the rhythm of his youth. His blood burned under his skin as people stared. Elbows poked ribs, hands covered mouths, failing to conceal the snickering behind them. He would force his hands into his pockets to keep his arms from swinging as he walked.

Now, with the late-July sun beating down through the high glass windows, he let Mae's words repeat in his head. *"It don't matter about them folks. You a damned good mechanic, and your work make room for you."* From across the room, Charles lifted his chin in his direction, a look of discomfort flitting across his face. Clyde swallowed his hope.

He wiped the sweat from his forehead and swallowed his anxiety, determined to put Mae's advice into practice. He focused on Charles. He wasn't overtly friendly, but his voice was silent when the hazing and ridicule began. It would be a start.

Clyde let the hood of the service Jeep fall shut, watching from beneath lowered eyelids as the other mechanics scattered away from him. He pushed the darkness back into its cage, the words he planned to say resting heavily in his mouth. He watched Charles's broad back as he walked away trailing the others, forcing himself to push his gait a little faster to close the gap between them.

He imagined the words coming unglued as he shared them with Charles, envisioning how he would laugh with him, not at him, when he caught up with him. However, the distance expanded, and Clyde damned his limbs, cursing his tongue for being too slow and tangled to tell Charles to wait, let alone bring forth the joke he had been practicing inside his head.

He blew air noisily through his thick lips, disappointment collapsing his shoulders as another plan burned to ash in his heart. Reaching upward to grab the tarnished silver handle above his head, he opened his locker, then jumped back awkwardly, arms pinwheeling as something tumbled out, landing at his feet. He looked down at it, and his jaw tightened. A vein in his forehead bulged.

Clyde stared up into his open locker, then down at the long, yellow banana lying at his feet, the skin spotted brown, the air thick with the overripe smell from sitting in the closed locker. On the other side of the lockers, he heard snatches of laughter and loud hoots as footsteps receded, moving toward the exit.

Snatching the banana from the floor, Clyde grabbed his lunch bag from the shelf and shoved the offending fruit into it before smashing the whole thing into the pocket of his overalls.

The sound of their laughter echoed in his head, chasing him from the room in a storm of hurt and shame, the darkness throbbing behind his eyes.

It thrived on his pain and pulled at him, draining his strength, the humiliation feeding it. Since his first sighting—the day they'd moved to this wretched hellhole, and he'd seen that woman—it had beat him down while he had grown weaker to his reawakened needs. The darkness smothered his desire for Mae, replacing it with a longing for that woman, Eva, leading him toward her. His dreams of a new life here with Mae crumbled and dissolved with his disappointment.

He stalked the streets, unaware of his destination, led by the darkness. He found himself walking past her apartment building like he did many days, slinking in the shadows, concealing himself in the darkness. He followed her smell, his mind a swirl of continuous fantasies of time and place. As he walked, he listened to the raucous sound of men hooting her name, their desire pulled by the sway of her hips as she passed them. Every day, she stopped at the storefront grocery below her apartment, picking up milk or bread and laughing with the pimply-faced clerk. He watched her hand pressing his arm, her head tilted back, dark lashes fluttering, unaware of Clyde seething in the alley, his eyes brimming with hatred.

The darkness shredded his mind relentlessly, tearing at his will, begging to be quenched. Dormant desires returning, gnawing and nibbling at him with promises of the power and greatness he had lost. From within the vortex of his thoughts, Fannie's voice resumed and overrode Mae's. "*She gon' be the ruination of you, baby boy.*"

Six days a week, eight hours a day, Eva labored washing clothes in the laundry where she worked. Clyde grunted in disgust at her attempts to make herself look respectable. As if all the washing in the world could hide the fact that she made most of her money lying flat on her back with her legs spread for anybody with the cash.

From his hiding place, he'd seen her johns creeping into the small, sweltering space where she waited behind the counter, clutching their crumpled bags of clothes. He'd seen their eyes sliding from side to side as they pressed a wad of balled-up dollar bills into her hand, a look passing between them. She would wait a few minutes, slipping out the back door of the laundry and walking ahead of her john, sometimes only as far as their car, other times, to her apartment.

Clyde imagined those men staring down at the small gold cross she wore, nestled between her breasts, as they plowed between her thighs. He would stand there in the shadows, his hands rubbing and tightening on his crotch, waiting for her to return. And she did, the reek of sex lingering in the air long after she passed him, his seed exploding inside his underwear.

Thoughts and memories of Eva cycloned through his mind, weaving in and out with the images of his coworkers as he forced his feet to move forward. He desperately wished that he could see her now. The darkness had marked her. It wanted her.

Minutes later, he was rewarded by her arrival as he lurked in the alley, almost crowing out loud for having remained vigilant and not giving up. There was Eva, framed in the early-evening light, pinpricks of darkness dancing around her. She stopped suddenly, alert, looking over her shoulder, prey scenting the predator. Clyde pressed his back against the wall and held his breath, his body tensing while he waited for her footsteps to begin again. Sweat poured from his brow, stinging his eyes.

Wiping it with the back of his hand, willing her not to see him, he looked around. He studied the depth of the passage he stood in, draped in black shadows. To his right, a large dumpster took up the back wall. Above him, he noticed the closest windows six feet over his head had been bricked up. Sweet silence encircled him, and he gasped aloud, then quickly covered his mouth. It was perfect.

He closed his eyes and visualized Eva with him, her body pulled tight against his chest, rubbing against his manhood as she struggled to escape. She would plead with him, beg him, and finally surrender to him. Then he would be benevolent and grant her a quick end. He would be merciful as he rendered justice. Then he would bury her in the dumpster, like the trash she was. Afterward, he would go home to Mae. He would drink from her body, leech the light from her, allowing her sex to quell the craving that would not stop.

Clyde wrung his hands in front of him, his head bobbing up and down, and yielded. He felt the darkness quivering in anticipation, then hesitated. A new idea formed and pushed its way to the forefront before being whispered into his eager mind. He listened intently while the darkness fermented its own plan. *Take her to your special place and bury her there. Bury her deep.*

He pictured his place, deep in Jackson Park, like the woods back home. The grass was wild and green, untouched by blades or man, tree branches hanging low to the ground and shielding him from the world. A place where he was able to forget the city that lay beyond it, shrouded by the leaves and breathing in the scent of earth and trees. A place he was alone by choice.

Yes, yes, he answered the dark. There would be no reason to rush. He would prolong it, hear her beg for mercy only he could grant her after she confessed her sins. Pleasure radiated through him, and he smiled, willing his aching legs to dance, and failed.

A small, persistent voice wormed at the back of his brain, boring into the darkness and trying to interject itself. Cocking his head to the left, straining to catch the sound again, his body trembled. It was Mae's voice—he was sure of it—a prayer pulling him back from his backslide into the pits of darkness.

The sound of Eva's retreating footsteps diminished and disappeared. He had lost her while vacillating, wrestling between the pull of the darkness and Mae. Clyde wrapped his arms around his torso, rocking violently as ragged sobs tore from his throat. Moving again to lean against the wall, he lifted his rough hands to his face, scrubbing away the tears.

He hated this city . . . the constant stink of the garbage and press of strangers against him. He hated that Mae had brought him here. Standing still, he let the darkness amplify his hearing and listened again to determine where the sound came from.

Behind the dumpster, the skittering sounds of rats filled the space. He straightened his body, attendant to a visceral desire demanding immediate satisfaction. Clyde moved silently on the balls of his feet, balancing awkwardly on his bent legs. He was upon the rats in a flash, his large hands grabbing one and locking around the struggling body. The sharp teeth snapped at his hand, the claws digging into flesh.

Clyde squeezed, the craving for the woman engorging his muscles as he twisted, grinding bone and fur as the rat squealed hideously, convulsed, and then went still. Reaching into the large pocket of his overalls, he pulled out the brown paper bag that had held his lunch. Opening it, he saw the banana lying across the bottom. The snickering sounds of his coworkers' laughter flooded his ears again, and he grimaced, rubbing his face in his hands.

Taking several deep breaths, he dropped the rat inside, blocking the sight of the banana, and folded the top shut. He forced himself to think of Mae, listening for her voice.

Mae, Mae, Mae. He thought her name repeatedly, clutching at the thread of salvation. He pictured her face, imagined her slight frame molded against him, her soft voice whispering close to his ear. He imagined her touch against his face, allowing it to soothe and calm him.

Moving to the mouth of the alley, he looked to the left and the right, assuring himself that no one noticed him. He retraced his footsteps until he was headed south again. He had to get home to Mae.

His legs windmilled slowly, propelling him forward. The rhythm of his heart slowed, calming him as each step brought him closer. If he could make it home, Mae would make it all right. He just needed to get there.

The darkness intruded, slipping stealthily across his mind, igniting the embers of doubt the day had placed in him. *Look how weak she done made you*, it whispered, its laugh raw and grating against his soul. *She ain't no different than the rest of them. She probably getting some more bananas for you.* Tilting his head to the side, Clyde pounded his palm against his ear, attempting to force the thoughts to roll free. *You know she don't loves you*, it chided.

"Her do loves me," he shouted into the air, startling a man walking near enough to hear him. He stared at Clyde until Clyde glared at him, causing him to pick up his speed and hurry past without looking back.

Twenty minutes later, his body shaking with rage and uncertainty, Clyde stood on the patch of dirt and weeds that passed for a yard at the rear of their apartment building. He stepped behind the stairs, stuffing the bloodstained brown paper bag beneath the bottom step. Contentment played across his features for a few brief seconds. Tomorrow, it would be his turn to have some laughs.

Climbing the back stairs to the wide first-floor porch, he listened as the wood creaked under the weight of his bulk. He let out a whoosh of relief, Mae's face drifting before him. He was safe, close enough to feel the strength of her presence. She would have a hot meal waiting for him one floor up. She would push the darkness back, and it would relinquish its claim on him. Mae would make it stop like she always did.

Ahead of him, a man stood on the first-floor landing. His face bent forward, his hand rapidly rising to his mouth, stuffing portions of bread into it from a bag clutched in his other hand. Clyde hesitated, one foot lifted in midair, blinking rapidly. Looking down at Clyde, the man grinned around the food in his mouth, interrupting his feast.

"Hey, how you, Clyde?" he asked, the words muffled by his chewing.

Clyde waited a few steps below the taller man, trying to place his face. He didn't respond, waiting for him to move so he could get to Mae.

"You probably don't remembers me, but I seen you before with that sweet little gal of yours." The man grinned, sticking his hand out toward Clyde. "My name be Jimmie. I lives down the hall, on the other side of Miss Ruby."

Clyde stiffened, not liking the fox-sly look on his sharp features when he mentioned Mae. Leaving Jimmie's hand hanging in the air, his eyes darted rapidly from side to side, impatient to be past him. He studied the look of the man, taking in the sharp crease of his tan slacks, cuffed and resting neatly over brown and white leather shoes. A yellow shirt with a wide collar was tucked neatly into the belted waist of his slacks. He brought his eyes back to the slick, conked hair shining on the man's head—city boy.

"I'm gon' needs you to move on out the way," Clyde said, moving sideways to get around Jimmie and casting his face into shadow, his body tense and coiled to spring.

Looking up at the taller man, Clyde watched darkness slide over Jimmie's features, clouding them.

"Man, I tell you, that wife of yours, Mae, she some woman!" Jimmie exclaimed, sucking his fingers and slapping the bag lightly against his thigh. Later, when he replayed the scene in his mind, asking himself what made him say it, he wouldn't have an answer. He leaned his head to the side as if listening to a distant voice, overcome by the need to provoke Clyde, something aggravating his spirit to "poke the bear."

Clyde froze in place, hearing his wife's name fouled on the man's lips. Moving up one step, he glowered up at him. "What you mean?" he growled low in his throat.

Jimmie stopped grinning, his eyes narrowing as he surveyed Clyde, sliding past his grease-splattered overalls and the black brogans on his feet, then back up to the squashed features of his face. He lifted the bag, twisted it open, and pulled another chunk of bread free, continuing to take great gulping bites and talking as he chewed.

"You best watch it, boy. Woman cook like she do and look that good, somebody be done stole her away from you."

Jimmie winked and stepped back, turning sideways so Clyde could advance past him, continuing to slowly lick the fingers of his now-empty hand, a deep laugh rumbling from his throat.

Clyde saw the darkness swimming around him before it slammed around his brain, a vice squeezing reason away, blinding him with visions of Mae and this man. He saw her leaning close to Jimmie, her face tilted back, her lips waiting for his kiss, and her hands stroking his long, straight limbs.

Clyde lurched up the last two steps, his bulk completely blocking Jimmie from moving around him. Bunching the material of Jimmie's shirt in his fists, he shook him, forcing the man backward as he glared into his face.

"Who the fuck you say you is?" he yelled, the city having made words that had once been foreign on his tongue, normalized. "And what you knows about my Mae?"

The smile slid from Jimmie's face, his mouth going dry, leaving him unable to swallow the last small piece of bread now stuck in his throat.

He choked, his throat working to bring the bread back up into his mouth, simultaneously clutching and pulling at Clyde's hands. Struggling, he finally managed to spit out the wad, where it landed with a heavy thump on the porch.

Jimmie stared into Clyde's face, his muscles flexing and straining as he pushed back against the bigger man, feeling his shirt ripping. Backpedaling, he two-stepped to remove himself from striking distance, checking how Clyde leaned forward with his fists balled at his side.

"What the fuck wrong with you, man?" Jimmy stared at Clyde, confusion wild in his eyes, and panted loudly. "This shirt costed me two dollars, Negro," he ranted indignantly, one hand pulling at the tear in the material, his other hand dropping the bag he carried. He rolled his shoulders and moved his neck from side to side, stretching the tendons. "Is you gon' pay for it?" he demanded, balling his hands tightly into fists, and bringing them up in front of him as he dropped into a fighter's crouch.

"I say, what you knows about my Mae?" Clyde ground the words out through clenched teeth, readying his body for the assault. The dark swam through him, swelling his muscles.

"You been with her?!" The question exploded between the two of them, hanging in the air.

Tendrils of fear crept into Jimmie's wide eyes as understanding settled over him, an awareness of what lay behind the bulging red-rimmed eyes crazed with anger and contorting Clyde's features. The taste of the sweet bread soured in his mouth, causing his stomach to clench and spasm. Jimmie tried to swallow again, his Adam's apple bobbing up and down. The vein in Clyde's forehead bulged purple, his hands clenching and unclenching into fists. Blood flushed and darkened his skin.

"Whoa, whoa, man, ain't nothing like that going on," Jimmie stammered, straightening and throwing both hands up in a surrendering motion, blinking away the dark that had clouded his vision. "I just got this banana bread she made this morning." He waved toward the bag containing the half-eaten loaf on the porch between them, kicking it with his toe until the contents spilled out. "Man, I was just playing. You know she be cooking for folks in the building?"

Jimmie swallowed hard, backing up another step, reason returning to his thoughts. He felt his own muscles tighten. Clyde was thick through the shoulders but stood a head shorter than Jimmie, resting on his stunted legs.

Jimmie had been raised to fight. His mother had taught him hard, saying, "*Boy, your ass better not never run from nobody. The streets ain't got no time for pussies. You run, and I'm gon' whop your ass myself when you gets back home. And you remembers,*" she would always pause there, neck jutting forward, staring directly into his eyes, her bony finger poking him in his narrow chest. "*No matter how big they is, they got to bring some ass to get some ass.*"

"It just some banana bread!" he yelled as Clyde seemed to grow and expand, looming over Jimmie. His skin glistened with sweat, a murderous outrage darkening his eyes.

Jimmie's eyes widened, sliding back and forth as he tried to circle away from Clyde, searching for escape. His heart pounded in his chest, his body trembling as he felt his bowels gurgling loosely, causing his face to flush with shame. Edging toward the steps, he prayed to his Mawmaw's God, that never answered him. The

God he'd abandoned when he still knelt on the side of the bed, parroting his grandmother's prayers. He begged for intervention.

Banana was the only word Clyde heard as he shot forward, startling Jimmie with the speed of his movement. Jimmie sidestepped, creating a space between them, kicking away the remainder of the loaf of banana bread in his haste to put some distance between him and Clyde. He slammed his shoulder into Clyde's chest, wincing at the pain flowing down his arm, and succeeded in knocking him off balance.

Seizing the opportunity the opening created, Jimmie whirled past Clyde and leaped down the first four stairs, just managing to duck a massive blow as Clyde's fist flew through the space where his head had been. Jimmie felt panic plant itself firmly, obliterating his courage.

"Shit, man! You crazy," he yelled over his shoulder as he stumbled forward, pounding down the remaining steps. Reaching the bottom, Jimmie turned to see Clyde—chest heaving—still standing at the top of the stairs but no longer moving in his direction.

"You out your country, pig-shit-eating mind!" Jimmie screamed, having reached the dead brown grass of the yard. Putting distance between them, his pride reasserted itself, demanding he make a show of resistance. Ignoring the foul trickle sliding between his buttocks into his shorts, he shouted, "And ain't nobody scared of your big ass!"

Clyde flexed his body forward, causing Jimmie to bolt across the grass and down the narrow passageway formed by the wall of the adjacent building leading to the street.

"You best stay your slick ass the hell away from my wife," Clyde bellowed, feeling the last of the darkness as it drew away from Jimmie's retreating figure. Turning, he yanked open the screen door and hesitated as he looked down the long, dimly lit passage. A young woman stood in the doorway at the end of the hall, a baby riding her hip, gawking at him. The baby began to fuss loudly and, seeing Clyde, the woman jostled him, then ducked and hid behind her apartment door before easing it shut. The heads of the other tenants, drawn by the chaos outside, quickly withdrew as well. His own door was the only one that remained open, Mae standing there, framed by the light from inside and wiping her hands on her apron.

"Lord God Almighty, what in the world was going on out there, Clyde Henry?" she cried, startled by the fire of anger illuminating his eyes. "Folks in heaven could hear you hollering."

"That what I wants to know," he thundered, grabbing her by the arm and yanking her into their apartment, the door thudding shut behind them. "Who this Jimmy, and what he know about you?"

Mae stared up into Clyde's face, stunned by the ferocity of his voice. She searched his face, her mind racing and heart stuttering.

"Clyde, baby, what wrong? Why you talking to me like that?"

Clyde felt her words tunneling through the darkness clamped around his mind, looking for an anchor. He breathed in her scent, allowing it to filter through his memories of her and him. But the darkness would not let go.

"Who Jimmie?!" he yelled, spittle flying between them as he shook her like a small rag doll. Mae whimpered, tears making splotches on her apron, her mind racing and trying to grasp what was wrong.

"Who Jimmie?" she echoed back at him, dismay forcing the tears to fall faster.

"Don't act like you don't know who that slick-head Negro be," he spat out, pushing her backward and releasing her from his grasp,

The memory of Jimmie flashed through her, and she inhaled deeply, relief halting the tears immediately. She reached out to stroke Clyde's face, startled when he slapped her hand away.

"Oh, he ain't nothing, Clyde." She tried to chuckle, hoping to ease the strain from her voice. "He ain't got no wife or peoples here, and I made a little extra banana bread today and give him some. Miss Ruby say she feel sorry for him."

She lied to Clyde more easily than she liked, a warning insinuating itself between them and reminding her of the need to keep the money she made a secret. She saw herself that morning giving Jimmie a fresh batch of banana bread. She charged him the usual twenty-five cents, the same price she had been selling it for since she found how popular it was among the workingmen in the building. A twinge of guilt pinged in her spirit, wedging itself between her and Clyde.

A voice attached itself to the memory. Verna, that cantankerous little tramp who lured her father away from her, had taught Mae by her example. *A woman needs to keep her something of her own because ain't no man that good. He leave your ass high and dry if you be that kind of fool.* And she'd kept a stash hidden from Mae's father that she probably kept to this day. Now, Verna's guilty secret bound them both.

"He been fucking you?" Clyde demanded, grimacing as he reached out and shook Mae again, her head wobbling on her neck before it hit the wall behind her. Mae let out a little yelp of pain, alarmed as much by the viciousness of his language as the physical assault. She tried to wriggle free, tears welling up once more in her eyes.

"No, Clyde, I swear he ain't been around me like that. Ain't nothing like that going on. You knows me better than that," Mae pleaded as the pressure increased on her arm, her fingers growing numb from the loss of blood flow.

"That why he say I gots to watch you because he gon' takes you. You done got a taste for these pretty city boys?"

Clyde's eyes rolled wildly, a black mist swirling in their depths. Wisps of fear crept through her.

"I don't know what you talking about, Clyde. You hurting me," she squeaked. He released one arm, still holding her firmly against the wall with the other. Mae watched, eyes rounding, her mouth hanging open, as his empty hand gathered into a fist.

"That goddamned Ruby." He screamed in her face. "I should have knowed she was behind it." His voice escalated, becoming impossibly loud as it boomed in her ears. "She pimping you out? Turning you into a whore?"

Shaking her head, she lifted her free arm, the one he no longer held, and used her hand to stroke his face. Her fingers began their familiar dance, trailing from his forehead to his cheek, moving softly down the length of his nose. She prayed silently.

Mae continued stroking. Her eyes squeezed shut, sensory memory guiding her movements. She waited for the blow, her breath held and making her light-headed until she heard Clyde's breathing begin to slow.

Opening her eyes to slits, she saw Clyde's eyes had returned to normal, muddy brown and calm. He released his grip on her other arm, leaving her able to use both hands to stroke his face. Slowly, her tremors ceased, and the dread drained from her.

"Clyde, you know it ain't never been nobody but you for me," she whispered, leaning into him. "You was my first and only. Cain't nobody never takes me away from you."

He inhaled her, the lavender smell of her hair from her shampoo, the rose scent of the soap she used, and his own musky smell still on her skin from their morning lovemaking. She felt him relax slightly, then tense again as he spoke over the top of her head.

"I kills him if I sees his narrow ass sniffing around you anymore," he mumbled, his breath hot on her scalp. "And don't be making no more goddamned banana bread." His fist slammed into the wall beside her head, a dent appearing in the plaster.

Mae jumped, bewildered at his demand, and glided sideways to get away from the pressure of his body.

"OK, Clyde," she stammered, nodding emphatically, desperate to reassure him of her love. "I be sorry, and I won't makes no more if you don't likes it. You knows I love you."

His hand reached out and stopped her movement, sliding slowly from her arms and down her body. He pulled her closer to him, feeling her quake against him, and forced the darkness to retreat deeper, letting himself believe her. That glow lit beneath her skin, bathing him, pushing back the dark, calming the chaos of his mind. She was his Mae. His and his alone. He pushed Jimmie's smug expression from his memory.

Looking up, she let him brush the remaining tears from her cheek. "Now, you gets ready for your supper. I be putting it on the table," she finished, giving his chest a final pat with her hand before sighing and gently pushing him toward the sink.

Standing across the room, Clyde began scrubbing his hands, watching the water turn pink and then clear as he washed away the rat's blood still visible beneath his nails. The darkness fell away in layers, and he felt the calm erase the residual bitterness as it always did with Mae. The dim spark of her light banished the last of the darkness to the furthest recesses of his soul . . . for now. He felt his loins tighten with raw desire.

Turning and looking at the bed, he inclined his head toward it and watched Mae move in that direction. Sitting on the edge, she scooted backward and waited, her legs spread wide, her eyes still wet. Unbuckling his belt, he allowed his pants and drawers to drop to the floor, then stepped out of them.

Crossing the few steps to reach Mae, he pushed up her dress until her breasts were free and yanked at her panties, ripping them in haste. Mae inhaled sharply as he invaded her body.

For the first time in their relationship, there was no tender loving between her and Clyde, just the harsh, abrasive rubbing of his manhood against her dryness, leaving her raw and aching. She turned her head to the side, trapping the tears behind her lids, accepting his brutality as no more than she deserved. Humiliated, she swallowed her remorse and waited, her eyes fixed on the ceiling above, until he was done.

Clyde heaved one final time, shuddered, rolled off her, and walked away. Mae stared at his buttocks clenching and relaxing. She reached to pull down her dress, wincing at the pain between her legs.

"What you got for my dinner?" he asked over his shoulder, bending to yank his underwear and pants back on. She cringed at the gruffness that remained in his voice. Be patient, she scolded herself. Clyde was struggling. He just needed more time. Rubbing her bruised arm as she limped to the hot plate, she picked up the spoon and stirred the contents of the pot on the single burner.

CHAPTER SIX

Clyde hummed tunelessly as he walked the length of the locker room. He glanced at Eugene's locker, a slight smile curving his lips as he remembered the younger man opening it just before the dead, disemboweled rat fell at his feet.

Again, he saw Eugene screeching and leaping up on the bench, the sound reverberating through the room and bringing the remainder of the six-man crew running. It had earned Clyde a few days of peace from the daily malice that usually surrounded him. Now, Eugene bore the brunt of their ridicule, with everyone mimicking him as they hopped from foot to foot and screamed in a high falsetto. Clyde knew they probably suspected him as the perpetrator, but he didn't care. No one dared to call him out.

As the day wore on, his anger began to resurface. It rumbled through him, a growing rash of discontent labeled "Mae." She'd been creeping through the apartment since the incident with Jimmie, too meek to say anything beyond yes or no. And lately, he noticed, she had been putting on airs, talking about getting a job. He drew a long breath, then exhaled as he walked to the pay phone on the corner. He hated Chicago more than he had ever hated anyplace, even Rayville.

At least, back there, he knew where he stood and where the hatred was. It wasn't hidden behind grins and smiles or whispered just loud enough to be heard. He knew how everyone in town had felt. They made sure that he did. Whatever they had to say, fear of him forced them to give him a wide berth.

Back in Delhi, Mae had made him believe she loved him no matter what. When they met in the woods, he thought she accepted him as he was. She wanted to be with him. She was sincere.

On their wedding night, the two had lain side by side, shoulders touching, thighs touching, and their fingers tracing each other's hands. Mae had rolled over and climbed atop him, stroking his head, his face, and back again—just like she had watched his mother do—until he felt his manhood rise, stiff and pulsating, waiting for her touch.

She'd slowly spread her legs, lifting herself until she could ease onto him. He felt her allow him to inch into the heated wetness between her thighs. Her body stiffened, going rigid at the resistance of her virginity, before she yielded, crying out and then sliding all the way down upon him. He had reeled and bucked with pleasure as she rode him, her small hands still cradling his face.

"My Mae," he had whispered, their bodies slick with sweat, him holding her against his chest.

"Always," she'd whispered back.

They should have stayed in Delhi, he pouted. Maybe they couldn't return to Rayville, but everything was fine in Delhi, close enough to still work at the garage with his father. But no, Mae had dreams and fed them to him every night, painting a new life for them both.

There had been no women, not one, since he started courting her. Like Adam being tempted in the garden, she had been his forbidden fruit. With her came the knowledge of his own sin. She had managed to eradicate the darkness, her light making killing wrong. He never spoke of it; she never knew what he had done, but the desire ebbed and dissipated. He'd left the darkness behind with Mama.

Then they came here, and the darkness crept back insidiously, first in his dreams, then here in this shit city. The darkness had begun invading his thoughts regularly, pointing out how Mae was changing. He could feel it, and he knew it was that skinny old bitch who was taking her away, pulling them apart.

Who can blame her? the darkness jeered at him. She was all citified, trying to sound all proper when she spoke. She'd even begun correcting him when he talked—or worse, talked *for* him, rushing to fill in the words his tangled tongue couldn't express.

She never said it, but it was clear to him that she didn't want somebody like him anymore. There was no way he believed she wasn't sniffing after Jimmie, with his conked hair and yellow, pretty-boy features. He should have smashed his face in while he had the chance. Smeared it until Mae wouldn't be able to look at him again.

The darkness showed him the disdain in her eyes as she looked at him when he came home, how she cringed as he tried to get his thick, heavy tongue to shape some loving words that would bring her back to him. Shaking his head angrily, he squeezed himself into the phone booth and closed the door.

He stared at the telephone receiver in his hand for several long minutes, the darkness torturing his mind and pushing between him and Mae. Finally, groaning miserably, he put it to his ear and dialed the number to the general store from memory, listening to the operator's voice that demanded his coins. Dropping his nickels, dimes, and quarters into the coin slots, he waited for the connection to ring through.

"Hey, hello, this Hattie's General Store. This here be Hattie."

Deep within his soul, his mother's voice climbed, whispering in his head and curling through the darkness. He covered the mouthpiece with his hand as he began to whimper softly, an almost suffocating longing to lay his head against her breasts, the smell of her milk surfacing and surrounding him. He sucked in his breath, the darkness rolled behind his closed eyes, and sighed, strengthening him.

"How do, Miss Hattie? This Clyde Henry." His words were short and breathless with despair. "Can you gets word to my mama? Tells her I be calling back day after tomorrow." Remembering his manners, he added, "If you please?"

He imagined Hattie's mouth screwed up in disgust, knowing that his polite words did nothing to endear him to her. She didn't like him, hadn't since he had punched her eldest boy in the mouth, caving in his nose and knocking out three of his teeth when he'd caught him staring at Mae last year.

Growling low in his throat when Hattie hesitated too long, he allowed his displeasure to telegraph itself across the miles of wire, willing the darkness to travel the distance and remind her of what he could do. He connected with her own bitter darkness.

"I sees what I can do," she mumbled into the phone, unable to hide the sudden quaking in her voice.

"Yes, ma'm, you do that, please." He let the fear continue to build in the gap of her silence. "I calls back then."

He was confident as the line went dead that she would obey him. He pushed the door to the phone booth open, glaring at the man standing impatiently in front of it.

"You ain't the only man what wants to use the phone." The man pushed forward, his body sticking with Clyde's as he reached for the phone.

Clyde stepped aside, grasping the man's shirt collar, and shoved him inside the booth, watching his arms flung forward, his feet scrambling to keep him standing. His head thumped against the metal phone.

"I a . . . ain't the one t . . . t . . . today," Clyde stammered and turned toward the street. He imagined that, in Delhi, one of Miss

Hattie's eight children had hightailed it out to his mother's shack to give her the message and smiled in satisfaction.

Over the last week, he had felt a connection with his mother for the first time since they had fallen out with each other, and he savored it. Maybe she had been right about all of it . . . Mae and his moving. As he walked back to the garage, Clyde whistled tunelessly. He'd never been good at it, but it soothed and reminded him of when his mama had hummed or sung for him.

He began unbuttoning his overalls as he walked toward his locker, images of Fannie flowing seamlessly through his memories, the helpless loneliness that had plagued him since arriving in Chicago abating. His thoughts of Mae continued to boil in a stew of confusion, the darkness stirring it restlessly. Pushing up the locker's handle with one hand, the other worked the button-down snaps of his coverall. He felt almost happy.

It sat on the top shelf, highlighted by the shaft of fluorescent light from overhead. The toy organ grinder's monkey filled the entire space, its large ears protruding from the neckless head resting squarely on its shoulders. Its round, sightless eyes protruded, yellow circling the black orbs. Short black fur covered the long arms and ended in paws that held metal cymbals, partially hiding the bright yellow vest that covered its chest. The short, bowed legs were covered in garish red-and-yellow striped pants that stopped just short of its lower paws.

He stopped, unaware of how long he stood staring into the locker, his breath hitching and then ceasing, arrested by the sight in front of him. His eyes bulged, focused straight ahead, and his brain rushed to assimilate information about the object before him, first stubbornly refusing it and then finally translating it into reality. The image seared itself onto the screen of his mind to slam him backward in time and place, back to Rayville, back to the last classroom he'd ever sat in, back to Robert, back to monkey boy.

Clyde's gaze drifted back to the wide mouth stretched across the monkey's face. The lips skinned back to reveal two rows of square white teeth and red gums. Beneath the arms raised to clang his instrument, he saw his name, "Clyde," crudely written with black marker on the yellow vest.

Gradually, the sound of the cymbals banging together penetrated his consciousness. He shook his head, trying to recall if the sound had been there all along. Laughter rained around him—rising over the tops of the lockers, soft at first—then quickly escalating into hoots.

The swell of darkness billowed over him, separating him from his movements as bitterness overtook him. He yanked the toy from the shelf, ripping the arms and legs free before slamming it to the floor and stomping on it. He felt the satisfying crunch as the metal cymbals bent and the monkey's body collapsed under his heel.

Clyde fell back heavily, landing on the wooden bench between the rows of lockers, feeling the rawness in his throat from his guttural screams as awareness of his surroundings returned. His chest expanded and contracted rapidly as he sucked in air, forcing him to lean forward—hands on knees, palms up—and stare at the grease beneath his nails.

He wiped his hands on his thighs, forcing deep breaths in and out. The darkness continued to swim before his eyes, hanging over the lockers like a cloud. The men's laughter echoed and burned his ears. Hatred and violence built unchecked until they erupted from his throat.

"LEAVE ME BE!" he roared, his hands balling into fists as he staggered to his feet. Air whistled in and out through his flared nostrils, his shoulders hunched up around his ears, and his muscles taut with the power the darkness fed through his blood.

Clyde's knee bent awkwardly as he climbed to the top of the bench, bringing his other leg up and leaning forward to grab the edge of the lockers, his fingertips stretching to pull them forward. They crashed to the floor, their metallic ring filling the room as they hit the floor.

Four of his coworkers stood on the other side, frozen into a tableau of astonished horror, naked to his anger. Their laughter disappeared, lost in the echo of the metal crashing around them.

Clyde jumped back to the floor with a nimbleness that belied his stunted legs. Straddling the remains of the monkey lying between his feet again, he watched their eyes moving uneasily, shifting from him to the shattered toy. Its crumpled cymbals were silent, its batteries lying on the floor next to it. Clyde's head swiveled from side to side, his body bowed tight, and his chin lowered to his chest.

"What the fuck?" one of the men closest to him shouted, having found his voice. He pushed past the others, knocking them off balance in his haste to make his way to the emergency exit behind them. His hand hit the steel bar as Clyde charged at them. The other three men piled into his back. The alarm blared into the room.

Clyde stretched his arms until his hands touched the door frame on either side, watching them run, leaving him alone with his anger for the space of a dozen heartbeats. He let the darkness rise, swirling around his feet until it obscured the room and the monkey's remains behind him. From within the dark mist, he heard running feet and raised voices. They propelled him onward through the open exit, the darkness leading and guiding him, reaching out to the chaos in the other men's souls. Darkness always found darkness. He loped forward, manic glee stretching his mouth in a wide grin.

Clyde stood in the mouth of an alley, his body trembling and his knuckles skinned raw and throbbing with pain. Blood and gore splattered the coveralls he still wore. In the distance, a church bell rang five times, disorienting him further. He remembered that he got off work at 4:30. It was a full thirty minutes later.

His eyes blinked rapidly and fluttered, and he felt light-headed, bewildered, and unaware of having come there. His thinking was blurred around the edges, replaced by an ever-increasing need that gnawed at him.

He raised his bloody knuckles, bits of flesh stuck in the skin, and scrutinized them. Flashes blinked in and out of his conscious memory: laughter, a monkey, his coworkers running and looking back over their shoulders as he closed the distance between them. Had he caught them?

He waited for his memory to catch up. When he heard them again, there was no laughter, only the sound of bones crunching and muffled screams for mercy and pleas that sent shivers of pleasure through his body. He smiled, licking his knuckles and tasting the blood. He felt power flowing back into him. He shivered in near ecstasy. Oh yes, he had caught them. The memories drifted together, puzzle pieces of pain, a dark thread strung between him and the still bodies he'd left in another alley somewhere behind him. The thread assured him they were alive.

Awareness bled into his reality, and he knew what he was waiting for. He was in *her* alley and had come for her. The darkness needed Eva. It had broken loose, rolling and declaring its dominance.

Already, he could feel her throat between his hands as he cleansed the world of her filth, purging it from her. No longer would the stench of her sin sully the air. Panic rose as her foul odor blended into his olfactory memory, mixing her scent with Mae's.

Outrage flash fired, ignited. He heard his mother's accusations. "*She done robbed you of your power. She done castrated you, just like Delilah did Samson. Done took your power. Stole your anointing, the special power God done give you at birth. Just like I warned you.*"

His conflicted emotions spun and spiraled as the sentient blackness ruled. He felt Mae's voice attempt to rise to the surface, colliding with his mother's voice.

A choked cry of anguish strangled in his throat as the darkness channeled his need for Eva, fusing it with the warped misery his life had become. The darkness had searched for culpability and found Mae.

She blinds you, it warned. *Took you from home and brought you here to this hellish place.* He heard her smooth lies woven around him, chaining him. *First, do Eva—then her*, it demanded.

Clyde began to tremble, clenching and unclenching his hands, then fisting them at his side. Sweat broke out on his forehead, dripping down his nose as he fought to master the churning turbulence. He tried to think of his good Mae, her touch on his skin, and how she made him feel safe and loved.

For a flickering moment, it worked, and he remembered his Mae, the way her deep dimples appeared on her cheeks when she smiled at him, how she lulled the darkness until it lay coiled and dormant, buried beneath his love for her.

Then he saw her face last night. Mouth drawn, eyes darting nervously around the room when he came in, withdrawing when he touched her. *The taint of sin is on her*, the darkness whispered. *Just like it is on Eva.*

Grasping his head with both hands, he squeezed. First, he had to deal with the one the darkness had chosen for him. The one he had been watching. He had to stop being a fool. The Creator abhorred a fool. He focused on the woman.

This one was Eva, just like the trifling woman that led Adam to his fall from grace, like Mae had led him to his fall. He'd heard men call to her, voices thick with the familiarity of where their hands and tongues and mouths had been and how they longed to be between her thighs again. Clyde had watched the sway of her hips, felt her in his man parts, and let the darkness persuade him.

The Creator's righteousness, absent for so long, was again his constant companion. The restraint of the last year dwindled as his mama's words enfolded him: *"You was created special for this."* He was the one who could stop them all. The needs of the darkness roared to full life.

Clyde stood still, pressed into the shadows, intently listening until he heard it—the rhythmic click of her heels against the concrete. He sighed. She had come. She wore a powder-blue sweater tossed over her shoulders against the unseasonable coolness of the summer evening. Reaching up, she smoothed the finger waves styled into her hair. A full-throated laugh rushed into the night as she waved over her shoulder at someone out of his line of vision.

He pushed back against the alley wall and remained still, the darkness concealing him as she passed by just within his reach. The shadows that had swallowed him hid him as he tensed to lunge.

Reaching out, the urgency heating his blood, Clyde grabbed her, slapping his hand over her mouth while he held her against his broad chest. Feebly struggling as she craned her head backward to look up at him, her eyes widened in terror.

"I gots you now, Jezebel." He breathed into her face, a bubble of freedom bursting in his chest as he pressed on her throat with one hand and watched her gasp for air. She choked, her eyes rolled upward, and her body went limp against him.

His mind was clear now, and he could think. He recalled parking his truck in the rear of the alley. Moving quickly, he pulled her semiconscious body to it, his arm wrapped around her waist like an affectionate lover. Opening the passenger door, he pushed her onto the seat, sat, and waited again. Sliding the key into the ignition, he looked from left to right, then drove out slowly onto the deserted street. Eva's body slid from the seat to the floor. Her eyes fluttered open, and she moaned, her hands reaching up to grasp the edge of the seat.

Clyde leaned sideways, his hand releasing from the steering wheel as he lifted his fist and slammed it into her face, the nose bone crunching and blood spurting outward, splashing warm across his lips. He shuddered in ecstasy, his tongue sliding over his lips, relishing the taste as he sucked off the red droplets.

The road was barren as he slowed the truck and drove over the grass into the park's wooded area, the truck concealed by the trees. Clyde pulled a blanket and a shovel from the backseat before opening the passenger door. He wrapped the blanket around her, hoisting her over his shoulder. He kicked the door shut and balanced the shovel he carried in his other hand before dropping the body to the ground. Walking quickly, he scanned the area repeatedly, reassuring himself that he was not seen. He walked deeper into the trees, finding the clearing he had marked on his previous visits.

Clyde heaved Eva, listening to the thud as her body hit the ground, swallowing his disappointment. She was already dead. She'd stopped breathing during the ride, denying him the pleasure of hearing her confession of her sins.

Whirling on the corpse, he kicked it, hearing the squelching sound as his steel-toed boot connected with her head. He stepped back as a deep red stain spread across the blanket.

Looking around him, he was temporarily transported, and an encroaching sense of safety swam through his blood. The closeness of the trees and the way they surrounded the clearing felt familiar, like home. The twilight of late summer blinked in and out through the leaves as he inhaled a deep lungful of air and let the tension begin to uncoil.

The fabric of his new world continued shredding at the seams, leaving him powerless to stop. Nothing had been right since they had arrived in Chicago. The laughter of the past and present pounded in his brain, making him desperate to hear Fannie's voice again.

Throwing his head back, he let his mouth fall open and howled, "Fuck!" then recoiled from the word. His language had deteriorated, tainted by the sin around him.

Turning, Clyde kicked out at the tree trunk looming near him before sliding to the ground. Pulling his knees up to his chest, he buried his face against his thighs and let the darkness envelop him. It pushed against every part of him until he felt it sliding out of each orifice and back into the night air. He found himself sobbing brokenly. The darkness demanded satisfaction.

Taking the shovel in his gloved hands, he began to dig, turning over heaps of earth and creating the hole she would lie in. More than she deserved, he thought. Better to be left in the streets where she whored, for the dogs to devour. But he could leave nothing to chance—no loose ends, no chances of being caught.

Bit by bit, with each shovelful of dirt, he felt the fear eroding. He shook himself, dropped the shovel, pounded his chest, and howled again at the sky, the laughter ringing in his ears.

"Stop being a pussy," he shouted into the night air, now relishing the way the foul, forbidden words sounded coming off his tongue. "I ain't no p . . . p . . . pussy."

He let the words rattle around his brain, the bad words pushing at the laughter, the ridicule, and the humiliation.

He walked around the body twice before shoving it with his toe and rolling it into the open grave, listening to the gratifying *thunk* as it hit the bottom. Whistling, he dropped clods of dirt from his shovel onto her ruined face as she stared wide eyed and unseeing at him.

He would bury her deep, let her disappear like every whore before her. Now, the darkness turned its attention to Mae and *her* transgressions.

CHAPTER SEVEN

Clyde watched Mae flinch as he stepped into the apartment almost two hours later, causing her to miss a stitch in the row of the Afghan she was crocheting. His eyes narrowed, daring her to question him about his lateness.

Mae let the yarn and crochet hook fall into her lap as she studied him, standing with the closed door behind him, trying to calibrate his mood and assess the level of danger he brought, wondering when and how everything had gone so incredibly wrong.

Clyde lowered his head, hiding his eyes from her view as his stride took him across the floor to the sink. He passed by the chair she sat in without leaning down to press a kiss to her forehead. She rose halfway and then flopped back into the cushions, clearing her throat to get his attention.

"Hey, Clyde, how you be?" she asked, her voice low and holding a quiver.

He grunted and continued to the sink, turning the water on full force before scrubbing his hands vigorously with the Lava soap from the dish.

Gathering her courage, Mae stood, dropping the yarn and unfinished Afghan into the chair. Approaching Clyde, she fought the urge to lean forward, touch his shoulder gently, and turn him around to face her. She would stroke his hair, feeling the silken curls slide through her fingers as they worked themselves to his cheeks, and found the soothing rhythm that would settle him and dissolve his troubles. Instead, she stood still and waited for him to turn.

He spun around, staring hard at her, his nostrils flaring impossibly wide as he inhaled, then shrank back, her smell repugnant.

"Why you smell like that?" he demanded, his nose wrinkling in disgust.

Mae lifted her arm upward, leaned down, and sniffed at her armpit, searching for that raw, musty scent.

"Smell like what?" she asked, her eyebrows raised, puzzled. "I done had a bath yesterday."

"Then you needs to take another one today. You stink." He slung the words at her as he went to the chair, throwing her crochet work to the floor and kicking it in her direction. "Pick this mess up. Cain't a man get no rest when he come home?"

"I get it up, Clyde," she said, rushing across the room, leaning to pick up her work and clasping it to her chest. "And I gots your dinner ready. Baked chicken and cabbage. I know you likes it."

His dark eyes seemed to dim, an edge of red showing on the rims. Mae felt a tremor begin deep in her belly, traveling upward and spreading down her arms to her hands. She fumbled the yarn as it slipped from her grasp.

"You makes it for me?" His voice was tinged with suspicion, his eyebrows lifting. "You ain't still feeding your mens, is you?"

"Clyde, I done told you, I don't cooks for them no more. Not since that trouble what we had."

Mae did not see him move; her thought cut off before she could continue it. Clyde's open-palmed slap cracked against her cheek. Dropping to her knees from the force, Mae's hand rubbed her stinging cheek.

Tears slid through her spread fingers, trailing down the back of her hand. She remained on the floor, dazed and disoriented. Slowly, she staggered to her feet and back across the room to the double-burner hot plate. Using two potholders, she lifted the pot of cabbage and carried it carefully to the table, where she ladled it into their waiting bowls.

Clyde joined her at the table, the chair groaning under his weight. Picking up his spoon, he shoveled the steaming cabbage into his mouth, not bothering to say grace.

"I should have listened to my mama," he mumbled. Mae lowered her head, her eyes focused on her plate as the tears continued to fall.

"And shut up that damned noise," Clyde growled, rising from his seat and looming over her, his hand raised.

Mae sniffled loudly, sucking down her tears, and went silent. Clyde fell heavily back into the chair, attacking his food. The clanking of spoons against plates was the only sound in the room.

Cora sat beside the window, the stirring of a slight breeze pushing through the screen. In the kitchen, the sound of porcelain against metal clanked through the house as Gal finished the dinner dishes, humming a gospel hymn. Cora strained to make out the words, comforted by the soothing alto of her voice.

She shifted restlessly in her chair, her spirit disturbed by her most recent dreams. She had been drawn to the glen again, the Knowing pulling her forward to find Clyde huddled in the grass. The light surrounding him was dimming, and she could see the darkness pushing against it, straining to escape. The morning found her staring at the ceiling, cold dread clutching her heart.

Sitting with the sun's heat still clinging to the glass of their living room window, Cora felt the room's temperature slowly fall, sending shivers through her body jangling her nerves. Her good leg and hand began to tremble simultaneously with enough force to shake the Afghan free of her shoulders. She stared down at it, unable to retrieve it.

Suddenly, she moaned and spittle came from her mouth as a glimmer of light near the door caught her attention. She cringed, her vulnerability exposed as she remained trapped within the confines of her wheelchair, waiting, defenseless, against whatever came.

The light shimmered and gathered itself into a wispy form, solidifying into the shape of a woman.

"Who you? Where I'm at?" The high-pitched screech reeked of the fear trapped in the residual remains of the woman who stood before her.

Cora recognized the horrified expression on her face immediately . . . the bulging, fear-filled eyes, the mangled throat, and the confusion.

"Calms yourself, child. I knows you all riled up right now."

"Who you? Where I be at?"

The number of these women mixed among the dead coming to her had grown for almost eleven years. First, slowly, only two during the year Clyde killed Robert and Baby Doll. Then, every two or three months, there would be another one. Always women or girls. All garishly dressed and hard used by the world.

Over nine years, he had never gone without killing. There was always some new lost soul drifting in. Thirty women weighed down with the bitterness of life cut short, a brevity not of their own making. They haunted the slow, tedious minutes and hours of each day, inescapable.

She thought back to when he had stopped. She'd first noticed it not too long after Gal said she ran into Fannie in town with some cute little girl hanging onto her. When she recollected the time, it aligned with the news of Clyde's marriage and the more than three months since anyone new had afflicted her.

Not too long after, Gal had come running in, filled with gossip from town, and told her they all had better pray for the mighty state of Mississippi because word was that was where Clyde and Mae had left for.

And then there was nothing. Month after month, and still nothing. The only newly dead are the result of old age, illness, or the suffering of life. They came to her searching for resolution or absolution with their loved ones or wandered in denial of their deaths. None were ushered across the threshold with any help from Clyde. No darkness draped their auras. Her connection with Clyde was inexplicably severed. She could no longer feel him for the first time since his birth had cursed her life.

The months bled into one another until they became six and then twelve. Cora had allowed herself to believe he had to be dead, taken out by a force more powerful than the evil that ran through him. She'd reasoned that only death could have kept him from killing. It was the blood that nourished him. He could not live without it, couldn't control it. So, Cora let herself believe it was over. The light had achieved victory without her . . . until now . . . until this woman appeared.

Cora let her gaze rove over the woman. Her black skirt hugged her hips down to her knees where it flared, the black stockings with a seam running up the back, and the black patent leather stiletto heels. A wide belt cinched an impossibly tiny waist above the soft white silk blouse spotted with blood that she wore.

Her clothing made her look different from the rest, but the buck-eyed horror, the splashes of blood, and the hysterical denial that death had indeed claimed her marked her as the same. It was the commonality she shared with the others. Only the clothes she wore marked her as foreign to the South.

Gal glanced over at Cora for a half second, watching her lean forward and motion with her left hand, muttering. She sighed before returning her attention to the radio. She'd long ago become accustomed to Cora's long, rambling sessions, where she mumbled and groaned to the air in front of her, sometimes for hours. It had bothered her at first when Cora started trying to talk again, making her jump and search the room for haunts and spooks.

The doctor said Cora's brain was scrambled and would never be right, and they better thank God she could talk at all. After years of being as still as stone, she—like Joe—was grateful to have any parts of Miss Cora back, so long as she wasn't just sitting in that chair like she used to. It didn't matter that they barely understood her words.

The spirit before Cora wailed loudly, her mouth wide open, head whipping back and forth. She fell backward, her heels drumming against the floor and her hands reaching up to grasp an unseen assailant as she writhed beneath him.

"You going to have to stop all that caterwauling, Miss Ma'm. Ain't nothing what can hurts you no more. You is dead," Cora snapped. She had learned it was pointless to draw the truth out.

The years had drained compassion from her. It served no purpose other than prolonging her aggravation and needlessly extending the turmoil surrounding the experience. The words she spoke to the spirit rang clearly, unimpeded by the partial paralysis that twisted her body and speech in the natural world.

The woman's scream cut off abruptly, chastised by Cora's tone.

"Who you and where you from?"

A kaleidoscope of emotion flowed over her face. "Eva. Chicago," her tear-choked voice whispered before she evaporated into nothingness.

Cora fell back against her chair and pounded her left fist on the arm of the wheelchair, startling Gal, who leaped up from the couch where she had settled after finishing the dishes. She rushed to her side.

"Miss Cora, you okay?" she asked nervously, grabbing the Afghan that had fallen to the floor. She smoothed the material over Cora's shoulders, her words soft and soothing. Cora was building herself into a fit.

Cora grunted, struggling to force the words up through her mangled vocal cords, rocking in frustration until Gal grabbed her and forcefully pushed her until her back rested against the chair. "You gots to stop this, Miss Cora," she cried. "You going to hurt yourself and me if you keeps it up."

A voice rang inside Cora's head, one that she had longed to hear, strong and familiar. "*It's time,*" Mi's disembodied words commanded.

The sounds of Gal and the radio faded as Cora slumped sideways, silence descending around her. She listened to the sound of her blood rushing through her veins, felt the snakes of power writhing under her skin, and watched the blinding light build against her closed eyelids.

The woman hadn't said Clyde's name, but Cora knew it was him. Knew by the darkness that shrouded the pale light of the dead woman's aura. Her previous failures resonated deep within, and she felt a tear trickling down the left side of her face. It had come at last. She felt her power building, stronger than it had been in ten years.

Her work was not done. The respite was over. She relaxed into her chair, allowing Gal to wrap her in her Afghan before falling into a deep sleep. Behind her closed eyelids, she thrilled as her new power reached out through her dreams.

The light bent and shimmered around Cora as she stood mutely among the trees, her large frame shrouded in a simple calico dress that hung just above her ankles. The broad brim of a hat concealed her face from the boy and man seated in the grass, except for her eyes. She felt them furiously blazing as she looked from one to another.

Clyde inhaled deeply, his lungs fit to burst with the sweet, satisfying scent of the woods around him, making his head swim. He knew this place; knew it well. For a moment, beside him, he saw the specter of his young self hover with him on the edge of the water. The grass beneath him was dead and brown from his constant presence. His face turned up to the warmth of the sun. This was where he sought solace from the hateful words and stares that comprised his life.

The boy Clyde cocked his head to the side, listening for the familiar sounds of insects and frogs that normally chorused through the air, and found only deafening silence. It struck a chord of wrongness. Both Clydes listened intently, bodies leaning forward.

A twig snapped, and young Clyde turned his head, staring mournfully past him into the woods. Someone was coming, someone who was trying to creep up on them, someone who wanted to do them harm.

Clyde's skin crawled, and he felt his shoulders squeeze with tension, his muscles contracting in preparation to flee. He waited, staring.

She was on him instantly, clinging to his back, one arm wrapped around his throat, both legs wound tightly about his waist as she fought to pull him backward, her other hand wielding a wickedly sharp blade pointed toward his throat.

Clyde bucked wildly, trying unsuccessfully to throw her off him, his hands grasping her muscular forearm and pulling. He struggled for air as she hung on. She couldn't be this damned strong, his mind screamed; no way could she hold him.

Her hand slashed down on an angle, the knife plunging through the back of his hand.

His howl split the night air, causing young Clyde to pull his knees up to his chest and cry out, holding his wounded hand up to his chest, blood leaking from the gash in his hand. Clyde bent forward until he was almost doubled over, then rolled forward until she flipped over him and landed on her back. Her legs scissored around him before he could run, and he found himself still locked in her savage embrace with her staring into his face.

Cora stared up at him, her eyes green pebbles of burning hatred, and her lips pulled back in a snarl as she brought her blade upward to his throat.

"I'm coming for you," she snarled. Cora smiled. Clyde was going to die.

He felt the sharp tip of the blade burn as it ripped into the tender skin of his throat, and the blood flowed out over her hand.

Clyde's eyes flew open, rolling wildly, as he screamed into the stillness of the room. His face twisted and contorted, his body bucking as it had been in the dream, both hands reaching for his throat and searching for blood.

"No, no, Mama, help me!" he cried out as the images flashed fresh through his mind.

Mae sat up in bed, cowering away from him, her newborn fear asserting itself and demanding safety.

"NO! I AIN'T DYING," Clyde shouted into the thick quiet of the room, plunging his hands between his thighs, locking them there, and struggling against himself.

Mae breathed deeply, fighting against her instincts to flee, and moved closer to him. She tried to calm his agitation, her hand circling the crown of his head and then dropping to his cheek, stroking gently.

"What's wrong with you, honey?" she queried, her voice ice smooth as she attempted to comfort him. Clyde slapped her hand away and shoved, pushing so hard that she flew from the bed onto the floor. Air bellowed in and out through his open mouth, forcing her to scramble farther away. His protuberant eyes tracked her movement, the whites standing out in the darkness, stark against his skin. The darkness that was there, more often lately than not, swirled in their depths.

Mae scooted backward until her back was against the wall, using it to push herself upward until she stood. Her fingers slipped from the knob several times as she attempted to turn on the table lamp, flooding the room with light.

His eyes narrowed and slid over her, the darkness beginning to clear as he seemed to recognize the familiar contours of the room. His features slackened but remained guarded. She leaned forward across the short distance between the table and the bed. Reaching tremulously for his face, she let her fingertips graze his cheek and find their rhythm again.

This time, he permitted it. His breathing slowed as the minutes ticked past, the wild back-and-forth darting replaced by a steady, fixed glare. He began to calm down. His labored breathing slowed, and his muscles unclenched. Clyde blinked rapidly at her, recognition seeming to creep across his face for the first time since he awakened.

Easing herself back into the bed, Mae sat beside him, rubbing his back gently, thrilled he welcomed her touch. Daring to hope the old warmth between them was returning, she watched him pull his legs back up onto the bed. Mae lowered her body next to his, snuggling against his chest, lulled by the tranquil peace that lay tentatively between them.

"What was you dreaming?" she asked, scooting up to kiss the corner of his mouth.

Clyde stilled and moved away abruptly, turning and giving her his back.

"Wasn't nothing. Just goes to sleep," he said over his shoulder.

Mae tried to drape her arm over his back, rubbing his ear until she felt him relaxing again. "Sure it wasn't no witch riding your chest?" she teased, attempting to lighten the mood again.

Clyde stiffened. She could not miss the rage signaling from him as the question hung in the air. When he spoke, his voice had gone cold. The warmth between them evaporated, retreating from her and sinking beneath the layers that had been building day after day, leaving this stranger in her bed . . . a man who terrified her.

"Turn off that damned light," he muttered, silencing any further questions or conversations. "Only witch around here be Miss Ruby."

Mae stretched out her arm, reaching to extinguish the light. The bed moved beneath her, dipping as Clyde turned back toward her. She heard the blow coming, whistling through the air before exploding against the side of her head.

She rolled from the bed and curled into herself—knees and head tucked to her chest, desperately attempting to protect herself—as he continued using his fist, leaning out of the bed to strike her body and arms. Mae waited for his rage to be spent, waited for him to pry her legs apart and drive into her. Tears poured onto the cotton of her nightgown as she choked on silent sobs.

The bed creaked and groaned as Clyde clamored back to his side of the mattress. Within a few minutes, his heavy snores filled the room.

Mae did not move. She remained on the floor, the pain throbbing with every beat of her heart while she stared out the window and waited, searching for the sun to bruise the sky.

CHAPTER EIGHT

Mae pulled the sleeve of her cardigan down over her hand, covering the remnants of a large bruise. Her eyes darted away from Ruby as she passed her walking the length of the hallway to the incinerator at its end. She stepped carefully, the soreness between her legs making her move awkwardly.

Ruby avoided eye contact as well, causing Mae to question how much the woman heard through the thinness of the walls. Did she hear his angry grunts as he thrust and pounded her flesh? Did she hear her holding in her cries? Shame reddened her cheeks.

"How you, Mae? I ain't seen much of you this past week," Ruby said, clearing her throat in the uncomfortable silence that blossomed between them.

"I been real behind in my housework. You know, it a little place, but it take a lot to keeps it clean. I been doing the windows and such."

"Humph," Ruby snorted, her eyes darting involuntarily to Mae's hand, watching her pull the sleeve down further and hold it tight with her fingers. "That's good, less work for me. I need to take a look. I bet you can see them shining from the street."

Mae shrugged and shifted her bag, looking longingly at the incinerator. All she wanted was to keep going, throw away her garbage, get back inside, and, most of all, stay away from Ruby.

Ruby shifted her weight, determined to force Mae to talk to her. She missed her friend.

"You know, you ain't the only one been missing around here. Jimmie ain't been here since it was all that ruckus with Clyde. He say anything to you about it?"

"Nah, not much," Mae muttered, shuffling forward and leaving Ruby standing at her own door.

In front of the incinerator, Mae stood, hip cocked to brace the hand holding the garbage bag. She watched as Ruby stood in the doorway of her room and stared hard in Mae's direction before moving toward her. Though only a few feet of the hallway's air—thick with the aroma of conflicting meals being cooked in private rooms—separated them, it formed a chasm between them. Ruby sighed. The hollow emptiness that had accompanied her days before she met Mae had returned.

"If I done something what made your husband mad with me, you can tells me, Mae. I ain't no babe. I knows him and Jimmie had words. Then you got 'busy' and been busy every day since. Ain't nobody stupid."

Mae searched the floor for the words to explain what she didn't understand herself, how Clyde had been changing every day since then. Yes, God, he had changed.

He stormed through their small room each evening, glaring at her, following her with eyes that burned with hatred. She didn't know him anymore, didn't *want* to know him. Her other hand rubbed absently at the bruise hidden beneath her sleeve, willing the pain away.

Her mind scrapped and shredded all the things she had done . . . eschewing time with Ruby, foregoing spending time with her, shunning even the mention of her name. She remained closeted inside their apartment, avoiding the other tenants while letting her secret meal cooking stagnate. Her life had deteriorated into one continuous nightmare of degradation, pain, and humiliation.

Clyde's hands had become his primary means of communication, printing his displeasure on her flesh, revealing the brutal, wild man she had heard whispered about back home. The one she had only occasionally glimpsed . . . until now.

The man she married had vanished into nonexistence, leaving this angry person who beat her savagely and screwed her until her womb ached from the pounding. His darkness roiled between them, smothering the life from her.

She shook herself, realizing she had been standing still, staring at a spot above Ruby's head, her eyes vacant. Ruby shot snuff into the can in her hand and wiped her mouth with her handkerchief.

"Is you okay, Mae?" she asked, hearing the underlying plea in her words. She wanted Mae to look at her, to see the wisdom in her eyes, see she had a story to tell, a tale that could save her.

Ruby sifted through the memories awakened of hands pummeling flesh and choked whimpers seeping through thin walls. Not Mae's, but her own. Her features scrunched, her brows coming together over her wrinkled nose. She pulled the courage to tell the truth about good men into the light. Good men who hid their badness from the world, saving it to unleash on the women who loved them.

"I'm gon' catch up with you, Miss Ruby." Mae sighed, her shoulders slumping. "You been a good friend to me and all. But, Miss Ruby, Clyde, he my husband. He ain't never been happy since we come here. My muhdeah say sometimes you got to let a man be a man and do what a man do." She paused, reading the air as she collected her thoughts, then continued. "And Clyde, he been having a hard time. I don't thinks he feel like the man he need to be. He be thinking we needs to go back to Louisiana. I wants to stay here, but he might be right. Us might needs to go back home."

She sighed again, finally lifting her eyes to Ruby's. "I'm gon' miss you if I do."

Ruby's gaze roamed, following the turmoil flowing across Mae's delicate features, waiting for her to finish. Her words diminished to a near whisper.

"He really do be a good man," Mae murmured. "He just having a real hard time right now."

"All right, then." Ruby felt her courage dissolve as the seconds ticked by, and the space between them grew, the chasm becoming an abyss. Straightening her posture, Ruby seemed to decide and raised her head, her chin jutting forward. "I understands what you saying, though, and I ain't one to come between a husband and wife." The silence stretched between them, and she waited. "If you gets a chance, that gal down in 110 got her a sick boy. You might see if your herbs can help. I done told her about you, and she be waiting."

She remembered the thumps against the thin wall again, followed by Mae's choked whimpers; remembered keeping her own pain a secret locked behind swollen lips and transparent lies. "You knows where I be, Mae. All you needs to do is knock on this here door if you needs me."

Mae smiled weakly, walking past Ruby and back to her own door.

CHAPTER NINE

Cora sat stiffly in the passenger seat of Joe's truck, her good eye combing the boardwalk and watching as the dead drifted over and between the living, some sidling up to the passenger door of the car to stare at her, hands outstretched and imploring her to hear them. She turned away and willed them to be gone. A curtain dropped over her mind, shielding her from the cacophony of need that threatened to swamp her and leaving her to mull over her most recent dreams of Clyde.

"You going to be all right here, Cora?" Joe smiled, reaching across to squeeze her hand.

"Yes." She forced the word through her mangled vocal cords and gave him a lopsided smile that did not reach her eyes.

"I should have brought Gal with us. Then you wouldn't be sitting here by yourself," he said, unable to keep the sigh from his voice.

Cora swallowed her frustration. He didn't know that it was just good to get out of the house, to look at something other than the walls of their living room and bedroom, and see someone other than him and Gal. Their sons seldom endured her presence beyond what was demanded. Even the church was absent from their lives. Joe didn't care, unwilling to sit under the hypocritical judgment that accompanied their visits. She tried to smile and make it reach him.

He squeezed her hand again and smiled back. "That's my girl. I won't be gone long."

He let go and slid out of the truck, closing the door firmly behind him. Giving her one final parting glance, he thanked God as he always did that Cora was alive, still with him despite the odds. Finally, with a heavy tread, he turned to walk toward Harold's Feed and Grain, planning his circuitous route to end up at Hattie's General Store, where the truck was parked. Unable to stop himself, his head swiveled around until he stared back at the vehicle, nodding at Cora as she leaned against the passenger window, showing the healthy side of her face. Up one side of the boardwalk and down the other, he told himself, and he'd be back.

Outside of Hattie's, Fannie stood still, allowing the waves of déjà vu to drift over her as she stood on the wooden boards of Main Street. She relived images that Clyde had shared with her so vividly they had become part of her own reality . . . Baby Doll and that woman locked in a swirl of skirts, the ice pick tearing through flesh. She was sucked back into a maelstrom of anger and hatred, the feelings as fresh as they were ten years ago. Knowing that nasty whore had deserved every bit of the death that found her filled Fannie with a deep satisfaction.

Stooping her slight frame forward so that her bonnet fell to conceal her face, she wiped the sweat from her palms on the starched apron that covered the front of her dress. Keeping her eyes fixed on the gray boards, she eased into Hattie's and stood, waiting as her vision adjusted to the dim interior. Hattie nodded in her direction, her three chins wobbling, as she completed the order of the man standing before her.

Fannie bounced on her toes, quivering with the anticipation of hearing Clyde's voice. She'd been just about out of her mind sitting in that shack with nothing but the rats and her memories to keep her company, convinced that God had abandoned her when he took Clyde, his anointed, away from her.

She saw herself lying facedown on the dirt floor and crying out her desperation over the last year. Cajoling, demanding, screaming, imploring the Creator until her throat was raw and her voice was hoarse. Both his blessings and his hand of protection continued to elude her, stripped away when Clyde had fallen to the curse of that little hussy.

Her hand fingered the gold cross around her neck as she whispered prayers quietly, seeking forgiveness for her doubt and disbelief. The lure Mae held between her thighs was strong but not as strong as the power of the bond between her and Clyde. He was hers.

A man pushed past her to the front door, distracted by his own thoughts. Fannie shifted uncomfortably and stepped back, ignoring the tingle of familiarity at the sight of his broad shoulders.

Hattie cleared her throat several times before she spoke. "How you, Miss Fannie? You welcome to sits there on that barrel and waits for your boy to call if you wants," she said, pointing her chins toward a large barrel beneath the black phone attached to the wall.

Hattie regarded Fannie with undisguised scrutiny, examining her from the broad-flowered bonnet, faded gingham dress, and immaculate apron to the dusty shoes on her feet. She raised one eyebrow at the harmless appearance Fannie presented.

Hattie's eyes followed her movement warily. Gal had filled her ears with a boatload of gossip about Fannie and that boy of hers when Fannie returned to town. She'd left it to swim around in Hattie's head, unanchored to anything substantial or real . . . until the day that Clyde called. She shivered, remembering the uneasiness that invaded her body, congealing into a dark mass that froze her blood. The fear resurfaced, and she turned to the shelves behind her, busying herself with shuffling items into empty spaces, keeping her eyes off Fannie.

Suddenly, the phone rang shrilly, and Hattie jumped, startled. Squeezing her immense bulk through the space that separated the counter from the shelves, she made her way to the phone, lifting it from its cradle.

"Hattie's General Store," she barked into the receiver, her voice elevated as though shouting made it easier for the person on the other end to both hear and understand her across the miles of distance.

"This be Clyde. My mama there?" The voice panted out the question.

"Hold on." Hattie watched as Fannie leaped from the top of the barrel where she had been sitting. She snatched the receiver from Hattie's outstretched hand, then glared at the woman until she turned away and began returning to the front of the store. Two small children scampered toward them, then stopped as their mother shooed them back in the opposite direction.

Fannie listened to the breathing on the other end of the line, synchronized it with her own, and felt the rhythm of his heartbeat across time and space. She inhaled deeply.

"Baby boy?" she whispered.

"Mama?" Clyde choked out the question.

Silence echoed across the damning words of the past and the 800-plus miles between them. And she waited to hear what he wanted to say, feeling his hurt and pain twisting in her gut.

"I wants to come home," he said, the words finally exploding into the phone's receiver as, on the other end, he squeezed it tightly in his hand.

Fannie felt her heart spasm in delight as the words she had longed to hear became a reality. She sucked them in, rolled them around in her own mouth, tasted the sweetness, and silently praised God for answering her prayers.

"No, baby boy, you ain't got to come back here. This place ain't home for you and me no more." Her jubilation changed the cadence of her words as she spoke rapidly into the phone, aware that they did not have much time. "I knowed you would come to your senses one day, and Lord be praised, I gots a plan for us."

Fannie licked her dry, chapped lips, feeling them cracking and bleeding as the beginning of a smile spread across her face. Her life—which had been hanging by a rope of regret tied to a bucket of misery—shuddered back into existence.

When Hattie's boy had come banging on her door with his message from Clyde, Fannie had stood reeling and blinking in the doorway, stunned by his words that flung her a lifeline. Walking to the center of the room, she had looked down at the form of her body imprinted into the floor's dust, worn by her lying prostrate on her face, day and night, fasting and praying for God's favor and the return of her boy.

She heard Clyde sigh through the connection, his relief palpable, and her heart fluttered in her chest. Fannie felt the first tentative threads of the link between them blossoming anew, encouraging her to continue.

"First, tell me what wrong?"

She heard the familiar growl, full-throated as he spoke. "Ain't nothing here like I expected. It just all the same as before. And—"

She didn't let him finish the sentence. "Don't say no more. You don't know who listening." Her eyes stared pointedly at the front of the store until Hattie lowered her head and looked away. "Ain't I always told you? It just be you, me, and God." Fannie let him absorb her words before she asked her next question. "What about *her*?"

His taciturn silence was all the answer she required. It didn't matter. Her body trembled with excitement as she heard him deposit more coins at the operator's request.

"Don't you worry none, baby boy. God been making a way for us. Um-hmmm." Her head bobbed up and down as she spoke, her free hand patting her chest. "I be taking in washing and baking bread. I gots us money saved. I just been waiting."

"Me, you, and Mae?" he inquired tersely.

Fannie swallowed the acrid hatred that tried to push its way up with her words. "I done said I been saving for us. And you know if you loves her, then I likes her."

She swallowed the desire to dig at him about Mae, to spew the bitter diatribe that assaulted her thoughts from the moment she awoke until she lay down in her narrow bed, her breasts aching for her lost son. Instead, she rejoiced in the benevolence of the moment. She allowed the "us" to remain intentionally ambiguous between them.

"Now, I'm going get the bus and the train and comes to Chicago. You meets me at the train station. I be done figured it all out by the time I gets there."

Her words tiptoed gingerly through her next thoughts, cautious of alienating him again. "Don't you worry none, baby boy. Everything be right soon as I get there. Won't be but about a week or two."

She listened to his harsh breathing as her mind began arranging the details for the Greyhound to Mississippi and the city of New Orleans to Chicago, laid out just as she had dreamed, conveniently eliminating Mae from her vision. She dug down into her apron pocket and pulled out the worn and wrinkled train schedule, smoothing it out in the palm of her hand while she cradled the phone between her neck and shoulder.

"Today be Tuesday," she continued. "Meets me at Union Station two weeks from today. It be a few things I got to arrange before I comes. But I gets it all ready. Us gon' be together again, baby boy."

Their hearts beat a sympathetic rhythm across the miles and swept them back to a space of unity, erasing the gulf of his betrayal with his need.

"I calls Miss Hattie if I needs to get word to you before you comes. And, Mama, I be sorry." Clyde's voice reverberated across the line, signaling his profound deprivation to her eager ears.

"Ain't no need to say nothing. I knows the truth. I done always knowed the truth. Don't you worry none. Mama be there, and everything be fine. Just fine." She hesitated, then added, "Don't tell Mae until I gets there. It be a surprise."

"We be waiting when you gets here." He finished, swallowing his disappointment that it would be two weeks, breaking the connection before she could reassure him of her love for him. She stood with the phone pressed against her chest and her mouth moving in wordless praise. It didn't matter. Her everything was being restored to her, and what was broken was mending itself. Her God had answered her prayers, and she was sure a solution to Mae would present itself.

Reaching up to place the receiver back into its cradle, striding quickly past Hattie, she almost floated from the store. Happiness dismissed everything beyond Clyde's words pulsating in her heart.

Fannie stood outside. The August sun blazed in a cloudless sky and heated her skin. She ripped loose the strings of the bonnet from her head and threw it back, laughing out loud. A moment later, a long, undulating shriek split the air, cutting into her joy. Fannie stopped, her head swiveling slowly on her neck and searching to find the source of the cries. Her eyes narrowed.

The screaming woman's face was skeletal, the skin dripping from the skull, an ill-fitting mask hinting at the person it hid. Something about the eyes clawed at her remembrance even though her brain screamed that it couldn't be. But it was Cora. The eyes in the cadaverous face still sparkled with hatred as they stared out at her from the remnants of the woman Fannie had known.

Fannie's visage tightened with anger as she stared at Cora sitting in the truck, her mouth stretched wide with the force of her scream. They locked eyes, and then Fannie smiled. Cora's eyes widened before she fell back against the seat, her body convulsing as it bounced around.

Fannie hawked and spat, the saliva sliding down the window. "Bitch, I hope you die for real this time."

She hysterically laughed as she grasped her skirts in both hands, lifted them above her ankles, and ran, disappearing around the corner of the building. Sensory memory guided her on a diagonal angle that would lead her out of sight and away from town.

Joe pushed his cap back from his forehead, wiping at the sweat from where the band sat as he exited the shoe repair shop adjacent to Hattie's. His body jolted, hearing the muffled sound of Cora's head banging against the truck window. His arms released the heavy bags, sugar and flour floating into the air as they crashed to the boards while Cora's screams slammed against his ears. His feet pulled him away from the shoe shop as he raced toward the truck, his eyes stretched wide, guilt twisting his stomach. He shouldn't have made that extra stop. His boots could have waited.

"Cora . . . Cora!" His own hoarse scream joined hers as he pounded on the window glass, watching her body bounce against the seat, a marionette yanked by a sadistic puppeteer.

He felt the thundering, erratic beat of his heart slamming against his rib cage as he fumbled with the door handle, then wrenched the passenger door open, pulling Cora to his chest.

Dragging Cora, he laid her down on the pale gray of the weathered boards beneath them. Her heels drummed against the wood, her head thrashed from side to side, and her fists rigid against her sides as her mouth stretched sideways in a scream.

Hattie appeared, framed in the doorway, a look of alarm etched across her face as she wrung her hands in front of her.

"What I can do, Joe?" she asked, her voice rising above the chaos.

"You gots a popsicle stick? I needs something for her to bite down on."

Cora's fit began to subside, becoming tremors, her limbs jerking and her head thumping against the boardwalk. She became aware of the rough callouses of Joe's palms rubbing down her arms and sliding on her bare skin. She worked her jaws, trying to force words free.

"That's okay. She be all right, Miss Hattie. Can you calls over to Doc Adams?" he asked, feeling his own body relax.

"I do that right now." Hattie spun on her heel and disappeared back inside.

"Fannie." Cora groaned, trusting Joe to understand.

A hard knot formed in his stomach as the garbled word translated itself into a name.

CHAPTER TEN

Cora sat still at the living room table, her right hand smoothing the lace and linen cloth that covered it, and stared out at the tree in the yard. She imagined herself walking through the hard brown grass, feeling it break under her toes as she made her way to the tree, picked pecans, held them in the hammock of her apron, and dreamed of the pecan pies she would bake.

She stared upward through the heavy branches soaring more than seventy feet into the sky, the thick canopy protecting the house as it had for over one hundred years, marking where her ancestors gathered to meet and exchange stories. Reaching out with her senses, she felt for the light around her. Felt for the blood of the long gone to lend her strength and wisdom.

The tangle of her emotions knotted, then frayed as she thought of Clyde, loose somewhere in Chicago. Was he stalking another victim while she sat trapped inside her body, the power of the Knowing locked within her? Her agitation escaped in moans of frustration, her mouth twitching uncontrollably, her good eye focused on Joe standing by the mantle.

"I thought sure we was through with Fannie after Gal seen her a year back. You remembers." Joe chewed on the stem of his pipe as he sucked on it, exhaling small puffs of smoke as he talked. "Gal said she was with some little cute child done married Clyde, and they was gone move to Mississippi," he continued, not really expecting more than the usual gargled noises from Cora. "Why the hell anybody marry him, I cain't tell you. I wish I had caught his ass or knowed Fannie was back around. I'd have killed her and done my time with a smile."

Rayville was a small town, with word traveling mouth to ear and back, limited only by transportation available to the speakers and listeners. "Ain't no telling how long she been hiding out there in them woods. I remembers when you got dead, Fannie had done hightailed it out that house before I gots there. I wish I knowed where she went." Joe stopped, searching Cora's face, hearing her grunting, the sounds coming faster and louder.

Gal stepped into the room, drying her hands on a cloth as she came from the kitchen, ignoring Cora and turning her comments toward Joe. "Mr. Joe, I done told Miss Cora about that girl what they say Clyde married. She been gone most about a year, but her peoples still in Delhi."

Joe paced, his thoughts racing. Clyde had been back in Rayville as recently as last year, and he hadn't known. "They say anything about her and him?" Joe asked, pacing back and forth across the room, chewing on the stem of his pipe.

"Yeah"—Gal grinned—"they say them was in Mississippi and then went to Chicago. Say that's where they at now. Her name be Mae." Gal squeezed the dish towel in her hands. "She real cute. I seen her that one time with Miss Fannie."

Joe grumbled low in his throat, stared over at Cora, then snapped his mouth shut. Cora's mouth hung open, and her good eye rolled wildly in its socket. Kneeling in front of her chair, he grasped her hands in his, rubbing them in his own.

"I'm sorry, Cora. It just bring it all back to me. Hearing his name. Knowing he been here where he might could hurt you again." He inhaled deeply, then leaned his forehead on her hands. Standing, he motioned to Gal before she could begin again.

Cora counted inside her head, seeking calm, praying until the Knowing rose like the tide. She knew what she needed to do.

She looked down at the sheets of writing paper in front of her and drew in a deep breath, thankful that her mind remained sharp within the withered shell of her broken body. She prepared herself for the ordeal of writing, her good hand shaking in anticipation of holding her pencil for such an extended period as the one that lay ahead.

"I done told you, you needs to get somebody else what knows they letters to write for you, Cora," Joe insisted, settling back into his rocker, blowing smoke rings from his pipe as he rocked the chair forward and back, tapping heel to toe with each motion.

Cora shook her head and grunted her no. They would never understand her mangled speech. She would write for herself, even if it took her all day. Her lamp stood ready for darkness. She glared at Joe, then bent her head to the task, sighing in resignation. She should have felt Clyde sooner. The Knowing should have informed her. Instead, it had let her fail once again.

Her head shot up at the sound of soft sobbing. She glanced past Joe to the couch, where the woman who called herself Eva sat with her ankles crossed primly, wiping the tears that streamed down her cheeks. Cora let her mind connect with her and waited for her words to flow.

"Why he kills me? I ain't never even seen him before. He just grab me and pulls me in the alley and start choking me."

"He ain't needs to know you," Cora answered as women began to assemble, filling the room with their ethereal forms, gliding around their newest member, and studying her intently.

"You make your money on your back?" Baby Doll inquired, one eyebrow arching upward. Eva sucked in air, her mouth rounding and her hand fluttering to her chest.

Baby Doll's laughter was loud and boisterous, joined by the women around her. "Girl, ain't no shame here. We cain't judge nobody, so you can stop putting on airs. We all did the same thing. Spreading our legs for all them righteous pricks. *That's* how he find us."

Eva bowed her head and sniffled again. "That's why he kill me because I be a whore?" She glared at the women around her. "What I'm supposed to do? I got two babies to send money for. How I'm supposed to take care of them?"

Cora cut through the chatter, her thoughts drowning out the others. "Where was you living?"

"Chicago over by Forty-Seventh Street." Her tears had stopped, and she wiggled a little on the couch, trying to make a dent in the cushions.

"You remembers what the man look like what done it?" Cora waited for the verification she knew would come as Eva shuddered.

"I cain't never forgets him, them bug eyes muddy yellow and red all around the edges. It was like it was something in them, something dark what was reaching out to me, trying to pull me in, and he smell like something dead."

Cora stopped listening. She didn't need to hear anything else. She should have told Joe when Gal told her about seeing Fannie. Should have let him go and find her, drag the information from her about where Clyde was. Maybe Eva would still be alive.

Joe was talking again, oblivious to the spirits around him. He cleared his throat, coughing loudly and pounding his chest with his free hand before sucking on his pipe again. Cora looked away from the women who crowded around Eva and obscured her from her sight. What Eva said aligned perfectly with Gal's information. Looking back at the paper, she raised her hand and began to write slowly and carefully.

Dear Miss Mae,

You don't know me. I be the midwife what brought Clyde into this world. I hear tell you married Clyde Henry. I don't know how that be possible, don't see how he get any woman to marry him, but I be guessing what I hear be true. What I'm sending you ain't going to be easy to swallow, but trust and know it be the truth.

Cora straightened her body as much as her muscles would allow and looked down at the sheets of paper filled with her neat, tight script. She had not seen the sun set outside the window or seen Joe turn on the lamp to banish the shadows crowding the table. The familiar weight of her Afghan rested on her shoulders, and beneath it, she felt the knots of pain from leaning over to write. She became aware of the muscles in her hands, cramped and spasming from the tight grip she'd held on the pencil. She felt Joe's warm lips brush against her forehead as he leaned over her.

"Is you finished, stubborn woman?" he asked, looking at the sheets beneath her hand.

She studied the sky, faded to purple and blue like bruised skin, the stars pinpoints of light winking at her. Cora looked up from the letter, wondering if she had said enough or too much.

She nodded at Joe and watched as he folded the pages and placed them in the envelope.

"Me and Gal ride over to that girl's daddy and give him this. Hope he send it to her."

Cora nodded and returned her gaze to the darkness beyond the window. Her breath hitched, and she leaned forward, catching a glimmer of light flickering through the trees.

CHAPTER ELEVEN

Sneaking through the hallways, feeling like a thief, Mae avoided Ruby and her neighbors as she eased shut the door to her room. She leaned back, feeling the press of the cool wood seeping through the thin material of her cotton dress, and took deep breaths. A thin sheen of sweat shone on her forehead as she entered the room.

The late-afternoon sun created bars of light across the table's surface standing in the corner across the room. Dust motes danced in the air, defying her constant cleaning. Walking to it, she lifted the tail end of her dress and wiped across the gleaming surface before reaching into her dress pocket and pulling the thick envelope free. She shook it, curious about its unusual weight. Smoothing it out, she immediately recognized her father's handwriting, the thin, spidery lines.

Glancing over her shoulder toward the door, then back at the clock sitting on the table's polished surface, she calculated Clyde's arrival. Her shoulders relaxed. It was still hours until he would be home.

Her eyes lingered lovingly on the gleaming surfaces of the table beneath the window, her red-and-white kitchen table with the matching upholstered chairs, and the brass headboard of their bed. She would never have had any of this back home.

Looking around the pristine room, Mae became aware of the disparity between her hopes and the dismal prison of fear and secrets that her life had become. It should have been good.

Her hands rubbed the swollen nipples of her breasts, tender from the abrasive sucking and biting Clyde had given them the previous night. Her face was a study in sadness as she sat, isolated in the midst of her bounty. She thought fleetingly of venturing out to find Ruby or one of the other neighbors she had just slid past, then dismissed it as she remembered Clyde's warning. Loneliness tugged at her until the dread of Clyde's appearance obliterated it.

Lowering herself into the wing-backed chair, a small smile of anticipation lifted the corners of her mouth, pushing away her lingering sadness. Tapping the envelope against the palm of her hand, she savored the joy bubbling in her gut.

A pang of yearning stirred as she thought of her father. She saw him in his heavy wooden chair pulled up to the round table with its faded red cloth, his nearly bald head bent in concentration as he carefully shaped each letter. She remembered her young self standing on tiptoe to kiss his bald spot while he laughed and chuckled. "*Grass don't grow on no busy street,*" he'd say. Back then, he was the father that existed before Verna, the babies, and his retreat into whiskey—the year of absence from him thinned the bad times between them. The hard edges of his flaws were softened, leaving only the desperate image of a love that past reality had denied. She missed him.

As she removed and unfolded the letter, two more sheets of paper and two creased dollar bills dropped into her lap. Her eyes squinted in curiosity as she lifted the second goldenrod sheet, noting the faint scent of lavender drifting to her nose. She allowed them to fall into her lap. Taking up her father's letter, she began to read.

Dear Mae,

Seem like you been gone a long time, and it ain't the same here no more. This here house ain't been cleaned good since you left, and I ain't had no good eating like I done when you was here. Verna, she doing her best, but is any chance you might changes your mind and come back? I makes sure she be treating you better if you do. She know now you was a big help around here.

Mae harumphed loudly, fanning the letter in front of her face, and tried to imagine Verna wanting her back home. Papa was thinking with his belly again, the only thing he thought with other than his man parts. She knew the only time Verna would welcome her back would be if she were dead, and then she would probably spit on her grave. She returned her eyes to the page and continued reading.

How that man treating you? I seen his mama the other day. She done come back here and staying somewhere between Rayville and Delhi. She hit me with a evil eye what made my man parts shrivel up. That boy better not be putting his hands on you neither. I ain't too old to whup some ass about my baby if I needs to.

Well, today, this man and this little skinny woman say her name is Gal stop by here and say Crazy Cora done sent them. She keep saying. 'Miss Cora say this the only way you gon' save your girl.' She push that letter I done sent you at me, told me don't read it and don't tell nobody about it.

You knows I ain't no scary man. But it be something in that letter for sure. I feels it. Every time I went to read it, something stop me.

Write and tell me what that woman say, but don't put too much store by it. You know she crazy as cat shit. Folks say she be talking to dead peoples. The babies send they love, and your mama Verna, well, she just herself. And I put a little something with this here letter in case you needs it.

Love, Pappy

Mae wiped the tears from the corners of her eyes, her father's final words assuaging her heart. Picking up the money, she rolled up the bills, tightly wadding them in her fist, then stepped to the large trunk at the foot of their bed. Kneeling, she lifted the lid.

Pushing aside the handmade quilts and clothes, she dug to the bottom until she found her only purse, which had belonged to her mother. She ran her hand lovingly over the smooth tan leather and opened it to the compartment for bills. Carefully, she added her father's to the ones she had collected from her tenant baking before Clyde had forced her to stop.

Admittedly, Verna was a miserable, conniving heifer the whole time she'd known her, even if her father couldn't see it. Still, she had occasionally spit out wisdom worth retaining. She saw Verna, her mouth twisted and her eyes narrow slits, as she snatched Mae's earnings from her hand. "*This be all of it?*" she'd asked before she slapped her. "*I know even you ain't stupid enough to give nobody all you got. I done told you before, don't be nobody's fool.*"

Mae stared at her father's letter and then read it again, an inexplicable fear and apprehension gathering at the base of her spine. She stood and paced the room, shaking her head intermittently, then collapsed back to the floor. Her mind raced, trying hard to make sense of what she had read in her father's words, Cora's letter waiting beneath her fingertips.

An hour later, the afternoon sun played across Mae's face, where she still sat on the floor in front of the trunk, Cora's letter scattered in the pool of her dress.

The letter stank of craziness. She lifted it and thought of tearing it up and throwing it away before the insanity reached out and grabbed hold of her mind. It forced her to start rethinking images that scurried around the edges of her brain. The missing pieces fought to fall into place, scattered puzzle pieces coming together to form a cohesive picture. She reread until the words jumped off the page at her.

Miss Mae, I know this be hard for you to hear and believe, but I ain't crazy like I might sounds. Clyde a killer with a soul black as hell. He try to kill me, and I know he done killed other women's because I done talked with them.

Pappy had to be right. The woman was crazy, must be. But at the same time, Cora's words made sense of her life, the way Clyde stared at her, his brows drawn together, his eyes dark and smoldering, his vicious assaults on her body. And his disgusting new sexual appetite growing and increasing along with the level of violence.

After leaving her raw and sore, he often got up and left their room when he thought she was asleep, never saying where he had been when he returned. Later, after he'd come back when the bed vibrated with his snores, she would roll over and sniff for the smell of another woman on his skin and find none.

She shook her head violently, freeing the scenes from her mind. She refused to accept it. She *knew* Clyde. He was no killer. She would have known it if he were, felt it. She read the last paragraph again.

Ain't nobody safe from him. You needs to watch him close as you can. You can see the dark if you looks. It be swimming in his eyes, like smoke, black smoke. The dark make him ugly mean too. You must got a lot of the light in you, so you can probably feels it your own self. It probably what done kept you safe so far, but I be the only one who can really help you.

Mae pushed the thoughts away, burying them in the back of her mind until she could bear to bring them out and examine them further. Looking at the small clock on the table, she hastily pushed the letters inside the purse with the money, then buried it back in the trunk beneath the other items.

Standing, Mae brushed down her dress and crossed the room to the dual hot plate. Lifting the lid on the cast-iron pot, she stared down at the chicken and dumplings simmering in the thick broth and inhaled normalcy.

Her ears perked as she recognized the sound of Clyde's footsteps, his heavy tread stopping at the door, followed by the key turning in the lock. Mae reached up to smooth her hair into place, bringing up a smile that she hoped looked real.

"Hey, honey." Her words floated toward him as she crossed the room and reached up to embrace him. Clyde grabbed her wrists, startling her, and held her away from him. His nostrils flared as he inhaled deeply, then studied her intently, his eyes roaming from her head to her feet. Seemingly satisfied, he let her go.

"What for dinner?" he asked, sniffing the air and ignoring the puzzled look on her face.

"I made chicken and dumplings today and them biscuits you like." Her words tumbled over one another. "It's all hot and ready for you whenever you wants it." The smile she'd pasted on felt false, pulling at the corners of her mouth but not touching any other part of her face as she walked back to the burner, the warnings from Cora's letter pushing into her thoughts.

Clyde came behind her, moving to the small sink to scrub his hands with the bar of lye soap she kept there. She watched the grease and dirt run into the bowl, noticing that the area beneath his fingernails remained black.

"How was your day? It go good?"

Clyde grunted, hunching his shoulders.

"That supervisor and them men still messing with you?"

He grunted again, and she sighed, almost missing his mumbled answer. "Since Eugene finded that dead rat in his locker with the stomach pulled out, they ain't laughing no more. Not none of them."

Mae shuddered. What Cora had written in her letter about Clyde killing small animals jumped to the forefront of her mind. She shook her head, tossing her bangs to the side.

"That terrible. Who do something like that?" she asked. Looking down to avoid his eyes, she studied a yellow stain on the tablecloth that she hadn't noticed, her thumbnail scratching at it.

Clyde's face hardened. "How I know?" She could feel him glaring at her, his gaze burning into the top of her skull.

"Fix my plate," he snarled. "I'm ready to eat."

Mae recoiled and turned, her thighs knocking against the table, causing the salt and pepper shakers to sway. Reaching out, she steadied them, glad to have something to do with her hands and a place to look other than at Clyde.

His eyes raked over her again, and she trembled, aware of what the night would bring. He felt the leash loosening on the darkness and grinned. He would set her right.

The sun sat high in the sky with a promise of the heat it would bring by noon, hot enough to make the hair oil on her scalp drip down her forehead. Mae felt a slight breeze caress her skin, blowing through her hair to cool her head. Ruby sat across from her, smug satisfaction stamped on her features for having successfully hounded her into coming out of her apartment. She'd rapped on the door like an errant woodpecker until Mae had relented and answered, speaking to her with the door still on its chain. Ruby refused to accept no for an answer.

Now she looked over at Mae, a large bowl of unsnapped green beans resting in her lap, unasked questions in her eyes. Her fingers moved rapidly, years of sensory memory kicking into habit and finding the right place to break the beans and the portion to discard. Mae held a similar bowl, untouched.

Ruby cleared her throat, and Mae jumped, startled. "What's the matter with you, child? You looking mighty peaked."

Mae's lips lifted in a wan smile, and she waved her hand in front of her face, dispersing her feelings into the wind. "Oh, it ain't nothing. I got a letter from my daddy back home, and it got me to missing my folks. You know how it is."

Ruby sat back in her chair, grunting, her fingers moving faster. "Naw, I ain't got no family no more. Everybody gone but me."

The silence dragged, filled with their shallow breaths of discomfort, until Ruby sighed and lifted her head to look at Mae, tears glistening in her eyes. "But I still miss my mama a lot of times. Think about the things she used to say to me."

"Me too, I mean, my real mama. She died when I was still a young gal. Had the typhoid. Then my daddy got up with Verna and married her like I told you. She want to act like she my real mama."

"Girl, sure enough?"

"She ain't, though. She was mean as hell, always making trouble for me. Like this one time, my daddy had bought her this dress for church. She done hung it up over the stove so she can look at it. When I come in from school, she be hollering about starting up the stove. I ain't know the top wasn't closed. Then *woosh*. I tried to put it out, but the whole bottom burned up. When Daddy come home, she still crying and swear I done did it on purpose. Daddy damn near beat the skin off me. Ain't nobody's real mama would have stood for it."

"Shouldn't no man be beating on a girl child or a woman like that." Ruby nodded, hesitating and taking in a breath, pausing to see the effect of her words on Mae. "Mae?" She nodded, chewing her bottom lip, and starting to speak again. "Mae."

The bowl of beans slid from Mae's lap as she leaped abruptly to her feet, the contents scattering. Bending forward, she quickly began scooping them into the bowl.

"Lord, I don't know what's wrong with me, Miss Ruby. It was a bee," she lied, fearing what Ruby would say next. She turned hastily, gesturing with her hand that Ruby should remain seated and not try to help as she gathered the beans. "I best get these inside and wash them. I'll be back." She called, halfway to the door as she spoke, reaching for the handle.

Ruby sat back in her chair, beans snapping and falling into the bowl while she stared at the fat white clouds drifting overhead, echoes of Mae's night cries resonating in her ears. Shame rose in goose bumps on her arms as she remembered how she had listened, curled up on her bed, her hands covering her ears, trying to block out the sounds from her ears and her heart. She'd heard the thud of Mae's body hitting the wall, the sharp slap of his palm against her flesh, and her pleading between the whimpers.

She'd rocked back and forth, her hands clasped around her knees, her prayers and supplications to God for his intervention stopped at the ceiling. Then the rhythmic sound of the bed springs creaking had replaced the sounds of assault, followed by a blanket of silence.

Today, Ruby had sworn to herself that she would not nod and pretend that she hadn't heard Mae screaming and begging. Not accept Mae issuing a self-deprecating laugh at her clumsiness and how she had run into the door or tripped over her big feet. No more having her hide in her apartment until the bruises faded to purple and mottled yellow, and she could walk again with a natural gait.

The screen door slammed behind her and Ruby watched her go, knowing Mae wouldn't return to the porch.

CHAPTER TWELVE

The sound of the trains rattled in his bones, making Clyde squeeze his arms into his sides and shove his hands deeper into his pockets to hold himself together. The darkness thrummed through him, in complete control.

He hunched his shoulders up toward his ears as metal squealed against metal, grating on his eardrums. His features collapsed into an angry scowl as he ground his teeth until his jaws ached, waiting for the train to pass beyond him. He felt the people staring down at him from behind the glass of the 'L' train windows while he stood frozen on the street below, bodies ebbing and flowing around him.

A voice boomed to his right, the owner shoulder-checking him as he hurried past. "Big country-ass Negro ain't got sense enough to move out the way."

Clyde's head pivoted around on his neck to follow the man's retreating back, watching the dip-glide, step-stride rhythm of his walk. It was the walk he could never imitate. The walk that distinguished Clyde as different from city men, the walk exaggerating the gait of his short legs when he tried.

The two men with the stranger guffawed loudly, slapping hands as they strolled away. Clyde waited, smoldering, as the sound of their chatter faded. He imagined his legs long and straight, his shoulder dipping, slide step, slide step, as he walked up beside them, emulating them perfectly.

Slide, step, slide, step. He'd first grab the one with the fast mouth, spinning him around and caving in his face with his fist. Then he'd stomp the other two, feeling their ribs cave in under the thick heels of his boots. See who'd be laughing then.

The pounding inside his head resounded with his heart's beat, growing heavier as his blood heated. The dark familiarity embraced him as his fingers flexed, then formed into fists inside his pockets. It eddied around his vision, threatening to blind him until he forced himself to pull it back. He inhaled and exhaled deeply, his chest expanding and contracting with the effort.

Finally, he came to himself, still standing in the street, gazing up at the now-empty tracks. Rolling the tension from his shoulders, he ambled forward, his knees knocking together as he walked.

The same old woman he passed every day, the proprietor of the newsstand, looked up at him from the crate where she sat huddled in a shawl despite the heat of the August evening. Her near-toothless mouth worked over her gums like she would ask him a question, then stopped as she caught his eye.

The stink of death that had dogged his steps since burying Eva swirled up from the street beneath him, the stench overwhelming. Reaching up with one massive hand, Clyde rubbed his nose viciously. The smell, like sewer rot, closed in around him, permeating his skin, plugging his pores, and choking him on its filth. No amount of scrubbing his skin raw with hot water and lye soap had freed him of it.

"What you looking at?" he asked, letting his eyes lock on the old woman, holding hers until she lowered her head to stare at the concrete beneath her feet and tightened her shawl. Sweat gathered on his scalp, then trickled down his forehead, leaving a wet, oily sheen on his face. He cringed, and his nostrils flared. The smell was coming from her too, old as she was.

"Whore," he cried out and backed away from her, his finger jabbing the air, pointing accusingly. The woman's eyes rounded, her shawl dropping from her shoulders as she gasped in horror.

His finger wavered, then dropped to his side as he turned to shamble away from her as quickly as his tired legs would allow. His hands throbbed with the desire to close around her scrawny neck and dig through the mass of wrinkled flesh until he felt bones crunching. He'd watch the light fade from her eyes and know, like the darkness knew, that she deserved the death it held for her. He was her only chance at salvation. He needed to deliver her. The darkness demanded it.

He tried to run, moving as fast as he could, desperate to escape as his mind screamed and fought the darkness with rationales. *Never this close to home; people will see, know it was you. Hell, even a dog know not to shit where he eat*, the darkness chided him.

Clyde slowed, reaching down to rub his knees to relieve the ache in his joints. As he rubbed, his mind wandered to Fannie, a lump rising in his throat and making it difficult to swallow around the sorrow trapped inside. He conjured the feel of her long, slender fingers massaging his scalp and sliding down his cheek. Sniffing the air, he remembered the scent of her milk, momentarily erasing the stink surrounding him. *Mama.*

He almost wept out loud, then paused and looked around, trying to recall if he had spoken the word out loud. But no one responded to him beyond a furtive glance before averting their eyes. People continued to move around him, their presence growing sparser as he neared his apartment building.

His feet continued their journey while his mind drifted, his knees magnetized to one another, one leg twisting to bring his foot around and pull him forward before the other leg rotated to complete the same action with his other foot, his body swaying from side to side with each step. Fatigue exaggerated his walk, and each arduous step on the unyielding concrete street reminded him that he did not belong here.

But Fannie was coming. His mother was coming. He would be special again. Things would be like they were before. When she got there, she would fix Mae and make her love him like she used to.

Looking up, he blinked several times against the evening sun. His head rocked back, surprised to find both that it was early evening and that he had arrived at home, staring up from the bottom of the stairs of his building.

He searched the brick walls for their window, the last one in the corner. Finding it, he watched Mae's silhouette behind the drawn shade as she moved around the room. He devoured her curvy image . . . until another flicker of motion caught his attention.

Straining his eyes, he saw a barely discernable shadow beside her. He tried and failed to blink it away. The shadows took on the shape of a man who followed Mae across the room. Clyde grunted and rubbed both fists into his eyes hard enough to cause spots to form, then looked again. It was still there. A man. In his house. With his Mae.

He forced his legs to take the stairs two at a time, the rotation against locked cartilage slow and painful as his joints resisted the motion. Reaching the first-floor landing, panting, he wrenched the screen door open, hearing it slam against the wall and bounce back as he pushed through it. He barreled down the hall, his head lowered, a growl built in his chest. The reeking smell amplified, growing stronger as he neared the apartment door.

His mind flared in anguish, his thoughts tumbling one over another. She had him in there, his mind shrieked—that Jimmie asshole. The scene unrolled on the picture screen of his mind: Mae against the wall, her legs spread wide and wrapped around his back, writhing against him as she moaned out his name.

Clyde jammed the key into the lock, the metal twisting until it bent, leaving it hanging as he stood panting wildly in the doorway. His eyes roamed past Mae standing near the hot plate.

Mae stopped, her hand hesitating in the air and holding the spoon over the pot she was stirring as Clyde burst into the room. She swallowed, turned, and unconsciously stepped backward away from him, her body tightening and shrinking in anticipation of the coming blow.

"Where he at?" he bellowed, wrenching the key from the lock before closing the distance between them in four strides. The spoon clattered to the floor as he pushed her out of his path, sauce splashing across her legs. Mae stumbled, her arms waving wildly for balance.

"Who?" she stammered, bewildered. Clyde pushed her again, silencing her.

"I seen him," he yelled, spittle flying from his mouth into her face. The sound of his open-handed slap against her cheek cracked the air. Mae stumbled backward, landing against the wall, her wrist twisted awkwardly beneath her as she hit it.

"Clyde, what *wrong* with you?" she squeaked, feeling his hands wrapped around her upper arms, iron bands that yanked her forward, lifted her from the floor, and shook her.

"Don't play me for stupid! I seen him. Where he at?"

"WHO?" she screamed, her head rocking back and forth and her teeth snapping together as he shook her.

"Ain't nobody here," she cried, fat tears leaking from her eyes to drop off her chin.

Clyde stopped, his breath wheezing, his eyes searching the cramped space and coming to rest on the closet door. Dropping Mae to land in a heap on the floor, he rushed forward. He yanked the door open and pushed his body inside amidst the clothes, hangars, and boxes that occupied the space. Mae watched, her eyes wide and horrified, her body shaking as she rubbed her wrist. Her body curled forward protectively, arms wrapped around her knees.

She looked longingly at the closed door to their apartment, her heart racing and brain urging her to move and do it quickly. Her mind screamed for survival, telling her to stand up and run while he was turned away, burrowing into the closet. Maybe, she thought frantically, she could make it into the hallway, to the back door, and down the stairs before he caught her. She could outrun him.

A box flew from the closet, narrowly missing her, yanking her from her paralysis. She began to crawl forward, scrambling to her feet as Clyde appeared. His head thrust forward as he gripped the edges of the closet's frame.

Clyde's eyes protruded in his head, the sclera a muddy yellow rimmed by red, the dark centers a writhing mass. His nose spread across his face, his nostrils flared, and his lips pulled back in a snarl over teeth grown sharp and pointed.

Mae blinked, trying to flush the image from her sight. Covering her face with both hands, she screamed, then ran.

Clyde's hand clamped down on Mae's shoulder, halting her as she reached for the door, her fingers stretching and straining for the knob.

"Clyde, please, please." She sobbed raggedly as he pulled her toward him, bringing her back against his chest. "What I done did wrong, Clyde? I . . . I loves you." She wept, tears squeezing through her tightly closed lids.

For a moment, time stopped around them. Clyde's breathing slowed, the thundering of his heart eased, and his grip lightened. He turned Mae so that she faced him, lifting her hand to place it against his cheek and holding it there.

Reluctantly, Mae opened her eyes, startled to find her hand resting against the smooth dark chocolate skin of Clyde's face, his eyes clear and his mouth trembling. She began to stroke, her fingers finding the familiar rhythm across his cheeks and caressing the curls on his head as he leaned forward, head lowered.

"It be all right, Clyde. It be all right." Mae's words were soft, caressing him, and her hands stroked as she talked, her thoughts colliding with stark denial as he pulled them both down to the floor. He rested his head on her lap, relaxing under her tender ministrations, both lulled into memories of better times.

"Mae," he whispered. The darkness receded in concentric circles, contracting and growing smaller. The faint scent of mother's milk drifted up from her breasts, exciting him just as it had the night before. It had driven him into a frenzy, causing him to suck and pull hard at her dry nipples. He sniffed once, twice, and again, thinking of Fannie.

"Mamma coming. She be here soon." He moaned, the words pulled into the air as Mae cradled his head.

Mae's body stiffened, her fingers caught in the curls of his hair, her mouth hanging open before it snapped shut, and she swallowed the hope that had blossomed while they sat. She looked down into his face, a plea forming on her lips.

An avalanche of stink crashed over Clyde, and he bolted upright, using his shoulder to shove her backward and away from him, the moment between them evaporating into nothingness.

An abrupt banging on the door shredded the sudden stillness, causing both of their heads to swivel toward it.

"Miss Mae?" A muffled voice strained with emotion seeped through the wood, followed by intermittent knocking, growing louder in the spaces of their silence.

Mae stared at Clyde. The banging became stronger and more persistent, demanding an audience. Breaking eye contact, he nodded slightly, raising his head and caterpillar crawling on his back away from her.

Mae stood and turned, rising from the floor, uncertainty dancing in her eyes as she looked back at him. He rose fluidly, a move discordant with his size and malformed legs. A chill shook her as she eased the door open.

The woman standing in the hallway was disheveled, her clothing wrinkled, damp, and covered with stains. A baby rested over her shoulder. Mae's nose wrinkled against the smell of urine and vomit, searching her memory to recall a name to match the familiar face, and failing. She opened the door wider.

"I sorry to be bothering you, Miss Mae," the woman said, leaning to look around Mae at Clyde as he moved toward the closet to renew his search. "And how you, Mr. Clyde?" she asked, then continued, not waiting for a response.

"I don't know what else to do, Miss Mae." She jostled the boy on her shoulder, making her voice shake with the motion and her own fear. "My boy, Jeremiah, here, he real sick, and we cain't affords no doctor. I heard tell you does some healing, least that's what Miss Ruby say when I asked her," she continued, her hands sliding up and down the child's back.

She let the boy's listless body slide down into her arms, shifting it to hold his head in the crook of her arm as it lolled from side to side. Her head turned to look first at Mae and then strayed to Clyde, watching the slope of his back as he moved toward the closet. Her movements became more agitated as she shifted from foot to foot.

"My name Sarah Anne. You remembers me?" Her eyebrows raised, and she released one hand from Jeremiah's back, extending it to Mae, then dropping it helplessly when Mae left it there. "I seen you when you was hanging sheets one day with Miss Ruby," she said, tears glimmering in her soft brown eyes. "I know I asking a lot, but I don't wants to lose my boy. He done stopped taking my bosom, and he burning up. Look." She squeezed his cheeks and turned his face toward Mae, displaying the tinge of blue around his mouth and nose. Her mouth trembled. "It be like he cain't hardly breathe," she pleaded.

Mae leaned forward, her hand pressed to the child's chest, and felt the heat radiating from him, noting how small and fragile he looked lying limp in his mother's arms.

"Who that?" Clyde yelled from deep within the closet where he had returned.

"It just Sara Anne from down the hall," she called over her shoulder, jerking her hand away. "Look like she got a croupy baby. She want me to look at him."

Clyde stepped back into the room, looking from Mae to the woman in the doorway, his eyes narrowed in suspicion.

"Who else with you? His daddy send you?" Clyde demanded, lumbering forward.

Sarah Anne shook her head and took a step back. "I ain't gots no husband. His daddy run off," she answered, her face coloring in embarrassment. "Ain't nobody but me and Jeremiah," she finished, her eyebrows bunching together, and gave Mae a puzzled look.

Clyde made his way to the winged chair, falling heavily into the cushions, his nostrils wide and his head swiveling to watch the women framed in the doorway. They both reeked. He could smell it, drifting down from between their clenched thighs where they tried to hold it in, hide it from him.

He stared at the boy, watching the slight rise of his chest as he took short, shallow breaths. The child's arms dangled over his mother's, the little fingers spasming and jerking.

Mae hovered over him, a barrier between Clyde, the mother, and the child. She ran her hand down the smooth wood of the door frame, sensing the danger still emanating from Clyde. It lurked just below the calm exterior he tried to present as he sat glowering at them from the chair. Dread jangled her nerves, the need to get away from him escalating, becoming an undercurrent pulsing with her heartbeat.

Then she looked at the boy again, the face of Verna's first baby, still and blue, superimposing itself over his. *Sometimes, babies just stop breathing.*

Her heart stuttered in her chest, adrenaline rushing through her system. Jeremiah gasped helplessly for breath, and Mae straightened her stance, rolling her shoulders to ease the tension, and prepared herself to defy Clyde.

"It won't takes me long, and I come right back." She wheedled, embarrassed at the weak sound of her voice. Her hands came together in front of her, twisting in concern and worry for the baby, willing him to continue breathing.

Moving to completely block Clyde's view, she patted Sarah Anne gently on her arm, whispering conspiratorially, "You go on and takes him back down to your place, and I come right down." She swallowed hard, imbuing truth into her words. "Let me gets my husband's dinner first."

Mae moved forward, forcing Sarah Anne to retreat until she was out of the doorway and back in the hall. "Don't you worry," she cautioned. Giving Jeremiah a final pat, she stepped away, then closed the door with her last words.

Clyde's gaze slid over Mae as she turned away from the door, freezing her in place, her hand still on the doorknob. He searched her face, seeing the twisted conniving of her thoughts painted there.

Her head drooped on her neck, and she stared down at the floor. "I done seen babies go real fast too." And she saw the dead baby lying next to her stepmother. "He real sick. I done seen my little brother and sister with the croup. But I thinks if I give him some steam, and some of my herbs, that might open him up some." Her hand released the doorknob, and she looked up at Clyde, running her hands over her arms, then clasping them across her breasts, waiting.

Time ticked by slowly, and Mae felt Jeremiah slipping from the world. She slid her back along the wall incrementally until she had inched her way to her blue trunk and the healing herbs that would help Jeremiah.

Mae knelt quickly, her back bent over the trunk. Pulling out a quilted bag, it quivered on the end of its pull string as her hand shook. Leaning farther in, she continued digging through the trunk's contents until she retrieved a jar of raw honey. Closing her mind to her fear, she concentrated on her search and sighed in relief when she found a vial into which she could pour a small portion of ginger.

She did not see Clyde rising from his chair, crossing the room to loom over her. His hand shot out in a flash, grabbing her by her hair, wrapping it around his hand, and pulling as she gasped and groaned. One of her hands flailed at the base of her scalp, where he held her tightly.

"I ain't said you could go nowhere," he screamed into her upturned face as he yanked her head backward. Mae clung to the trunk with her other hand, desperate to keep from being pulled onto her back.

"Please, Clyde, he a baby." She forced the words through teeth gritted against the pain.

Suddenly, the lid of the trunk came down, catching her hand before she could pull it away.

"Father, help me," she groaned, twisting and feeling her hair ripping from the roots.

Clyde latched onto her injured hand and squeezed, grinding the bones together. The scream she had been holding in split the air, and she saw him smile.

Grunting, he let go of her hand and hair simultaneously. She watched the emotions playing across his face: joy, rage, and disgust. She crawled on her knees and one arm, her other hand clutched against her chest, frantic to escape him. Pain radiated up her arm from her throbbing fingers and across her scalp. She reached up for the doorknob, an arm's length away from escape, a petition of pleas and prayers to a benevolent God looping through her mind.

"He do be a baby." His voice growled from where he stood behind her, his lungs tightening, a distant sensory memory pressing into his own lungs, bringing a sensation of breathlessness clawing its way up from his subconcious. "You best fix him right. And bring your ass right back, or else." He let the implied threat hang between them.

Mae collapsed, groaning. Her stomach churned, nausea making her roll from side to side. Clyde stepped away from her with another grunt and turned away. "Don't make me have to come and get you."

She thought of Jeremiah again, knowing his breaths grew shorter and his life was fading. She pulled herself up, waited for the throbbing in her hand to subside enough to move it, then rose to go back to her trunk. Bent over it again, she dug around for a poultice. Finding it, she stood straight, limped back across the room, and pulled her apron from its hook by the front door, awkwardly placing it over her head.

Clyde stood and came up behind her, yanking the ties of the apron and tying it tightly. She didn't respond, puffing and expanding her stomach to loosen the material. She leaned against the wall for support and placed all the items into the apron's big pockets. Scurrying to the door, her damaged hand pressed against her chest, she tried not to run, fearful that Clyde would change his mind or come after her again. She looked at him again and swallowed her fear of what might happen if she didn't come back.

"Do what you needs to do and come right back," he added, his eyes heavily lidded and dark.

Mae waited until she was on the other side of door to lean against it and collect her thoughts, wiping the fear from her face. She pushed the pain away and ran her fingers through her hair, smoothing it back into some semblance of order. She forced Clyde from her mind, stepping forward resolutely. Jeremiah was all that mattered.

CHAPTER THIRTEEN

Hurry, hurry, hurry, hurry, the rhythm of the train wheels chanted urgently to Fannie as she leaned her forehead against the glass window, the scenery flying by in a blur. Pushing the tip of her tongue out, she licked her lips and smiled, feeling her renewed connection to Clyde thrumming across the miles.

Soon. She would be with him again soon. She kneaded her breasts and reached for her bag under the seat. She pulled her breast pump free and went to the small bathroom.

The vacancy sign turned as she twisted the latch and sat on the cold metal seat. Unbuttoning her dress, she lifted her bra and let her breasts hang free, the nipples puckering in the cold air.

Fannie cupped her left breast, applied the plastic funnel, and began squeezing the rubber bulb, watching the stream of white liquid fill the attached bottle. She rocked back and forth, remembering the tug of Clyde's mouth, the low, soft whimper of satisfaction as he suckled, and she rubbed his hair.

After twenty years of being perfect together, Mae broke them. She'd come shaking her ass into Clyde's life like the miserable little slut she was and dragged him away, severing their connection. She'd felt it snap, a chasm opening between them and inside of her. She remembered their last night as she huddled on the floor, sobbing and begging, her fingers clutching at the empty air as he strode away from her.

The pain and anger of seeing Cora alive again that afternoon had almost been erased from her mind. Still, stomach acid bubbled with the memories. They became a tight burning sensation in her chest, churning upward into her throat as they bled into images of both Cora and Mae.

Fannie squeezed hard, causing a spurt of liquid to shoot into the bottle just as the train lurched and caused the suction to break. She switched breasts, attached the pump, squeezed vigorously, and grinned. She'd kept his milk this whole time, never letting it dry up, even when the one-year anniversary of his leaving came and went. When she got there, she'd be ready for him.

A whole year, she thought, of long days leaning over a hot tub—lye burning her hands—scrubbing the shit out of white folks' drawers, saving her money for this day, the day he came to his senses and realized that he needed her. She'd heard it in his voice when he called. His plea. He was ready to let the Jezebel go.

This was the day. The train sped her steadily northward, each revolution of the wheels bringing her closer to her baby boy. Her mouth moved in praise. Her prayers finally had been answered.

Her mind searched for their connection until she felt it again, tingling through her. The tentative tendrils had continued to grow in strength every day. She felt his struggle—his fear, his anger—building, hastening her actions as she sold her few belongings and called on favors among their people in Chicago to make arrangements. Her boy was in trouble. He needed her.

Standing, Fannie unscrewed the pump from its jar, turning in the narrow space to pour the contents into the silver toilet basin. She tapped the floor pedal and watched the bottom open, the water swirling and releasing her milk to cascade onto the railroad tracks speeding beneath the train.

I'm coming, I'm coming, I'm coming. She let her thoughts flow with the clickety-clack of the wheels rushing her forward to Clyde.

The L train screeched in the distance, brakes squealing as it neared the platform two blocks away, and Clyde jerked, reminded of his humiliating walk home. The men's laughter echoed inside his head, and he raised his fist, bringing it down on the arm of the chair with enough force to crack the wood. Leaning over, he planted his elbows on his thighs and rubbed his face with his other hand, oblivious to the pain tracing up his arm. The darkness crowded his brain, pulsing until he felt it would explode, leaking from his ears, his eyes, his nostrils, and his mouth. He let his jaw drop, unhinged, leaving an open path to free the darkness.

The sounds were indiscernible at first, not clearly inside his head or in the room. He lifted his head, his ear turned to the window, and listened urgently. The sounds ceased to be incomprehensible jabber with the voices of the many, gathering to form words, thoughts, and images that blazed along his soul. Leaping to his feet, he turned in a full circle, looking wildly around the room. He took one step forward, paused, then threw his head back and laughed out loud.

Mama. He'd heard her thoughts as distinctly as if she stood beside him in the room. She was coming. The darkness danced.

Clyde stood utterly still, then shook his head against the cloud of confusion descending and muddling his thoughts until he remembered the man, Jimmie, again. He sniffed the air, inhaling the stench of that other Mae, the whore Mae. His eyes narrowed to slits as he clapped his hands together, nodding his head up and down.

Oh yes, the darkness assured him. Jimmie had been there. He knew what he had seen with his own eyes. That man, in his apartment, following his wife like a lapdog.

His rapidly darting eyes stopped, resting on Mae's prized blue trunk. She cared more about it than him, not letting him touch it. He stared at it hard, awareness filtering through the empty spaces left in his thoughts. The trunk was big enough. A man could hide in it.

Clyde shuffled forward, slamming his open palm against his forehead. *Dummy.* The voices congealed, chanting it simultaneously in the distant past and his tortured present—*stupid monkey boy.*

But he wasn't stupid; oh no, not by a long shot. He'd just been blind, stripped of his power, and disconnected. His eyes narrowed as he saw Mae's actions with cunning clarity.

He should have looked in the trunk first. *That's why she acted like she was digging in that damned trunk. She hiding Jimmie in there, covering him up.* His footsteps became quiet, like when he tracked animals in the woods. He was silent as he crept up to the trunk.

"I gots your black ass now!" he trumpeted, jerking up the lid. His eyes eagerly scanned from left to right, anticipating the sight of the man scrunched down like a gopher in his hidey hole. He'd tear his shit out from between his legs.

A carefully folded quilt lay innocuously across the expanse of the trunk. Prodding it with his fingers, he stepped back, waiting for movement.

"Get up!" he screamed, spit flying from his mouth with the force of his words. Grabbing the quilt, he bunched the fabric against his chest, then ripped it, tossing it behind him. Rage flushed his face a deep purple.

The trunk's contents that had lain beneath the quilt sat mute in their place—a layer of lace curtains, blue and white dish towels, and sheets embroidered with delicate flowers on their edges. He recognized Mae's Sunday dress pressed beneath the nightgown she had worn on their wedding night.

He let his fingers linger lovingly over the silken material and remembered her lifting the hem to reveal her caramel skin underneath, the soft patch of black curls between her thighs slick with moisture. He remembered how she had guided his manhood to slide into her heat. *How she tempted you with her sex, made you want her until you didn't think of nothing else but being between those thighs, her holding you tight and hot while she squirmed underneath you.*

The sound of the material tearing between his hands filled the room as Clyde threw his head back and howled, shredding the garment before tossing it to the floor. His eyes continued to scour the insides of the trunk in frustration, arrested by the sight of leather peeking out from deep within a corner.

His big hands pawed at the remaining clothing until it closed around Mae's purse, hefting it in his palm. One eyebrow shifted upward, and he stared at the bag, stunned by its weight. Shaking it, he heard coins clinking against one another.

Clyde sat down hard on his backside, the purse resting on his thighs, coiled like a snake. An uneasy fear tugged at his spirit, and the darkness whispered, *Treachery.*

The purse seemed so small in his hands, the gold metal clasp fragile and awkward between his finger and thumb as he pushed it back. Reaching behind the seemingly empty interior, he felt inside the silk lining and pulled out a handful of letters, a wallet, and a worn leather coin purse.

He opened the small pouch that had weighed the purse down, heavy with coins, and turned it upside down. Quarters, nickels, dimes, and pennies cascaded into his lap, some slipping between his open legs and bouncing on the wooden floor. Clyde leaned forward, gathered them all back to himself, and then began counting, stacking each denomination separately. Twelve dollars and twenty-five cents.

In a haze of denial, he opened the purple wallet with a black clock embossed on its vinyl hide. He ignored the pictures in their plastic sheathes and opened the section for bills, snatching them out and counting them quickly before balling them up in his fist. His breathing became labored as he looked at the crumpled bills and the change before him. So much money. More money than he had, and only one way she could have made it. *Flat on her back.*

Picking up the letters with one hand, Clyde felt himself sliding headfirst into the darkness and cursed his ignorance. Reaching down, he grabbed his manhood and yanked with the other hand, relishing the pain. It had betrayed him. *Thinking with the wrong head, letting that girl lead you around by your dick when your mama raised you better.*

Clyde growled, grinding his teeth in anguish. The letters crumpled in his hand. *Read it*, the darkness demanded. Clyde leaned his back against Mae's open trunk. The diminishing rays of the sun glinted off the window, offering just enough light for him to read.

He opened the first one from Mae's father, postmarked a few days ago. He let the extra pages enfolded within the letter flutter past him to land on the floor between his sprawled legs. He read quickly, scanning the inconsequential rambling until his eyes snagged on Cora's name.

He stopped, dropped Mae's father's letter, then snatched the other pages that had fallen to the floor and began to read, the power of Cora's words bridging her from death and back into his world. He read each sentence carefully, incredulously, as reality shuffled, distorted, and realigned itself with each line. Pulling his legs beneath him into a crouch, he leaped to his feet, shaking his head in stupefaction.

Since I come back from the dead, after Clyde done killed me, I been plagued with spirits. When I first come back, I cain't talk with nobody but dead folks. Well, least until I seen Fannie. When I seen her, it give me back the parts of my mind what was lost when I died. Helped me to remembers everything about Clyde and what I needs to do.

She was alive. Had been alive all these years, and somehow, he hadn't known it. He thought back, remembering that day behind her house. He saw her again, crumpled in the grass, and felt the satisfying thump as his foot struck her skull and the bone gave in. He'd seen the light of life leave her eyes. He'd watched as the breath left her body, leaving it empty and still.

But here, in his hands, was another truth. One written by Mae's father's hand that contradicted what he believed, and one written by Cora's own hand. The darkness had failed to reveal it to him. His mama hadn't told him. *She's alive.*

He paced the room, moving back and forth, occasionally looking back at the letter and remembering. The words branded into his brain. The final sheets glimmered in the dim light from the window, seeming to glow with an ambience of their own. Clyde scooped up the pages and turned on the bedside lamp. The mattress sank, springs squeaking, as he sat on the edge of the bed to read—the pages burned in his hands.

Clyde stared down, expecting to find his hands scorched and blackened. Instead, they remained the same as always, palms pink against the dark skin of his hands, the pages trembling in his grasp.

His mind reeled beneath the increasingly familiar fear and panic that had begun to dog his heels over the last few weeks, exacerbated by the letter he held. *Rip it.* The voices tried to break through the darkness, whispering to his tortured brain.

"No!" he shouted to the empty room. "Not before I knows what she done said." Pieces began to fall into place for him, and the days and months began to make sense. *She* was the one. She'd come into his dreams, casting juju in his life without his knowledge and poisoning him by using Mae.

Clyde's knee bobbed up and down restlessly, and he hummed. He allowed his mind to drift again to Cora. He saw himself bending over her, pulling something from her pockets. His eyes squinted shut as he concentrated and forced himself to see the object and feel it.

Standing, he walked to the closet again, pushing through the boxes until he found the one he was looking for, the only one he had packed when he left his mama's house. Taking it back to the bed, he sat and opened the carton, folding the flaps to reveal what was inside. Cora's journal lay on top.

He picked it up and ran his hand over the leather cover, then dropped it as it heated, scalding his hands more intensely than the letter had. He'd carried it with him over the years, never reading it, his talisman of success. His victory over the ones who would see him destroyed.

Realization dawned. Her journal was her juju, infused with her spirit and connecting her to him. It wasn't the darkness that had failed; it was him. He had not killed her, and he had kept the journal.

Even now, it had helped her invade his dreams. His brows lifted in realization. That was how she brought Jimmie here. He was convinced now that the witch was the one who had brought him into the apartment and then snatched him out using her juju. *And Mae is a part of it*, the darkness whispered, *making like she making herbs for that baby when she know she's gon' use them against you.*

His hatred manifested into physical pain, tightening in his stomach and liquifying his bowels. Clyde leaned forward, doubling himself in half as he rocked and moaned. Clutching the letter to his chest, he waited for the spasm to pass. Finally, as it released him, he sat up straight and began to read again, the darkness fully descending both outside . . . and within.

Outside their room, three doors down, Mae stood framed in the meager light from the hallway lamps and repeated her instructions to Sarah Anne.

"He doing better now. That steam done really opened him up. You massages him with that there lavender oil and gives him that lemon juice and raw honey. See if he take your bosom. That be the best thing for him."

Sarah Anne kept nodding, looking back over her shoulder to the crib tucked in the corner of the room, and listening to the sounds of Jeremiah's breathing.

"You remembers he need that ginger and cinnamon I made, three times a day."

Sarah Anne reached out and grasped Mae's hands between her own, pressing a crumpled dollar bill against her palm, tears welling in her eyes.

"It ain't much, I knows, and I cain't thanks you enough."

"No, you keeps it." Mae tried to push the money back into Sarah Anne's hand.

"No, ma'm. Don't shames me by not taking it. I ain't going to forget how you helped us."

Seeing her determination, Mae nodded, folding the money carefully before depositing it in her apron pocket. She would need it to leave, she thought, her plans solidifying. She glanced over Sarah Anne's shoulder at the small boy, sprawled on his back and breathing deeply in and out. A smile teased the corner of her lips as she blew a kiss through the air toward him.

The women parted, Mae turning to walk down the hall and Sarah Anne shutting the door quietly behind her. Her mind raced, crashing against the impossibilities that faced her. If she could get through the night, she could be gone before he returned from work, even if it meant returning to Papa and Verna.

Mae's feet barely lifted from the carpet as she trudged slowly down the hallway, her mind picking at the threads of her life. Cora's letter and her father's worry gathered in her spirit, conspiring to make her run. Her injured hand throbbed, reminding her of Clyde's brutality. And now, Fannie was coming.

Her thoughts tugged at one another as Fannie wove herself into her memories. She heard the woman's voice screeching her rancor as it echoed through the bus station while she and Clyde tried to leave.

You trifling bitch. You gon' be the death of my Clyde. You hears me? She kept screaming, running beside the bus after they had boarded to bang on the window as they took their seats. Clyde stared straight ahead while Mae shrank into her seat as Fannie continued yelling. The veins stood out in her neck, her mouth stretched wide, and the sound penetrated the thick glass. *She using juju on you, Clyde!*

"How you, Mae?"

Mae was startled, her uninjured hand going to her mouth to stifle a scream as Ruby stepped into the hall, her door open behind her.

"Clyde ain't sounding too good in there," she warned, shaking her head.

Mae's eyebrows lifted as she lowered her hand, watching Ruby as she stared at her—searching for a way around her without being rude or hurtful.

"What happen to your hand?" The snuff behind Ruby's lower lip rolled as she prepared to spit into her can.

"Oh." Mae looked in the direction of Sarah Anne's room. "Sarah Anne come to get me for little Jeremiah. He was real sick just like you told me he was, and I gots to rushing so bad, I slammed the top of my trunk on my hand. It all right, though; just need some salve on it."

Ruby grunted and rolled her eyes, then spit into the can again. "Hmm, you *sure* you and Clyde all right?"

Mae pulled up a smile, the dimples in her cheeks deepening with the effort. "Of course, we fine. I done told you he a good man, Miss Ruby."

The door to her room flew open, Clyde filling the door frame. Mae shrank in upon herself, pulling in her limbs as she crossed her arms to wrap around her body, any hope of fleeing dissolving. She lifted her head, holding the smile that did not reach her fear-filled eyes. Clyde grabbed her by her elbow, pulling her into their room before Ruby could open her mouth or say goodbye to her friend. *A damned no-good man more like it*, Ruby spat at the closed door.

Back in her own room, Ruby pushed the wad of snuff up with the tip of her tongue, spit it into the can in her hand, and then sat it on the floor near her rocking chair. Lowering herself into the deep cushions, she twisted her body and reached over to turn on the radio that sat on the table beside her. Finding a strong signal, she turned the volume up to its highest, a blues song blaring across the room, drowning out the sounds leaking through the walls. Lifting her knitting from the basket on the floor, she set the needles to flying in tempo with the rocking chair.

She shook her head slowly, attempting to free herself of her negative thoughts. Mae would be all right. She always was, and no matter what, like she always reminded her, he was still her husband. "Leave and cleave," the Bible said. It wasn't her place to come between a man and his wife.

CHAPTER FOURTEEN

Mae stared at the destruction strewn around her. Everything from her trunk was flung around the room. Her grandmother's quilt had been torn and tossed haphazardly on the floor, her nightgown ripped to shreds, the lace and linen sheets covered with muddy footprints, and piles of coins and dollar bills sprinkled throughout. A sob caught in her throat at the catastrophic debris scattered around her.

Clyde loomed over her, one hand squeezing her elbow, the other holding sheaths of paper crumpled in his fist that he waved in her face.

"Your daddy got a lot to say, I see," he sneered.

"What you mean?" Mae sniffed, blinking rapidly and wiping at her eyes with her free hand. She ignored how the grip on her elbow made her sore hand thrum with pain.

Clyde's features slid into the sly, calculating look that had become his norm.

"You wants to act like you don't know about *her*?" He smashed the pages into her face, grinding the rough paper into her skin and trying to force her lips apart. "I needs to make your lying ass eat it!"

Mae yanked her elbow free, staggering away and spitting the pieces of paper that had been jammed past her lips onto the floor, her mind racing and her heart galloping as it pounded against her rib cage.

"Why?" he howled, the sound of a wounded animal in a trap. "Why you lie?"

Mae stared at him helplessly, trying to follow his thoughts.

"She had him in here—then *poof.* He gone. She the only one what could do it." He paced, kicking through the detritus of her life. "Him, that little scrawny bastard. That's who you cheating on me with?"

"She who? Clyde, I ain't doing nothing with nobody. I done told you, I just sells Jimmie some bread, and he ain't been back. He don't even lives here no more." Her words fell over one another in their haste to be out.

"LIAR!" he screamed, lifting her by both arms and then dropping her back to the floor. "You been letting that witch Cora uses you, and you knows it."

Mae's body slammed against the door with the force of his slap across her face, her head thumping against the door and bouncing back. She slid down the wall, her legs spread out in front of her, and her dress pulled up to expose her thighs. Before she could draw breath, Clyde grabbed her by the front of her dress, lifting her into the air again before him and shaking her. Her head flopped back and forth on her thin neck.

"Clyde, please . . . Ain't nobody been here. Mens don't mean nothing to me . . . just you," Mae sobbed, trying to control her head and limbs. "And I ain't never even hear nothing about no Cora until I got them letters from my daddy." Looking through her blurred vision, she tried to capture his eyes.

Finding them, she searched, then recoiled from what she saw. Darkness swam in the depths, reaching out to her, and she knew. *This* was the man the woman Cora had written her about.

"Oh God," she moaned, then opened her mouth wide and screamed.

His meaty fist found her face again, and her front teeth shattered. "Don't you blaspheme, witch."

Blood, saliva, and mucus ran down her chin, and she coughed to keep from choking on the blood running backward down her throat. Words no longer formed through the haze of pain as he dropped her to the floor.

Climbing to her hands and knees—her throat raw from screaming, praying that someone would hear her, help her— she began slowly crawling toward the door. Clyde's booted foot connected with her stomach, lifting her half a foot into the air before she landed on her side, one arm thrown over her face to protect it and her other clutching her stomach as life seeped from her womb to stain the inside of her thighs. Falling onto her back, she spewed vomit from her mouth. Mae tried to turn her head away from the stinking pool.

Clyde leaned over, his breath bellowing in and out, and his hands circled her neck as he lifted her and dragged her back across the room to the bed, screaming words into her face as he slammed her onto the bed.

"You ain't never loved me! You just used me like they all do. My mama done told me. I should have listened. I should have listened. You full of sin!"

She felt his hands tightening on her neck, pressing harder as she struggled for air, her legs kicking at him. It was too late. She should have run. Her eyes distended in their sockets, locked on his, and she saw the pure hatred in his face. His lips twisted in a snarl. She tried to lift her arm to reach up and stroke his face one last time to bring him back to himself. But it was a dead weight, dangling ineffectively beside her as her vision dimmed . . . and the light of life fled.

Clyde allowed her limp body to drop back on the bed, staring down at her sightless eyes and feeling her judgment.

Don't let the witch fool you like Cora did. Make sure she dead.

Clyde nodded and moved to the small sink and counter across the room. He searched through the few utensils until he found the knife Mae used to cut up chickens. He strode back, climbing onto the bed, and straddled her body. His arm flew up and down repeatedly, slamming the blade through tissue and bone. Tears and snot flowed into his open mouth, splashing in the blood on her chest as he sobbed.

Ruby slowly lowered her hands from her ears where she had placed them as Mae's screams escalated higher and higher. She had heard his fists pounding flesh, heard Mae's muffled cries between her screams, sounds that the radio could not drown out.

The desperation in Mae's screams vibrated through her body, different this time, unlike the ones on other nights. These urged Ruby to move, to help. Then, the screams stopped, cut off like the click of a radio knob. The sudden silence that descended horrified her worse than the screams.

Ruby heard the bed springs creaking again. Later, the sound of something being dragged across the floor penetrated the walls. She heard footsteps shuffle across the room several times before she heard the door open and a heavy tread that could only be Clyde going toward the communal bathroom. The footsteps returned to the room, and the door opened and closed several times before silence enveloped the whole floor again.

Rising, Ruby walked to the closet and began peeling the clothes from her body, carefully placing them on their padded hangers. Standing at the basin, she used a washcloth to wipe her face, rinse her arms, and wash between her legs before slipping her peignoir over her head. Lying down, she felt the weight of loneliness crushing her into the mattress. She stared first at the ceiling, then at the room's only window, and waited for night to abandon the sky.

Clyde inhaled deeply, took one final look, and then firmly pulled the door shut to his and Mae's room. Using Mae's key to lock it behind him, he reached for his connection to Fannie and smiled. As he had awakened, the first rays of the day's light warm on his face, he felt her presence. She was near, and the uneasiness that saturated the space around him lifted. The darkness tingled in eager anticipation of seeing her, having her make it all right again. He felt Mae's memory attempting to force its way into his mind, pushing doubt through the darkness. He stopped, tilting his head to the side. Had he heard Mae call his name? He looked back at the closed door, listened carefully, then sighed when no further sounds followed him and continued walking to the incinerator.

Clutching Cora's journal tightly in his gloved hand, Clyde felt the darkness simmering, no longer turbulent as it had been the day before but welcoming. He grabbed the metal handle and pulled the door downward, gazing at the orange flames dancing inside. The image of the fire reflected in the inky spheres of his eyes as they narrowed, and the darkness fed the anger brewing within him. Anger for the years he had carried his own pain and damnation with him, hatred for every word on every page that chronicled the turmoil and devastation of his life. Not once had Cora ever considered helping or saving him, only coveting his destruction. He tossed the journal inside and watched, mesmerized, as the inferno licked the leather cover, the pages blackening and curling.

Turning away, he began shuffling the long, painful walk to the rear of the building. Black tendrils leaked from beneath the door of his apartment, with still more gathering at Ruby's door, shifting and swirling toward him as he made his way to his job for his last day. They could fire him if they wanted to. He was done with this place. He would shake the dust from his heels.

Mama here, and I'm coming for you soon, witch, it whispered across his conscious mind. Clyde began to whistle. Everything was going to be all right. Fannie was almost here. This time, there would be no mistakes.

Ruby planted herself on the back porch, her eyes gritty from lack of sleep. Morning had arrived, clouds coming to make the sky a leaden gray, obscuring the sun from her world. Earlier, she'd sat on the side of the bed, paralyzed, shrouded by a loathing so deep, she thought never to move again. Mae's cries echoed in her head, shredding any peace she sought.

"*He a good man.*" Mae's words and her own formed a bitter ash in her thoughts. Both lies. The only time Amos was a good man was in her memories, and if Clyde was ever a good man, it wasn't during the time that Ruby had known him. She needed to help Mae. She had to get Clyde to tell her what was going on, and this time, she would not be dissuaded like yesterday. Then, she'd stood in front of Mae's door, knocking timidly, then beating against it, demanding Mae to appear. She imagined her opening the door just wide enough to show her face, her eyes downcast and shadowed with shame.

But it didn't happen. She'd swallowed the temptation to use her master key to barge into the apartment and check on Mae, but she hesitated, remembering how embarrassed she was when

Clyde started beating her. Ruby had instead gone back to her own rooms and continued to cower inside her apartment for the remainder of the day. She recalled her own bruises, the ones she had hidden from her own family and friends; the false tales about the "accidents" she seemed to have all too frequently, the number of missed opportunities she'd had to talk to Mae.

She sat now, watching the last tinge of orange sunlight dimming the horizon before the skies became the color of her soul, determined that Clyde would not get past her. She'd seated herself in one of the chairs where she and Mae had sat so many days, laughing and gossiping in the sunlight. She saw Mae's face, those deep dimples imprinting themselves on her cheeks, her eyes bright with warmth and humor. She felt the tears pooling in her eyes as she waited for Clyde to return from work.

Hearing the heavy tread of footsteps, she looked down the stairs to see Clyde, that lopsided walk propelling him toward her. For a brief moment, his face pulled downward in sadness, and she felt a twinge of sorrow for him. Then she remembered him pulling Mae away from her, not allowing her to say goodbye. She saw herself, her body curled up on the bed, trying to drown out the sound of Mae's cries.

Drawing in a deep breath, she gathered her courage and stood, pulling herself up to her full height, which left him still a head taller. Undaunted, she cleared her throat and began talking as he stepped up onto the porch, the words pouring forth before her courage faltered.

"I see Mae ain't been out since the other day, Clyde." She would not let him intimidate her today. "And we was planning on looking in on that baby boy Jeremiah together." She continued, then paused, waiting for his response. "She ain't sick or nothing, is she?" she asked, her voice heavy with concern, her expression cautiously blank.

"Her done left me." Clyde looked down at her, his eyes red-rimmed and sorrowful. "She done went back to her peoples, I expect."

Ruby's eyes drooped at his words. Mae was really and truly gone. Her body sagged in disappointment, remembering the sound of something heavy sliding across the floor, probably Mae's trunk.

Ruby searched his face as he licked his lips, his tongue leaving a trail of saliva behind, his dark eyes darting nervously from side to side. She'd seen that look before. Seen it when Amos crept back into their bedroom, filled with false bravado, daring her to question him about where he'd been, his lies held behind his teeth. She would see his eyes flash in disgust as they roamed over her body. His hands would be next, she knew, open palms heavy on her skin, followed by fists pounding against frail bone.

Clyde stared at Ruby, his nose wrinkled against the smell of her. The air in the hallway reeked with the stink of her Jezebel spirit. *She the reason Mae dead. She Cora's puppet pulling the strings and poisoning her against you*, the darkness whispered. He wished they had never come here, had never met her. He swallowed his hatred of Ruby and schooled his features to look contrite once more, wishing he'd taken his suitcase with him when he'd left that morning.

As Ruby stood there remembering, she felt a dark rage growing inside her as she continued to study Clyde's bowed head. Her hand slipped inside her apron, the pocket slightly lopsided with the weight of what she carried, fingering and stroking it. She allowed the fury to swell in her veins. Looking up, she watched his features slide and distort until her husband Amos's face grinned at her, darkness swirling around him. Her mind screamed a warning. Violence would not take her today, not ever again.

"LIAR! YOU DON'T CARE!" she shouted into his face. Fabric rustled as her hand dove deeper, her fingers tightening around the solid handle of the stiletto blade nestled there where she had hidden it, prepared to defend herself.

Ruby's scream paralyzed him where he stood. Sound fueled by rage and anguish that echoed in her body, recalling every blow Mae took, every fist against innocent flesh. Confusion clouded Clyde's expression for an instant as his eyes jerked from the wicked point of the blade in her hand to the hatred on her face. A flicker of fear danced in his eyes before the darkness gathered and swirled, rising up in protection against the crazed woman before him.

Ruby plunged the razor-sharp metal tip into Clyde's chest, sinking it all the way to the hilt, throwing her entire weight behind the blow. "You'll never hurt me again!" she sobbed into Clyde's face, seeing only Amos.

Clyde staggered and fell back against the rail, the slender blade protruding from his chest, his horrified eyes stretched wide in terror, then collapsed into the chair Ruby had abandoned. The pain bloomed and throbbed, spreading through his chest, strangling his heart. He had never been hurt like this before, never felt pain like this. He felt the darkness that had always shielded him failing.

Clyde watched Ruby from beneath lowered lids, her chest heaving as she backed away from him. He grunted in agony and attempted to stand, one hand wrapped around the handle of the dagger, blind instinct warning him not to remove it. His other hand waved helplessly in the air.

Ruby staggered, her heart tripping rapidly, walking backward until she felt the screen door at her back as Clyde's face became his own again. Fear blazed in her soul as he tried again to gain his feet, his one hand reaching toward her, grasping at empty air. Fumbling for the door handle, she wrenched it sideways, slamming the door open. Ruby fled down the hallway, not daring to look back to see if Clyde followed.

Clyde lurched upright as he tried again to raise himself from the chair, sucking in great gasps of air. Soft whimpers leaked from his mouth as his free hand fell to his side, Ruby now out of reach.

His hand began a frantic search in his pants pocket until his fingers curled around a scrap of silk from Mae's gown. He yanked it free, sending a stabbing pain to his chest with the movement that elicited another moan of agony. Holding it tightly in his fist, he raised it to his nose, suddenly desperate for the remembered comfort of a time when Mae had held him close. A time before Cora and Ruby, a time when she had forced the darkness to retreat from him. Pain pulsated with each beat of his heart from the wound in his chest.

Moving the piece of silk to his nose, he inhaled deeply. For just a moment, it smelled like she used to, and his eyes fluttered with the sweet memory. Then he recoiled as it changed, and he hurled the offending rag to the floor. His nose wrinkled at the repugnant smell that wafted up from where it lay at his feet. It stank, a miasma rising upward with the scent of Cora's corruption.

Suddenly, the darkness surged through his muscles, engorging them with strength and power. He thrilled. It had not left him alone to die. Instead, it enabled him to rise and remain on his feet, swaying unsteadily toward the stairs. The darkness urged him to get to the train. He needed Fannie.

"Damn Cora!" He almost wept, his eyes narrowed. The darkness knew she was behind it all. He pushed himself forward, the darkness dragging him. He looked back at the screen door, his mind conflicted between images of Ruby's throat in his hands and getting to Fannie.

No, Mama was first. He would get to her, and she would make the pain go away. She would fix it. Then, together, they would come back and deal with Ruby, and finally, they would get to Cora and give her the death she was so eager to deliver to him.

CHAPTER FIFTEEN

Joe stared at Cora, examining her profile as she sat staring into the deep purple twilight outside their window, little dots of light emerging to twinkle on its surface. This had been her posture for the better part of the last week since they had sent off the letter: not moving from the window, taking little food or water, refusing to be taken to bed, staring as though she could look through time itself. Gal cleared her throat behind him.

"I sorry, Mr. Joe. She ain't been no better today. You thinks I should get Doc Adams to come out?"

Joe shrugged. "It ain't nothing he can do. She come out of it, or she don't." He sighed and walked to Cora, resting his hand on her thin shoulder and squeezing gently. She no longer spoke, mute again after finishing the letter to Clyde's wife. He wondered if she'd had a stroke but sensed it was more of a refusal to speak than an inability. Walking away, he left her to ponder the night skies.

Cora's eyes searched the horizon, awaiting a glimpse of light as she continued her prayer vigil. Surrounding her, row upon row of Clyde's victims arrayed themselves, eyes silent and accusing, waiting. She knew with a certainty that she had not known or felt since she was first purposed with her task that help was coming. The Knowing was incontrovertible.

The sound manifested first, a screaming, then a wailing at decibels unsustainable by a human voice. She continued to wait, not turning from the window until she felt the subtle cooling of the air on her skin. She slammed her fist on the edge of her chair, a signal to Gal, who ran forward and turned her so that she faced the room, excitement tickling against her working nerve endings.

The air shimmered, and Cora watched as it cohered, becoming a small woman's body with her head wobbling on a crushed neck. Her mouth dropped open, and Cora knew that the screaming would begin again if she didn't act.

"Clyde?" she whispered into the woman's mind.

The woman nodded toward Cora and then relaxed as she said her name aloud. "Mae." Light blazed around her, surging and filling the room and momentarily rendering Cora sightless. As her vision returned, her mouth lifted in a crooked smile. The light had arrived. Clyde would come. Clyde would die.

The mantle clock continued to tick off the time. Still, she wasn't sure if hours or minutes had passed. Cora shifted in her chair, her bladder nearly bursting, yet she refused its release. She would not meet Clyde, sitting in her own filth, wrapped in the heavy ammonia scent of urine as she waited for Joe and Gal to come and attend to her. She turned her head to look over at Joe, whose long body stretched across the couch. He snorted in his sleep.

Behind her, Clyde's victims remained, a litany of accusations on their lips. The one called Mae remained mute, her eyes deep pools of sorrow. She could feel the eyes of the others boring into her. They sensed his presence—his nearness—too, just as she did.

She waited. She let the Knowing probe the night and bring him to her. Her own eyes grainy with sleeplessness, her head finally nodded, and she fell into a restless sleep.

Scanning the horizon of the dreamscape, Cora caught a glimpse of movement in the shadow of the trees, a cloud of darkness moving toward her. Her heart rate accelerated, previous discomfort forgotten, as she leaned forward, squinting, wavering between the world of dreams and the reality of the room she sat in. She felt the tug of the Knowing build in anticipation.

She watched as the darkness took human shape, lurching side to side as it advanced, and she felt its attempt to seep into her spirit, growing stronger as the form came closer. Sitting rigid in her chair, she could discern Clyde as he continued forward, now close enough to reveal his features. He looked the same. Age had not affected him. She braced herself, allowing the Knowing to flood her. She watched him come toward her.

Clyde closed the distance until he stood in front of Cora, seated in front of her window. Her body listed to one side, her shoulder hunched, and her skeletal face twisted in a sneer. Still as a statue, his dark eyes glared directly into her own, pushing the darkness that swirled around him until it rose waist high. A grin stretched his wide mouth. His lips pulled back in a snarl, baring his teeth. Then he raised both hands, and the darkness surged toward her.

Cora flinched, transfixed in his stare, her good hand lifted, palm out to combat the darkness leeching through the flimsy barrier of the glass between them and encircling her heart, bending her light. She felt herself once again succumbing, shame flooding her face with heat. A sob hitched in her broken throat.

Mae drifted across the room and stared through the darkness watching as the form of her husband solidified before her. She searched his face for traces of the man she had known, the gentleness she had claimed as her own, and found only a savage atrocity twisted by loathing.

Standing beside Cora, her radiance flared again, and Cora felt her body loosen, feeling flowing down through her useless arm. She turned her head slightly to find Mae beside her, her body pulsing a brilliant light that flowed through her. Cora's muscles warmed as unused nerves fired, and the Knowing sent additional strength and movement to her limbs.

Grasping the arms of her chair, she pushed upward until she stood on her feet, vibrating with power, eyes glowing, her hands mirroring Clyde's. The aura around Mae gleamed, and another burst of brilliance blazed from her.

Behind them, the chorus of the dead that surrounded Cora day and night ceased to speak, their murmuring silencing as they joined the battle. They became a unified light, forming a shimmering vanguard augmenting the attack. Mae extended her small hands to grasp Cora's wrist, pouring out her power, her face pinched with regret as the light magnified, blinding Clyde and obliterating the darkness surrounding him. "I loved you," she wailed mournfully.

"*Mae!*" Clyde cried, his eyes bulging in terror. He felt the darkness waning, undone by Mae's final betrayal. The light filled his nostrils, slithering down his throat, coating his skin, sealing his pores, and denying him the breath of life.

He was submerged in the darkness, a blackness different from the familiar form he'd known his entire life. One he would never escape. At first, it seemed infinite, stretching beyond the perception of his senses, his eyes unable to penetrate it. Still, he did not fear it. Instead, it comforted him, warm as the womb. He listened intently, sure that he heard the echo of his mother's heartbeat in the distance. Lying down, he drew his knees to his chest, wrapped his arms around them, and rested his chin. His eyes closed.

There was no sense of time, and he drifted in this darkness until a pinpoint of light in the distance moved toward him. He disregarded it, no more than an irritation against his closed eyelids. But it grew as it advanced toward him in undulating waves, bringing with it a feeling of dread and trepidation.

Clyde squeezed his eyes tightly against the radiance of the advancing light, the darkness around him pulsing outward, pushing the light back, then relenting. It forced his eyes to open.

Mae stood over him, a nimbus of light around her as she stared down at him, light glowing beneath her skin and the power of it leaking from her pores. Clyde blinked rapidly at her. Her face was drawn into harsh lines of sorrow and bitterness.

Clyde struggled to free himself from his position—to straighten his legs, stand, and confront her—but found himself bound by bands of light. He strained, grunting, as the light tightened and squeezed his muscles, draining his strength.

Mae leaned over him, then stood erect, her image morphing as her stomach rounded to become a perfectly round ball, her small hands smoothing, then resting beneath it. A moment later, her stomach flattened, and she held a small bundle against her chest as she stared down at him, her face a study of misery. She turned the infant toward him, and Clyde knew.

He gazed upon the child's perfect features beneath a mop of unruly curls. The contours of his tiny chest, the proportionate length of his arms and legs were miniature versions of his own, unblemished by the effects of the darkness. His seed lay nestled against Mae's body—his son.

"Mae," he moaned, reaching toward what could have been as she backed away. She aligned herself with many women who had stepped out of the darkness, and each face was frozen in a rictus of hatred encircling him.

Clyde lifted his head and peered through the ebbing darkness swirling around him. His body was leaning against the alley wall where he had collapsed. The same one where he had waited for Eva. He didn't remember walking there, just that he had to get to his mother so she could help him, could save him. His head flopped on his neck and he dropped his chin to his chest, seeing the black dagger embedded there.

The pain enveloped him, growing worse each moment, screaming at him to remove the blade and relieve the agony. Shreds of the battle with Cora floated through his mind, the light assaulting the tendrils of darkness that remained in his brain. The battle was over. His will faded with the darkness, the light stamping him in defeat. And he could still hear them, a multiplicity of voices, urging him to remove the dagger. "*It's over for you,*" they chanted. "*Die.*"

One voice rose above all the rest, and he saw Mae's face before him, her eyes filled with mourning, her hand stretched outward to him. "*Pull it out and let go. Let the light come, and the darkness will never claim you again.*" *Silent beside her, Cora simply stared, the Knowing had made its judgement.*

Wrapping both hands around the smooth bone handle, Clyde yanked it free and watched as blood spurted with each faltering beat of his heart. His body bucked wildly, choking sounds emitting from his closed throat. He flailed helplessly, his lungs starving for oxygen . . . and Clyde knew fear. The darkness blasted in his head, surging a final time and then faltering under the onslaught of the light that illuminated his soul. The faces of Cora and Mae floated before him, the light haloing them, and they watched as life departed from his eyes.

Fannie stared, checking the time on the large clock on the wall of Union station. Her eyes remained glued to the door as people streamed in and past her, where she sat on the hard wooden bench, searching for Clyde. She waited to see the familiar lopsided gait singling him out from the crowd.

"Clyde! Clyde!" she shouted as she thought she saw him for a moment, her face lighting with joy. She hurried forward. He pushed his stunted legs to move faster, something akin to delight shimmering in his features at the sight of his mother's face. Fannie held her arms out toward him as he barreled into her. Her arms snatched at him . . . only to seize empty air.

Fannie stopped, balanced on a precipice between reality and desire. "Clyde!" she shouted as her mind frantically reached for the connection between them. Where Clyde should have been . . . there was nothing. The cord dangled uselessly in her mind . . . severed. She leaned forward, a strangled moan building in her throat as she raised both hands to clutch her breasts. She felt their emptiness.

"Clyde, baby boy, Clyde," she cried, then, "Jesus, Jesus, please, Jesus." She beseeched God to give her favor, not to let her fears become truth. Fannie mashed her breasts together. She twisted them, attempting to wring milk for Clyde, then lifted her hands to tear at her hair when none came forth. They remained dry and devoid of milk for the first time since his birth. The meaning of it bore into her heart with a cold certainty.

Fannie stood there on legs that threatened to fold beneath her. A scream tore from her soul, ululating through the train station, calling her son back from the dead. Her fingernails dragged bloody rivulets down her cheeks as she continued to shudder and sob, her empty arms wrapped around her body.

Finally, her throat raw, she bent to pick up her Bible from where it had fallen when she stood, then collapsed to her knees on the hard polished floor. She knelt, weeping, begging, and finally demanding her God to intervene on behalf of her son. Silence reverberated around her, mocking her prayers. She had failed. She had not protected him.

Falling forward, she lay facedown on the floor. Around her, people gathered, whispering as they ringed her in. Fannie wept and waited for death to find her.

Behind Cora, Joe tumbled off the couch, snatched from sleep by the sound of a heavy thump as Cora dropped back into her wheelchair. Hearing him, she turned to stare at him. Her features flowed through a range of emotions, ending in grim satisfaction. His eyebrows slammed together in confusion at what his bewildered mind thought he saw.

"Clyde." Cora spoke his name clearly without pause or hesitation. The sound of her voice, his Cora's voice, galvanized Joe into action. Gaining his feet, he flew across the room, grabbing her around her shoulders. Leaning back, he stared at her. Her skin no longer dripped like melted wax on one side. Her shoulders squared evenly, and both hands rested in her lap. Tears rolled unchecked to drip off his chin.

Cora reached within and felt the Knowing flow through her unimpeded. She knew that Clyde lay still and dead somewhere, an empty shell. She pushed the Knowing outward to access the dreamscape where she found his remains. Nothing emanated from him. He was no more.

The dead who had filled the room winked out of existence one by one, except for Mae. She drifted for a moment, a look of abject sadness in her eyes. Then she too was gone.

Across from Cora, Gal screamed, having come into the room at the sound of Cora's voice. She threw both hands upward, tilting her head back.

"What done happened? Lord have mercy, what done happened to you, Miss Cora?" She fired her questions unchecked at her employers.

Cora lifted her chin to stare in Joe's direction and nodded. Her full mouth lifted in a smile before returning her attention to the girl in front of her.

"Hush all that foolishness, Gal," she scolded as Gal collapsed in a heap beside her chair, a look of stunned amazement on her face at hearing Cora speak clearly.

"It be done," Cora said, nodding again at Joe before leaning back in her chair and lifting her face to the rays of morning light flowing in from the sun riding high in the sky. "Everything be all right."

EPILOGUE

Ruby shifted her stance and lifted a handkerchief dipped in a sachet to cover her nose and mouth. Six days had passed since she had seen Mae. One more than the day since she left Clyde on the porch, her stiletto stuck deep in his chest—seven days since she had buried another secret in her heart. Clyde and Mae's apartment remained eerily silent, a sentinel accusing her each time she passed. Her heart trembled. What would Mae think when she found out what happened to Clyde? Would she grieve and mourn?

When she had ventured back to the porch, Clyde was gone, a set of bloody boot prints leading to the stairs and out of the yard. Grabbing a bucket of hot water, she descended and worked on the stains, vengefully scrubbing any evidence away—no body, no crime.

The next day, there was a small article about an unidentified man found stabbed in an alley a few blocks away. Ruby smiled, grateful for the acknowledgment, assured that Mae was free. She had done what Ruby had been too weak to do. She had left and gotten away. Now, Clyde would never hurt her or anyone else again. The darkness Amos had left behind had gone with him as well, as if the remnants Clyde had anchored to haunt her died in that alley with him.

Then there came the smell. It was initially subtle, riding a stray breeze wafting through the hallway. Then it grew stronger daily until finally, it coated your tongue with its stench whenever you tried to draw a breath. Today, she had finally called Mr. Elliott, who, after smelling the odor himself, had notified the police.

People crowded the hallway, their curiosity overriding the repulsive smell that should have driven them away. Ruby pushed her way through them until she stood beside Mr. Elliott.

"You got the key, Ruby?" he asked, rolling his cigar around in his mouth, sweat gleaming on his round face. Ruby narrowed her eyes at him, wondering who he was posturing for. Of course, she had the key. Her hands trembled as she attempted to push the key into the lock, fear washing over her, the sound of Mae's cries echoing inside her head.

The smell crashed over them as hands covered both nose and mouth or reached for handkerchiefs to cover their faces. The stink pushed out into the hall, forming a wall that halted movement until Mr. Elliott and the officers poured into the room. They blocked her view for a moment as inquisitive tenants pressed in from behind, muttering.

Ruby squeezed herself between them, allowing herself to be part of the human tide as it filled the space. The combination of the smell from the apartment and Mr. Elliott's cigar smoke mingled, threatening to cause Ruby to retch and making her glad she had her snuff can.

Her gaze took in the overturned table, the torn linen and clothing spread across the floor, and the broken chair. She could almost hear Mr. Elliott calculating the repair cost and whether the deposit would cover it. She clicked her tongue in disgust.

Her eyes hooked on Mae's blue trunk, a puzzled expression on her face. Mae would never have left without it. She studied the lid first, then the floor underneath it, shuddering. As she peered through the bodies pressing into the room, she saw it . . . blood, black and tacky looking, pooled beneath the trunk.

"Sweet Jesus," she'd cried into the silent air of the room before they pushed her backward, but not before she had seen the contents of the trunk when they raised the lid.

Mae's sightless eyes stared upward from the bloated and decomposing flesh of her once-beautiful face. Her blood-covered body lay folded impossibly, like discarded clothing inside the trunk.

Mr. Elliott and one of the police officers bolted past her, rushing from the room and vomiting into their hands before they could reach the bathroom in the middle of the hall. Later, the newspapers would quote the coroner's report, claiming strangulation, a broken neck, and fifteen stab wounds.

For days afterward, the hall churned with the sounds of more police officers, detectives, the coroner, and members of the press. Ruby hid within the walls of her apartment, refusing to answer the door. Sometimes, she rocked in her chair, or sometimes, lay on her bed, conjuring the murder into reality again and again. She heard the bed's headboard slamming against the wall and Mae's screams, unearthly in their fear, shattering the air. They constantly played every night, as consistent as a radio broadcast.

Today, Ruby steeled herself for her task. The yellow police tape was finally gone, and she had been ordered to clean the room. Mae was her friend, and she needed to do this for her. It was the only way she knew to make amends with the dead. *This is for you, Mae*, played in an unrelenting spool in her mind, overcoming the fear and dread of what she might see in the apartment.

Tears rolled down Ruby's cheeks as she hauled another bucket of hot, soapy water and her other cleaning solutions into the room. She scrubbed the floor with vinegar, rinsed it, then scrubbed again with baking soda and hydrogen peroxide, following the same steps she had taken to remove Clyde's blood. Now, she ran her scrub brush over the hardwood floor until no residue was found.

Following the process, she scoured the inside of the trunk, discarded after the investigation, and returned it to its former pristine condition, the way that it had looked when Mae first showed it to her . . . before it became her casket.

On her hands and knees, tears dripping into the soapy water, she felt a faint chill in the room, the window having lost the sun's heat. She'd lost track of time. Backing up on her stiff knees, she rested on her heels and took in a deep breath, which became a gasp as the air beside the trunk shimmered and pulsed, becoming the image of Mae.

Ruby's hand raised to her open mouth as she fought to stifle both a scream and a sob at the sight of her friend. Slowly, her fear subsided as her gaze lingered on the sadness in Mae's eyes, and she let the tears break free.

"Mae, Mae, I'm sorry I wasn't soon enough when I could have saved you if I tells you the truth about good men." Her body shook with the force of her sobs as she plopped down next to the bucket. Mae looked toward her and shook her head.

"But he won't never hurt nobody again, I swears to that truth," Ruby cried. She lumbered to her feet, gathering her cleaning supplies, wiping at her tears, then stopped so that she could stare directly into the eyes of the apparition. "And, Mae, I just wants you to know, whatever good they was in Clyde, if it was some, it was from you. You was a good woman."

Mae smiled, her cheeks dimpling. The glow surrounding her flared brightly, and then she was gone, leaving Ruby standing in the silent room.

ACKNOWLEDGEMENTS

Acknowledgement must begin and end somewhere. First to the Creator and my ancestors, and then to Dorothy Mae and Ruthie Mae, my two mothers. One who saw the need to release me and one who accepted the call to embrace me. Onward to Joanne Bowser who recognized my ability to write at age eleven, and Judith Stein who pushed that ability further in high school by referring me to Urban Gateways Writer's Workshop. Next to Colombia College Chicago who accepted me into their master's program and provided a faculty of writing instructors who emboldened me, especially and including Alexis Pride who gently prodded me along regardless of my resistance and motivated me to submit my work; and Don DeGrazia in whose class this story began.

Thank you to my agent Harvey Klinger for seeing something in my story that made him want to keep reading and, stuck with me through all the 'beautiful' rejections we received. I thank him for aligning me with Black Odyssey Media who has worked with me and beside me, providing inspiration and respect for the craft of writing. These women are incredible. Thank you for giving my voice a space to be in.

And of course, I thank my family and friends for everything they have done, both large and small to encourage me along the way. My husband, Barry, who has never wavered in his belief that I could in fact become a writer in this winter season of my life. Our children Stephan, CeeJay, Danielle and Kisa who cheer me on always. They are the first to celebrate me and the loudest applause in the house. And of course, my friend and fellow writer, Jeff Hoffman. As iron sharpens iron, Jeff keeps me on my toes and provides feedback without flinching. Thanks for pointing me towards Harvey and continuing to show me the way forward on the author's road.

Darrielle, Fran, Laverne, Linda, and Ramona, my Greek Chorus who have provided the rhyme, reason, and unconditional friendship throughout this journey, thank you for being with me.

If your name is not here, it's not because your contribution is not valued, I just ran out of space.

WWW.BLACKODYSSEY.NET

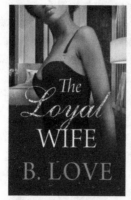

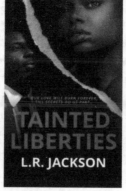